RED SAILS IN THE FALLOUT

PAUL KIDD

A

GAMMA WORLD

NOVEL

Dungeons & Dragons
Gamma World: Red Sails in the Fallout

©2011 Wizards of the Coast LLC

Published by Wizards of the Coast LLC

DUNGEONS & DRAGONS, D&D, FORGOTTEN REALMS, GREYHAWK, GAMMA WORLD, WIZARDS OF THE COAST, and their respective logos are trademarks of Wizards of the Coast LLC in the U.S.A. and other countries. Other trademarks are property of their respective owners.

Printed in the U.S.A.

Cover art by Jason Chan

First Printing: July 2011

9 8 7 6 5 4 3 2 1

ISBN: 978-0-7869-5792-7
ISBN: 978-0-7869-5921-1 (e-book)
620-31417000-001-EN

U.S., CANADA, ASIA, PACIFIC,
& LATIN AMERICA
Wizards of the Coast LLC
P.O. Box 707
Renton, WA 98057-0707
+1-800-324-6496

EUROPEAN HEADQUARTERS
Hasbro UK Ltd
Caswell Way
Newport, Gwent NP9 0YH
GREAT BRITAIN
Save this address for your records.

Visit our web site at www.wizards.com

Apocalypse means never having to say you're sorry . . .

As far as accidents went, it had certainly been colorful. One moment, happy little researchers were stomping on atoms and making "universe particles." Seconds later, they had fed the multiverse into an nth-dimensional blender and hit frappé. Countless alternative Earths had been smashed together. Bits and chunks collided in bright and interesting ways. Environments withered, cities warped, oceans went belly up and died. Civilization gave an embarrassed sneeze and simply disappeared.

In its place there were radioactive wastelands and a shattered wilderness. Predators and nightmares from different versions of Earth grappled in spectacular battles to survive. Mutagenic particles warped the survivors into countless new shapes and forms.

Ah well, there went the neighborhood . . .

Mind you, things were not all bad. A century and a half later, things seemed to have adjusted to a weird and colorful status quo. The new world, Gamma Terra, was a very odd place. It was a dangerous place, the kind of place where a man could tend his flocks and prune his own fig tree provided he didn't mind the fig tree pruning him back.

Radioactive wastelands, ancient ruins, weird mutations, three-headed monsters . . . What's not to like?

For Tornassuk, with much joy and thanks.

GAMMA WORLD

Welcome to the post-apocalyptic world of Gamma Terra

IN THE FALL OF 2012, scientists at the Large Hadron Collider in Geneva, Switzerland, embarked on a new series of high-energy experiments. No one knows exactly what they were attempting to do, but a little after 3 p.m. on a Thursday afternoon came the Big Mistake, and in the blink of an eye, many possible universes all condensed into a single reality.

In some of these universes, little had changed; it didn't make a big difference, for example, which team won the 2011 World Series. In other universes, there were more important divergences: the Gray Emissary, carrying gifts of advanced technology, wasn't shot down at Roswell in 1947; the Black Death didn't devastate Europe in the fourteenth century; the dinosaurs didn't die out; Nikola Tesla conquered the world with a robot army, and so on. The Cold War went nuclear in eighty-three percent of the possible universes, and in three percent the French unloaded their entire nuclear arsenal on the town of Peshtigo, Wisconsin, because it had to be done.

The year is now 2162 (or 151, or 32,173, or Six Monkey Slap-Slap, depending on your point of view). Fluctuating time lines, lingering radiation and toxins, and strange creatures and technology transposed from alternate dimensions have combined to create a world the Ancients would think of as the height of fantasy. But to the inhabitants of Gamma Terra, fantasy is the reality.

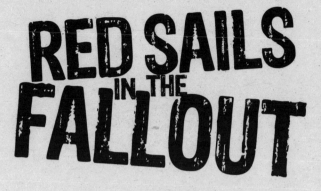

CHAPTER 1

It was another glorious, dusty, postapocalyptic day.

Mornings in the desert were always the best of times. The world felt cool and fresh, with a delicate kiss of dew. The sands gave off a sharp, delicious scent of earth and dust. Here and there, the last few desert creatures moved about their business, little critters bustling happily about, hoping to make breakfast out of one another.

It was another beautiful day on the sands.

Soft, gray light spread out over the endless ocean of rock, scrub, and sand. Standing in her saddle, Xoota pushed up her sand goggles and dug at her belt for her binoculars. One lens was smashed, but the other still worked. Using the thing as a telescope, she scanned the desert for anything of interest—a sharp angle, a glint of metal, the tinge of rust in the soil. Below her, Budgie fluffed out his feathers then made a little side step as he decided to investigate a bush. With her view jolted, Xoota glowered down at the critter in displeasure.

"Must you?"

The bird chirruped, utterly unconcerned. Xoota shook her head and went back to scanning the horizon.

To the west, there was only the great salt plains. To the north and east, the restless sands. Here and there a rock outcrop jutted from the ground. Spindly bushes looked more alive than dead. Xoota sucked one fang then decided to move west, in the direction of the morning wind. Perhaps the sands had shifted and uncovered something new. She put her binoculars away and tried to draw a bead on images of many possible futures.

West *felt* right. There was an immanence in the air; something pervasive was settling on Gamma Terra. Xoota settled her weapons and flicked at Budgie's reins.

"Come on, birdbrain. Let's go."

She kicked the giant blue budgerigar into a trot. The bird ambled happily across the sands, heading toward the dark, cool west. He wagged little flightless wings and loped off on his way.

Peace and quiet. Xoota told herself that she loved it.

As far as mutant humanoid animals went, Xoota was a fairly typical, fun-loving child of the apocalypse. She was a mutated quoll: a short, compact female figure dressed in sun veil and leathers. Xoota had the thighs of a rider, an archer's muscles, and tawny fur covered in bright white spots. Across her belly, below the navel, she had a neat little marsupial pouch, and a handful of whiskers jutted from her scruffy muzzle. Her nose was pink, her ears long, and her prehensile tail often twitched in irritation. She wore a leather halter around her breasts, a ragged cloth around her head, and at her belt hung a mace made from metal cogs. A powerful crossbow rode across her lap.

The wastes were no place for the incautious.

She smelled none too fresh. Were it not for a pair of feathery antennae jutting from her head, she would have been perfectly hard-core and predatory. The antennae were inarguably cute, which irritated Xoota to no end. As said, that irritation often was evident in her twitching tail, but sometimes it led to more grievous action. The citizens of Watering Hole, her hometown, had in fact voted Xoota "Sentient Creature Most Likely to Punch You in the Neck" three years running.

Still, at least there were no particularly absurd alpha mutations in the wind. There were days when one could wake up purple, with tentacles, or covered in a crusty shell. It was all part of the fun of life in the wastelands.

Xoota and Budgie trotted their way westward, up over the sands and into a land of short, brittle shrub. Here and there an immense plant jutted a stalk high into the air, usually with one or more eyes blinking on the top. Xoota gave the things a wide berth. The Great Sky-Bunny only knew what the things were looking for. Most likely it was breakfast, and a mutant quoll on a riding budgie might score pretty high on the list of desirable cuisine.

Budgie trotted happily along, chattering madly to himself, as budgerigars do. He seemed to have the parakeet version of Tourette's. Xoota just endured the noise and watched the world, her eyes sharp, her antennae questing. She sniffed about for any sense of something different, dangerous, or wrong.

When chunks of ancient asphalt peeked up through the sands, Xoota was immediately interested. She followed the line of the ancient road, hoping to come across something worth digging from the soil.

Finally she came to a hollow in the ground. Half buried under the rust-streaked sand were the bodies of several cars. Keeping her distance, Xoota stood up in her stirrups and scanned the shrubbery.

The wind gusted, hissing as it swept through the dead, dry bushes. Xoota pulled off her head cloth, baring her tall ears to listen carefully. She heard no untoward sounds, no movement.

She circled the site carefully, moving downwind, sniffing for any signs. She shushed Budgie and dismounted. Crossbow at the ready, she edged slowly toward the cars.

Budgie kept quiet but he fluffed his feathers in warning. Xoota sank down into cover.

The old cars were total wrecks. Someone had ripped away the engine blocks, seats, and doors, leaving the chassis gutted like rabbits. The cars formed a windbreak, and in the middle of the sand was a campfire—just a mound of cold ashes but still fairly fresh, no more than a day old.

There were bones around the campfire, big ones. They were humanoid. Something with a taste for sentient prey had sat down for a barbecue.

Razorbacks.

Most of the year, the pig mutants kept to the outer desert. But the Big Dry had arrived early. If the desert watering holes were drying up early in the season, then the pig tribes might migrate closer to civilization, and that could mean trouble.

Xoota moved in and began to inspect the ruined cars.

One of the cars had been a "hybrid"—useless on Gamma Terra to man or beast, even for parts. But there were a few tools in a cubbyhole in the trunk—always good. She found a combination tire iron and nut wrench, two screwdrivers, and something that looked like two metal octopuses wrestling but was probably a collapsible jack.

Not too bad.

There was nothing left in the other cars—no tires, no light bulbs. Seat belt webbing was always useful, though, and the buckles were intact. There were two side mirrors that were worth taking. Xoota was wondering if it was worth the effort of trying to strip the battery out of the hybrid, when she suddenly spied a little glitter of red beneath the sand.

Nyaha. Treasure.

There was an old road sign beneath one of the cars. The pole was bent, but there was an octagonal sign on top, made from a wonderfully tough piece of Kevlar sheet. It looked light and sturdy. One side was red and covered in runes. Xoota dusted it off then took out her tools and undid screw fastenings, freeing the thing from its pole. It would make a perfect shield—light and handy. All it needed were arm straps and a bit of glue.

Excellent.

Xoota secured her finds on Budgie's saddle then unshipped her tools, ready to cannibalize the transmissions of the old cars. They were not much of a find, but at least they were something. The days of finding spectacular treasures seemed to be long past. With razorbacks on the loose, it was time to go home.

One of the penalties of being the sole sensible creature in a land of nitwits was a lack of bosom buddies. So Xoota spent her time out on the sands and in the scrub, prospecting for junk. She found scrap metal and little artifacts then dragged them back to Watering Hole for trade. Watering Hole was a backwater burg, but it was the most populated for kilometers in any direction. Scrapping was a radical improvement over farming or water prospecting, and it had the added bonus of keeping her far away from idiots. With a little bit of salvage in hand, she could head back and cash in the scrap for essential supplies—bug bars, meat, and tea. She would think about hunting her way south to the rim of the Great Rift and see if the tremors had unearthed anything of interest.

A couple of chunks of old scrap steel was a pretty poor return for two weeks in the field. Being a quoll had its disadvantages. She needed decent food—bugs and other meat, preferably dead. A regular morning and evening cup of tea, *with milk,* was essential. Without it, she was even more foul tempered than usual.

It was getting harder and harder to scrape a living out of the desert. Unfortunately her world was bound by hard and deadly walls. No one had ever crossed the northern and eastern deserts and returned. No one could possibly survive the endless salt plains to the west. To the south, a vast landslide had plunged the world away down a sheer drop that was at least a thousand meters' fall. Everything was dust, death, and radiation, and the only things that ever came out of the desert were gamma moths . . . and sandstorms.

Thinking of gamma moths, Xoota made a quick scan of the skies. The morning sun was on the rise, and the temperature would soon be up. It was time to camp: to dig a deep, cool scrape in the dirt, set up the sun shields, and try to rest through the heat of the day. Xoota jerked her shovel down from Budgie's saddle packs but stopped when a distant, tinny sound tinkled in her ears.

The quoll went stiff. The sound made no damned sense. But there was a ripple in Xoota's perception, a twist in the world. Her antennae were picking up a shift in probabilities.

It was odd. Damned odd.

What was that noise? Singing? The sound came and went, carried on the breeze, caught only by the quoll girl's huge, sensitive ears.

Music. Bad music and bad singing. Razorbacks were on the loose, the deadly heat of the day was about to smash down over the sands, and someone was out there apparently happy as a lark. Xoota clambered up onto Budgie and stood on the saddle, boosting her modest height far above the tallest scrub. There, far off to the west, she saw a little blink of light and a regular flash of motion.

Was that out on the salt? It couldn't be. The whole shoreline was radioactive.

Xoota used her binoculars, making the image slowly worm into focus. There was something out there, just a hundred meters or so away from the shore. Mounds of dirt, some regular shapes . . .

Whoever it was, they were going to get themselves killed. If Xoota could hear it, then every predator, weird-ass mutant, and razorback in the area must be tuning in as well. Xoota kicked Budgie into gear and raced toward the distant sound of song.

The bird sped through the brush, leaping over rocks and fallen wood, past a fat bluetongue skink that was shooting berries off the bushes with its laser eyes. When they reached the edge of the sands, Xoota kicked her bird out onto the salt.

The bird balked, dancing back from the radiation. There was a good reason desert riders preferred budgerigars. But Xoota had no time to argue. She kicked Budgie in the flanks, driving her mount out onto the salt plains, hoping to rescue an absolute idiot from disaster.

"*Hi-yah.* Go, Budgie. *Yah!*"

Budgie charged hard and fast across the salt. Radiation prickled—it wasn't hurting yet, but it was there. Xoota's skin crawled yet she urged Budgie on to greater speed.

Budgie said, *"Arrrrrk,"* his standard interjection.

"I know. I know."

Xoota swerved Budgie past an outcrop of rocks, past an ancient boat lying rotting on its side, then saw a weird little campsite just ahead. A massive, rusting, steel tube was jutting up out of the salt. Beside it, some idiot had set up for a holiday. A bicycle had been propped neatly in the shade of the steel tube, next to a rather natty parasol. There was a carefully weighted picnic rug and some sort of little box that bellowed out the music. It was loudly playing one of the majestic, ancient classics: "Tainted Love." Xoota brought Budgie to a panicked, skidding halt beside the rug and vaulted from the saddle. She grabbed the music box but could see no way of turning the damned thing off. Xoota looked around in panic, expecting mutant hordes to be racing toward her. She felt horribly exposed out on the flat, white salt plains.

A voice was singing raucously in tune to the music. Dirt flew as someone dug away inside a hole excavated beside the steel tube. Feeling radiation stinging at her skin, Xoota ran over toward the hole.

"Hey. Hey, you."

There was a crunching, crumbling sound. A considerable disc of rusting steel was tossed up out of the hole. It was followed by a pink nose and a spray of whiskers attached to a neat, narrow, white-furred face. She had a broad straw hat, and the inevitable sand goggles. Happy as a lark, a rat girl dusted off her gloves and greeted Xoota with an enthusiastic wave.

"Hallo. Dropping in for some tea?"

The rat girl was pure white and pink eyed, limber and full of guileless energy. Her features were very humanoid, despite a long, expressive tail and a pointed, delicately pretty rat face. She wore a cotton singlet, voluminous shorts with many pockets, and clunky work boots. She used her meager cleavage to stow an ancient penlight. She had delightfully long, white hair plaited back into a ponytail. The rat girl planted her shovel in the salt, pushed a pair of spectacles up on her nose, and climbed happily out to greet her guest.

"Jolly glad to see you. It was getting a tad lonely. This is a bit of a find, what?"

The music still clanged and thumped out across the wilds, echoing perfectly off the hard-packed salt. Xoota almost danced in anger.

"Turn it off." She waved in panic at the music machine. "Get it the hell off. Now."

The rat cocked an ear. "Can't hear you. Sorry. Just a mo." She pulled a tiny control out of one pocket and pressed a button. The music instantly shut off. "That's better. Sorry. Whistle while you work and all that."

Oh, *scrote*. Xoota seethed. Four hundred kilometers from home, and she still managed to find the one idiot in the entire desert.

The rat girl pulled off her gloves, and Xoota found herself numbly shaking the girl's pink hand.

"Shaani. Name's Shaani." The rat instantly presumed they were colleagues. "Charmed. How do you do? Didn't catch your name."

"Xoota." The quoll's antennae were flat with droll displeasure. "So you're prospecting, are you?"

"No, no—investigating. Research. Scientific process." Shaani the rat had somehow managed to dig through salt, dust, and rust and emerge remarkably clean. She saw Budgie and was delighted, fearlessly going over to scratch him behind the head. "Oh my. Who's a pretty boy, then? Who's a pretty boy?" She looked back at Xoota. "Beautiful. Does he talk?"

"He doesn't talk." Xoota was so tired of idiots. "Now look. You have to get out of here. This whole area is exposed. What the hell are you doing out here?"

Shaani was already back in her hole, levering rust chinks out of the side of the wide tube.

"Well, I'm a lab rat." The girl seemed surprised anyone would ask. "It's the mission. *Noblesse oblige* and all that." She passed a large chunk of rust up from the hole. "Here. Hold that, will you?"

"This area is irradiated."

"Oh—fairly immune to all that sort of thing, old horse. I mentioned I'm a lab rat? Special breed. Science ever forward and all that." The rat's face reappeared in the hole. "I say, you might not want to hover here too long, though. Unless you don't mind it. Some folks don't. Tickle the old genes and all that. But radiation can be dangerous, you know."

"I know." Xoota felt as though a hand were crushing her brain. "You're just lucky that damned music didn't bring anything down on you."

"Oh, no bother. The salt makes a sound conductor. I'd have heard anything coming."

"Over the music?"

"Oh, well, I see your point. Stand corrected." The rat had broken a sizable hole into the side of the wide tube. "Excellent. Here we go."

Xoota peered down at the hole in the tube.

"What is that?"

"Ah, a point of egress."

"Egrets?"

"*Egress*. Entry. Or is it exit? I can never remember. Whatever it is, it's an invitation to adventure." The rat switched on her entirely inadequate penlight. "Splendid."

Xoota took another look at the steel tube. She could see it was a funnel. The rat was digging into the side of a funnel. It was the top of a vast, old ship, somehow buried in the salt.

"You found this?" Xoota was amazed. "How?"

"Oh, simple deduction. This used to be a sea, old bean. Some documents back home said these were what's called 'gauge roads,' where ships sort of parked while waiting to unload in port. So it was a matter of following up the gauge roads and seeing if anything had somehow gotten stuck."

"Following the 'roads'?"

"Yes."

"Through hard radiation?"

"That's the way." The rat was pleased. "Well, if it was easy, someone would already have found it."

The technique was impressively simple. Xoota was annoyed that she had never thought of it herself. However, her skin was starting to burn. Although creatures on Gamma Terra could laugh off radiation that would have fried their ancestors to a bubbling paste, it was still not a good idea to dance around in it, particularly if one wanted to limit the number of tentacles festooning one's children. Xoota irritably shoved dirt and rust aside and squatted by the hole.

"Anything down there will be radioactive, you know. No one will trade for it."

"Trade? Oh. No, no. This is a time capsule. A veritable museum. With luck the power generators and drives will be intact."

"They'll be too big to drag home." Xoota blinked. "Wait— you know how these things ran?"

"Well, of course. Perfectly simple principles. It's just all in the engineering." The rat poked her head up out of the hole. "Coming?"

Xoota blew a sharp, sour breath through her whiskers. "Where did you come from, anyway?"

"Oh, here and there. From the Rookery, down south of Watering Hole. But no research to be done down there. No, it's all up here. Improve the world . . . sacred calling. I'm a lab rat, you know."

"So you've never really left the villages before?"

"No, no. Just starting field operations now."

"Did you even bring a weapon?"

"I have the shovel." Shaani had a slightly battered entrenching tool. "Oh, and these would do at a pinch." She pointed at a few homemade pipe bombs jutting through her belt. "But observation is the key. No need to run about being disruptive."

Xoota's tail thrashed.

"Look, rat girl. There are certain rules out here if you want—"

The rat was tugging away at the rusty sides of the funnel.

"Will you listen to me?"

"Listening in, old girl. All ears."

"Look, you can't expect to survive unless you take extreme care. It takes a real veteran to know just how dangerous the wilds are." Xoota paced back and forth, waving an expressive hand in the air. "Now look, survival in the wilds is a matter of wits, of perception. You need to be like me: stealthy, cautious, switched on."

Xoota had a sudden flash of the future: teeth exploding up around the ground at her feet. She did an instant dive and roll. "Bleedin' heck!"

Right on her heels, huge jaws burst up from the ground where she had been standing. They clashed shut with a noise like ringing steel. Xoota had leaped pell-mell and knocked Shaani off her feet. Out on the salt, Budgie frantically climbed to the top of the steel funnel. He sat up there, screeching in alarm.

The ground rumbled as the ravening snout of a sand shark snapped its jaws at the two. As they tumbled through the hole, their progress was slowed by a rusted grill that gave way under their weight. The metal crumbled, spilling them down again, where Xoota caught hold of Shaani as they fell through the dark, but she was able to lash out with her prehensile tail and catch a protruding metal strut. Shaani was almost ripped from her grasp and ended up hanging from her hand.

They swung from an ancient, rusted metal strut in the darkness. The metal creaked, and a little shower of rust flakes fell.

Xoota's tail felt as if it were being pulled out by the roots. Below her, Shaani swung back and forth with her penlight still awkwardly clamped in her mouth.

"Wot th' deuce was zat?"

"Sand shark." Xoota's tail shifted. She clung tighter in panic. "Can you reach anything to hold on to?"

"'Kay." The rat immediately began to climb up over Xoota, using the quoll girl's armpits and backside as footholds. "'Scuse 'e."

The metal strut slowly began to sag. Paralyzed by fright, Xoota could only stare into the dark. Suddenly Shaani was scrabbling off her into the blackness. An instant later, the rat grabbed Xoota's belt and hauled her up into a hole rusted through the wall. They tumbled back into a reeking, old corridor and sat there in the glow of the little penlight, both dazed with fright.

Shaani pulled spectacles from her cleavage and settled them back on her nose. "What's a sand shark?"

"Mutated . . . fish . . . thing." Xoota could still feel her heart hammering, but at least the danger was over. She took a bio light stick from her belt and shook it into life. "We're safe now. This whole hull's made of steel."

They looked carefully around themselves. They were inside a dark corridor sheathed entirely in rust. The rat's penlight showed some yellowed posters clinging to the walls. Xoota dusted rust from her fur and looked at the light in interest.

"Hey, how are you powering that? Have you got batteries?"

"Mmm? No, no, personal voltage. I generate electricity. It's a lab rat thing." The rat girl waggled her light. "Specialized evolution."

"Oh." Xoota blinked. "Wacko."

The two women edged slowly into the long corridor before them, hearing the ancient ship all around them groan and echo. Shaani seemed fascinated by it all.

" 'So . . . sand sharks. Would you say that's a typical local life form?"

Xoota rolled her eyes. "Well, along the shoreline, yes. That's why we keep things quiet."

"So it could be homing in on us by sound?"

The quoll made a droll face and rapped her knuckles hard against the steel walls.

"Well, not *now*. We're inside a steel ship. We're perfectly safe."

Something exploded through the wall beside them. A vast, ravening sand shark with a mouth like a guillotine burst through the rusted, collapsing hull. Twelve meters long and mad with hunger, the monster smashed its way into the hall.

Screaming like nestlings, the two girls flung themselves down the corridor. The flooring was giving way beneath their feet. Behind them, the shark turned and thrust itself along the corridor, splitting the walls and ceiling as it came.

The lab rat cast a glance behind her as she ran. "I think the salt may have had a detrimental effect on the structural strength of the steel."

"Really? How bloody fascinating."

They came to a wide gulf in the floor. Corridors and cabin doors opened all around them. Shaani jumped and hit the edge of the decking. The floor instantly collapsed beneath her. She fell one level, landing on her rump. Xoota simply dived down after her, grabbed her by the scruff on the neck, and ran.

The sand shark plunged down after them, wriggling as it tried to fit into the new corridor. Xoota pulled her crossbow from her back, a bolt held in her teeth, and frantically cranked the cocking handle as she ran.

Xoota took aim and fired. She hit the beast right between the eyes. The crossbow bolt was on target, beautifully fast, and achieved absolutely nothing. The shark fixed her with an insane glare then lunged toward her. It came down the corridor at a terrifying speed.

The girls fled. Shaani took a sudden right turn, leading the way off through a vast, old chamber littered with tables and chairs. There were stairs. The two women raced up them two by two. The shark came right after them, floundering as it tried to take the stairs. Xoota danced away, desperately searching for ideas.

"The bombs. Light the bombs."

Shaani reached for a pipe bomb on her belt then hesitated. "Have you got any matches?"

"What?"

"Matches."

"No, I don't have any damned matches."

"Flint and tinder?"

The shark actually leaped. It gathered like a spring and lunged up the stairs, jaws shearing clean through the railings as the two girls fled madly away. Xoota took the lead.

"I can't believe you don't have matches. What use are bombs without matches?"

The rat girl squeaked as she ran through cobwebs black with dust. "They're on my bicycle. In the pack."

Xoota swore.

Quite suddenly, the sand shark burst up out of the deck beneath them. Teeth fastened on Xoota's leg. A chunk of wreckage stopped the jaws just short of clashing shut. The giant fangs gripped Xoota's leather armor. The shark jerked its head, yanking her off her feet and dragging her deeper into its mouth. Her legs were already halfway down its throat.

Shaani raced up and beat the shark about the snout with her shovel. She rained blows on it, shouting at it. "Drop it. Drop it. Down." Shaani backed off and leveled one hand. "Take that, you blighter."

A shot of green radiation blasted from the girl's hand and smashed into the shark's head, singeing it all down one side. The radiation blast cut out with a disappointing *fizz*.

The shark instantly spit out Xoota and turned on the lab rat. Covered from the waist down in shark drool, Xoota rolled aside and blinked. Shaani squealed and leaped as the beast snapped for her. She clung to the nose of the shark, which bucked like mad. It slammed the rat against the ceiling, plunging her up through the rusted deck and onto the floor above. Amazed that its prey had escaped, the shark remembered the quoll and whirled. Xoota picked herself up and ran as fast as she could.

Metal bent and shattered behind her. The sand shark roared. Struts collapsed and rusted panels burst open. Teeth slammed closed behind Xoota with a clash. Then she was leaping and scrabbling over fallen pipes that cluttered the hallway. She looked back to see the shark slamming itself against the blockage. There were three side hallways leading off into the dark. Heart hammering, Xoota wondered what the hell she should do.

The rat girl plunged down through the ceiling in a shower of rust. She landed on her backside, dazed, and saw Xoota.

"Oh, hello."

The sand shark burst through the old pipes with a savage roar.

"Oh, bloody hell." Shaani grabbed Xoota by the hand. "Come on. This way."

"Where?"

"Engineering. The bulkheads will be stronger."

They raced down a long passageway, ducking beneath fallen pipes and wreckage. Behind them, the sand shark floundered, sometimes gaining, sometimes falling behind. As they raced past a cabin, the lab rat screeched to a halt and sparked with glee.

"Ooh, books."

Fallen shelves had spilled old paper books over the floor. The rat instantly plunged into the room and snatched an armload of books. Xoota almost had a heart attack.

"Are you crazy?"

"But this is information."

"Run."

She propelled the rat down the corridor. Shaani kept two huge books clamped to her chest. The sand shark was only a few meters behind them. The women ran until an enormous, steel door blocked their path. Xoota took a run at the door and slammed her shoulder against it, rebounding with a yelp of pain. Shaani looked at her and yanked on a hefty handle. It squealed and moved slowly.

"Try now."

Swearing, Xoota slammed herself against the door again. It budged a few centimeters. She tried again with Shaani helping. Bit by bit, it squealed open. The shark came hopping and raging toward them. The girls squeezed through the crack and stumbled into a great space that stank of old machinery. The shark crashed against the door, bursting it from its hinges. The door cartwheeled into the room, narrowly missing the women. But the doorway was too small to admit their pursuer. Xoota backed away then felt a wave of relief wash through her.

Safe.

The lab rat polished her spectacles. She waved her little penlight over the vast cavern all around them. The chamber was filled with machinery—titanic engines, sitting silent and dead in the bowels of the ancient ship. Still clutching her books, the rat touched an engine and marveled then swung her light to point toward one wall.

"That's the funnel. We can make another hole in it and climb out."

"Climb how?"

"Well, there should actually be rungs or something inside it, so they could clean and inspect it back in the day." The shark was still making a horrendous noise, trying to shove itself through the bulkhead door. "The point remains: How do we escape the shark once we're on the salt?"

Xoota looked up at the ceiling and scowled. "Budgie can outrun it. We just double mount and ride off, providing the little coward is still up there."

"Oh. Right-o, then." The rat seemed perfectly happy. She pulled a string bag from a pocket, put her books in it, and slung it behind herself like a backpack. "Well, this has been a success, then. Shall we go?"

"Oh, by all means." The quoll sniffed. "After you."

Something in the chamber smelled decidedly sour. Xoota followed the rat as she clambered up and over machinery. The sand shark raged and roared, making an appalling din. Shaani found her way to a wall and began to tap on it experimentally, one pink ear pressed against the metal, seeking out the worst areas of rust. The shark was making her investigations more difficult than strictly necessary. Eventually she tapped with her little fist then bashed the wall with her shovel. A rotten chunk of metal buckled away, and she was able to tear open a hole into the funnel and peer around with her light. Gray daylight filtered in from high above.

"Excellent." The rat paused and gave a sniff. "Eww. I think something's been nesting in here. It smells horrid."

"Is there a ladder?"

"Um, sort of." The rat shone her light awkwardly up the shaft. "Looks intact."

Suddenly the shark was gone. Xoota could feel the distant crash and smash of its maneuvering for a new route into the engine room.

Shaani gave a frown. "Did it just give up?"

"Maybe." Xoota hesitated. Her antennae were tingling. "Wait. I'm having a moment."

"Ah . . . Triumph? Satisfaction?"

"Hypercognition." The quoll's antennae flicked. "Shush."

She had a clear image of a tentacle smashing her to a pulp. She grabbed the rat by the tail and yanked hard. "Down."

Something long and large whipped through the dark, smashing into the walls, gouging open the rotten hull plates. The light showed only a glimpse of tentacle, suckers and dripping slime. The two women stared then plunged into the hole in the funnel's side. Xoota scrabbled up the ladder with Shaani hard on her heels. High above, a wide oval of daylight promised sweet, sweet safety.

The girls went into overdrive, clambering like roaches up the soot-encrusted ladder. A rung came clean off in Xoota's hands. She started to slip, but Shaani caught her backside from below and gave a shove. Xoota latched on to the rungs above, blew rust out of her whiskers, and climbed for all she was worth.

Shaani stopped and started to hammer her entrenching tool against the side of the funnel. Xoota gaped down at her in shock.

"What the hell are you doing?

"This."

The metal wall shook. Shaani sped up the ladder like lightning. Just below her, the sand shark came bursting in through the side of the funnel. It missed Shaani and plunged down to the bottom of the shaft. The green tentacle lashed out, and the shark bit the thing with mighty teeth. Suddenly an epic battle was being waged down in the dark. Xoota didn't bother stopping to watch. She climbed fast, yelping as another rung almost pulled free. The patch of brightness above grew closer and closer. She yelled up at the sky.

"Budgie. Budgie, where the hell are you?"

Up above her, the bird gave a chirp. Thank the sacred Space Goat for that one. Xoota clambered to the rim of the funnel and out into the blinding glare of day. Shaani joined her, producing little dark lenses that she clipped over her spectacles. Apparently pink eyes were not the best choice for functional eyesight.

Budgie was perched on the edge of the funnel nearby, feathers fluffed out and feeling burned by radiation. The ground was half a dozen meters below. All three beings chose a landing zone and jumped down. The impact stung Xoota's feet like hell.

Somewhere far below, the monsters still raged. Xoota gave a sigh.

"Come on. Let's get the hell off the salt."

The rat collected her speaker box, picnic rug, parasol, and bicycle. All packed up and happy to go, she walked the bike along beside Xoota and Budgie as they plodded wearily toward the nearby sand.

Xoota spared the girl a dire glance. "You seem happy."

"Information. We have successfully plumbed the vault of ages and have discovered knowledge."

"And what knowledge is that, exactly?"

"Oh." The rat wrenched her string bag around and read the mildewed titles, her glasses perched on the end of her nose. "Ah, *Principles of Sailing, Volume One* and the *Nautical Almanac.*"

"Oh, very useful . . ."

Xoota plodded along, antennae flat, fur fluffed out—injured, burned, and seething with ill humor. The eternal cheeriness of the damned rat grated on her nerves. Xoota held out one hand and saw that her pink skin was turning beet red.

"Damn it. I'm rad burned."

"Never mind. It will mend. You've only had half an hour." The rat offered bottled lemon tea to her companion. "Chins up. We can't all be lab rats."

Xoota took the proffered drink of tea. "Why is it you don't even have any scrapes or bruises?"

"Oh, luck of the draw, old bean. Alpha mutations. See, I'm already healed."

"Lovely." Xoota was covered in scrapes and bruises from head to foot, and radiation would probably make her wake up the next day with two heads. "I'm so happy for you."

Shaani waved her hand happily out toward the salt. "Well, never mind. Soon have you to safety, old horse. At least it's peaceful and quiet now."

It *was* quiet. Not a sound disturbed the world except the soft sigh of the wind. Shaani looked at Xoota. Xoota looked at Shaani. A sudden thought prickled through their minds.

Budgie took off in a panic, leaving the girls behind. The women sprinted for the sand shore. Behind them on the salt, the surface suddenly split as a curved fin broke up from the ground. Wailing, the women raced madly for the sand with the sand shark in hot pursuit. Xoota swore at Budgie as she ran for her life.

Bicycle bouncing in her hands, Shaani led the charge. As she headed away from the sands, Xoota could only stare at her in shock. But the shark roared, and Xoota ran after the rat. Shaani jounced madly along the shore, onto yellow rocks then up into a promontory crammed with boulders. She tossed her bike aside and hauled Xoota up. She sat them both down and patted at the stone.

"Solid sandstone. It can't tunnel here, and it can't climb. So we're safe. QED."

"QED?"

"*Quod erat demonstrandum*, old bean. It's Latin. What was to be demonstrated."

Xoota stood, puffing too hard to speak, leaning on her knees while she tried to catch her breath. Down below the rocks, the sand shark roared in frustrated hunger.

Budgie strutted toward her, chirping merrily. Xoota fixed him with a dire glare.

"You'll keep, you ingrate."

The day's excitement was clearly over. Xoota rose and grabbed Budgie's halter. She looked and saw that her water skin and packet of rations had somehow come free and fallen off the bird's saddle. They must be lying somewhere back on the salt.

Perfect, just perfect.

Shaani watched innocently from off to one side. "Is everything all right?"

"It's fine." Xoota sighed. Darwin only knew what she was going to eat and drink. It was eight days back to Watering Hole. The quoll rubbed her eyes and tried to figure out what to do.

Shaani settled her string bag and looked to the south. "Are you headed back to town? We can go together. Companions in the wild and all that. I can extend you some hospitality. Plenty of food and water for all."

Xoota accepted the inevitable. She wearily nodded her head. The rat girl clapped her hands together, pleased, and led the way, pushing her bicycle jouncingly across the rocks. Xoota trudged after her, feeling thoroughly tired.

"A good expedition." The rat was thoroughly pleased. "A first jaunt into the wilds. Monsters beaten, dangers overcome. One more sliver of information gained."

"Really?"

"Really." Shaani took a deep breath of the desert air, feeling refreshed despite the building heat. "Knowledge is the foundation. Upon the foundation, we build a better world. That's the creed of science."

"Right . . ." Xoota decided to increase the pace, hoping it might make the rat shut up. She led Budgie over to where a stand of tall, spiky plants grew in the shadow of the rocks, where she could mount the bird more easily. She climbed a rock, and Shaani called out to her from below.

"Oh, watch out for the pink ones."

The what?

A pink, spiny plant a few meters away suddenly bulged. Xoota blinked then flung herself into cover. Long spines hissed overhead. One lanced right into her exposed buttocks, jutting out like a second tail.

Oh, for kack's sake.

Shaani appeared, full of concern. Budgie emerged from behind a rock and gave the spine plants a wide berth. They both approached Xoota, who was much the worse for wear.

Budgie blinked. "Chirrup?" said the bird, expanding the limits of his vocabulary.

The rat girl saw the great, jagged quill jutting from Xoota's rear.

"Ooh, did that get your bottom? I mean, did that just alpha mutate there, or . . . ?"

It hurt like fire, but Xoota just felt tired. "Yes, it's a plant spine. Yes, it's in my arse."

"Right. I'll handle it. Never fear. A bit of simple first aid." Shaani grabbed hold of the quill. "Eyes front and think of science."

Xoota's eyes went wide in alarm. "Wait! Don't just—"

Shaani yanked the quill free. The thing had barbs. Xoota squealed like a piglet. She screeched again as Shaani poured alcohol from a first-aid kit all over the wound and patted it dry. The rat admired her handiwork.

"There we are. Good as new." Shaani patted Xoota's sturdy bottom. "With a bit of luck, you'll mutate overnight, develop regeneration for a day or two, and just be right as rain. Odder things have happened." The rat girl cheerfully clapped her hands together. "Let's make camp. Who's for lunch?"

Xoota felt dizzy. There was a concept—a thought so profound, so simple it almost defied expression, but somehow Xoota managed to articulate it. She looked at the rat girl and groped for words, and finally they came.

"I . . . *hate* you."

Sitting beside her on the rocks, Budgie puffed out his feathers and beamed. "Who's a pretty boy, then?"

Where did he learn that?

CHAPTER 2

Late afternoon in the desert: the shadows were growing long, termite mounds stood tall and stark against the sky. Off in the distance, something blue, carnivorous, and hairy drifted through the skies. A few errant clouds gathered, all touched with a soft glow of radioactive green.

Another wonderful day in the wilds . . .

A row of termite-eaten poles stretched off into the south, following the path of an ancient blacktop road. Beside the road, beneath a flowering acorn myrtle, Shaani had dug out a delightful little camp. She had plumped up two little pillows filled with gel and dampened them with water from her canteen, which caused a chemical reaction that kept the pillows sinfully cool. She set up a shade cloth and a parasol, put her music on low, and solicitously parked Xoota in the choicest piece of shade. There was even room for Budgie, who immediately tucked his head into his feathers and went to sleep. Xoota lay on her stomach and scowled, determined not to enjoy the comforts of the day.

A tiny sand gecko raced past, hungrily chasing a beetle. Five seconds later the gecko ran past again, pursued by zaps of electricity shot from the horribly mutated beetle. The world was that sort of place. Xoota ignored the spectacle and sighed.

Shaani had a solar still set up nearby, converting a cactus into a bucket full of water. She had clearly designed and made the system herself, just as she had built the little fan she plugged into a homemade battery to blow a soothing breeze across the camp.

Xoota's backside stung. Her skin was healing slowly. Shaani remained cheerful, self-possessed, and hospitable, in short the perfect companion. It drove Xoota to distraction.

The rat wrapped one of her odd little cooling pillows around a canteen. She poured a glass—nicely cooled—added lemon cordial, and proffered it genially to her guest. "Lemon barley water?"

Why anyone would put grain in a cool drink was beyond her, but Xoota's mouth watered at the sight of the cold, dew-beaded glass. It was incredibly delicious. She drank like a horse only to find another glass waiting for her once she had finished. Shaani laid a cold compress upon Xoota's throbbing rear and settled it happily in place.

"There we are. Should keep the swelling down." The rat waved one neat, elegant hand. "It's a cooling pack. Once you moisten it, the thing stays cold."

It was a miracle. Xoota blinked in surprise. "Where did you get those?"

"Oh, I found them. A lot of ruins—the buildings most people don't bother with—have them. Old camping stores, clinics . . . I tested the beads, found what they did, and put them to use. QED." The rat clinked a cool glass against Xoota's drink. "Cheers."

All right, Xoota had to concede that the rat had a certain gift. Nevertheless, she *was* annoying; bright and chipper people always were. The Great Sky-Bunny only knew how many scavengers had looked at those damned little clear beads in the past and dismissed them as packing material. The rat was clearly something of a genius. Well, perhaps an idiot savant. But she was still a damned liability in the wilds.

The long afternoon finally drew toward night. Xoota seethed, even as a wonderfully varied dinner was prepared from sets of premade meal packets that the rat, of course, had prepared far in advance.

Xoota was more of a take-away food fan. She would find an animal, take away its life, take away its skin, heat it, and eat it. The rat's cooking—mouthwatering with herbs, spices, and sauce—was a definite shock to the system.

Shaani served her guest first, giving her the correct cutlery, then ate happily in the shade beneath her parasol. She peered genially over the edge of her glasses at her scruffy, scowling guest. "Feeling anything?"

"What, a pain in the bum?"

"No, alpha mutation?" The rat wriggled her toes, perfectly happy with life. "You know, shifts in the old DNA. Dark essences surging through your soul?"

"No, not really."

"Ah, well. Can't be helped." The rat stretched deliciously, gaping her chisel teeth in a wide yawn. "Shall we get moving? The heat seems to have bogged off at last."

Xoota rose, wincing as her backside twinged with pain. Budgie tried to pretend that he was fast asleep. Xoota rapped him on the head to let him know that she was on to him and hobbled off to fetch the pack and saddle. She stood and scanned the horizon. Nothing moved; nothing stood out. There was only the long line of poles and occasional patches of ancient asphalt road.

"Who's a pretty boy, then?"

Shaani was messing around with Budgie again. Xoota flattened her ears and ignored it. She changed clothes, swapping one stained singlet for another, ready to armor up and hit the road. Shaani bustled by with her blankets and parasol and looked at the quoll's midriff in delight. "Oh, that's so cute.

"What?" Xoota looked down at herself and covered up. "Quit looking at my pouch."

"Sorry. But the marsupial thing is fascinating." Shaani made a closer inspection. "So technically I guess you'd have three breasts?"

"No, technically I have two breasts and a pouch." The quoll pulled her shirt as far down as it could reach. "Could we forgo the reproductive curiosity?"

"All in the name of science, old horse. To the inquiring mind shall come the treasures of wisdom."

Xoota muttered a curse, threw on her armor—making sure it covered her damned midriff—then buckled on her knives, mace, binoculars, and a quiver of crossbow bolts.

Dressed in a red and white bobble hat, her pocket-smothered shorts, and a neat new singlet, Shaani trundled her bicycle over onto the hard sand and mounted up. She rang the bell, much to Budgie's delight. Xoota swung up into the saddle and took another sharp look around the horizon. Then the two women moved south.

The shadows grew long and rich with orange light. In the evening, insects began to stir. Overhead, a few wisps of cloud streamed rose pink into the west. The sands were hushed and quiet; it was the desert at its best. Xoota heaved a sigh, glad to just be riding through the quiet of the day.

Shaani kept pace with the giant budgerigar, cycling along happily, taking in the view. The white rat drew in a breath of sheer delight. Then, inevitably, she began to chat.

"Ah, marvelous. So good to get out and do real field research at last."

Xoota glanced down at the slender white rat. "I'm not sure you're suited to it."

"Of course I am. It's in the blood, in the soul. We were the first mutants, you see. Rats, made into the partners of mankind."

Xoota raised one antenna. "Really?"

"Really." Shaani warmed to her subject. "We are the very embodiment of science."

"Is that good?"

"Of course it's good. It's pure. It's noble." Shaani waved one hand in enthusiasm, almost steering into a rock. "Science is liberty. The breath of freedom. The noble reach of minds seeking to make a better world."

"I'm fairly certain that dried-up seas, mutant porcupine plants, and killer sand sharks have not made this place a better world."

"Ah, but that was not because of science. That was cruel fate. It is up to science to make us a new home in these new lands, to open horizons."

Xoota sucked on a fang. "And you'll be orchestrating this because you're some sort of hereditary genius?"

"*Evolved.* Evolved as a help mate, as a *partner.*" Shaani looked eagerly up at the quoll. "You see, once upon a time, long before the Great Disaster, a perfect union was formed. Humans and laboratory rats worked hand in hand to try and further the benefits of science. Both races working together. Humanity created the laboratory rats to be beings of science, to help both species onward to a better future.

"Then came the Great Disaster. The humans are no longer the only evolved creature, so now the noble task falls upon us, their partners. Lab rats are here to carry on the noble tradition. To learn, to research, to benefit and heal the world."

They had drawn to a halt on a low rise of sandstone. Shaani excitedly fished into her pockets for her spare glasses. Kept lovingly inside the case was an ancient, yellowed piece of newspaper. She unfolded it carefully. With reverent hands, she pressed the paper flat, looking at it with love.

"I found this in an ancient archive when I was a nestling."

Xoota had no idea how to read. "What does it say?"

The rat girl gently stroked the ancient headline. "Laboratory rats give final proof: cure for ovarian cancer found." Shaani's eyes looked from a perfect past into a glorious new future. "A partnership. Humans and rats—one family, researching together, side by side, trying to make a better tomorrow."

Shaani gazed at the paper a moment longer then folded it back up and put it away as carefully as she'd taken it out.

They rode along together in silence. Xoota heaved a sigh and kept her thoughts to herself.

They moved steadily down the old, ruined road, carefully watching the world around them. Here and there, luminous bugs perched in the scrub, stretching their wings. Small creatures were on the loose—speedy-snails and geckos—moving around under a huge full moon. The light was excellent, predators and scavengers would all be out and on the job.

The broken wooden poles beside the road gave way to a row of tall, spindly pylons, each one topped by an ancient street light. There were some hillocks in the dirt nearby, possibly an entire string of old houses covered over by sand. Alternatively, it might actually *be* sand. Shaani stood up on her pedals and looked over the site with glee, her hat with two red bobbles gleaming absurdly in the dark.

"Excellent. You know, I have a feeling those might be buildings."

"Just hang back." Xoota tested the night breeze. There was a faint scent of moisture and a weird tingle of danger. She looked for a way to circle downwind of the ruins unseen. "Lots of things like ruins. You have to approach these places cautiously."

"Oh, wacko." The rat was not really listening. "Never fear. I'll be the soul of caution."

Xoota turned to carefully examine the local desert. By the time she turned around, Shaani was already pedaling off toward the sand mounds. Xoota cursed, kicked Budgie into a canter, and raced to cut the girl off.

"Hey!"

Budgie suddenly came to a halt, absolutely refusing to step any closer to the ruins. At least someone had some sense.

Xoota planted her fists on her hips and glowered at the rat. "Now look, I am the wilderness expert. You are the . . . the technical dude. You do not approach ruins unless they have been personally cleared as safe by my say-so."

Shaani looked a little chagrined. "Oh, yes, yes, yes. If you say so."

"Right." Xoota dismounted. She slung her shield across her back, took her crossbow in her arms, and loaded it. "So we do this properly, skilled and aware. You stay right there until I give you an 'all clear.' Do you understand?"

The rat rolled her eyes. "I understand."

"Fantastic." With mace, knives, shield, crossbow, and armor, Xoota headed toward the ruins.

The ground instantly fell out beneath her feet.

Something had cast an illusion across an expanse of sand. What had looked like flat sand was actually a deep, conical pit with sides made from cascading, slippery dust. Xoota lost her crossbow. She fell slipping down the slope. One brief glimpse at the bottom of the pit showed a great pair of insect mandibles jutting up from beneath the ground, clashing hungrily as its dinner slid toward it.

Xoota yanked out her two knives and jammed them into the dirt, frenziedly trying to claw her way back to the top of the pit. "Help me."

From a few meters away from the pit, Shaani called out uncertainly. "Is that an 'all clear'?"

"No, that's a 'help me.' " Xoota scrabbled for purchase on the shifting sand. Below her, massive mandibles scissored at the bottom of the pit. The enormous ant-lion larva made a delighted growling sound, anticipating quoll for dinner. Xoota desperately tried to climb. "Get me out. There's a bug in here."

Shaani poked her head over the edge of the pit. She looked at the carnivorous insect ravening away at the bottom of the pit, sucked her incisors in thought, then disappeared.

Xoota bellowed for her again, only to see a little fizzing firefly go whirling through the air above her, trailing sparks. It landed at the bottom of the pit.

Pipe bomb.

Xoota tried to hunch beneath the shield across her back. Moments later, there was an immense boom. The ground bucked and something slammed hard against Xoota's back. Debris crashed off her shield, one chunk of something moist and ghastly hit the back of her head. The breath was knocked clean out of her.

A cascade of bug juice came *gooshing* down all over her. Xoota, covered with bug innards, saw stars as she slowly slid down the side of the pit. Unable to move, she heard Shaani's voice through the ringing in her ears.

"How was that?"

"That's good. Thanks." Dazed, Xoota lay at the bottom of the pit. "Perfect."

The ant-lion larva was missing its head and a large chunk of its forequarters. The rest of it was twitching in an appalling lack of sympathy for Xoota's condition. The quoll girl's head spun. She tried to move her toes. "Shaani? I can't move."

"Ah, that's shock. Sorry. I used the bomb that had no casing—you know, no nails and chains and scrap metal? But it has a bigger bang."

"What the hell is this stuff all over me?"

"Juice."

"Juice? What do you mean 'juice'?"

"Juice." The rat seemed happy to explain. "Technically the liquid part of a vegetable, fruit, or insect. Which is why I normally only drink tea."

Xoota's stomach jerked. "I think I'm going to be sick."

"That might be good. You could gum the sides of the pit together and climb out."

"You're not helping." Xoota swallowed hard. The stench of bug guts was utterly nauseating. Normally she didn't mind eating insects, but the insides of the ant-lion larva smelled like a dead dingo's rectum. "Get me out."

A rope—newly plaited from tent cords—sailed down into the pit. It flopped onto the ground beside Xoota. Shaani called down happily from above. "Right. Grab on."

"What part of *'I can't move'* just refused to sink into your synapses?"

"Sorry. I wasn't sure whether it was just a turn of phrase." From the edge of the pit up above, Shaani adjusted her spectacles. "Hmm, I could make a loop. Or a lariat. I might be able to snag you."

"I don't think looping a noose around my neck is a great way to get me free."

"Ah, point taken, point taken." Shaani cast around and suddenly seemed pleased. "Here we go. Just wait there. I'll just nip off and get help."

The rat disappeared. Xoota lay and stared at the stars then frowned. "What help?"

There was no answer.

"Rat girl? What help?"

They were in the middle of an empty desert. Magnanimous passersby were going to be few and far between. Xoota was clearly the one stable creature adrift in an ocean of total morons.

Somewhere behind her, the ant-lion larva's body thrashed and jerked. It seemed to be going on and on; there was no actual sign of its dying. Xoota began to feel a nasty, crawling suspicion filter from her antennae down to her shoes.

"Is that thing regenerating?" She strained to hear if anyone was paying her the least attention. "Hello? Anybody? Listen, I think that giant bug is growing back its head."

There was a sudden bustle of motion at the top of the pit. Xoota felt a huge surge of relief. She relaxed back. Rescue at last.

A swarm of earwigs, each the size of a well-fed mouse, came running up over her toes. Several dozen of them perched on her chest and waved their feelers.

"Hi." The creatures spoke all at once in a high, soft, squeaky voice.

Xoota froze. Oh, kack, they were going to eat her brain. "Shaani?"

"Whee." Earwigs moved in a group, grabbing the end of the rope. "Helping. I and I helping." The bugs seemed pleased. "Very good help."

"Shaani!?"

Xoota's terror seemed to trigger off the bugs. They recoiled from her, scrambling at the sides of the pit, wailing and covering their eyes with their front legs. Shaani the rat poked her head over the side of the pit, out of breath from having run across the sand.

"Oh, good. They're here."

"What, you brought these?" Xoota was paralyzed. She could hear the cerci on the earwig's backsides clashing like knives. "They're going to eat me."

"Oh, tush. Don't be such a baby. This is a very helpful local resident I found over at the ruins. They want to help."

"How do you know that?"

"They told me."

"Well, of course they *told* you that." Xoota's skin crawled. "What the hell makes you sit up there and think it's true?"

"What, just because people come from a postapocalyptic radiation desert, they can't be nice?" Shaani tied her end of the rope to Budgie's saddle. "Now do hold still. We'll have you out in a mo'."

Bugs ran over to try to tie the end of the rope around Xoota's left foot. They scampered all over her legs. Xoota's fur stood on end. The bugs immediately began to squeal and churn. They crowded away from Xoota in revulsion.

Shaani gave an irritated sigh. She planted her fists on her hips and glowered down from the rim of the pit. "Well, now you've upset them." Shaani tapped her foot. "We really must work on those people skills of yours. Folk will start to think you truly don't like them."

"I don't like them."

"Shush." Shaani bent down to talk to the tail end of the sentient earwig swarm. "I do apologize, my dears. She's a tad distraught. Let's heft her out, and we can all have a spot of tea."

Invigorated by Shaani, the earwigs tromped down in a determined procession. Some clambered up onto Xoota's chest to oversee the operation, while others dragged the rope and tied it around her boot. Xoota glowered at the things.

One of the earwigs actually seemed to blow a raspberry at her. It turned its back and clashed its pincers.

Xoota gave a sniff. Fine, be like that.

The earwigs tugged the knot tight. A chorus of them called and waved to Shaani. The rat girl looked down into the pit then signaled Budgie to back away.

"Up we come. Haul away."

The rope tightened and creaked. Upside down and damned annoyed, Xoota was dragged up the side of the pit. She tried to blow back the sand that tried to cascade up her nose; too much of it found its way up her trouser legs. Attended by a swarm of busy bugs, she was finally hauled up onto the surface. She lay there and glowered over at Budgie, who tried to look innocent.

"You and I need to have a little talk about this trap-finding ability of yours."

The bird looked at her blankly. "Who's a pretty boy, then?"

"Right . . ."

 . . . . .

Long minutes later, Xoota lay on the sand, still unable to move. The earwigs bustled constantly around her, forming a sort of pyramid to help lift up her head. Others had brought over a bottle of cold, lemon tea with a long straw. The earwigs seemed very keen to help.

"Here we go, marsupial lady. Drinky drink."

Earwigs scuttled all over her, forceps clacking. Xoota felt sheer helplessness writhing through her skin. "Oh, crud."

The earwigs all looked at each other in concern. "Oh, crud."

The quoll girl fixed them with one eye and scowled. "Stop copying me."

The nearest earwigs scowled right back at her. "Okay."

Xoota just gave in. The earwigs scuttled forward and gave her a drink. It was Shaani's tea, extremely good. Xoota drank it with gratitude. "All right. Thank you."

"Welcome." The earwigs set the bottle upright in the sand. They lowered Xoota's head back down. "Welcome, welcome."

"Where is Shaani? You know, the rat lady? The thin one with the white fur and the ponytail? With glasses?"

"Pretty rat." The earwigs chorused happily. "Wig-wig helped pretty rat go down into the hole. Science."

Oh no, *more* science.

The earwigs were apparently helpfully trying to massage some life into her legs and feet. She rolled her eyes and stared up at the stars. It was not so bad. She just had to imagine that it was something other than earwigs . . .

Shaani came traipsing up out of the ant-lion pit, sounding pleased. She tossed jars and equipment onto the sand beside her. "So how are you doing, old gal? Still a tad stiff?"

"I still can't move, if that's what you mean."

"Thought not, thought not." The rat seemed tired but elated. "The critter had a paralytic poison it was intending to inject you with. When it blew up, it ended up all over your clothes and fur. Soaked into the skin, you see." The rat waved a sealed jar. "I have a sample, all airtight and sealed. I got it from the guts."

"Lovely." Xoota rolled her eyes toward the earwigs. "Why are they still here?"

"They're interesting." Shaani seemed pleased. "And 'they' might not be quite the correct term. The entire swarm refers to itself as 'I.' Possibly a shared consciousness. Fascinating."

"Oh, fascinating."

"Well, think how useful a swarm of little happy companions will be."

Xoota closed her eyes and winced. Oh, gods, make this end . . .

Shaani rummaged inside the packs of her bicycle and came out with a long bar of homemade soap. "Soon be fixed. Wig-wig, my dear, could you do the honors?"

The earwigs plunged in and wormed beneath Xoota. She suddenly found herself being transported across the sand, whisked along by a bustling horde of really large earwigs. She blinked in amazement.

"Where the hell are we going?

Shaani trundled her bike along at Xoota's side without a care in the world. "To wash you off, old bean. Get the toxins off you. Bath time. And we'll do your laundry. You should be right as rain in a while."

A bath? Xoota's eyes opened in panic. "Wait. We should talk about this."

"Nothing to discuss. Basic procedures, old gal."

"But I can't move. You can't just chuck me in the water."

"I'll hold your head up. Don't be such a baby."

The earwigs chorused happily beneath Xoota. "Baby?"

The quoll swallowed in panic. "Bathing can make you sick."

"Sick?" The earwigs suddenly seemed concerned. "Oh, no."

The rat girl looked drolly down at Xoota. "It most certainly does not."

"Can too."

"Yes, well, I wasn't going to say anything. But hygiene in the field is always a top priority." Shaani smelled clean and neat, with well-combed whiskers and beautifully plaited hair. By contrast, Xoota decidedly did *not* smell like desert roses. "Come along. In you go."

They plunged through a crack in a concrete wall and down into a building hidden underneath the ground. The sand mounds had hidden old concrete buildings. Something from an alternate earth had sort of appeared half inside a more mundane building. The merger had done neither structure the least bit of good. A sort of ceramic egg shape had been stuck through an ancient garage and grocery store. Cracked concrete ceilings still held the sand at bay, but the vast ceramic egg held a shallow pool of water.

Shaani found an old trough that looked as if it might do for a bath. Working with the help of the earwigs, she pulled old pots and buckets full of water up out of the cistern and filled the bath. They admired their handiwork as Shaani went to fetch some gloves out of her baggage.

Budgie had already plunged into the cistern and was splashing around, enjoying a wash. Xoota made a note to boil the water before drinking. She sighed then saw Shaani approaching her. The rat had a scarf around her head, an apron made out of an old sack, and elbow-length rubber gloves.

"Right, old bean. Let's get you out of your kit."

Xoota wailed in protest. The earwigs busily swarmed all over her, untying buckles and laces. Her boots were tugged off her feet, which was not the best of smells. Shaani went to work pulling off Xoota's armor, ignoring her curses, pleas, and wails.

"Stop. Just put me in my clothes."

"No. It all gets cleaned properly."

"Wait, no!" Xoota's visible skin blushed pink. "Close your eyes. Don't look at my pouch."

Shaani rolled her eyes. "We're not looking. Now do just be sensible."

"Eyes closed."

"Oh, very well." Shaani pretended to close her eyes. The earwigs could do no such damned fool thing, although Xoota apparently didn't realize it. They finally wrestled the quoll out of her bug-sticky clothing. Shaani then had the hard task of trying to lift a limp, paralyzed quoll woman up and into the bath.

"*Oof*. I say, you're rather compact."

Xoota sounded hurt. "I'm not that fat."

"I didn't say 'fat,' just compact. Like you're made of teak." Shaani managed to roll Xoota over into the water. "There we go."

With a splash, Xoota was in the tub. She floated with her head resting on the rim. The damned water was cold and found its way straight through her fur. The quoll immediately grumbled. "It's too cold."

"Don't be such a baby. It's lovely after the daytime heat."

"You're looking."

"Hush. I'm a scientist." Shaani grabbed her long, hard bar of soap. "Right, here we go. Eyes front and think of progress." Shaani began to scrub.

Xoota gave a plaintive wail. "Stop. Just let it soak off."

"No, it has to be soap."

A host of little earwigs suddenly peered over the edge of the tub.

"Wig-wig will help."

There was a tickling sensation inside Xoota's mind. Suddenly she felt a wave of lazy happiness spreading through her. It felt good to be lying there, with someone scrubbing hard at her fur with the soap. Delicious to just let someone else do the work. To just float there, without a care in the—

Xoota gave a jerk of shock and outrage. "Hey." She glared at the earwigs. "You knock that off."

"I helping," said Wig-wig.

"Leave my brain alone."

Shaani kept right on working. "Thank you, Wig-wig, dear. It was a nice thought. I have some apricots in my pack. Perhaps you would like to have them?"

The earwigs bustled off to investigate. Budgie, wet and refreshed, strutted over to watch the fun as Xoota made her first acquaintance with the wonderful world of soap.

The bug goo was all through Xoota's facial fur, her hair, her hands, her neck. Those were cleaned quickly. Shaani soldiered on, mercilessly scrubbing the quoll clean from head to toe. The bath water had turned a rather unpleasant gray. And after the old water was bailed out and new water poured in, the rat sat back in satisfaction.

"There. Can you feel your toes?"

She could. Xoota's eyes lit with happiness. She actually managed to move fingers and toes. Hell, she could almost sit up. "Yes. Hey, I can move."

"You're all right to sit there?" The rat wiped her face then used a stick to transport Xoota's clothes to an old, plastic bin she was using as a washtub. "Just sit there and soak while I do these. And we'll do your blankets and spare clothes while we're at it."

"But what will I wear when I get out?"

"Well, I'm not letting you get back into that filthy gear. You can borrow some of mine."

The rat girl set to work. She scrubbed at old, leather armor; underwear that was more dirt than cloth; singlet; shirts; pants; socks. It was sheer hard work. All the while, Xoota sat in her bath, life returning to her legs. The rat girl had managed to fold a little boat out of waxed paper, and had left it floating in the bath. Xoota heard the tough, unglamorous sounds of clothes being washed. She felt her skin tingling with cleanliness. She kept her eyes focused on her toes, feeling uncomfortable.

"Shaani?"

"Yes, yes?"

"Thank you." Xoota dragged the words out of her darkest, most cobweb-slathered mental archives.

The rat wiped her tired face. "No problem, old horse. A pleasure."

• • • • •

Half an hour later and two shades lighter, Xoota sat beside a little campfire sipping hot tea and eating damper, a bush bread made from grain and wattle seeds, and even a few bugs, herbs, and perhaps a rock or two. Her clothing and armor hung from a dozen different sticks and rails, all drip-drying in the cool, night air. Dressed in a blanket knotted at her shoulder, Xoota wriggled her toes at the fire, admiring the shine of her pink feet.

The earwig swarm sat on the rocks nearby, welcoming a load of warm damper Shaani had diced into cubes. The creatures ate with relish. They ranged in size from tiny babies to large adults; it was obviously a self-sustaining colony. The swarm was eager to be helpful. She glanced at her crossbow on a rock nearby; the colony had been kind enough to retrieve it from the ant-lion pit right after Xoota began her bath.

Xoota spread quince jam onto her bread and waved it at the earwigs.

"So, hey. You actually live here, yes? Here in this ruin?"

"For little bit. Sometimes in another place down road. Sometimes in the bushes, when rains come." Several insects spoke at once, all in chorus, sitting up on their forked backsides while other bugs ate like starving wolves. "This place is good in Big Dry. Wig-wig stay here for water. Water is almost gone now."

Xoota inspected the cracked ceiling. "So the reservoir must fill up during the winter rain."

"But this year, no rains come. Only little bit. So water be almost gone. Maybe two months, then be bye-bye." Several bugs sighed. "But boring. Boring. No one for I to talk to. Nothing new to do."

Shaani poured soup into a saucer for the bugs to drink. "Well, you should come with us. Come to the villages. There's always water there. And things to do."

"Glee." Bugs began to dance. "Glee. Glee."

"Wait, we are partnering up with bug swarms now?" Xoota lifted one finger, about to pontificate, when one of her antennae twitched.

Danger.

Xoota cursed. Never stay *at* a water source. Stay nearby. Too many things like to come to the water and drink. Earwigs flowed in a carpet, moving alongside a crack in the concrete, some of them looking outside onto the sand, and others hanging back to pass on the news. Xoota grabbed her mace and her plastic shield. She was rummaging around, trying to find her crossbow, when Shaani went running past her with a pipe bomb in her hand. The quoll pointed at Shaani with her mace.

"No bombs. Not in here. One more of those things, and I'll smack you." She waved Shaani into cover. "Over there. Get your shovel. Douse the fire."

The earwigs came bustling back. They seemed to always stay in fairly close proximity to one another. "Wig-wig saw. Is big pigs, maybe five, with stinky birds."

"Have they got a krunch wagon?"

"What is wagon?"

"Okay, thanks." Xoota hitched up her blanket and flitted over to the one point of exit into the upper world. She crept slowly, carefully up into the night air, moving with immense stealth. She settled between some sprigs of spinifex and carefully scanned the outside world.

Razorbacks.

There were five of them, war pigs in armor made from leather and metal. They were mounted on ragged, black cockatoos, which were aggressive and flightless, and they smelled bad enough to make the desert bushes wilt.

The war pigs were armed with flails and cleavers and crude bows slung across their backs. There was no sign of a wagon, though; razorbacks could sometimes pack some fairly heavy artillery. They were scouts for a war band, checking out the water supply, which meant a lot more razorbacks were on the way.

Two of them stayed mounted, while three others fanned out cautiously toward the ruins. The three incoming razorbacks readied cleavers and shook out their flails, the chains clanking in the dark.

Shaani stayed hidden in the crevice. She gave a polite, concerned whisper. "Is it bad?"

"Bad. We've got five of 'em."

"Are they butch?"

"Well, fairly heavy on the muscular side of things, yes."

"Should we use a bomb?"

Xoota bit her lip. "The ones on bird-back would ride off and summon the entire tribe."

"Can we just nip off unseen?"

"Not a chance." Xoota read the ground. The sand was too open to give any cover. She felt for her spare crossbow bolts. "I don't suppose you feel any neat new mutations coming on? Laser eyes, mind control—that sort of thing?"

"Um, no. Just the usual quickie healing. You?"

"Genius-level synapses—the usual." Xoota tried to somehow make a plan. The only thing she could think of was damned risky. "Right, okay. I'll open fire and draw them off. You sneak off west with the gear. I'll try to join you later."

"Most certainly not." The rat gave her a lofty glance. "I can't have you putting yourself at that sort of risk."

"Well, what else can we do?"

"Well, certainly nothing that leaves you facing the foe alone. A rat is ever faithful." Shaani prepared her shovel. "Species characteristic, old girl."

Five huge razorbacks were closing in. Shaani and Xoota despaired, when earwigs popped onto the sand.

"Never mind. Wig-wig will fix it," said the bug swarm.

Suddenly the air was swarming with earwigs.

Oversized earwigs, hundreds of them, glossy brown and black, wings whirring, pincers clashing, rose up from the sand and swarmed madly all around the razorbacks, buzzing, swerving, nipping, squealing. The pigs ducked and tried to cover their eyes, roaring as sharp forceps nipped at tender parts of their anatomies.

Xoota stared.

"They fly? I didn't know earwigs flew."

"Well, of course they do."

Some nearby earwigs climbed onto a rock and their wings flicked open like switchblades. The bugs waved to Xoota and Shaani, then joined the swarm, making gleeful noises as they sped in to the attack.

"Squee!"

Razorbacks cursed and swatted.

Some earwigs were already nipping the riding birds, making them screech and rear. The loose birds broke and ran. Cursing, the razorbacks still on bird-back tried to get their mounts under control, only to have the birds bolt off into the wilderness. Of the remaining three razorbacks, two ran off madly after their cockatoos, bellowing and cursing. Only one war pig—the biggest—decided not to run. Shielding its eyes, it staggered into the shelter of the ruins, roaring in rage.

Xoota cracked it on the rib cage with her mace.

The gigantic pig staggered then swung wildly at Xoota with its flail. Xoota ducked and took the blow on her shield. Earwigs buzzed around the razorback's eyes, making the monster snarl and curse. Xoota swatted the creature's flail aside and hammered her mace down onto its neck. The blow simply rebounded off the creature's hide.

Shaani smacked the razorback across its lumpy snout. Her spade made a noise like a ringing bell when she hit it, but the razorback simply shook its head and ignored her.

Xoota landed a solid blow on the enemy's skull. Her cog mace was no laughing matter. The razorback staggered, half stunned. It shook its head, saw Xoota, and gave a savage roar.

Shaani looked behind the pig and brightened.

The ant-lion pit.

Shaani held her little shovel like a battering ram and charged. She hit the razorback as it ducked beneath Xoota's mace. The razorback staggered and its footing gave way. It spilled, tumbling down the side of the ant-lion pit, and landed in a crash and tangle of armor.

Two giant mandibles lashed up from beneath the sand, almost cutting the razorback in two. An instant later the creature had been yanked under the sand. Xoota could only stare.

Exhausted, Shaani leaned on her shovel. She wiped her brow then peered into the pit.

"Oh, it *did* regenerate. I say, you were spot on."

The earwigs landed *en masse* on the sands. A few were bent and damaged but seemed to be healing. One battered creature simply stretched, glowed purple, and popped its cracked carapace back in place before trotting off to join the swarm.

Still stunned by the violence of the razorback attack, Xoota looked down at the little bugs. "Hey. Ah . . . thank you."

Wig-wig seemed well pleased.

The other razorbacks would be back soon. Xoota and Shaani swiftly gathered up their goods. Budgie kept glancing off to the north, where the noises of a distant war band could be heard on the breeze.

It was time to go. As the two women mounted up, the earwig swarm gathered all around.

"Wig-wig will come too." The bugs seemed excited to be off. "Which way? Which way?"

"South, old bug." Shaani pointed with her entrenching tool. "South and away."

"Glee." The earwigs flowed around them like a carpet as the women rode off to the south. They headed away from the deep desert, down an ancient, broken road. Xoota rode with her head held high; Shaani rode with a smile.

The quoll sneaked a suspicious glance. "What?"

Shaani's whiskers gleamed. "You have underwear with little hearts all over them."

With immense yet fragile dignity, Xoota lifted up her chin. "I *found* them in a ruin. They fitted me."

The budgerigar flapped his little wings. "Who's a pretty boy, then?"

"Oh, shut up."

CHAPTER 3

Watering Hole.

Not so much a town as a sad accident, the settlement had been formed on the Great Disaster, when a large tidal bore dumped an assorted collection of shipping right on top of a picturesque, seaside resort. To add insult to injury, a space vessel from a parallel dimension had materialized overhead and crashed down on top of the entire pile, splitting into three pieces and irradiating everything for three hundred kilometers downwind. With the entire ocean drying up and the death of all known civilization, the tourist trade had decidedly dropped off. It was, however, the site of the one and only constant water source in the entire desert lands.

Apart from that, it had absolutely nothing to recommend it. The village was home to a population of perhaps three hundred, spread across an intriguing collection of families, species, and sub phyla. There was a sturdy, fortified wall made from vehicles, old junk, and rubble. Beside the front gates there was a radioactive dust pit avoided by all except the few people who actually *lived* in it.

Most residences were inside either old, half-buried boats or one of the tall chunks of ruined spaceship. A collection of bamboo ladders, balconies, and laundry lines removed any sense of grandeur the old ship might once have had, but such is life.

There were smithies, stables for budgerigars and ambulatory riding plants, scrap dealers, street stalls, and a tannery. It all centered on the great stone watering hole—a deep, smooth-sided hole from which an old hand pump gushed water into buckets carried by the locals. Every morning, farmers worked to fill the water carts that took the precious liquid to the fields.

A tavern had pride of place for the village, carved into the side of a rusty tramp freighter. A painted board swung above the entry hole: *Snappy's Tavern—best in the west!* Famous for its potluck stews and barium meals, it served as a hotel and impromptu meeting hall. The tavern was also home to a number of female "dance artists" who were not so much exotic as downright weird. Still, the lunchtime cat girl show always drew a steady crowd. The owner was an easy-going mutant crayfish, her bouncer was eight feet tall and sheathed in rock, and the waitresses could temporarily clone themselves during rush hour. All in all, it was a homey place—provided your home was inside a boat filled with weirdoes.

Dusty, hot, and tired, Xoota and Shaani tramped in through the door with Wig-wig swarming along at their heels. They brought with them baggage, a considerable amount of dust, and a good deal of thirst. Xoota headed over to the tables against the bulkhead wall, picking one as far from the dance stage as possible.

The tavern had high ceilings with a series of fans that dispelled a little of the heat. It was still an hour until dusk, but most life in the desert was nocturnal. The only patrons at the time were a group of locals avidly playing cards, three traders eating cheese, the cat girl snoring in one corner, and a man with light blue skin who sat at the bar, weeping into his beer.

Shaani took it all in with interest—an anthropologist studying her specimens. "Fascinating. So this is a tavern?"

"This is it." Xoota swung a considering glance at the rat. "Surely you've been in a tavern?"

"Well, not really. The settlements down south have a few—but they weren't really my kind of place."

"Well, here's where you get food, drink, a place to stay. You can do business, meet clients, make trades—"

"I much admire the lizards."

Two slim gecko girls moved through the room, collecting glasses from tables. Xoota planted her booted feet up on the table. "Echo-gecko One, and Echo-gecko Two. They're twins. Actually, sometimes they're more than twins. There always seem to be a few of them around."

Wig-wig was fascinated. There were a great many things to do and see. The swarm of glossy bugs flowing over the floor beneath the tables found some interesting discarded nuts and snacks then swept up and onto the bar. The insects sat themselves beside the blue man, who turned them a miserable glance and shoved a glass of beer in their direction.

"What can you do, man? What can you do?"

Multiple earwigs looked up at him and nodded solemnly. "Do," they said in unison.

"She was supposed to meet me here. The bridal suite . . . our one-year anniversary. All booked and paid for. And now all I have is a note, a lousy note breaking it all off." The man half collapsed over the bar. "Just right out of my life. Just like that. One minute she's there then *pow*. Next minute she's gone." The man waved to the crayfish barkeep. "A round for my friend." He hung his head. "She said *I* wasn't able to understand her. She said *he* has two brains. That's twice as much to 'get' her. But I got her. Me. Old one-brain. We had good times. I mean, does that all count for nothing?"

"Nothing." Wig-wig looked distressed. A long chain of earwigs took turns drinking beer from a tankard made out of a dingo's skull. Others clustered around the blue skinned man and wrung their forefeet in distress. "How could she do this to you?"

At the gambling tables nearby, several burly scrap miners were swapping predatory looks. A thin, gangly boy was playing cards with them, losing steadily. He was anxious and confused, unable to comprehend why every single hand was going against him. The laughter of the miners only made him more determined and confused.

Over at the dinner table, Xoota waved a finger and drew the attention of a gecko waitress.

"Geck. This is Shaani. She's a scientist from down south. And, ah . . ." Xoota looked to Wig-wig over at the bar. "Yeah, the insect swarm is with us as well. Keep them away from the live food tank."

The gecko wiped her hands on a grubby apron. "So . . . what can I get you?"

Shaani brightened. "Oh. Can I see a menu?"

Xoota cleared her throat. "Can we have three meals, please? One carni-insectivore, one omnivore, and . . ." What *did* earwigs eat, anyway? "Make that two omnivore. And three omega ales, please."

"Ooh." Shaani happily adjusted her spectacles. "Do you have any cheese?"

"I believe some has just spawned, madam."

"Ah, excellent. Do please bring us some."

The waitress left. Xoota looked uneasy. "I don't have much money . . ."

"Oh, I have a little. What's mine is thine. Never worry."

"That's just it, you never worry." The quoll fixed Shaani with a dire glare. She looked around. "Where did that earwig swarm go, anyway?"

· · · · ·

Up at the bar, the blue drunk poured his life's woes out to Wig-wig, who sat there beside him, agreeing with every word.

"She never loved me."

"Never." The insects wailed. "Never never. Waaah."

"She was just using me all along."

"She betrayed you." Earwigs waved their forefeet. "Stabbed you in the back."

"My life is pointless."

"A total waste. Eeeee—no point going on."

Xoota stomped up to the bar and pointed a commanding finger. "Will you stop that? Knock it off. You're making things worse."

"But she left us."

"She didn't leave you; she left him." The quoll chased the bugs away from the weeping drunk. "Sorry, man. You just go right on with enjoying your evening."

The blue-skinned drunk collapsed. The bouncer grabbed him by one ankle and dragged him off, transferring him to the back shed where he could sleep it off. Xoota returned to find their table filled with bowls of stewed, gray lumps; bread made with locusts and grasshoppers; and a platter of cactus-fried potatoes for those who ate vegetables. Tankards of beer gave off a faint green glow—omega ale at its best. Ignoring the biohazard runes on the tankard, Xoota drank gratefully and deeply, feeling it tingle right down to her toes.

"Ah." Xoota put down her half-empty tankard. "Drink up. It puts hairs on your chest."

"I have hairs on my chest already."

"Well, it puts a chest on your chest." Xoota drank again. "Cheers."

Shaani drank then smiled at the pleasant taste—not sour, not sweet, with just a hint of omega particles. Beside her, Wig-wig tucked in to a full meal of stew, grasshopper bread, vegetables, and beer. Shaani ate and drank with delicate decorum, keeping her long whiskers clear of foam.

Xoota poked a long spoon at Shaani's plate. "Are you going to eat your locust bread?"

"What? Oh, no, do be my guest." She jabbed at the stew with her spoon then stirred it and sniffed the nice aroma. "So this is your tavern? Your haunt?"

"This is the place." Xoota sighed. Kack, she was broke. The meal was going to wipe out the last of her funds. "More ale?" She might as well drink while she had the opportunity.

"I'm not sure we should," cautioned Shaani.

"Oh, live while you can." More ale came, thicker stuff from the bottom of the keg that glowed an interesting hue of green. "Drink up. Here's to friendly encounters."

Shaani drank her ale. She continued to poke at her stew, but she downed the cactus-fried potatoes enthusiastically. The earwigs ran around, cleaning everybody's plates. Relaxing somewhat, the rat gazed around, watching the tavern slowly fill up with the evening crowd.

She blinked then checked under her arms. "I'm growing tentacles. What a bother."

Xoota shrugged happily, drinking another ale. "Had to happen eventually."

"I suppose so . . . Still, it is better than the time I accidentally grew a rubbery shell. I suppose they'll wear off eventually."

"'Spose so. Meanwhile pass the cheese."

A long tentacle pushed the cheese platter in Xoota's direction. All over the table, contented earwigs rested on their swollen abdomens and sighed.

Xoota flopped, tired and contented. "Well, with this feast, I'm broke."

"I'm afraid I'm running dry on funds as well." Shaani rested her head, propping her face up with a tentacle. "We should find somewhere to stay."

"We can has a room." An earwig waved a lazy foot. "Bridal suite."

"Really? The blue man told you that?" asked Xoota.

"All paid for. No one using it."

"Sounds good. Let's pay for this and scoot."

It had been a long, eventful trek through the desert, but she didn't bring anything home to barter. Xoota was going to have to find a paying job just to cover her own food and seed for Budgie. It didn't bear thinking about until morning. Bone weary, she collected Shaani and the earwig swarm and headed up the rusty steps that led to the rooms.

Sharing accommodation with a rat and a swarm of empathic bugs . . .

Ah, well. How bad could it possibly be?

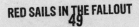

The immense bed came with an actual sheet and anteapoca-
lypse feather pillows. There was enough bed for two people
to sprawl and feel happy.

It was best to keep your distance when sleeping near Shaani,
she was good enough to inform Xoota. For one thing, she
sometimes gave off an odd, green glow at night. For another,
when she dreamed happy dreams, she gave off electric sparks.
Luckily the bed was big enough that she thought it wouldn't
be a problem.

Having accommodations for the night meant Xoota did
not have to wake up long before dawn, saddle a chattering
budgerigar and tramp off into the dust. She could sleep in,
luxuriating in actual sheets and an ancient mattress with actual
springs. She sprawled, naked and happy, drifting off into the
wonderful oblivion of sleep—until a noise ripped right through
her skull like a buzz saw.

It was like someone using a file on an upright metal
spike, like nails dragging down a sheet of slate. The noise
actually made Xoota's eyeballs bulge. She jerked upright
in the absurdly huge bridal bed, its canopy festooned with
snoozing earwigs.

Over beside the speckled mirror and wash stand, Shaani
was looking at herself in the mirror, industriously working
away on her incisors with a great, old file. The noise was utterly
appalling. Xoota felt horrified.

"What the hell are you doing?"

"Ah. G'morning." The rat cheerfully waved, apparently ready
for yet another day of high adventure. "Doing the full grooming
thing. Sorry. Do you need the mirror?"

Xoota rubbed at her eyes. It wasn't even dawn, and she
already had a headache. Her antennae flopped down to either
side of her head. "Why are you doing that to your teeth?"

"Ah. My incisors grow at a set rate per week. If I don't keep
them down, they might eventually pierce the roof of my mouth
and impale my brain."

Xoota collapsed back onto bed and seethed. Darwin, let it be soon . . .

Anyway, it was time to get up. She was broke, not even enough for a stake to get back out there and explore, which meant going out and making some sort of deal with idiots out there in the town—courier work or caravan escort to the south.

Damn.

The room had a bucket shower suspended above an old bathtub. Shaani flicked a significant glance from the bucket to Xoota. The quoll bowed to the inevitable and levered herself up out of bed. Working a bad taste from her mouth, she trudged over to the tub, poured a bucket of water up into the overhead, and endured being made wet and miserable.

Whiskers drooping, she soaped herself. At least all the bathing seemed to have exterminated her fleas. She held up one hand, rubbed at her eyes, and examined her fingers.

A little glimmer of light flickered about her fingertips. When she concentrated, it grew brighter. Xoota gave a sigh. "Damn it. Why do I never get any cool alphas?"

Alpha mutations were the periodic and unpredictable effects that resulted from the different energies at play in the world. Sometimes they altered a creature's physical nature, activating a piece of junk DNA, for instance, turning the mitochondria into something new and different. Sometimes they altered the mind's ability to affect reality. Sometimes it was a matter of unlocking the secrets of the dark matter in the universe. Whatever the case, it was usually something weird, and not always helpful, but it was seldom permanent.

"Hmm?" The rat girl had removed the braids from her hair. Loose, it cascaded all the way down past her rear. She still had her silly tentacles from the night before, waving sinuously from her back. "Did you get a change in the night?"

"That stupid omega ale." Xoota rinsed off under a second bucket of water. It tasted a little brackish in her mouth. "Some people? Laser vision. Me? *No.* I just have to go all sparkly at the edges. Could that *be* any more lame?"

"Some might find it appealing."

"Then they're idiots." Xoota found a well-worn piece of sacking to use as a towel and rubbed herself dry. Her newly cleaned fur stuck out at a thousand silly angles. She shook herself in an effort to make the stuff behave. "Why don't the damned earwigs have to bathe?"

"They groom themselves very nicely, thank you." Some of the female earwigs were sleeping with their own young stacked on top of them. "Wig-wig is really rather neat."

Wig-wig had also managed to sleep through all the noise. Many of the earwigs snored—truth be told, in imitation of Xoota. Others worked their pincers and blearily gazed around before deciding to go back to sleep.

Xoota found underwear, boots, and trousers.

"We'd better get the hell out of here before the blue guy gets over his DTs." She managed to open a hole in one of her socks as she tried to pull it on. Damn. "I guess I'll see you around."

The rat was braiding her hair, her fingers skilled and nimble. "We're broke," said Shaani.

"No, *I'm* broke and *you're* broke," said Xoota, sitting in her heart-spotted underwear. "Two very separate things. Two unconnected individuals." She jerked on her pants.

"Ah, can any individuals be truly unconnected? When each particle can influence every other, when each observer changes the universe simply by the act of observation, does that mean any of us can truly claim disconnection from our fellows?"

"True." Several earwigs peered over the bed, waving their feet. "Science."

"Science." Shaani took an earwig into her hand and tickled it under the chin. "Quite so, dear chap."

"Glee."

"Who asked you?" Xoota speared the earwig swarm with a dark glance.

"He is empathic. He senses a deeper truth." Shaani was dressed for action. "The three of us, all together. Companions in adversity." The rat girl pulled on her straw hat and settled her goggles on the crown. She slammed her entrenching tool into its sheath at her side. "Never fear. Science will show the way."

"Science will show the way . . ." Xoota grumbled and gathered up her gear. "All right, mighty scientists. Well, I have to go and look for work. Alone, if you please."

"An excellent concept. We can distribute our efforts more efficiently if we spread out and conduct an individual search." Shaani and the earwigs hastened after Xoota as she stomped down the stairs. "We'll meet at the well. Midday."

Xoota headed out into the dusty streets.

・　・　・　・　・

Shaani watched Xoota leave the common room then girded her loins and looked around the tavern. She found a single waitress quietly enjoying breakfast in one corner and marched over to address herself to business.

Wig-wig, meanwhile, swarmed merrily up and over tables. In a gloomy corner of the bar, the gambling boy from the night before rested his horned head in his hands. He sat, glumly regarding a meager, glittering pile containing his last few coins.

Earwigs climbed up to sit on the table beside him. "Aw, down on luck?"

"Not for long." The boy seemed determined. "I'll get my money back. Just you see."

The earwigs clustered around the boy and beamed. "We'll see. We'll see." The earwigs began to dance. "Glee."

・　・　・　・　・

Out in the stark light of the morning, Xoota stomped about her business. She made sure Budgie had a new seed bell from her store of feed and fresh water, though the water smelled a little strange. Then she walked off to see a few contacts and try to rustle up some coin.

The scrap dealers and artifact merchants weren't interested in subsidizing any journeys. It had been years since the last decent store of omega tech had been found, which had given the town an official tally of two laser pistols and an energy whip that worked only one time out of ten. Still, it helped keep the razorbacks at bay. But no one had any confidence anymore. The desert was all played out—there were no more bright, new treasures to be found just under the sands. The world was bounded by thirst, sand, and salt, and the days of rich pickings had come and gone.

Xoota tromped over to the general store, where there was sometimes news of caravans that needed a guard or two or a parcel that required delivery to another village. As she stepped into the store, she drew a blank. All travel seemed to be halted; the Big Dry was upon them, and no one wanted to travel during the dry season.

She ended up at the mechanist's forge, where she sold off the gears and cogs she had found out in the desert. The fat, genial store owner had a metallic skin caused by a nanite plague he had picked up in an unfortunate sexual encounter as a youth. He seemed to have come to terms with the affliction and had a metallic wife who helped him mind the store.

Xoota sat and discontentedly counted out the coins she had just been paid. They were trade tokens in silver and gold, fifty *domars.* Polishing his newly acquired cogs, the store owner sat himself down at his bench.

"Good stuff. Good stuff. Looks like they might be useful."

Xoota wrinkled her snout. "Yeah, well, I'll be charging more for those in the future. There's less and less out there these days."

"Work's drying up?"

"I'm open to commissions."

The shop owner brightened. "Well now. Well now, well now, well now. Had a chap in here earlier today who might have work. Human chap. Jolly good skin. Asking about guides for a trip into the wilderness. Cash in plenty. Seemed the genuine thing."

Xoota's antennae tested for pitfalls and found nothing but a tingle. "Really?"

"Absolutely. He's getting tailor-made armor being crafted across the street. Had all the gear . . ."

"Can you point him out to me?"

The merchant beamed. " 'Course I can. 'Course I can, 'course I can, 'course I can. That's him right over there." He pointed to the armorer's across the way. "With the chin that looks like a backside."

Over the road, a massive figure emerged from the armorer's. He was huge for a human, far over two meters tall, broad and horribly powerful. The man had cold eyes and stark, blond hair. With perfect human teeth and unblemished skin, he was the most photogenic individual to accidentally step into budgerigar poop in the town of Watering Hole. Xoota examined the man, feeling a tad confused, and rubbed at her neck.

"That's him? He looks a bit . . . well polished."

"That's the man." The merchant shook his head in admiration. "Beautiful speaking voice."

"Oh goodie."

Ah, well, it might be just what the sawbones ordered. Xoota gathered up her coins and headed out into the street.

Mister Adonis—the world's most perfect man—was admiring the fit of his brand new, tailor-made plate armor. His gear seemed high on polish and low on practicality.

Xoota twiddled her long whiskers then walked over to the man and gave a nod of her head. "G'day. The guy over the road said you were looking for guides?"

The strong man turned. He looked down at Xoota from on high, towering over her. His sheer bulk of muscle would have intimidated anyone less foul tempered and ornery than a quoll.

The human seemed to hesitate before he spoke, as if wondering if it was worthwhile speaking down to her. "I do not normally work with *animals*." The man's voice seemed to dwell on the term. He drew in a sour breath. "However, I am told that entering the desert requires a guide. I need the services of the most skilled personnel possible."

Xoota measured the man for a swift kick to the happy sacks. But she needed money. "Well, we can discuss it. Where are you thinking of heading, Mister?"

"Benek." The man did not look at her as he spoke. "You may know me as Benek."

"Well, you may know me as Xoota."

"Is that your title?"

The quoll sucked on a fang. "Well, my actual title is Great Sage, Equal of Heaven. I tend to just let it drop."

Benek gave an uncaring shrug. "Xoota will suffice."

Oh, this is going to be fun. Xoota's antennae drooped ill temperedly beside her face. "Well, Benek. Should we go to the tavern to discuss your business?"

"I do not pollute my body with alcohol. My germ-plasm must remain utterly pure."

"Fine. How about a bun and a cup of tea?"

"That would be acceptable."

They made their way over to a nearby bakery. Although Xoota was essentially a carnivore, she did like to gnaw on something sweet. She had also missed her morning mug of tea, which might possibly have explained her fraying temper. She led the way over to the settlement's little bakery, asked for tea and a sweet pepper-seed bun, and sat herself down on a bench beside the shop. A eucalyptus tree spread shady branches above, making the whole place tolerably cool.

Benek chose a multigrain bread roll and contented himself with pure water poured from his own canteen. Xoota sipped her tea and made a face; the damned stuff was strangely salty.

"So, Benek. You have a mission in mind?"

"I do. A mission of the gravest import." The constant breeze stirred the air beside the shop. Benek checked his perfectly set hair in the bakery window's reflection. "I have to be taken to an ancient installation, a slice of an omega world."

He produced a bag and poured its contents out across the table. There were several bright, new photographs printed on stiff plastic; a small, oblong box with a window in it; and an old power cell with a decent amount of charge left on the meter.

Xoota poked at the odd box. "What is this?"

"Ah, it's a military training tool of the ancients. In this small screen, mutants and zombies approach. The trainee must destroy them before they reach his base." The man put the little machine away. "I have the current high score."

"Wonderful." Xoota pulled over one of the photographs. It showed a line of tall, cylindrical structures that gleamed red and copper, white and gold. "And these?"

"Those are our target."

The man spread out the photographs. There were three main points of view, all from along a fence line that ran beside a series of flamboyant buildings. Beside the buildings, a row of immense, gleaming darts stood on their tails with their noses pointed at the sky. Benek ran a thoughtful hand over the images.

"It is unlikely that you would recognize the technology, but this is a starport, what you would term an omega-tech facility."

Xoota restrained an urge to bite the man. Was he talking down to her because she wasn't human? "I see."

"What you won't see from the photographs is the desolate surrounding area. Clearly its sheer isolation has kept the site from vandalism," Benek said pedantically.

That isolation might be the teeny, *tiny* detail of difficulty about the job. Xoota tapped a photograph against the table. "If the site is isolated, then where are these photos coming from?" she asked.

"Downloaded in real time from an ancient device. The screen worked for three days before it finally failed." Benek drew forth another photograph. He looked at the image in reverence. "The treasure of the ages . . ."

The photograph showed a long, dark cavern, an enormous hollow lit by a cold, blue glow. The walls of the cavern were covered in booths, frost-smothered glass cylinders festooned with power cables. Benek looked at the image and smiled.

"Cryogenic booths—still operating. These hold two thousand female colonists, genetically perfect human women once destined to populate the stars. But now they shall help reclaim the savage earth." The man slowly flexed his fists. "So when I say I have a mission, understand that it is my genetic destiny to restart the human race."

Xoota looked at Benek over her sticky bun. "Restart the race?"

"Yes."

"You mean *you* restart the race. You intend to father children by two thousand different women?"

"Of course."

"Well, at least your free time will be spoken for." Xoota felt a creeping sensation of aversion rippling beneath her fur; most simply articulated, it would have made a sound something like *eww*. His was the creepiest proposal she had heard in years. In fact, she had a little trouble not throwing up into her mouth. Swallowing tea, she winced and tried to go back to business.

"So, Mister Benek, you . . . ah . . . you want a guide to help you reach this . . . this treasure trove?"

"Indeed." Benek swept a giant hand out to indicate he owned time, space, and the stars. "I have prepared the essentials. I have a storage tank containing a thousand liters of pure water. I have dried rations to last for months. And now I have combat gear that will allow me to overcome the monsters of the wastelands. I need only secure guides to assist me in my travels."

"Mmm-hmm." The quoll leaned back in her seat, annoying sparkles twinkling in her fur. "And where exactly *is* this treasure trove of yours?"

The massive, perfect man looked off toward the horizon, pointing with one iron-muscled arm. "There, at the far side of the great desert."

Somehow Xoota managed to keep a straight face, although her tail sparkled. "The far side of the desert?" she said with a measure of incredulity.

"Indeed."

"The uncrossable desert?"

"Quite so."

"The uncrossable desert, called that because it cannot be crossed?" Xoota thought the point was worth reiterating; she had been dealing with lesser intellects for most of her life. "The waterless desert, lacking, as it were, in water."

Benek patiently nodded his head. "Ah, yes, but as I have said, I have stockpiled a thousand liters of pure drinking water."

"Which would make for a portage load of one ton." Xoota wearily tried to explain basic logistics to yet another moron traveler. "Look, your problem is basic portage, loads carried. A pack budgerigar can carry about one hundred and sixty kilograms. One-thirty if you're out for a long haul. So that's about . . . what? Eight budgies to carry that load of water? But the budgies themselves will need to drink water. They drink about three liters a day. So for every five days you plan to be out, you will end up needing another budgie load of water to supply the budgies—and then some budgies to supply the budgies who are supplying the budgies. Not to mention the budgie handlers—one man leading every two birds." Xoota waved a finger. "Now also figure about four liters of water per person, per day out there in the dry. We're starting to get an entourage larger than the entire pack budgerigar population of the known world. And the desert just goes on and on. I've gone out one month in every direction, and it was all just the same. Only drier. We are surrounded by an impenetrable wall of dust."

"But it does end." Benek was adamant. "The photographs prove it."

"Do we know they're really from the other side of the desert?"

The man seemed pleased. "Oh, yes. Time codes on the photographs showed that sunset arrives there about three hours before local sunset here at the villages."

"Three hours." Holy kack. That was . . . Actually Xoota had no idea how far away that would be. What, one-eighth the width of the entire planet? Shaani would know. "That's too far to go by budgie."

"But has anyone ever tried to cross the desert?"

"I've come across the bones of several who thought it was worth a shot. It's not a pretty sight."

Benek sipped his distilled water and pondered. "The solution seems simple enough. Clearly a means of transport other than pack beasts is required." He nodded. "Perhaps you could turn your thoughts to this. Serve me in this, and I will see that you are well provided for."

Xoota rose from her seat. "Yes, well, I'll certainly let you know if any inspiration comes my way. We wouldn't want to see you miss out on your procreative adventure." Xoota raised her tea mug in farewell salute. "Good day to you, Benek."

"Good day." Benek rose too. He did not offer to shake hands. The man strode off into the village, casting dark, condemning glances at the mutants quietly walking the streets.

Xoota watched him go and shook her head. Sadly Xoota was forever doomed to engage against inferior intellects . . .

Ah, well, time to start rethinking the whole job search. Xoota sank back down and finished her tea. She made a face at the awful taste.

What the hell was wrong with the water?

· · · · ·

"Salt."

With goggles, gloves, and fantastic industry, Shaani had set up shop beside the Watering Hole. She was at the center of an anxious crowd of onlookers. The rat pushed up her goggles and peered into her glass retort then carefully tasted the powder inside it.

"Sodium chloride . . . A few other additives. But it's salt."

She had boiled ten liters of well water, distilling it down further and further until the liquid had all gone. What remained was a crust of white crystals. Shaani carefully scraped the crystals out onto a delicate set of scales, measuring the results. "Ten grams per liter. That's bad. Very, very bad."

The town mayor listened, his long face ashen gray. Other citizens from the settlement gathered around the rat.

The mayor looked at the well—utterly appalled. "Is it drinkable?"

Shaani wrinkled her long snout. "Just within tolerance but you say it's gotten worse and worse over the last week?"

"Well, yes, yes it has."

The rat was damned unhappy. "This is only just short of being poisonous. Much saltier than this, and you will dehydrate; you'll expel more liquid in urine than you take in by drinking."

The mayor swallowed. "And if it gets worse?"

"If it grows three times this salty, it would be quite deadly." Shaani sniffed at the salt. "This isn't pure sodium chloride. I'd say it's sea salt."

"Sea salt?"

"Much like the salt out there on the great salt flats." The rat pondered. "Could the groundwater have become contaminated by the salt plains?"

"It's always been fresh. Perfectly fresh."

The rat was totally fearless. She clapped the mayor on one armored shoulder. "Never fear, old chap. We can rig you a solar still, use it to purify drinking water for the town. Should last you a while."

A lizard woman spread her frilled neck fringes in alarm. "But what about the crops? The fields. We can't distill enough water to keep the fields irrigated."

"Well, there is always a solution. Science will show the way." Shaani, the bold avatar of scientific spirit, gathered up her equipment. "More data is needed. We must investigate." The rat slapped one hand against the rim of the well. "I have a crack science and exploration team. We shall make a proper study. If I could trouble you gentlefolk for a very long and sturdy rope and a few stout hands to help haul it? We will take ourselves down the hole and investigate the water at its source."

The mayor shouted. People bustled over to the stables and noisily searched for rope. "How long does it have to be?"

"Hold on. We'll see," said Shaani. She dropped a rock into the well and counted. It took an awfully long time to make a splash. The rat bit her lip in thought.

"Ah, D equals sixteen T squared . . ." She totted up the math on the rock face of the well. "Can you stretch to three hundred meters?"

"I . . . I suppose so." Men began splicing ropes, cords, and even some hairy string into one long rope. "Is it really that far?"

"Sounds like it." Shaani looked at the activity in approval. "Right, bring me a pulley, and we'll set it up here. I shall just go and rouse my team."

Feeling thoroughly useful, Shaani strode over to the tavern. There, she found a card game in motion, with a dozen locals flinging down cards, pushing coins across the table, and sweating in tension. A thin boy with a fine pair of horns on his head seemed to be winning. There were quite a few earwigs stationed all around the area—apparently able to clandestinely watch everybody's cards. Shaani sought one out and politely drew its attention.

"Wig-wig, old trout. Would you be up for a bit of pot-holing?"

"Sounds fun."

The white rat peered over her glasses at the cards. "What actually are you doing?"

"Wig-wig gets monies for helping." The earwigs seemed pleased. "Wig-wig likes helping."

"Right-o, then. Have fun."

For once, Shaani had money in her pockets: As paid scientific consultant to the local water supply committee, she could finally afford a decent breakfast for the whole team. She set someone scampering off to make her eggs and bacon, toast and tea. And thankfully the place did have a decent nonmutagenic beverage or three. She ordered the coldest the house could provide and sank herself down at an outside table where she could watch the rope being prepared.

Xoota appeared, looking harassed and annoyed. Shaani lifted her glass of ginger beer.

"There you are, old girl. I was about to send out a search party." She waved at the table. "Bacon and eggs are on. Toast. And if we're lucky, a sausage or three. Ecstasy."

Utterly amazed, Xoota sank down into a chair. She was immediately presented with food. "Where did you get the cash for all of this?"

"Our cash. We are scientific investigators to the Watering Hole community. Comes with a room at the hotel while we need it and full board. Lovely." Shaani passed over some coin. "There. A third of the advance they gave us. Lovely to be needed, what?"

"A third of . . . ?"

"Three hundred domars paid in advance. So I thought I'd divvy it between you, myself, and the earwigs. But I'm pretty well set for kit, so if you need any adventuring gear, what's mine is yours." She raised her glass and clinked it against Xoota's. "Partners. Cheers."

Bemused, Xoota sank back into her chair. Somewhere inside, bacon and sausages were frying. They smelled damned good.

"Well, you certainly had better luck than I did. I just sat and listened to the creepiest commission I've ever heard." She sipped the ginger beer and blinked. It was fiery. "What's this about adventuring gear? Where are we going?"

"Well, for a starters, we're going to take a quick look at the source of the town's water supply and see if anything there is contaminating it."

"Is it far?

"Three hundred meters."

"Ha." Xoota relaxed, suddenly quite pleased with life. "Excellent."

From inside the tavern, they heard fighting. A thin boy with horns on his head came sailing out of the window to land in the budgie trough, scaring the birds. Men piled out of the tavern to hurtle themselves atop the boy. There were breaking chairs and bellowing waitresses. The bouncer waded in and plucked people out of the chaos, throwing them aside as if he were picking daisies. Unseen by the melee, Wig-wig came cascading out of a side window, the earwigs all carrying a good number of gold coins and plastic domars. Some earwigs stopped to salute Xoota and Shaani as they passed.

"We can has money."

Xoota watched the creatures flee into the woodpile to hide. "He's a worry." She sighed then sat up eagerly as the sausages arrived. "Ah, the onion bratwurst. Wonderful."

Xoota tore into her sausages and bacon, watched over benevolently by Shaani. The rat looked off down the street toward the town's ragged walls. A huge, old exploration buggy from the town's shattered spaceship had been used to make the nearest chunk of ramparts, a long, spindly truck fitted with eight balloon tires. It lay on its side beside shattered boats and an upside-down sign that read *Shop n' Save*.

Shaani looked in fascination at the old, beached yachts. "Ships. How wonderful."

"They didn't have any of these where you came from?"

"Oh no, up in the hills, old bean. But now that I have these books, I've been able to study them." The rat patted her haul from the wrecked merchant ship out on the salt. "Fascinating stuff."

Xoota ate her way eagerly through a plate of crunchy bacon. Food mellowed her. "I always loved the idea of boats. I wonder what it was like, to steer something like that. To feel it move and glide, to have the world slide gracefully by . . ." She shook her head. The world around her was sand and dust. The oceans had long gone. "Ah, well."

Shaani poured tea. "You seem a bit more chipper."

The quoll looked up at Shaani and gave a grin.

"Things are looking up. Breakfast, a room, a hundred domars—all for messing with some water."

"Quite so, my dear. Science shall prevail." Shaani looked out in the courtyard where they were making the horrible, hairy rope. "This should be damned interesting."

"Excellent." Xoota crunched into a sausage and gave herself over to ecstasy. "Well, I'm glad you didn't agree to anything silly."

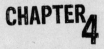

CHAPTER 4

I don't like it."

Swaying on a creaking rope made out of old nylon cordage and braided hair, Xoota's wailing echoed down the shaft. She kept her eyes screwed shut, clinging to the rope with a death grip.

The well shaft was a scant few meters wide and plunged three hundred meters straight down into the earth. The slick, stone walls echoed with the sounds of water. Lowered gradually down by the work team above, Xoota was absolutely not enjoying the ride.

"Why did I let you talk me into this?"

"Because it's fun." Standing far below, Shaani's voice echoed cheerfully up the shaft. "Come along. A change is as good as a holiday."

"The rope is going to break, and I'm going to fall."

"Oh, don't be such a baby. This is for science."

"Damn you and your science."

Shaani did not take offense. "Science ennobles us. In science, the unthinkable becomes possible. The boundaries of dreams expand"—her hands helped Xoota's feet touch the ground—"and we can even get to the ground with our eyes closed."

Xoota hesitantly opened up her eyes. She stood ankle deep in water, in a round chamber that echoed with the sounds of running water. The quoll splashed her feet and looked pouty. "I don't like hanging like that."

"I thought you quoll chaps were arboreal?" The rat was holding a glowing light bulb in one of her new tentacles. "Anyway, it was depth, not height. Nothing to worry about."

"It doesn't make a difference to the *ahs.*"

" 'Ahs'?"

Xoota grumpily pulled her shield onto her arm. "Falls are measured in *ahs.* That's how long you scream before you finally hit the bottom and go splat."

"Well, there are no more *ahs,* dear. Let's get on. You're all sparkly. So sparkle."

Xoota irritably let her newly luminescent self glitter and twinkle. She would be glad when that particular little alpha did its dash and disappeared. Still, the increased lighting helped. They looked around the cavern and took stock.

It was a great, wide hemisphere cut through bedrock and lined with concrete. The pipe from the pump high above ended beneath the water in the center of the chamber. The place had a distinctly brackish smell.

There were two tunnels leading out of the chamber. One was dry, raised above the floor. The other was a large, round tunnel with water flowing steadily into the chamber. Shaani knelt and filled a jug full of water. She touched wet fingers to her mouth. "Taste that."

Xoota knelt and tried a handful of water. She spit it straight back out. "Gah. Salty."

"Don't spit. That's the town water supply."

"Salt is a disinfectant."

"Ooh, nicely observed. But be careful. Don't pollute." Shaani lifted her light, her tentacles snaking sinuously. "I can't see any salt encrustation on the walls."

She tasted the water flowing out of the nearby tunnel. It, too, was salty. The contamination had to be coming from farther afield.

The air clattered as a cloud of earwigs came flying down the well. They settled all over Xoota and Shaani.

"Hi hi."

"Hey, Wig-wig." Shaani fixed one earwig with a considering eye, looking over the rim of her spectacles. "Were you cheating at cards?"

"No no. Wig-wig was merely helping. Boy was the one who cheated." The bugs puffed up with pride. "No, Wig-wig stole all the monies on the floor when big fight began."

Shaani was scandalized. "Wig-wig!"

The bugs sitting on her wilted. "I ashamed."

Xoota came to the insects' defense. "What's wrong with making off with the loot? Hey, that's just initiative."

Earwigs puffed up with sly pride. "Yeah." The earwigs seemed distinctly influenced by whomever they stood closest to.

Shaani combed her whiskers thoughtfully then cleared her throat. "Very well. Just don't cause any trouble. It might rebound on us." She lifted up her light. "The salt is being carried downstream from the water tunnel. We shall investigate."

Light held high, Shaani led the way into the tunnel, which was high enough to let them stand. Water gurgled past their feet in a slow, continuous flow. Here and there, a cobweb stretched across the tunnel, but there was no sign of the actual spiders. Wig-wig was careful to keep to the tunnel walls.

From far ahead, there came a sudden low, guttural moan. The explorers froze in their tracks.

Xoota's antennae jittered. She was sensing something decidedly unpleasant ahead. "What was that?"

Shaani shrugged. "It's probably nothing."

"Are those buck teeth of yours digging into your head?"

Once again, the deep moan sounded. Xoota readied her mace. "There can't be anything living down here, can there?" she asked.

"Highly unlikely."

"Highly unlikely means there is a definite possibility."

Shaani quickly took a step behind the quoll. "Agreed. Ah, well, you have the defensive equipment. You go first."

Great. Xoota cursed and held up her shield. She shuffled forward carefully, pace by pace, with Shaani and the earwigs crowding close behind to peer around her shoulders. They advanced forward in a group, moving toward the sound.

Ahead, the tunnel seemed to take on an eerie, green glow, the walls twinkling occasionally with bio lights where little fungi and medusa plants grew. Wig-wig investigated, but the earwigs jumped back as the little medusae grabbed at them with their tentacles.

A wider chamber suddenly opened out before them. The floor had been fashioned into a vast set of stairs. A meter-wide pipe gushed water in a cascade down the steps, forming a deep pool at the center of the floor. Old tunnels led off into the gloom. The fungus there grew thick and lush, giving off a weird, blue-green glow.

Sitting on the steps were a pair of enormous frogs.

They were covered in glowing, green spots and were each at least the size of a human being. Xoota dropped into a crouch. Quoll, rat, and earwigs all tried to hide behind the one shield.

One of the frogs tilted its head. "May we help you?"

Shaani rose up out of cover, her tall ears followed by her bobble hat, goggles, and face. "Ah, hello. What are you doing down here?"

"We live here. It's a well."

"Yes, yes, I suppose it is." Shaani stood up. The deep-throated rumble of the frogs was clearly the noise they had heard from down the tunnel. "Pardon us. Shaani, Xoota, and Wig-wig," she said, indicating each, "scientific investigators. How do you do?"

"Quite well, thank you." The frogs had some boxes and pieces of furniture over by one dry wall. "Do come in."

Xoota stood, feeling decidedly weirded out. "Sorry. We thought there were monsters down here."

One frog frowned. "Oh, yes, we do have those."

"Down!" Xoota caught a sudden premonition and ducked. Five long, horrible flesh tubes erupted out of the water. Sucking mouths gaped at the tips as they came right at Shaani and Xoota. Shaani squealed and dodged. One of the horrible creatures missed her by a whisker's breadth. Xoota let one monster crash into her shield. She met another head-on with her mace, the hard cogs pounding into the creature's rubbery flesh. But another one of the beasts stuck on to her leg. She cursed as it bit through her hide.

Wig-wig descended all over one of the horrible serpent creatures, slicing and nipping with countless earwig forceps. The monster bucked and squealed. Earwigs held on grimly as the monster tried to slam itself against the walls.

Shaani fled backward, whacking at one slithering eel creature with her entrenching spade. Her long tentacles found loose rocks and threw them at the creature, driving it back. Suddenly the monster reared and flung itself at her like a javelin. Shaani struck it with full force after a magnificent windup, the blow making her shovel ring like a bell. The monster catapulted back onto the ground and lay still. It was immediately consumed by one of the frogs.

Xoota was driven back by two of the rubbery monsters. A third hung off her leg, sucking blood. Shaani gave a shout, pointed her hand, and shot a blast of pure radiation straight at the creature crawling up over Xoota's shield. The monster fell aside, burned to a cinder.

The other two clung on. A second monster lunged for Xoota's face. She caught the thing's sucker-mouthed head in her bare hand. It spit goo right in her eye.

"Kack damn it."

Wildly angry, Xoota bunched her fists, and her fur blazed brightly. Shaani and the earwigs ducked aside as a brilliant flash flooded the room.

Xoota stood, seething and annoyed, smoke rising from her blackened fur. Scorched, rubbery monsters dropped off her and lay smoldering on the ground. They smelled strangely tasty. Shaani raised her head from behind a rock, totally dazzled by the flash.

"Oh, wacko."

"Damn it." Xoota no longer sparkled. It hadn't been such a lame alpha mutation after all. She kicked at one of the dead monsters and sent it flying.

The frogs had been horribly dazzled by the light. "Ow."

"Serves you right." Xoota was in a fine, foul mood. "What the hell were those things?"

"Leeches." The frogs shrugged. "We eat them so they keep away from us. They must like you."

"Thanks for the heads-up." Xoota saw blood running down her thigh. "Damn it. I'm bit."

Earwigs emerged out of hiding. "Ow. Hurt." Several danced around Xoota. "Owie."

Xoota swore and pressed the injury, which seemed determined to keep bleeding. "Damn it. Somebody help me fix this."

"Wig-wig can fix it."

Earwigs clustered around Xoota, pointing their little antennae. The quoll's leg instantly felt weird, tickling and jerking up and down.

She waved a hand in panic. "Wait. What are you doing?"

Shaani had come running over with her first-aid kit. She scooped a tin cup into the water, ready to wash Xoota's wound clean.

The quoll frantically tried to wave the water away. "No, those frogs have been peeing in it."

"Don't be such a baby. Salt is a disinfectant." Shaani carefully bathed Xoota's thigh. Much to their surprise, Xoota's wound was already perfectly healed. Even her fur had grown back. Shaani inspected the bite site in amazement. "I say. Wig-wig, did you do that?"

The earwigs beamed. "Wig-wig did it."

Xoota blinked. The wound had gone. "That's . . . actually, that's amazing."

The earwigs beamed. "Wig-wig be useful."

The lab rat was delighted. "Empathic healing. He's an empath." Shaani pointed an admonishing finger at Xoota. "He picks up on emotional radiations. You have to be more careful with your attitudes."

"What?" Xoota bridled. "Why mine? Why not yours?"

The rat made a lofty gesture. "Mine are motivated by science and benevolence. They cannot possibly be harmful."

Xoota muttered curses under her breath. She stomped off to take guard against any more sudden leech attacks while Shaani ambled over to the frogs, who sat casually on old, plastic lawn tables, their throat pouches wobbling in and out. They seemed to be keeping carefully out of the water.

One of them turned to face Shaani. "Did you come about the water?"

"Yes." Shaani knelt beside the frog. "You've noticed the change?"

"Indeed. We have to keep up out of the water now. It's hurting our skins."

Shaani carefully tasted the water gushing out of the pipe. It was salty. "When did this first start happening?"

"It became a little brackish a week ago. It's been getting worse and worse." The smaller frog had a higher, more musical voice. "It burns my feet."

"Hmm." Shaani looked at the pipe. It was the same vintage technology as the surrounding chambers. "Have you chaps always lived down here?"

"Oh, yes. It's the only place an amphibian can live, really. But there's a long-necked tortoise who lives here too."

"So no one upstairs knows about you?"

"Well, in a sense. We come up to the tavern from time to time. We just don't like to tell anyone we're living in the town water supply."

Xoota grumbled. "They probably know; that's why they all drink at the tavern." The quoll glowered. "Look, that pipe, there. Do you idiots know where all that water is coming from?"

The smaller frog puffed up in self-importance. "Of course. It's on the map."

"All right, show me the map."

The frogs led the way, making long leaps into one of the dry side tunnels.

Mounted on one wall was a plastic plate that depicted a series of lines snaking and branching off from one great central route. Shaani produced a broad brush and began industriously cleaning away a deep layer of dust and grime.

Xoota blinked at the runes written on the plastic. "What does it say?"

The rat peered through her glasses. "It says 'National grid conduit—western power line.'"

"What's a grid conduit?"

"A means of transferring electrical power from one place to another. They must have been making underground power lines." Shaani blew more dust away from the runes. "See this? 'Proposed completion date' . . ." She mused. "They never completed the project."

Xoota scratched her hairy chin. "So if this was for power, why is water coming through it?"

"A water source must have started flowing into the far end of the empty power pipe."

They stood together and looked at the map.

Xoota sucked on one fang. "So do you think salt is somehow leaking into the pipe?"

Shaani pondered. "Well, the pipe is intact, otherwise the water wouldn't flow. So contamination must be getting in via the water source at the far end." She tapped at the upper end of the map. "What we have to do is locate that water source, which will be . . . well, here, at the only other open point in the line."

There was an awful lot of space between the top and bottom parts of the pipe. Xoota scratched at her head. "What distance is that?"

"Hmm. Well, it heads east out beneath the desert . . ." There was a scale on one side of the map. Shaani took a piece of string and measured the scale then measured the distance on the map.

Xoota frowned. "Well?"

"Oh, it's a wee bit of a way. I'm sure we could make it."

Xoota grew suspicious. She folded up her arms. "How damned far?"

"Ahem." Shaani tried to look innocent. "About three thousand kilometers."

Xoota gave the girl a level glare. "Three thousand?"

"Give or take."

"I see." Xoota gestured back at the pipe. "Were you planning on crawling? How long can you hold your breath?"

The lab rat was not downhearted. She settled her bobble hat and goggles and took on a wild, determined look in her pink eyes. "It can be done. We can just go overland."

"Nope, sorry. I'm going to play the 'bones bleaching in the sand' card here." Xoota leaned against one wall. "This is not something we can fix."

"It's just a problem in mechanics." Shaani unrolled paper and took a rubbing of the map. "The pipe has been laid in a straight line. We merely proceed on the same compass bearing for three thousand kilometers."

"See, that's the part I don't think you're grasping."

Wig-wig clustered happily around Shaani, echoing her eagerness. "It can be done. It can be done."

"Hush, you." Xoota glared. "There's no way pack animals can carry enough water to cross the sands."

"Quite so. Quite so . . ." Shaani was no longer listening. She was alive with the seeds of an idea. "Come on. Let's get upstairs and get busy."

Shaani nodded a good-bye to the frogs. She walked off, so possessed by thought that she took a wrong turn. Wig-wig happily led her off in the right direction.

Xoota hung back, kicking at the rubble. Finally she made an exasperated noise and followed the others. She called down the tunnel after Shaani. "It can't be done."

"Can."

"Can't." Xoota stamped a foot. "Can't can't can't can't can't."

The only answer was a distant noise of delight from Shaani. "Ooh, my tentacles have gone."

Xoota shook her head. "Bleeding hell."

She stomped off after the others, certain that the day would end in tears.

. . . . .

Sitting in the tavern nursing a large omega ale, Xoota was decidedly out of sorts. She was right. She was always right. Other people were basically idiots. Why Shaani couldn't see that elemental truth was utterly beyond her. Ha. Let her learn.

The rat was out in the town somewhere, probably talking to caravaners, trying to find some fool who would risk making the desert trek. Well, she wouldn't find anyone. And if she did, then Xoota wasn't following them to pick up the corpses. If she had to, she would tie the rat up and lock her in a cellar. That ought to put some sense into her.

Two gecko girls came and presented Xoota with her dinner. The geckos were both wreathed in smiles. "Dinner, science adviser. The best in the house."

"What? Oh, thank you." Xoota felt a stab of guilt; being antisocial, it took her a moment to recognize the source of the emotion. She was a hero even though she hadn't saved the town's water supply. How was she ever going to live down their expectations?

Happy as a prairie oyster in chowder, Shaani came bopping into the room, surrounded by earwigs. She had an old blanket coat on as protection from the stiff, night breeze, and her spectacles shone bright. She plunked herself into a seat beside Xoota.

"Top ho. I've just been up on the tavern rooftop."

Xoota drank, possibly mutating as she swallowed. "What the hell have you been doing up there?"

"Measuring the wind."

"What, in a bag?"

"No, in some cups." The rat held out her latest gizmo, a crosswork of sticks with cups on the end, designed to catch the breeze and turn like a windmill. "An *anemometer*. I count the RPMs to get the wind strength. Did you know we get a persistent wind in the five-meter band above the ground, more at ten meters."

"Well, that's nice." Xoota looked at her dinner: sand prawns and a four-legged chicken. "Why is this relevant?"

"It is relevant because it is a delivered system of energy. We may transfer this energy into a machine and convert energy to motion."

"What?"

"We can use the wind to make something go."

Xoota rolled her eyes. "I know that. I mean, what are you going to make go?"

"Ah, I shall create a revolution." Shaani sampled her dinner and made a face. "I say, this is a bit odd. How's yours?"

"The chicken tastes like beef."

"This beef tastes like chicken."

They looked at each other for a moment then swapped plates. The results were far more satisfying. Shaani ate like a starving monster, getting her food down quickly so she could talk.

"It's all coming along swimmingly. The village council is cooperative. They say we can take what we need if it gets the job done. So for a start, I shall be wanting that." Shaani pointed toward the town fortifications. "It's perfect. I can't believe it's in such good condition."

"What, the village wall?"

"No, the giant moon buggy." Shaani waved for a stone jug of ginger beer, anything but the water or the omega ale. "Here. Finish up and I'll show you."

The rat wolfed down a last mouthful of food and tugged Xoota to her feet. Wig-wig smothered her plate and finished her dinner then started on the leftovers at another table. Xoota hurried after Shaani, collecting the earwigs before they started eating up the patrons.

Outside in the streets, the nighttime sky blazed with stars. An aurora australis shimmered brilliantly high above the south horizon. Xoota stood for a moment to admire the sight then followed the earwigs as they stampeded off in pursuit of Shaani.

The white rat stood beside the village wall. The town guard, citizens drafted to walk the walls, kept watch for threats from the outside world. Others were standing and discussing the wall, pointing and talking. They seemed to have already been in consultation with Shaani. Shaani borrowed a broom that was leaning against the side of the tavern stables, swept a patch of dirt to make a drawing board, and squatted down to scribble in the dust with a stick.

Budgie strutted over to the fence, chortling away. The bird chattered merrily at Xoota as she scratched him behind the skull.

"Hello, Budgie," the bird said to her.

"Yeah, hello, Budgie."

"Hello. Hello, Budgie." The bird twittered and bobbed in glee. "Hello. Hello."

Xoota grimaced. Like *that* wasn't going to get annoying. "Did you teach him that?"

"Yes, he's a very quick learner. Later on we shall try to teach him to whistle." Shaani had finished preparing her drawing board. "Right. The plan. For a start, we shall need *that.*" She pointed to the moon buggy. The thing had been a vast truck designed to explore far-off worlds. The damned thing was almost twenty-five meters long.

Xoota pushed her goggles to the back of her head in puzzlement. "You do know that thing doesn't go, don't you?"

"Not now." Shaani looked up at the vehicle in delight. "But look at it. It's perfect." She tapped her big chisel teeth in thought. "Oh, and I'll need a work party. Um, a wheelwright, a mechanist, a blacksmith, and a seamstress. I think the locals will all pitch in."

Xoota was intrigued. She squatted down beside the rat, suddenly admiring her. "Pitch in? What are you making?"

"Here." Shaani began to sketch. "We work with just the frame of the moon buggy. Eight wheels, balloon tires, spring suspension . . ." She pointed to the ruins and the rubble. "We take masts from the old yachts, leftover sails. To our wheelbase, we fit a bowsprit and two masts. Rig her as a gaff-rigged schooner. We can even try a sky sail." She began modifying the sketch of the buggy, turning the long-bodied, ungainly looking vehicle into a ship. "We enclose the hull with cabins taken from wrecked ships and yachts. The water tank will act as a low center of gravity for ballast. As we remove water, we replace the weight with sand bags as necessary."

Xoota was enthralled. "Will it move?"

"In a decent breeze, I can't see why we wouldn't get a good thirty kph out of her. In a full breeze or a gale, she'd race like lightning."

"What happens if she gets becalmed?"

"Ah. Now this is the clever bit." The rat drew a diagram full of symbols and lines. "The moon buggy runs off electric power. There are motors sealed in the wheel hubs." The rat sketched again. "Now we don't have power generators, but we do have metal and glass, so we can make banks of capacitors to store a charge. When we use the wind, the magnets and wire in the wheels will be generating electricity. We store that in the capacitor plates. If we need to move the ship without wind, we reverse the power flow and use the capacitors to power the motors. QED."

"QED . . ." Xoota was amazed. "You can do this? You can actually do this?"

"Of course I can. It's science." The rat was happier than Xoota had ever seen her. "You see? It's your ship. You get to captain a ship at last. You get your dream."

The quoll blinked. "You did this for me?"

"Of course I did. You're my friend." The rat stood up, dusting off her hands. "We'll have to work fast, though. We'll need you to find us our masts, sails, and parts; take them from anywhere you need to."

"You've got it." Xoota cleared her throat. "Will there be room for Budgie?"

"Of course. For scouting. And every ship needs a parrot. There'll be plenty of room."

Xoota felt an odd emotion. She looked down at her boots. "Shaani . . . thank you."

Villagers began levering rubble away from the wall. It would take a lot of manpower to tilt the old moon buggy out of position and back onto its wheels; the thing was more than twice the length of an ancient semi trailer. Thankfully, it was made from a light omega alloy.

It could be done. Still, Shaani seemed concerned. Xoota watched her from the corner of one eye. "What's the matter?"

"Supplies. We can make the ship; the ship can carry enough water to get us across the desert. But where do we find the water? I'm showing the locals how to make stills, so they can get minimal drinking water while we're gone. But there's no way to stockpile the sort of liters we'll need for the voyage."

Xoota bit her lip. "How much will we need?"

"Say we have a crew of four. In the heat, each person consumes four liters per day. Now let's say we average a hundred kilometers a day. That's a thirty-day trip. That would mean five hundred liters, twice that if we allow for a return trip. That's a thousand liters."

The quoll closed her eyes and heaved a sigh. "I know where we can get the water."

"Really?"

"If we don't mind making a side trip, a really icky side trip." Xoota rubbed her eyes. Oh crud. "This is not going to be fun."

· · · · ·

The village square was a churning hive of activity. Shaani presumed upon the enthusiasm of the local residents, racing around and stirring up the workers all in the name of science. Wig-wig raced after her, echoing her enthusiasm. Not surprisingly he was extremely useful for knotting, splicing, and running cables. Shaani ran her hands over the electrical system in the moon buggy wheels. Sparks clicked and flashed from her hands as she felt out the systems, finding the breaks in the circuits. She thieved solder from ancient, ruined machines and reconnected wires. Once the main construction began, all that could normally be seen of Shaani was her backside, legs and tail sticking up out of the hull.

The vessel was going to be impressive. The eight-wheeled chassis stood on wide, sprawling legs, the balloon tires rising higher than a man's head. Filling the entire village square, the chassis swarmed with people as plywood sheets were screwed in place. Earwigs ran messages, children chased each other between the wheels. The scene was total chaos.

Xoota did the unglamorous job of salvaging parts from the ruins. Among the piles of wrecked shipping, she found sturdy masts and pylons. Sails were more problematic; most had been cut up to make hammocks, water bags, and street awnings. Local weaving technique was not up to anything more complex than woolen blankets and homespun cotton.

It was a problem that caused Xoota a great deal of gloom. She sat at the tent makers, looking through fabrics and feeling a little demoralized. The tent maker, a rather delightful mutant rock wallaby who had a row of electroshock quills down her back and a decided lisp, tried to be as much help as she could. The problem was that local fabrics were made to be light and airy, not wind tight and robust. Most tents were made of wool, cotton sheets, or even woven grass.

The wallaby woman pondered, sparks racing up and down her back. The store had a distinct scent of ozone. "What about old rain jackets? A lot of the old boat wrecks have lots of nylon clothing in them. Old waterproofs?"

"How big an area could we cover?"

"Well, maybe enough for one of the little sails." The tent maker sat back, kangaroo style, using her tail as a seat.

"Have you found any other old tech cloth?" asked Xoota.

"There are two parachutes, from the old starship's ejection seats. Those are a godsend."

"It isn't enough?"

"Only for the mainsail. This thing's going to need a lot of fabric."

Xoota sighed, frustrated. "We still need the top sails, the jibs for the bowsprit thingy, and the ... whatever it's called, the sail for the second mast." Xoota really needed to find someone who could read and have some of Shaani's nautical books read to her. That way she might actually understand half of what the rat was talking about. "We need cloth and lots of it."

"Well, we could get some weaving going. Try and make a much heavier cotton than normal. That might make good sails."

"How long will that take?"

"A few months."

"No, we don't have that much time." Xoota rubbed at her eyes. The water problem would be critical in a matter of weeks. "What else do people use for big sheets of cloth?"

"Hmm . . ." The wallaby rubbed her nose. "Leather?"

"Too heavy."

"What you really need are sharkskins." The wallaby sighed. "Fat chance of any of those."

Sand sharks cast off their skins regularly as they grew. Razorbacks salvaged the thin, tough inner membranes and used them to make their huge sunshade tents. But the razorbacks never, ever traded. They merely killed any traveler they could find, ate his flesh, and stole his equipment. Xoota could think of no one who might have captured a tent or accidentally found a pile of discarded sharkskins.

She clambered onto her feet. "I'll keep thinking. There'll be something out there."

"Good luck."

. . . . .

Xoota was still trying to turn fantasies into practical solutions an hour later. She sat in the shade of the tavern wall, watching the ship being built. Budgie lay at her feet, making happy noises as Xoota carefully groomed his feathers. She was still obsessing about sails when a massive presence suddenly loomed overhead.

The shadow that fell over Xoota was lumpy in a way that simply annoyed her. The quoll gave a sigh. "Hello, Benek."

"Scout Xoota. Well met." The colossal human posed with his fists on his hips, surveying the growing shape of the sand ship with a masterful air. "So this is the vessel?"

"It is indeed."

"The design is surprisingly cunning." Benek looked the ship up and down. "Taken from old sources, no doubt."

"No, no, an original design. All Shaani's work."

"You surprise me. I had not thought animals capable of such."

Xoota looked Benek over and wondered what he would look like inside out. "We find ourselves quite capable."

"And I approve of your efforts." Benek leaned back on his heels, inspecting the two large masts that had been hauled up into position just an hour before. Braces and rigging made out of home-woven cable were still being winched up into place. "You have gone to great efforts to ensure the success of my expedition."

"Yes . . . well . . ." Xoota's droll antennae spoke volumes. "Future of your race and all that. Can't deny the world more humans. After all, look what they did for the place."

Benek had a backpack sheathed entirely in a pink, translucent membrane. Xoota looked at it in puzzlement then fingered the outer covering. It was tough, light, amazingly strong . . .

"Benek, what is this? Sharkskin?"

"It is a waterproof covering." The man was coldly proud of all his *fixtures.* "The superior intellect prepares for all eventualities."

The quoll's temper was at its customary low boiling point. "I don't need to know *why* you got it. I just need to know *where* you got it."

Benek arrogantly smoothed his golden hair. "I bought it from a half-human herdsman. It's an off-cut. The creature found it in the desert." Benek brushed his piece of sharkskin clean. "Apparently his clan of scavengers often find old razorback castoffs. They seem to know where to look."

"They do, do they?" Xoota stood. "Do tell, where can I find this herdsman of yours?"

* * * * *

Half an hour later, Xoota wandered back toward the ship, towing Budgie behind her. Shaani was down beneath the hull, licking the end of a copper wire to see if there was any electrical current. She made a spark on the tip of her tongue and touched it to the wire. Her homemade voltmeter gave her a reading she felt happy with. Grease-stained and gleeful, the rat looked up at Xoota.

"Xoota, old thing. Had some successes with supplies?"

"I have. I have. I've found us sailcloth at last." Xoota spotted a box and sat down. Budgie sat down beside her, apparently quite satisfied with his life. Xoota used him as a backrest. "There's a local leather—thin, light, immensely tough, waterproof. It doesn't stretch or shrink with the cold or sun. And it is available in bulk."

"Sterling stuff." The rat was overjoyed. "Can we get hold of a sufficient quantity?"

"I think we can secure all that we'll need." Xoota steepled her fingertips, her antennae making sly little motions above her skull. "How would you feel about taking a jaunt into the desert?"

"Oh. Tonight?"

"Mmm, starting this afternoon. We need to cover fifty K by tomorrow midday."

"Midday?" The rat wasn't really paying attention. She was sorting through a box of rusty screws and bolts salvaged from a dozen different wrecks. "If you like."

"Good." Xoota wriggled her toes. "By the way, how go the mutations? No amusing alphas today?"

"No, no. I do feel a tad spry, though. Might be a burst of extra speed in reserve here somewhere."

"Oh, good." The quoll plumped up Budgie like a giant pillow and relaxed. "That ought to come in very useful."

• • • • •

Two long damned days in the desert later, and Shaani was frying inside her skin. The Big Dry was in full force, with the sun burning pitilessly down upon the sand. Anything with the slightest bit of common sense was deep under cover, looking for cool.

Shaani and Xoota, of course, were traipsing around on the sands and trying not to be burned to a cinder.

The rat sheltered beneath her parasol. Wig-wig clung to her, afraid to burn his little feet on the sands. Both women wore thick oversoles of woven dry grass to insulate their boot soles from the sizzling-hot sands. The air shimmered with silver curtains of mirage, and the steady wind sucked moisture right out of the skin. Walking awkwardly in his grass overshoes, Budgie waved his little wings and wilted in the sun.

The two days' travel saw them far past the belt of huts and shelters used by herdsmen in the winter. The watering holes were drying up in the outer desert, and the razorbacks were closing in on the southern settlements. They moved at night in scattered groups, using secret water caches they had planted months before. By day, they spread out their slick, shiny tents of sand-shark skin and slept through the desert heat.

Hidden behind the crest of a sand dune, Xoota used her binoculars to carefully inspect a distant encampment. There were four or five huge, broad awnings sheltering a dark mass of razorbacks and their riding cockatoos. It was a band of forty, maybe fifty war pigs. They had a krunch wagon parked beside the biggest tent, a balloon-tired cart designed to be dragged along behind a team of cockatoos. A rough-and-ready ballista had been mounted on the cart, but the guards and operators had all fled beneath the awnings. Only the cockatoos seemed to be awake, grumbling and croaking in the heat.

Benek strode up behind Xoota, gazing at the razorback tribe. "Excellent. The mutant scum are at our mercy."

Xoota didn't bother looking at him. She was examining the enemy camp. "Benek, go put a hat on. You'll fry your brain."

"My neural pathways are not like those of other men."

"We noticed." Xoota lowered her binoculars. She spoke for the benefit of Shaani and Wig-wig. "I make it three squadrons, plus what looks like a chief and some sows. One krunch wagon with a ballista."

Shaani walked awkwardly over the sand, wincing at the heat radiating up from the ground. "Do they have sentries?"

"Nope. They're not that organized. But the cockatoos will raise the alarm the instant they sense anything." The quoll tested with her antennae, looking for clear images of dangerous futures, but everything was all a-jangle. "If we can approach downwind, we should be able to get in close. But what we need to do is make the cockatoos scatter and run. Then the razorbacks can't come after us."

Shaani stroked her snout. "A bomb?"

"Yep, throw a bomb. But only after we hitch their tents up to the budgies."

For the purposes of the expedition, Shaani had been loaned a bright green riding budgerigar. Benek had another one, and each rider also led a pack animal, ready to haul away the loot.

Xoota clambered down the sand dune and hauled herself back into the saddle. She waited for Shaani to find her stirrups and get up onto her own bird then waved the expedition forward, aiming to circle the razorback camp.

"Budgies, *yo.*"

The column moved out with Xoota at the point, Benek guarding the rear, and Shaani juggling a parasol and telescope in the middle. Wig-wig clung onto Shaani's budgerigar, making every possible use of the shade.

The sand was hard packed and dotted with sprigs of dead, dry grass. Dense stands of spinifex bush stood dry and dense between the hills of sand. It was good, hard footing, dense and dusty. Here and there a termite mound stood out against the sky. Nothing moved. No predators cross the sky. The ground seemed to tremble with the awful heat.

The temperature was making Shaani dizzy, and her mouth was dry. As Xoota led the way between two dunes, Shaani poured herself a drink. She poured yet more into a bowl, and swarms of large, brown earwigs came gratefully down to drink.

"Thanking rat. Thanking much."

The expedition made a long, circling route around the razorback camp. The stench of the pigs began to fill the air, a stink thickened up by their noisome riding cockatoos. Xoota motioned the others to absolute silence and edged her bird skillfully up beneath the crest of a rise of sand. She peered just over the crest, carefully spying out the enemy camp.

Yes, the positioning was good.

There were three colossal tents filled with warriors, all tangled in snorting, grunting heaps in the shade of their broad tent awnings. The chief was upwind of his warriors. His tent held nothing but his armor, weapons, and a harem of half a dozen razorback females. The riding cockatoos, all sleeping with their heads down and twitching in aggravation at the heat, were in a tent off to one side.

Some broken brick walls stood a few hundred meters away from Shaani's rear. She moved quietly over to investigate. There, lying on the dust outside the ruins, was a strange object: a great, egg-shaped thing spun out of some sort of thick, coarse wool. The end was missing, the insides were empty, and the surface was shiny. Shaani dismounted and knelt down to investigate.

The object was radioactive. She could feel its warmth. The rat turned her face toward the nearby ruins and pondered.

Benek joined her.

"What is it? An egg?"

"A pupal casing. Radioactive."

Xoota rode over.

Shaani held up her find. "Radioactive. Quite hot. Benek, you should probably move back."

"Are you not affected?"

"Of course not; I'm a scientist." The white rat turned her face toward the brick walls. She held out her hand, palm first. "Those are radioactive too."

Xoota looked at the ruins. "Gamma moths?"

"Gamma moths."

The radiation and electromagnetic pulse given off from moths were enough to turn most people into decorative green ash. It was likely there was an underground space where the moths had made a colony. It was not a good place to make loud disturbances. It also limited the options for attacking the camp. Once the action began, the team would have to move and keep moving to escape any moths that took flight and became all touchy.

"How shall we divide the attack?" Benek had a crossbow of far more complex design than Xoota's, with strings and wheels and pulleys. "The rodent could bomb the tents; then we could slaughter the mutants as they try to recover."

"Yes, let's call that 'discarded option B.' " Xoota had no desire to spread mass slaughter on the sands. "We'll be taking 'smart-arse mutant option A.' " The quoll sketched out her intentions. "Wig-wig, if you can dig out around the tether stakes of the tents there and there." She pointed. "Just take them until they're almost ready to pull free. Then Benek and I ride through. Benek, go straight in to the far side of the tents, tie the main guy rope to your saddle bow, and spur the hell out of there and head for town. You take the left tent; I'll take the right." The quoll pointed to the cockatoos. "Shaani, your job: smoke candles to give us cover. Then as we snag the tents, you throw a bomb near the cockatoos. We want to chase them out into the desert. Once they scatter, you ride straight on to safety. Do not stop. We are not here to take on the entire razorback nation single-handed. Are we clear?"

Shaani was listening. Wig-wig seemed delighted. Benek was flexing his muscles. Xoota's antennae jingled with a sudden inkling of disaster.

"Benek, I mean it. Tents now; obey genetic imperative later."

"Of course." The man settled a helmet over his long, blond locks. "I have heard your opinions."

Xoota hated it when he said that. She made an irritable noise and turned away.

Earwigs scissored open their wings and fluttered up into the baking sky. They drifted silently through the air, landing in ones and twos all over the guy ropes of the nearest tents. The insects filtered stealthily down, halting as a pig near the edge of one tent rolled over in the heat and groaned. The beast farted, making the bugs duck and move hastily away.

The earwigs began digging in the sand, sending little plumes of dust flying upward as they undermined the tent pegs. They worked in turns, sparing their feet from the hot sands.

Shaani took another drink, offering some to her mount before climbing back into the saddle. She fumbled out a bomb from her belt and straightened out the wick, making sure she had raw gunpowder exposed on the end of the wick.

Over at the tents, Wig-wig moved on from his first tent and started work on the second. Bugs dug away industriously, having the time of their lives. Several earwigs waved back toward the rest of the team in joy.

There was a sudden grunt from the tents.

A razorback stood blinking in the light, his trousers half down around his waist; he had stepped out of the third tent to have a pee. Two hundred kilograms of porcine muscle was staring in bleary confusion at the jets of sand flying up from all the tent pegs in front of him.

Xoota gave a curse and kicked Budgie into the charge. "Benek, go."

Xoota and Benek charged.

The razorback gave a loud roar of alarm. A second later Budgie cannoned into him, hurtling the pig back into the piles of sleeping razorbacks. Xoota turned Budgie around and snatched at one of the tent ropes. She tied it in place at her saddle horn and urged Budgie onward. The rope strained and heaved, and suddenly the entire tent came free. Xoota gave a whoop of joy. She rode forward, dragging the cover off a churning pile of razorbacks, who all woke up, roaring in rage.

Hurtling smoke bombs left, right, and center, Shaani rode her skittering budgerigar right into the camp. She rode pell-mell toward the awning that sheltered the black riding cockatoos. The big, ragged birds were churning to their feet, screaming in alarm. Shaani made a spark crack from her fingertip and into the head of her bomb fuse. The wick sputtered furiously, burning far faster than she had planned. She hastily tossed the bomb away, but the fizzing fuse made her own budgerigar turn around in panic. The rat girl cursed and fought to get the creature under control, when suddenly the bomb exploded with a deafening *bang*. Her budgerigar reared in panic, throwing her off to land on her silky backside right in the sand.

Cockatoos scattered in panic, dragging their tent awning with them. Smoke candles belched dense, white clouds as dust from the bomb made a choking fog. Razorbacks ran past, chasing after the cockatoos. Shaani scrabbled to her feet and ran, crouching, in the dust. A huge warrior loomed over her; she cracked the razorback in the shins with her entrenching tool, making the monster hop away, holding its leg and yammering. She ran forward, blinded by the smoke, and fell right over a tent rope.

Benek gave a mighty war cry. He had never tried to seize a tent. Instead he drew a long sword and charged into the razorbacks, crashing his blade down into the creatures as they tried to rise from bed. His mount sideswiped Shaani as she ran, bowling her sideways into another tent. Benek hacked and swung; razorbacks grabbed at his mount and bogged it down.

An immense razorback with a two-handed flail whirled his weapon in a savage arc and slammed it against Benek's shield. The human staggered, half falling from his saddle. He shook his head and roared in rage. He got his hands around the neck of one razorback warrior, crushed the thing in his massive grasp, then hurtled the beast aside.

The mammoth flail struck again. Benek reeled, hurt, his budgerigar screeching as it tried to claw free from the melee.

Xoota looked back, saw Benek was in trouble, and gave a curse. She cut free her tent, turned, and rode like lightning crossways past the melee. She fired her crossbow from the saddle, and the bolt slammed into the flail-wielding pig. The razorback snarled and staggered away.

Xoota reloaded in the saddle, the spare bolt clenched in her teeth as she swung around at a gallop. Suddenly her antennae twitched. Xoota whipped around in the saddle and fired into the bushes. A razorback armed with bolas reeled aside, shot clean through the chest. The quoll slung her crossbow, pulled her shield on to her arm, and charged into the smoke clouds to save Benek.

Budgie crashed into the razorbacks, tearing at them with his beak. Rising in her stirrups, Xoota hammered her mace down onto one war pig's head. She had made an opening for Benek's bird, and the budgerigar took it. The bird clawed through the melee and lumbered into the dust. It ran south, the direction Benek should have damned well taken in the first place. Xoota hammered another mace blow at a razorback then stood in her saddle and called out to Shaani over the chaos.

. . . . .

The smoke was getting thicker. Coughing, the rat staggered to her feet. Razorbacks were all around her, but a swarm of earwigs made them stagger, cursing and swatting wildly with their clubs and flails.

Shaani blundered through the chieftain's tent. There was a scattering of silks; blankets; leather armor; and a number of very, very large razorback sows screaming like frightened girls. A great, naked razorback chieftain bellowed at his men. Shaani fired her radiation bolt past him and knocked down the tent pole, effectively burying the pig beneath his own tent. The rat girl saw a wooden crate lying open in the middle of the blankets, and she immediately leaned over to peek inside.

Xoota raced up on Budgie. "Shaani, run," Xoota said as she snared the chieftain's tent and tied the ropes to her saddle. "Get up behind me."

Shaani, however, had found a collection of rust and broken junk the razorbacks had been unable to understand. She plunged her head into the crate, her tail sticking up in glee. "Ooh. Spiffy."

"Shaani!"

She was focused on some sort of chain-sword with a knuckle guard and razor-sharp teeth made out of duralloy. The words "Mister Fusion" were printed on the weapon's power generator. She remembered something about this from a book. Shaani poured water from her canteen into the tank, and the "on" light instantly came to life. The rat was delighted.

Beside her, the earwigs danced and wheeled. "Glee. We found a happy."

Fighting free from beneath the tent, the razorback chieftain stood up, saw the rat, and roared. Shaani shut the chainsaw's cover plate, flicked a switch, and the weapon started with a roar. The chieftain took one look and fled. Shaani ran after the razorback, waving the chainsaw and cackling with glee.

The fleeing chieftain reached the ranks of armed and armored friends. Thirty war pigs roared in hate. Faced with the overwhelming numbers, Shaani decided the time had come to turn and flee.

Wig-wig surrounded her, suddenly just as keen to be out of the fight. "Run away! Run away!" the earwigs shouted.

Shaani felt something tweak inside her. Ah. That good old alpha moment. The rat took off at a sprint like a champion, her legs going like drumsticks as she ran. She passed Xoota and headed for all points south. Wig-wig gleefully flew along with her, imitating the roar of the chainsaw. Xoota spurred after them, dragging the unwieldy mass of the chieftain's tent behind her.

Flushed from her amazing run, Shaani found her budgerigar, mounted up, and rode off, dragging the tent Xoota had previously abandoned. It trailed behind her, meter after meter of prime sharkskin. Between the two tents, they had enough to give their schooner a full set of sails.

Benek, injured and hanging in his saddle with blood running down one broken arm, was waiting for them. His sword hung by a strap from his injured hand.

Furious, Xoota rode up to the human and looked him over. "Wig-wig can probably fix it. You were lucky." Xoota spurred away. "Don't disobey my orders again."

Xoota rode on. Benek glared after her. He gripped his broken arm and wrenched it straight, the bone clicking into place.

Far behind, the razorback camp was still in chaos. Benek turned his back on the barbarians and rode south.

CHAPTER 5

It was a wonderful, cool, clear dawn. The auroras had faded away; the last stars were slowly disappearing from view. The sky was lit a beautiful, soft, dove gray.

Wearing a blanket poncho against the morning chill, Shaani, in her bobble hat, were standing in pleased contemplation of her achievement. Walking out from the tavern to stand beside her, Xoota, Budgie, and the earwigs stood and looked up at the ship in awe.

The vessel looked strange, almost ungainly. She sat on eight balloon tires with her bare masts soaring high above the village. Her bowsprit jutted forward like a mighty horn. The vehicle towered over her visitors. She was bigger than a house, almost the size of the rusting ship that housed the village tavern. Two huge spare tires and metal water tanks were slung low as ballast between her axles. There were headlights, bumper bars, and coils of rope. The ship had a weird look of power and grace about her that was simply spellbinding. Xoota could have never imagined anything like it before.

"Wow."

Wig-wig echoed Xoota's stunned amazement. "Wow."

"Fantastic. Simply fantastic." Xoota craned her head back to look at the masthead, far overhead. "Shaani, you have outdone yourself."

The rat surveyed her handiwork. "Yes, I think this will do the job. She came out rather well."

"You think on a rather different scale to other people. Have I told you that?"

"Science." The rat was pleased. "Nothing is impossible with science."

The rear of the ship had a long ramp, a legacy of the moon buggy chassis. Shaani worked a control, and the ramp slowly lowered, offering a steep slope to access the ship's hold.

Shaani trotted up onto the vessel. Xoota had to coax Budgie on board, moving him only when the ramp began to close without him. The bird raced on board and tried to preserve his dignity by ordering his striped blue feathers.

Upstairs, Wig-wig settled in the rigging, looking happily around. "Does it go?"

"Yes, it should do. Now we have to test her under field conditions. We'll take her for a shakedown." Shaani gave her friends the full guided tour. "Right. So she steers from the front, looking out of those windows. The steering wheel swivels the front two sets of wheels; we have a wide turning circle, so be careful. Brakes are operated by foot pedal. Parking brake—that's this handle here." The rat walked along with her tail twirling. "Electric winches raise and lower the sails. We can control thrust by dropping the sails or by changing the angle of attack so that less thrust is produced. We'll have to learn that as we go. We need one driver and one or more people on deck to trim the sails." The rat looked around, wondering what to point out next. "The accommodations are in the cabin here at the stern. Cargo is stored beneath the decks, accessed by the ramp. That's where we can house Budgie, bicycles, that sort of thing. We have some grass awnings to spread above the deck to shade it in the daytime. Oh, a hand pump here, to wet down the sails in case of fire."

Xoota was simply amazed. "What about armament?"

Shaani airily waved her hand. She wore her chainsaw across her back. It gave her a decidedly psychopathic air. "I made a catapult. Good for about five hundred meters with a three-kilo shot."

"A catapult?" Xoota was delighted. She leaned over to inspect the weapon in question; it looked a little like a torture rack spliced with a crossbow. The windlass system had been taken from an old car's gearbox. The bow seemed to have been made out of the leaf springs from an old truck. "What does it fire?"

"Ah, now these are special." Shaani opened a locker. "I could only make six. It's hard to make bombs; no sulfur to make gunpowder, you know. So I made acid and soaked it into cotton to make a sort of gun cotton. These are three-kilo bombs, light blue touch paper and fire. Should give a cracker of a good bang." The rat sighed. "It's a shame there are only six."

"Why not just fire rocks?" Xoota looked the weapon over. "A three-kilo rock is no laughing matter."

"Oh, well, I suppose you could." Shaani had never really thought of the low-tech solution. "We can bring some rocks along if you like."

Several villagers had come drifting out of their homes to watch the activity on the strange, ungainly ship. Shaani gave her ship one last inspection then called down to the villagers below.

"I say. Might we have the village gates open, please? We're just taking her for a spin."

In the control cabin, Wig-wig was bustling all over the dashboard. Xoota looked at the confusing selection of chairs, wheels, levers, and pedals only to have Shaani usher her into a seat.

"Right. You do the honors. Throw that knife switch. It will engage the power to the engines. The wheel steers left and right. The pedal there controls the brakes."

Xoota felt a surge of panic. "How do I slow?"

"Uh, use the brakes, I guess. And toggle the power on and off . . . I suppose I should fix up something more elaborate." Shaani frowned. "This is sort of a working beta model, I'm afraid. Never mind." She patted the quoll on the shoulder. "Yoiks and away."

Nervous of the electric switch, Xoota gingerly lowered the contacts. There was a flash and a spark and suddenly the ship jerked forward. Xoota gave a squawk of panic and disconnected the switch. She tried it again, surging power awkwardly. The ship jerked in a series of hefty bunny hops, her masts swaying high above. From up on deck, Shaani called down into the cabin.

"Ha! She moves. Perhaps a rheostat? That would moderate the amount of power going into the wheels."

Xoota engaged the engines and grimly took hold of the steering wheel. The ship slid forward, faster and faster, her electric engines giving off only the faintest whir. Children ran along beside her in the street, laughing and hooting with joy. On the main deck, Budgie looked down over the rails, utterly amazed. More villagers came running out of doors, cheering as the ship slid by. Xoota took a slight turn at far too high a speed, somehow managing to miss the bakery, and headed for the village gates.

Sitting happily on the railing above, Shaani doffed her cap to the village guard. The ship rolled merrily onward, off into a lovely morning breeze. The rat waggled her feet above the ground and simply enjoyed the ride.

> Jolly boating weather.
> And a hay harvest breeze.
> Blades on the feather.
> Shade off the trees.
> Swing, swing together,
> With your bodies between your knees.
> Swing, swing together,
> With your bodies between your knees . . .

Off and down the dusty road, the ship rode smoothly over the uneven ground, the stalk suspension moving up and down like a caterpillar's legs. It took some getting used to, but one could walk the decks. Shaani and Wig-wig enjoyed the morning breeze then slid down to the back of the control cabin.

"Now head to the high ground over there, past the wattle trees. Bring her to a halt, and we'll test her under sail."

The ship turned uphill. She immediately slowed down. Under electrical power, she was no racehorse; a jogging man could have easily caught up with her. Xoota let her slowly climb to the hill crest, looking down upon the little town.

The morning breeze was its usual steady self. The quoll jerkily worked the brake, feeling the vehicle slow. With engines disengaged, the ship drifted slowly to a halt. Xoota remembered the hand brake and yanked at the thing; it was as stiff as all hell but seemed to do the job.

"How fast were we going?" Shaani asked.

Xoota blinked. "How should I know?"

"The dials on the moon buggy control panel. It still has a speedometer and odometer. Should give speed and also distance traveled."

"Oh." Xoota had noticed no such damned fool thing. She had been terrified of crashing and ruining the last two weeks of hard work. "Right. So what now?"

"We set the sails." Shaani led the way back out on deck. The view was magnificent. The ship gave a wonderful vantage point for observing the desert. Budgie was taking advantage of the fact, sitting on his backside beside the mainmast and chortling happily away. Shaani stood beside one of the winches and explained the sail plan to Xoota.

"Right. The mainmast is actually at the rear. It's taller. So that's the foremast." She pointed. "Bowsprit out the front. We can run with mainsail, fore and main, topsails on both masts, jibs running from the bowsprit to the foremast . . ." A switch hauled a triangular sail up out of a locker and stretched it on a line running from the bowsprit. "Just a jib and the mainsail for starters, I think."

The electric winch whirred. The big mainsail, made from a blue and gold parachute, soared up the mast. It immediately made a cracking noise in the wind, the fabric turning stiff as a board. The deck took on a decided tilt. Shaani kept her eyes fixed on the sails.

"Right. Ooh, good. Feel her trying to tilt in the wind? That's why the ballast can be pumped from port to starboard." The rat waved a hand. "Wig-wig, can you watch the instruments? Xoota, let's make history."

Xoota returned to her control cabin. Releasing the hand brake almost gave her a hernia, but she managed it. She felt the ship give a slight lurch. It moved ever so slightly forward. "The brakes are off."

"Right." Shaani let the boom swing to her right. "I'm letting her go full sails. Turn to port and we're away."

Xoota turned the wheel to the right, pointing the ship's nose toward the town. The hull creaked, there was a groan from the masts, and the ship began rolling backward. Eyes wide with panic, Xoota abandoned the steering wheel and hauled on the hand brake.

Outside on the deck, Shaani made a noise of panic. "No, wrong way." The rat ran around, tugging on ropes and trying to spill wind from the sails. "What are you doing? I said port."

Xoota looked at the rat, quite mystified. "I thought you meant steer for home. You know, head back to port."

"No, no, turn to *the* port. Port, that way. Left."

Xoota planted her fists on her hips. "Well, if you mean left, then say left. Don't be obtuse."

The rat looked at Xoota over the rims of her spectacles. "Did you bother to read any of the instructional material I laid out for you?"

"Yes." Xoota grumbled. "Well, no. I can only read if someone does it out loud for me."

The rat gave a patient sigh. "Well, *port* is a term we use on ships. Look, left could mean to *your* left, but port always means to the left side of the ship, facing forward. Right?"

"Right?"

"Stop that." Shaani's patience did have its limits. "Now we want the breeze blowing three-quarters from our rear. Use the brakes if we go too fast. Yell out to drop the sails if you think she's running away from us." The rat pointed to the left of the ship. "Now that way—to *port*. With the wind fair off our stern."

The quoll grumbled and returned to the control cabin. Port, starboard, bow, stern . . . the boat seemed to be having a damned silly effect on people's command of the English language. She looked out the windows, made sure her scarf was tied tightly around her head, and disengaged the hand brake.

"The brake's off." Xoota found a sliding panel in the roof and hauled it back. It allowed her to stand up with her head out on the breeze. "Can I put the roof down?"

"Absolutely." Shaani stood by at the pulleys, controlling the mainsail boom. "Shall I let her fill?"

"Let go."

The boom swung and the sail billowed and filled. The ship's hull creaked, seemed to gather, then suddenly she was rolling along the hard-packed sand. Dirt crunched; the wheels rumbled. Wind sighed beautifully through the rigging. Xoota changed course a little and felt the speed increase. The ship leaned slightly off to one side but not dangerously so. She moved happily along the ground, her suspension effortlessly absorbing the rise and fall of the land.

Shaani yelled down to her in joy. "How does she feel?"

"She feels good." Xoota was overjoyed. "Really good."

The rat called out to Wig-wig, who had several dozen of himself sitting with noses in the breeze. "Wig-wig. What's our speed?"

"Mister dial, he says twenty-five."

"Excellent."

Xoota tried some long, slow turns. The ship curved gracefully. Cautious at first, Xoota felt the balance change, the ship tilting. She came onto another tack, feeling the booms shift to the opposite side of the ship, the sails cracking home.

Shaani gave a squawk and ducked, narrowly missing being given impromptu brain surgery by the boom. Xoota called back across her shoulder. "Sorry."

They rode for half an hour, testing the ship against the wind, with wind astern and abeam. She could come up to about thirty degrees into the wind, but her speed dropped to almost nothing.

Moving into the wind would be a laborious task, although the electric engines would be handy. Darwin only knew how long the batteries would power the engines, certainly for only half an hour or so.

They turned the ship and angled back toward the town. Shaani yelled forward to the cabin. "Ready for the second sail?"

"Raise and let go."

The rat called happily back. "Aye, aye."

Another sail shot up the rear mast. The ship surged forward, rumbling at speed along the sand plain. The ride was smooth; the equipment was holding true.

Shaani climbed up into the rigging to check the masts. She looked at the world around her in absolute delight. "I think it works."

With her scarf tied around her head and an earwig on her shoulder, Captain Xoota steered her trusty ship for the horizon.

· · · · ·

They came back into town at midday, rolling forward under minimal sail, coasting easily forward. The electric engines engaged and cruised the ship in through the village gates. Xoota took the ship on a great, wide circuit inside the village walls, heading back to the tavern square with her bowsprit pointed at the gates. The quoll shut off the engines and braked, bringing the ship to a halt a dozen meters from the tavern door.

Xoota raised her goggles, put on the hand brake, and heaved a satisfied sigh. With happy earwigs swirling all around her, she walked contentedly aft to greet Shaani.

"A name. We should give the boat a name."

"Yes." The rat girl looked over her craft. "Whatever shall we call it?"

"She, all vessels are 'she.' "

Wig-wig clustered happily on the rigging. "How about *Fred?*"

"*Fred?*" Xoota was confused. "Why *Fred?*"

"Wig-wig once met a man called Fred."

"No, it has to be something more exciting. More evocative." Xoota waved her hands. "Something that makes you think about adventure."

"Hmm." Shaani agreed. "Well, it was a huge effort to make it, and it was a very good idea. How about *Enterprise?*"

"No, that sounds silly."

"Spooverwekki?"

Xoota was taken aback. *"Spooverwekki?"*

"I just like the sound." The rat looked up and down the ship, feeling a little lost. "I'm not really very good at names."

Xoota thought back to the day she and Shaani first met.

"How about *Sand Shark*"?

"Sand Shark." Shaani looked at the ship and smiled. It had a good sound. "Ooh, I say. I like that."

They christened her with a jar of omega ale. With the foam still fizzing green and purple on the sands, the crew of the *Sand Shark* headed in to the tavern to organize their supplies, meet the village council, and make their preparations to depart.

· · · · ·

It was a long afternoon of hard, unglamorous drudge work, all except for Wig-wig, who was utterly unsuited to packing supplies into a ship. Wig-wig enjoyed himself, sticking his multiple noses into boxes, bales, and bags until someone finally requested he get the hell out from underfoot.

With villagers helping, Xoota and Shaani struggled to load the vessel with food for a two-month journey. It was all dried, preserved, and desiccated stuff: potluck stew from the tavern somehow dried into powder, dried meats, and sausages made of pounded insects for the quoll. There were boxes of hard ship's biscuits made with flour and bone meal and dried sand fish, dried berries, and goober nuts for the budgerigar. A thousand liters of water, all carried bucket by bucket from Benek's private stores, were dumped into the cistern. Finally they took on two kegs of ginger beer, and the inevitable omega ale. Xoota topped it all off with precious boxes of tea leaves.

They worked through the night, loading by the light of a windmill-powered electric lamp and a light bulb hanging from Shaani's tail. Xoota took a careful stock of her equipment, spending cash to replace anything that looked too scuffed or broken.

Carefully stowing her chemical lab equipment in baskets full of dried grass, Shaani locked everything down.

Snappy, the crustacean owner of the tavern, helped by cutting twine and cord with her pincers. She was working grimly, trying to be of help. "How long will the journey take?" she asked Shaani.

"Ah, problematic." Shaani made a knot learned from her book on nautical skills. "Our top speed is far higher than I estimated. But there are so many variables—wind, terrain . . ." Shaani had found herself a decent rabbit-fur blanket in case the far east should be cold. "I'm hoping one month. If we then fix the water, fresh water should appear here within a few days after that. So keep pumping the entire well dry to clear out the brine. Ask the frogs to help."

"Frogs?"

"Just yell down the well. Should be the easiest way." Shaani took a last check of her pockets to make sure she had sufficient notebooks and pens. "Right. We're off. We'll fix the water; never fear. Science ever forward."

Visitors tramped off the ship. There were boys from the tavern, some children, and the tent merchant. Xoota counted them all off; the last thing she wanted was stowaways. She hefted her shield and crossbow then saw Benek striding purposefully toward the ship. The man was outfitted in his gleaming metal armor with sword, knives, daggers, a short sword, a crossbow . . . apparently he was preparing for a second apocalypse. Xoota nodded to him, hoping he would just climb aboard ship and shut up, but instead, Benek came to stand beside her and inspect the ship. He looked her over with a dark, dismissive eye.

"This has taken longer than I had hoped."

Xoota watched Shaani heft heavy bales up into the hold. "Well, it's a miracle of postapocalyptic engineering, Benek. We're sorry if that took you slightly over your schedule."

The man gave a sniff. "Are you certain that the rat's engineering skills can be trusted?"

Xoota gave the man a sidelong glance. "Yes, Benek. I'm trusting her with my life."

"I hope your guidance has been worth the wait."

The quoll's shoulder gave a hunch. "Well, if not entirely satisfied with our service, you are always at liberty to jump off and walk."

Wig-wig came racing from the tavern carrying several bags of coins. Xoota gave Wig-wig a considering glance as she watched him bustle by.

"Wig-wig, have you been stealing again?"

"No. Yes. A little. Wig-wig won at a game." The bugs clustered happily around Xoota's feet. "Then found coins in floor."

"All right. You're a kleptomaniac. You know that?" She waved the bug swarm to climb aboard. "All aboard. We're making sail in ten minutes."

Xoota and Benek mounted the ramp. It rose behind them, locking into place.

Standing tall, vast, and arrogant, Benek looked along the deck and scratched his jaw. "Which cabin is mine?"

"Well, there's a choice of accommodation." Xoota checked that a dagger was properly sheathed beside her boot. "You can sleep in the common cabin or up on deck."

Benek gave Xoota level glance. "The *common* cabin?"

"That's the way. We all bunk in together." Shaani bustled past. The rat revved her chainsaw, purely for the fun of it. "Top ho."

Benek hesitated then strode after Shaani. "I am an over-man. The genetic elite of Gamma Terra. I can't share a cabin with mere animals."

Filled with the joy of departure, Shaani seemed immune to insult. "Cheer up, old chap. We're giving you the big bed."

Benek disappeared belowdecks. Xoota rolled her eyes.

Hanging upside down in the rigging, earwigs jostled back and forth in glee. "Are we there yet?"

The quoll glared. "Don't make me stop this damned thing. Because I will."

All gear was stored. Xoota called down to the villagers, making sure everyone had cleared out of the way. The first hint of dawn gave just enough light for her to steer. Shaani sounded the ship's bell. Xoota fed power into the newly installed engine rheostat. The ship moved slowly forward, guided carefully down the streets. Villagers—mutant humans, mutant animals, even the frogs from the well—waved. Their faces were anxious. The well water grew saltier and saltier every day.

There were more warriors on the walls; razorbacks had been seen not far down the coast. Shaani doffed her bobble hat as she passed them. The men on the walls waved.

They were off. The sails soared up the masts, quickly filling in the breeze. With her wheels humming, the *Sand Shark* rode the breeze, gaining speed as she headed up the slopes and out into the desert. By the time the sunrise came, the little town of Watering Hole was out of view.

· · · · ·

The *Sand Shark* performed beautifully, rumbling softly out over the desert. The wind sighed through the rigging, making a wonderful, restful sound. With the wind off the stern quarter, the ship had only the slightest lean. The wheels were spaced widely enough to keep her stable, and springs let her ride smoothly. The ship crested a sandstone rise, steering wide around a stand of quill bushes. The wind over the hill came in at a new angle. The booms turned and slammed into place, all according to design.

Budgie and Wig-wig were down in the hold, resting atop the water tanks. The hold was a lovely, dark, cool space, made mysterious by all the smells of the food stores and electrical engines. The water tanks made the place far, far cooler than the deck. Budgie was splayed over the water tanks, watching in fascination as Wig-wig clustered around a handheld computer game. The earwigs worked madly away at the controls, some pressing buttons, others working stick controls, all with an entire chorus cheering, heckling, and giving advice. The earwigs squealed in delight as something flashed on the ancient, discolored screen.

Shaani came in from the deck and leaned over in puzzlement. "What ho, chaps. What on Gamma Terra have you got there?"

Something blew up on the screen. The earwigs gave a chorus of disappointment. Several of the larger adults turned and waved hello to Shaani. "Is game. I has gotten high score. But I died before I got to next part of story."

"Died?" Shaani blinked, her eyes still dazed by the contrast between the harsh light of the desert and the shadows of the cargo hold. "Oh, I see. It's a computer game. Did you get that from Benek?"

"He writing in a book. Writing all his plans for how to make new world." The earwigs seemed pleased. "So we borrowed game."

"Well, you really should have asked, dear. People can get a little touchy about their tech treasures." The rat sat down politely with the earwigs all around her and picked up the game. She pressed a button on the old computer unit, and lurid graphics sprung up onto the screen. "Marvelous. All this data, stored inside some tiny, little thing . . ."

"I like it when the bad guys' head come off." The earwigs danced in glee. *"Raaaar."*

"Heads come off?" Shaani wasn't quite sure she approved. She held the little computer screen at arm's length and focused on the writing.

"Gene Warrior." She felt a little ill. "Oh, dear. 'Destroy the mutants. All must be purified.' Lovely."

"Wig-wig play the other side. He be the mutants." The earwigs nudged at the computer. "You want turn?"

"No, no. I shall leave you to it. But do put it quietly back where it came from when you're finished." The rat stood up, wiping her hands clean against her shorts. "Don't play too long, or you'll warp Budgie's mind."

The rat rose and climbed the steps back up to the deck. She shook off a vague sense of dissatisfaction and walked forward to the front of the hull.

The sounds of ancient music drifted happily through the air. Xoota was playing Shaani's music box in the control cabin. She was singing along to a song at the top of her voice, though she had no ear for music at all.

Shaani smiled.

The control cabin was also surprisingly cool; a little wind generator up on the hull was providing enough current to run the cabin's air conditioner. It was pure luxury—cool air in the desert. Xoota drove with her goggles up, sunglasses on her nose, and her armor sitting behind her on the floor. A shirt well open at the cleavage and a pair of loose desert trousers were the best driving gear. Singing away and delighted with the view, she seemed to be quite happy at the wheel.

Shaani came into the cabin, holding overhead handholds as the ship lurched up over some rocks. Its ability to handle rough terrain was excellent. The rat sank down into the copilot's chair, fanning her tank top and taking the full blast of the air conditioner.

Xoota smiled. Her antennae rested easily; with her ability to see a flash of unhappy futures, she was proving to be an excellent driver.

"Hey, rattie rat. What's it like up on deck?"

"Hot. Not too bad, though." Shaani relaxed in the cool. "I'm glad the coolant system still works."

"It only works on low, but it's a godsend." The way ahead was long and smooth. Xoota had picked a path that ran along firm ground, bracketed by two ranges of hills a kilometer apart. The ground was dotted with spinifex, smoke bush, and dead grass. "Are the others helping?"

"Well, Budgie and Wig-wig are sort of available. Benek seems to be in hiding in the sleeping cabin. I asked him to take a turn as sail trimmer, but he never answered."

"Bastard."

The ship needed a second crewman on call out on deck, ready to trim the angle of the sails if it was needed. Though with the current nice, smooth run, it was hardly likely to be needed. Shaani gave a shrug. "Ah, well, can't be helped."

Hanging from a wire above the center of the windscreen was an ancient talisman rescued from old ruins: two oversized dice cubes fashioned out of fur. Shaani blinked in the softer light of the cabin, lowered her sunglasses, and looked at the dice.

"Ooh. What are these?"

"Ah, votive images to the gods of fortune. The tent maker gave them to me."

"Oh, wacko." Shaani had no time for superstition, but the furry dice did give the cabin a highly cultural air. "Well done." The way ahead was fairly flat and empty. Shaani polished her sunglasses. "Do you need me to spell you at the wheel?"

"I'm happy here for a while." It wasn't that hard a job. And Shaani's strange, little music box took the boredom away. "I figure we'll make it two-hour watches, you and I swap."

"What about Benek?"

"I not want that man at the helm of our ship. No, not Benek. Anyway, he wouldn't do it. He sees himself as a mighty autarch; we're just the servants."

"Ah, I see." Shaani carefully poured Xoota a drink of lemon barley water. "That would explain why he won't talk to me."

"Really?"

"Oh, yes. He's set himself up in the coolest bit of the cabin with a blanket hung up to divide his living space from ours."

"Lovely."

"He's not very sociable. I find that odd. Humans and rats have cohabited for thousands of years. We evolved as partners." The white rat pulled her long, white ponytail down into her lap. "Odd that he doesn't want to mingle with me."

Xoota folded her arms. "That man needs watching. He at least needs to be made aware of just who the hell runs this expedition. As far as I'm concerned, the chain of command runs from me and you, down through the earwigs, Budgie, the algae in the water tanks, several pantheons of gods, and finally ends up with Benek."

Shaani chuckled slightly but completely agreed. Benek was definitely not interested at all in science.

The quoll scratched a moment at her spotted fur then stood up in her chair to hand over the controls. "Did you want to try the helm?"

"Oh, yes, please." Shaani took notes, looking at the trip meter, the speedometer, and the sand timer. "Heading one zero one zero for the last hour, at . . . thirty-five kph. Excellent."

"Right, off you go." Xoota eased out of her chair. She took her mace, crossbow, and drinking bottle. "Steady as she goes."

"Aye, aye."

"Hmm." Xoota looked at the rat girl in puzzlement. "Is that another nautical phrase?"

"I think so."

"What does it mean?"

"I'm not sure. But it seems ever so adventurous." The rat selected a new track on the music box and took the wheel. "Stretch your legs. Have fun."

· · · · ·

Xoota was happy to leave Shaani at the wheel. She knew the rat girl could handle the ship. She knotted her shirt beneath her breasts, making sure her pants were pulled up high enough to cover her pouch. With spotted fur shining in the sun, she climbed out of the control cabin and up onto the deck. The outside world instantly sucked at her with its great, dry breeze. She pulled down her sunglasses and made sure her head cloth was on tightly. Her long, moth antennae stirred and tasted the sky.

The sails were drawing well; speed was steady. Xoota looked over the railings at the balloon tires, made from some sort of solid omega stuff. The copper wire running along the top of the railings was all intact. The catapult had been stowed properly with a dozen rocks stored beside it in a plastic drum.

Excellent.

Budgie and Wig-wig were enjoying themselves down in the cool of the hold. Xoota waved them a hello as she walked past. Her backside was a little numb from the control seat. She walked along, stretching her back, heading for the sleeping cabin at the back of the ship.

The crew cabin had been lifted from the back of an ancient, nomadic vehicle apparently christened *Winnebago*. There was a small common room, a kitchen, a shower, a toilet, a laboratory set up for Shaani's books work, and a sleeping cabin set up with one double bed, a double bunk, and a tray full of nice, damp bark and leaves for Wig-wig to nest in. Benek had rather ostentatiously seized the double bed as his own. He had also hung a felt blanket across the middle of the sleeping room, taking three quarters of it as his own personal space, including the little dressing table, cracked mirror, and the outlet for the cabin's air conditioner. Xoota used her prehensile tail as an anchor, gripping a handhold with it, as she planted her fists on her hips and surveyed the arrangement with dissatisfaction. She unhooked the line that supported the blanket, letting it fall.

Benek sat at the dressing table, writing in a large, black journal. He looked up at the quoll in irritation. "Do you mind? This area is private."

Xoota looked at the man in growing dislike. "Benek. A word, if you please."

He was massively muscled, and there was an air of barely controlled violence about the man. Xoota tasted the world with her antennae, feeling a few flashes of possible violence. She chose the best route and sat herself down upon the bunk bed.

Her mace was held innocently out of sight behind her back.

"Benek, I need to be able to draft you as part of the deck watch with Shaani. Two hours out of every six when we're under way."

The huge man looked at her scathingly. "I am the mission's patron, not a crewman."

"Well, we are going into very dangerous territory. I would like you to contribute to this team."

"I have no interest in teams."

Xoota sat cross-legged on the bunk, watching the man. He was strong, perfectly groomed, and utterly self-concerned. The quoll waved her long, black-furred tail. "Benek, are you quite serious about this 'date' of yours? These two thousand brides?" She tilted her head, her predator's eyes sharp and considering. "It seems a pretty big ambition."

The man began cleaning his weapons. "My mission is my own affair. Deliver me to the site; then you may depart."

"Mmm." The quoll's eyes narrowed. "Well, let me put it this way. If we have an accident because you're not there on deck when we need you, you will never reach those brides of yours. With you *on* the roster, our odds are just that much greater."

She rose to go, not waiting for him to agree, simply expecting compliance. "You will be on deck two hours out of six. I have the deck now. Relieve me in two hours." She rehung the blanket so it screened off just his chosen bed. "And the cabin space is for everyone. We have limited facilities; we all need access to them."

She left the cabin, feeling his eyes boring into her all the way. The quoll gave a malicious, little smile, full of fangs. Her antennae twirled as she made her way back up onto the deck.

The *Sand Shark* had caught a nice breeze that channeled between the two long sandstone ridges. The wheels hummed, jouncing slightly as they rode effortlessly over dips and mounds. The ship really was a pleasure to behold. Xoota hung up in the rigging of the rear mast and scanned the horizon but saw nothing worthy of alarm. She dropped down to the deck and went below to check on the others.

Down in the hold, Budgie had decided to sleep. He lay sprawled over the water tanks, making a contented noise. Wig-wig was making himself useful, scuttling around the place and checking the brake lines and electrical connections. He had turned into a very able assistant in Shaani's technical endeavors. He was also ludicrously eager and happy, another trait apparently transmitted to him via Shaani. Shaani's enthusiasm for life, people, and the world in general never seemed to fade.

Lunchtime was a "help yourself" affair. Xoota swung into the hold, found an insect stick, dried fruit, and some ship's biscuits for Shaani. She carried the food forward with a flask of tea, thinking the cabin might be the coolest place to enjoy a nibble for lunch.

The cabin door muffled the sounds of the music box. Xoota opened the door with her tail and backed through, carrying an armload of food. She put it all down on the little map table at the back of the cabin. "Benek is now on the roster for sail trimming."

"Oh, jolly good." Shaani leaned forward as she drove, concentrating just a little too much on keeping a tight grip on the wheel. "Is that lunch?"

"Bug sticks, tea, and biscuits."

"Ooh, spiffy."

Shaani absently took hold of a biscuit, crunching into it with teeth as sharp as chisels. It was a bit of a shock at times, realizing just how much power the neat, little rat had in her teeth. She nibbled rapidly, took a cup of tea, and suddenly took an interest in something in the road just up ahead. "There it is again."

Xoota cocked her head, her mouth full of pounded, dried grasshoppers. "Hmm?"

"Dust. Just a little bit. Just over to port."

"Where?" Xoota looked out a window.

"No, no, to port. Just over there."

There was the tiniest little smidge of dust about a kilometer ahead, so low to the ground that it was nothing but a haze. Xoota rose, a bug stick in her jaws, and clambered out onto the deck.

Shaani's voice pursued her through the door. "Port. That means the ship's *left*."

"I know, I know."

The foremast rigging made a quick and easy ladder. Xoota climbed up into the air with her binoculars dangling from her neck. She wrapped her tail securely in the rigging then used both hands to steady the binoculars as she carefully searched the port-side hills.

She could just see the barest hint of dust hanging low above the sand ridges. It was just a wisp, but not too far from thick stands of bushes that grew near the *Sand Shark*'s path. Xoota narrowed her eyes then slid swiftly down on deck.

"Shaani. Go hard right. To starboard." She rang the ship's alarm bell. "All hands on deck, please. Arms and armor."

Xoota ducked into the control cabin for her armor. She yanked on her leggings and swiftly buckled up.

Shaani had started the ship on a long curve to the right, away from the spinifex. "What's happening?"

"Dust behind the spinifex dead ahead. Someone might be waiting for us to pass." Xoota shrugged on her leather tunic. "We're manning topside. Careful of the ridges to starboard. We want to stay out of bowshot. Three hundred meters, at least."

Shaani checked her dials. "She's losing speed. We need the sails opened out more."

"I'm on it."

With crossbow, mace, and shield, Xoota hastened back on deck. Benek and Wig-wig had emerged. The earwigs manned the stern, a little pile of pipe bombs beside them.

Benek loaded his overly complex crossbow. He looked loftily out over the desert. "Where are all of these imminent enemies?"

"We're being cautious." Xoota turned a crank on a winch, giving the foresail about a meter more play to starboard. She pointed Benek at the rear mast. "Let that rope out about a meter. We need to keep our speed."

Something stirred in the spinifex. Suddenly a dozen huge shapes mounted on black cockatoos erupted up out of the bare desert sand. A whole squadron of razorbacks, dressed in heavy leathers, prepared to attack.

"Yeah, there you are." Xoota grinned.

The razorbacks fired bows. They were well out of range, but it made an impressive display. Xoota uncovered the ship's catapult. She opened a locker, found a bomb, and slotted it into the firing channel, fuse side up. "Wig-wig. Are there matches? How do you light this thing?"

Some earwigs fluttered over and pointed to a knob mounted on the side of the catapult. It was a cigarette lighter ripped from an old car. "Push in and wait little minute."

"Oh, thanks."

Xoota checked the wind. The ship was changing course to keep three hundred meters between them and the razorbacks. Xoota swung the catapult starboard, much to Benek's rage.

"Idiot animal. Fire at the barbarians."

"I intend to." Xoota's eye was on a stand of spinifex on the ridges almost six hundred meters away. She plucked out the cigarette lighter and saw the end was glowing cherry red. She touched it to the fuse, and it began to splutter. Xoota tilted the catapult high, aimed at the hills, and fired. The catapult springs made an almighty *clunk,* and the big, black bomb went whizzing away into the sky.

The bomb flew to the crest of the ridge and bounced down among the spinifex before exploding in a shocking ball of flame.

The violence of the explosion was stunning. Shaani had exceeded herself with the design of the bomb. Shards of scrap metal had scythed through the bushes, and a great gout of sand and dust clouded the air.

There was panic all over the hill crest. A cockatoo reared, and figures could be seen running back over ridge to hide. Xoota furiously worked the catapult crank, gears and ratchets clanking as she hauled the leaf springs back.

Benek glared at the starboard hills. "More of them?"

"That's the main body. The attack from the bushes was supposed to drive us right into them." Loading the catapult was no mean feat. The ship had crossed another few hundred meters before the springs were finally cocked. Off to port, a dozen mounted razorbacks were racing in pursuit.

Wig-wig gave a little cry of alarm. Sailing into the air from the starboard came a giant spear launched by a ballista. The razorbacks had their krunch wagon hidden up in the spinifex bushes, and the damned thing was dangerous.

Shaani hit the brakes. The ship shuddered as it lost speed, the masts bowing forward. The spear flew past a scant few meters in front of the ship and plowed into the sand.

Xoota loaded her next missile—a rock bound with rags soaked in oil. She set the thing afire, let it burn like a mad thing, then fired at the spinifex. The flaming ball shot flat and true as smashed into the dried brush. It bounced and rolled, showering the area with flame.

The dry brush caught fire and the flames spread, burning so hot that they shimmered visibly under the desert sun. Razorbacks jumped from the burning spinifex like fleas from vermin. Still, random shots came at the *Sand Shark,* all falling short. Cockatoos screamed as they surged to their feet and danced back from the fire. At the far end of the battle line, the krunch wagon suddenly emerged, dragged by a team of ragged cockatoos. The wagon moved hastily away from the spreading fire and disappeared down the far side of the hill.

The ambush to the right was looking much the worse for wear, but the twelve razorbacks who had begun to give chase rode hard and fast for the ship. Shaani curved the ship to port, bringing the catapult to bear on the advancing riders. The razorbacks, feeling threatened, instantly fanned out wide and scattered. They fired a few petulant shots before slithering to a halt and arguing furiously with one another over whose fault the disaster had been.

Shaani came back on course. Xoota secured the catapult then checked the trim of the sails. She walked past Benek, who stood at the railings with his crossbow unfired.

"Thanks, Benek. Moral support, mate. Couldn't have done it without you."

The man watched the razorbacks arguing in the distant dust. "We have killed none of them. We could turn back and reengage."

"Yes, we could but won't. Not a mission-positive activity. And it also might get us all killed." The quoll looked at the razorbacks through her binoculars. "You know, I think those are the ones we stole the tents from. We must have really pissed them off." She heaved a grateful sigh. "Right. Now back to lunch, I think. I'll head up the masts and keep a watch out on our snouty friends."

The ship rolled onward. Benek went back to his affairs. Xoota found her half-chewed bug stick and climbed up into the rigging, sitting happily aloft and watching the razorbacks disappear into her wake.

CHAPTER 6

The *Sand Shark* rolled on, up over a rise in the sandy desert then off down the vast slopes beyond. They moved past sand dunes and rock outcrops, past the stubs of shattered, ancient walls. At one point, they steered wide around a vast, jagged tumble of rocks, where lizards clung and countless quill bushes grew. The ship tacked with the wind steady at her back, zigzagging her way along beneath her noble spread of sail.

Even there, so far from water, the desert was alive. Thousands of flies plagued the ship, clinging to it like a long-lost brother. The little bastards settled on every flat surface they could find— all except for the ones that came too close to Wig-wig. Those flies were summarily snipped in two and eaten. The insects buzzed the ship until the sun finally started to go down; then they left as quickly as they had appeared. Apparently even flies need their beauty sleep.

Gunmetal and scarlet, eggplant blue and gold, the desert sunset unreeled glorious banners of color across the sky. The wind cooled, backing fitfully and making the ship quest back and forth as she tried to catch the breeze. With no moon due to rise, the desert became a little too dangerous to navigate, but they rolled on for a while then picked a fine vantage point atop a rise to bring the ship slowly to a halt. Xoota tugged on the mighty hand brake; the sails were furled, and the *Sand Shark* settled down to camp for the night.

It was odd not to be moving; the motion of the ship had seemed so permanent, so natural, that to be standing still felt almost strange. Budgie came out to strut the decks then paraded off onto the desert sands to forage for grubs and goober pods beneath the bushes. The crew of the *Sand Shark* decided to make its meal on the open upper deck beneath the stars. The last wisps of sunset hung dark and glorious in the sky. Strands of spinifex made stark, black shapes against the horizon.

Shaani made the dinner, cooking with the same easy aplomb with which she handled everything in life. Humble rations were somehow turned into delicious rolls of chapati bread filled with meat, spices, and cheese. She had even managed to chill the fruit yogurt she had made out of dried curds. The crew sat with deep satisfaction, watching the sun go down and the desert grow blue and mysterious with night.

Shaani brewed tea and served it with condensed milk, rich and creamy. She sat back, wriggled pink toes at the stars, and gave a satisfied sigh.

"Not bad at all. Day one, three hundred and two kilometers. We're moving at an angle to our destination, so that brings us two hundred and twenty-nine kilometers closer to the mission objective." The rat was pleased. "An excellent day's run."

Shaani told herself that she should walk around the ship and inspect the tires, the brakes, the wheels, but she put it off until morning. It was too peaceful, too perfect an evening. It would be a shame to break the spell. Still, it had been a long, long day. Bedtime beckoned. The rat gave a huge yawn.

Xoota noticed and heaved herself up to her feet. "We'll keep one person on guard at all times. Two-hour shifts. I'd like the drivers to rest their eyes. Benek, if you could take first watch then Wig-wig. I'll take third; my night vision is good. Shaani can take the last watch and do her teeth out on the main deck where we won't be tempted to stuff her tooth file up her backside sideways."

Benek gave a scowl. "Why am I on first watch? Why not last?"

"Because desert creatures are at their most active after sundown, and we need our best man armed and ready."

Benek approved. He laid out his weapons, ready for his first stint.

So there would be peace for a little while at least. Xoota took one last look at the horizon. Shaani took one last glance over the ship, and they retired to the sleeping cabin. Xoota tore off her boots and clothes and flopped into the upper bunk. Shaani neatly folded her clothing, topped them with her spectacles, and slid herself into bed. They kept the doors and windows wide open, letting in a cool, night breeze.

Wig-wig was down in the hold, clandestinely playing the computer game again. Apart from that, the ship was quiet. The two girls heard Benek's boots clomping along the deck as he marched around on guard. Somewhere out on the sands, a gecko called.

It was wonderful just to rest. Xoota lay back and enjoyed the desert breeze. "Hey, Shaani."

"Yes, old bean?"

"Your ship is wonderful."

"Oh." She sounded embarrassed. "Thank you."

"Good night." The quoll scratched herself, gave a vast yawn, and went to sleep.

Below her in the dark, Shaani smiled. She turned her pillow over to the cool side and settled down to sleep.

■ ■ ■ ■ ■

The night progressed peacefully. Benek came into bed after his stint on guard, ostentatiously ignoring the women sleeping in their bunk beds. Xoota dangled one leg over the side of her bed, snoring as though her life depended on it. Up on deck, Wig-wig tramped around the ship, scuttling up and down the rigging, mostly for the fun of jumping off and gliding back down again. Benek shook his head in disgust. He made sure that his weapons all lay close to hand and slept wearing his boots and combat pants.

Sometime in the wee hours of the morning, Shaani felt Xoota come down from standing guard and nudge her awake. The rat gave a vast, chisel-toothed yawn and nodded to show that she was up and about. It was easiest to just grip an old flashlight globe and let power tingle down into her fingertips; providing her own illumination, Shaani groped around for the morning's clothing—big, hairy socks; hiking boots; shorts; singlet; and poncho. She settled her glasses on her nose and reached for her bobble hat.

"So how's the desert? All's well?"

"All's quiet." Xoota propped her weapons up beside her bed, tore off her clothes, and flopped into her bunk. Since she would be up again in two hours, she left on her underwear, yet another set decorated with little hearts. "See you in two. We'll get an early start and get breakfast on the move."

"Right-o." Shaani slung her beloved chainsaw over her back. "Sweet dreams."

The rat took her night bag up on deck. The skies were a magnificent, velvety black with just a hint of glorious aurora australis. Shaani climbed up to sit upon the roof of the cabin. Feeling mightily pleased with the world, she took out her tooth file and proceeded to trim her incisors, the noise a horrible scar upon the quiet desert night.

The muffled voice of Xoota came up from the cabin. "Further."

Shaani walked a few paces away.

Xoota's muffled voice pursued her. "Much, *much* further . . ."

Shaani grumbled. She packed up her toiletries and moved away to the bow of the ship, where she sat upon the control cabin roof in peace and quiet.

Ever a neat rat, she groomed herself. She washed her face with a piece of flannel cloth then combed her fur with a damp currycomb until it shone bright and fine as silver. She washed her whiskers and her ears; combed her face; and unbound her streaming, white ponytail. She let her glorious hair flow in the desert breeze, enjoying the quiet and the freedom.

A mighty mission was being performed. Science was on the march, trying to make a better world. Shaani was fulfilling the great, noble vision of her ancestors. As long as one lab rat held on to the dream, the adventure was not dead. The rat propped herself up to watch the desert shadows, enjoying the peace of the night.

It was her ship. She had designed it; she had built it. She could feel every tiny part of it around her. When she felt the suspension move ever so slightly, she first flicked her glance at the wind anemometer mounted atop the mainmast, but it still turned at the same rate as before. Wind direction had not changed. She swiveled around on her bottom and turned to look along the length of the ship.

Something dark was crouching on the deck. A second and third shadow followed. Yet more figures were climbing over the rails. Shaani stood, staring, wondering if her eyes were playing tricks on her.

There was one simple way to tell. The rat put her hand on the copper wire that ran along the railings, gathered up her energy, and let an electric shock sear into the rails.

Down on the deck, figures were frozen halfway through climbing across the rails. Some screamed, some snarled. Two fell crashing to the sands. One of the figures up on the deck stood and roared, waving a cleaver as it charged toward the cabin. Shaani screamed at the top of her voice, raising the alarm, but she was still the only person up on deck.

Brave far beyond her means, Shaani seized her fusion-powered chainsaw. She pulled the trigger, and the razor-sharp blades roared and whirred. The device seemed to fill her with a wild, manic glee. She raced forward, holding the chainsaw like a battering ram. "Tally ho!"

A titanic razorback met her face-to-face, swinging at her with a hefty club. He collapsed backward as Shaani crashed into him, chainsaw first, the blade doing perfectly awful things. The razorback slammed against other war pigs, screaming and squealing as the rat leaped over him and crashed her chainsaw into another skull.

There was a roar from out on the desert sands; there were dozens of them, in fact. Shaani fought wildly in the dark against huge war pigs that swarmed onto her ship's decks.

Her chainsaw growled like a demon as sparks and body parts showered the deck. The blade bit and clawed at razorback armor, razorback shields, and razorback internal plumbing until one vast war pig in full plate armor slammed into her with his shoulder. The rat squealed and fell, sliding and skittering across the deck. She slammed against the control cabin door. The armored razorback came for her, tusks bared.

Dazed, Shaani pointed a finger. "Take that, you blighter." She fired her radiation blast at the monster, hitting it right in the head. Blinded, the monster staggered toward her as she scrabbled her find her feet. His war flail crashed against her, sending her tumbling across the deck. Stars danced before her eyes; her ribs felt broken, stabbing with pain. The armored razorback shook his head, cleared his vision, and charged at her, flinging himself on her in a rabid avalanche. The rat lunged upward with her chainsaw. The blade point skipped, lodged, then plunged in. The monster roared and grabbed Shaani's throat in his hands. He choked her, making her vision turn bright red. The rat yanked her chainsaw upward, and suddenly she found herself rolling free, hacking and coughing as she fought for breath.

The night rang to the sounds of weapons slamming into armor. Shaani's ribs speared her with agony; her vision danced with stars. She staggered to her feet and blinked at the melee.

Earwigs soared and flew, pinching and nipping, squealing and snarling. Razorbacks slapped and fought at the creatures, leaving themselves open for Xoota. Dressed in her heart-spotted underwear, the quoll fought ferociously with cog mace and shield, slamming her weapon home into razorback helms. She battered one to his knees but slipped, and suddenly a razorback warrior loomed over her. Wig-wig enveloped the razorback's face with dozens of wings and pincers, and the beast reeled aside.

Benek fought alone, making no move to help Shaani. He slammed his sword into razorbacks as they tried to climb up the railings. There were more war pigs down on the sands, yelling like demons as they raced toward the ship.

• • • • •

Rocking backward as a flail crashed into her shield, Xoota tried to make sense out of the melee. More and more razorbacks were closing in. She tried to see where Shaani had gone.

"Shaani, get us under way! Go go go go go!"

She saw the rat, staggering in a daze, blank and concussed. A war pig charged toward Shaani with a massive, two-handed cleaver.

Xoota gave a roar of warning. Quite suddenly long claws shot from her fingertips. She hurtled herself at Shaani's foe.

Xoota's claws were sharp enough to shear clean through steel. She screamed in feral glee and leaped onto her enemy, ripping his armor apart. The pig staggered and fell screaming. Xoota leaped from her victim and instantly felled another razorback with her claws. Her whole face lit up with delight.

"Yeah! Now that's what I call an alpha mutation." But her claws shrank and disappeared just as quickly as they had appeared. "Oh, bugger . . ."

• • • • •

Shaani staggered toward the control cabin. Budgie had erupted up out of the hold, kicking and biting at the enemy. He bowled into one razorback and sent the monster tumbling across the railings. Shaani stumbled past, into the control cabin, and threw the knife switch that fed the electric engines.

The ship refused to move.

Hand brake. The rat attacked the lever, putting her whole back into it. She had nowhere near Xoota's strength, but she managed to squeeze the locking handle open and pushed her weight against the lever.

The ship lurched. The *Sand Shark* picked up speed only slowly—a walk, then jogging speed, then slightly faster . . .

slightly faster . . . Razorbacks down on the sand broke into a run. They were all visible in the graying light. Some swung grappling hooks; others fired at the railings. Shaani abandoned the steering wheel and lurched her way back out onto the deck.

Benek, Budgie, Xoota, and Wig-wig were fighting a savage action against half a dozen war pigs all around the central deck. Shaani blinked, half blinded with concussion, then made her way to the catapult. She worked the crank handle, jacking back the titanic, steel springs, then slapped a rock into place. She swiveled the weapon around, took aim, and fired.

The rock slammed into the razorbacks who surrounded Xoota. The missile took one pig's head clean off before slamming into a second, who fell into a third.

Missed by a hair's breadth, Xoota stared at Shaani in shock and outrage. "Holy kack." She slammed her shield against another razorback, crashing him over the railing and onto the sand below.

Shaani ignored the fight. She staggered to the mainmast and hit the winch control. The mainsail soared upward, filling to the wind. The boom whipped across the deck, smashing two war pigs overboard.

"Who's driving this thing?" Xoota's yell carried across the chaos of the fight.

"No one." Sick and exhausted, Shaani restarted her chainsaw. "Right. Here I come." She collapsed against the mainmast.

∎ ∎ ∎ ∎ ∎

Three razorbacks were left. Benek smashed one down, savaging the monster where it fell. The last two pigs abandoned ship, leaping down into the sands. Benek fired his crossbow after them. Xoota ignored the razorbacks and raced over to Shaani.

"Shaani!" Her voice cracked with panic. "Wig-wig, get over to Shaani!"

The rat was covered in pig's blood; her chainsaw was dripping gore. She had a determined look in her pink eyes as she did her best to stand. But she was shaking; she was in shock and badly hurt.

Xoota caught her in her arms. "Easy. Easy now. They've gone. You chased them off."

Earwigs came flocking down around them. Wig-wig instantly caught Xoota's mood and raced around and around Shaani in fright, patting her with his feelers. The earwigs glowed, working their strange mutation, healing her as best they could.

Xoota watched carefully and made Shaani drink. She took a damp cloth and wiped the rat's face and whiskers clean. "You need a bath."

"A-a what?"

"A bath. You're a wreck."

Shaani tried to struggle up off the deck. "Are they gone? The razorbacks."

"Falling behind. Benek set the fore sail." The ship was bounding along. "I have to go steer. Wig-wig, look after her. Make her lie down."

The quoll raced off, still in her underwear, and threw herself into the control cabin. The ship had been bouncing off downwind, heading for sandstone boulders. The *Sand Shark* came back under control, curving away, leaning as she caught the wind diagonally from the stern.

. . . . .

Out on the sands far behind, the razorback tribe gave a vengeful yell. Cockatoos screamed as the warriors mounted to pursue the sand ship. Lying on the deck, Shaani groped for the flask of cold tea that Wig-wig handed her, and stared dazedly up at the sails.

"Wig-wig, can you . . . can you ask Benek to please set jib and fore staysail?"

"Benek be shooting at pigs. Pigs too far away, but Benek is shooting."

"Well, could you please ask him to stop it? We need full sail."

A ballista bolt from the razorbacks' krunch wagon flew past the ship. Shot from a wildly bucking wagon, it had gone wide but only just. The artillery shot was enough to finally move

Benek into action. Jibs began to whip up into place at the bow, followed by topsails at the heads of all the masts. The vessel leaned dangerously over to starboard, tilting hard. But her wheels sang faster, the springs absorbing the ripples of the hard-packed sand.

"Thank you, gentlemen. Wig-wig, go downstairs to the electric pump and shift all water to the portside tanks, please."

"Shaani must rest first. Into bed . . . lie down."

The rat swallowed. "I need to . . . to check the hull for damage. Check the tires . . ."

Wig-wig and Budgie were taking no arguments. Shaani suddenly felt the bugs swarm beneath her and carry her off across the sloping deck. He swept her down into the cabin. While they could not get her up into her bunk, they could set her up on the floor with blankets, sheets, and a pillow. They checked her broken ribs, quite distraught, wanting to help.

"Wig-wig, the water tanks . . ."

"We must heal you."

"Shift the water to port."

The earwigs gave in as they caught wind of Shaani's concern for the ship. They flowed off toward the hold. Minutes later the ship began to right herself a little, losing some of her extreme tilt.

By the time Wig-wig came back, Shaani was trying to sit. She had apparently taken quite a crack on her skull; the whole room was spinning.

The earwigs made a noise of protest and tried to make her lie back down. "Rat lady, be still. Be still and heal."

Shaani's tongue felt thick. For some reason, her words seemed to slur. "There are some tools. I can make caltrops . . . maybe land mines."

"No, no, rattie wants to go to sleep."

"Don't be silly. Of course I don't."

But apparently she did. The rat suddenly felt a great gush of images—soothing water, rustling leaves, and for some reason an infinity of sheep stupidly bouncing over a fence. It was odd, really. The only sheep she knew were three brothers, all called Kevin, who ran a farm in her home village. And the Kevins were all bright green . . .

Wig-wig. The little blighter was doing his brain-tweaking trick. Shaani felt her eyelids grow heavy and lifted up a finger to protest. "I shall have words with you about this . . ."

Seconds later she was asleep.

Wig-wig bustled all over her, pulling a sheet across her, making sure the fans were blowing cool air on her. One earwig bustled quietly up, kissed the rat on one cheek, and left her to her sleep.

The ship raced onward with her sails spread full. Far behind, a horde of razorbacks snarled in her wake.

. . . . .

All through a long, hot morning, the *Sand Shark* skimmed east-southeast, steering off course to take the wind full force into her stern quarter. The wind was moderate but steady. The ship moved at an average of thirty kilometers per hour, slowing as she reached rough ground or moved into the wind shadow of rock outcrops and sand hills.

At midday the wind died away almost completely. The sails jerked and flapped, leaving the ship to coast to a stop. Xoota engaged the electric drive, rolling the ship slowly onward at a dazzling eight kilometers per hour. But the ship began to slow after fifteen minutes of battery drain. She finally ground to a halt as she tried to reach the top of a sand dune, groaning, shuddering, and starting to roll backward.

They were stalled. Xoota hauled on the hand brake, gave an irritated sigh, and decided to make the best use of time by checking the ship for damage.

Out on deck, Benek was glaring out over the desert. The sails hung flaccid in the still, hot air. The little generator windmills for the air conditioners had also stopped. On top of the mainmast, Shaani's little wind-speed meter stood completely still.

Xoota shook her head in irritation and walked aft. "Benek, any sign of the razorbacks?"

"Nothing." The huge human had tossed razorback corpses overboard, but had made no move to swab the deck. "We have outrun them."

While leaving a set of tire tracks that could be followed by a blind man, Xoota thought. If the razorbacks were insane enough to pursue them into the deep desert, then they might be crazy enough to keep on coming. That would imply the creatures were seriously pissed off. The whole tent-theft incident seemed to have sparked a serious vendetta.

Xoota took the chance to head back to the cabin and visit Shaani. She found the rat fast asleep. She knelt beside her, checking her bandages. Wig-wig surrounded the rat girl, fanning her with dozens of giant earwig wings. It made the air surprisingly cool.

A representative earwig climbed onto Xoota's shoulder. He spoke in a whisper. "She can has sleeping. Is good."

"How bad is she?"

"Broken ribs. Bash on head. And skin had lots of big, black marks." The earwig was a little puzzled by mammalian structure. "Is that a disease?"

"Those are bruises. I think it's broken blood vessels beneath the skin."

"Not good design." The earwigs looked over Shaani's bandages, gently neatening them. "I shall fix."

"How soon do you think you can fix her?"

The earwigs looked unhappy. "Tomorrow, I can has more power. Make little bit better. A day after, little bit more better. Maybe four days."

"Does she need anything?"

"Just sleepings." The bugs sighed. "I needs food. Energy. Must have sugar nom noms." Wing-wagging was hard, hot work. "Tired."

"Okay, well, we might as well break for lunch. I can bring you some of that condensed milk?"

"Ooh, *nommy.*"

Xoota put the kettle on the stove and boiled tea. She made soup from a packet; found some of Shaani's homemade, deliciously crusty locust bread; and carried the food down into the hold, where they could eat in the cool.

Benek ate in one corner, fastidiously keeping to his own stores. Xoota couldn't have cared less.

The wind seemed determined to stay on holiday. Xoota checked on Shaani then went back up on deck, where she checked on the wind meter; climbed the mainmast; and made a long, careful study of the empty desert all around her. The tracks of the *Sand Shark* were clearly visible stretching back off across the hills. Xoota pulled out her binoculars and carefully studied the horizon, looking for anything that might spell danger.

A dust plume hung low on the west horizon. Small, it was low to the ground, with a broad base. But it looked as if it came from a large body of riders, moving fast.

Razorbacks.

Xoota watched them for a while, trying to estimate the distance. The cloud might hang twenty meters above the ground. Xoota was high, high up in the mainmast atop a fairly high hill.

Forty kilometers?

The razorbacks would take two hours to cross the distance galloping, three hours at a hard trot. Their arrival time depended on just how psychotic they felt.

There was no sign of any wind. No sand drifted from the dunes. The place felt as still and hot as an oven. Thrashing her tail in dissatisfaction, Xoota looked once more at the sky, hoping for a telltale trace of wind. She finally slid down a backstay and landed with a thump upon the deck.

Wig-wig, not blessed with wonderful distance vision, clustered around her for news. "Be they gone?"

"No, I see them. About forty K back on our trail." Budgie was sitting down in the hold, making free with the supplies of goober nuts. Xoota dismissed the idea of having the lazy avian bastard tow the entire ship. "Never mind. The wind should pick up in an hour or two."

Greatly relieved, Wig-wig hastened off to attend to Shaani. Meanwhile, Xoota replenished her stock of crossbow bolts and made sure the catapult bombs were ready.

There was nothing to do except to watch the wind meter and curse. Benek assembled his arms and armor, sharpened his sword, and walked up and down the deck in confidence. Xoota thrashed her tail, always keeping an eye on the wind. From time to time, she clambered all the way up the mainmast and watched the enemy slowly closing in.

The dust cloud was following right up along the *Sand Shark*'s tracks. After an hour, the cloud had halved the distance to the ship. Xoota managed to catch one glimpse of dark figures crossing a sand hill; razorback battle riders, fanned well out around a krunch wagon pulled by far too many cockatoos.

They were coming on hard and fast.

The quoll stalked along the deck. Benek was sitting stiff-backed in the shade, playing his computer game with intense concentration. Xoota cleared her throat.

"Benek, you feel any decent alphas coming on today?" The quoll wriggled her shoulders. It was as if some sort of mental power were brewing briefly in her skull. It was a shame the claws had gone; *those* had been fun. "You know, any mutations for combat?"

"I am a genetically perfect human." The man kept his eyes on the game. "I do not experience 'alpha mutations.' "

That was a shame. They might have found something that remodeled his personality from scratch. Xoota stroked her long whiskers and peered down at the computer game. "This is your training aid?"

"There appears to be something odd happening. The mutants in this game somehow now register high score." He pondered. "Initials have appeared on the high score chart. 'G.I.A.N.T.' I wonder if it might be some sort of sign?"

"Well, these things happen." Xoota nodded. "Stay sharp. Those razorbacks are closing in." The quoll wrinkled her nose in thought, then poked her head into the sleeping cabin. She whispered to the nearest earwig. "Psst. Wig-wig." Xoota cocked her head. "G.I.A.N.T.?"

"Greatest Insect of All Nature and Time." Wig-wig was carefully arranging a cool, wet cloth on Shaani's forehead. "Is me."

"Thought so."

Xoota paced back and forth on the decks. Still the wind refused to come. The quoll kicked at a backstay then stomped into the empty control cabin. She went so far as to peer at the furry dice hanging from the windscreen. Xoota made sure that the control cabin door was closed and sidled up to the dice, clearing her throat.

"Look. A bit of wind, needed now. Not an option." She pointed a commanding finger at the dice. "Right?"

The ship gave a creak. Suddenly the air conditioner began to blow cool air. Xoota froze. Then her antennae perked up as she heard the sound of the sails cracking in the breeze.

"*Yes.*" She kissed the fuzzy dice. "Thank you."

A quick peek on deck showed nothing but good news. The razorbacks had closed to ten kilometers away and were racing to close the gap at full speed. But the sails were no longer hanging limply. They were swelling, growing tighter and tighter. The little cups of the wind meter began to spin fast and steady at the mainmast. Xoota gave a grin.

"All right. Stand by to roll."

The ship heeled a little in the breeze, the springs creaking. Xoota happily yanked off the hand brake and flung herself into the control chair. She gripped the steering wheel, ready to roll.

Nothing happened.

The ship creaked but didn't move an inch. Nothing seemed to be happening. Xoota yanked the hand brake on and off again and pumped at the foot pedal. The ship creaked and leaned in the wind but never budged.

Xoota cursed long and hard, blistering paint off the walls with her tongue. She messed around with the brakes one more time then ran out on deck to see what the other idiots had done to the damned sails. She expected some sort of moronic activity, but the sails were all properly set and drawing. The ship actually began heeling too far over to starboard. Xoota dropped the staysail and had Benek take down the mizzen.

"Why the hell aren't we moving?"

Xoota leaned over the railings and looked at the wheels. The starboard side was perfectly clear; all was well. But on the port side . . .

The port lead wheel was half buried in sand.

"Son of a Blaash."

The ship was bogged.

The press of sail was only digging the tire in deeper, pushing down and driving her into the sand. Xoota tried to think how to free the ship. Dig it out? That would just make the hole deeper. Tow her? She tried to imagine Budgie, Benek, and herself having enough muscle power to move the entire ship and wilted.

Damn.

Minute by minute, the razorbacks were drawing closer.

Shaani would know what to do. Xoota ran past Benek and into the sleeping cabin. The rat girl was still lying asleep on the floor, tended by the conscientious little earwig swarm.

Xoota hated to do it, but she had to awaken Shaani. She stroked her face, her hands insistent, trying to be gentle. "Shaani? Shaani, wake up. I need to talk to you."

The rat blinked. She drew in a breath and turned a little green. She swallowed and tried to focus her eyes. "My head hurts."

"Shaani. The ship is bogged. Razorbacks are closing in." Xoota helped her friend lift up her head. "Shaani, tell me you knew this could happen. How do we un-bog the ship?"

"The ship . . . ?" Shaani screwed up her eyes, trying to concentrate. "Which wheels? All of them?"

"Left—ah, the front port wheel."

Shaani closed her eyes, clearly wanting to go back to sleep. "Just one wheel, easy . . . Shift ballast to the stern. Should lift the wheel out. And . . . reverse out of the . . . soft . . . dirt . . . thing."

"Shift the ballast." Okay, that could be done. The water was . . . Actually, doable. There was an empty tank at the back of the ship. She could run a siphon hose between the tanks.

How to reverse the ship?

"Shaani, how do we reverse the ship?"

"Reverse the electric engines."

"We're out of power."

"No power?"

"All gone. And there's no wind for the little wind generators."

The white rat tried to rise but was too dizzy to do more than sit up in bed. "Get my . . . chainsaw. Top the tank with water. You can run a power wire from the chainsaw's outlet to the capacitors."

She started drifting off again. Xoota tried to keep her awake.

"How long? Shaani? How long will the chainsaw need to charge the battery?"

"Oh, a long time . . ." Shaani sighed. "Hours."

She licked her lips. Wig-wig gave her cold peach tea to drink. The rat swallowed gratefully and rested her head back on her pillow.

"The planks on the starboard side of the hull. Unpeg them. Pull them off. Use them beneath the bogged wheels." She had thought of everything. "QED."

Xoota dropped Shaani's wet cloth back on her forehead, pushed her back into bed, and left her with the bugs. The quoll ran off to see to the ship.

"Benek. There's work to do."

She dropped the rear ramp and fetched Budgie, some coils of rope, and a folding shovel. The dust from the approaching razorback horde could be seen from the ground. Xoota found a hose and shoved one end of it into the main water tank. She sucked on it to drag water up and start it siphoning into the rear tank over the ship's back wheels.

"Benek."

He was up on the deck, standing proud and ready to fight, the ultimate peak of genetically perfect manhood, ready to take on the mutant hordes face-to-face. Xoota glared up at him.

"Benek, we're getting out of here. Pull the pegs on the port upper side planks and let the board drop down here to me."

Water was shifting to the back of the ship, and the board was finally on its way. Xoota tried to ignore the onrushing wave of enemies and simply set to work. Benek lowered her a solid wooden plank. Xoota dragged the thing awkwardly over to the front wheel. She dug away soft sand and struggled to ram the board beneath the bogged front tire.

The ship's stern was pointing downhill. If they could just get her rolling back and forth a little, the front wheel should ride up out of the damned hole it had dug for itself. Xoota fitted on Budgie's harness and saddle, looped a rope to the saddle horn, and tied the other end of the rope to the rear axle.

Benek and Wig-wig came running down the rear ramp. The human glowered. "What are you doing?"

"Working us free." The quoll had everything in hand. "Right. Benek, we need you up front at the front wheel. We're going to rock her back and forth. Once she rolls free, go up the access ladder and into the control cabin. We need you at the wheel. Steer us back about a hundred meters, put on the hand brake, then set the sails. I'll be back on board to help."

"What of the razorbacks?"

"Forget the damned razorbacks." Xoota raced back to Budgie, wrapped a tow rope around her own arm, and made ready to pull. "All right. Get behind the front wheel and push."

Budgie lunged against the tow rope, pulling for all he was worth. Xoota hauled on her own rope. The ship barely shifted. She let the rope go slack then heaved again, yelling to Budgie and Benek. They hauled, released, hauled, released . . .

The ship was hardly moving.

Wig-wig tried to help, holding the ship and whirring his wings. The thought was appreciated at least. Xoota heaved again and again. Each time they pulled, the ship shifted just a little then rolled back into its hole. The water was slowly shifting to the back of the ship. They pulled, released, pulled, released. Each time, the *Sand Shark* rocked just a little more. But she poised just short of being able the lurch out of the hole. Time and time again, she teetered on the brink and failed.

Xoota's boots slipped and slithered in the sand. Budgie hurtled himself into action. Benek put his back against the front axle and shoved, his huge muscles bulging. But the ship refused to make the last, tiny shift. Xoota heaved, her whole body straining, the muscles of her legs on fire as she tried to make her ship shift the last few precious centimeters.

There was a sudden surge of power from the wheels. Sand spurted from under the tires, and the ship started to move. Budgie and Xoota flung themselves against the tow ropes, and suddenly the ship was rolling. Xoota cast off the tow ropes, hauling Budgie aside as the ship slowly started to roll past.

Shaani was on her knees on deck, holding an electric cable. There was a sharp smell of ozone and a blue crackle coming from the rat's body. She must have generated her own power surge and fed it to the engines. Wig-wig swirled up to help her as Shaani collapsed to the deck.

A spear whipped past Xoota and plunged into the ground nearby. The quoll ran, scooping up equipment and hurling it onto the ship. The *Sand Shark* moved slowly onward as the razorbacks reloaded their artillery.

Xoota looked around. Twenty razorbacks were thundering toward the ship on cockatoo back. The ship rolled slowly downhill—closer and closer to the charging pigs.

Xoota bellowed up toward the decks. "Raise sails! Raise sails!"

The wheels squeaked as the hand brake came on. There were too few crew members to do too many jobs. Benek came on deck, reaching for his crossbow.

Xoota yelled up to him in command. "No firing! Raise the damned sails!"

The foremast winch was working slowly—too slowly. It had to be Shaani, still trying to help. Xoota mounted Budgie, ignored the ship, and charged straight toward the razorback hordes.

She was a rider and a shooter, and she was good. Budgie sped along the sands, faster and smoother than the raucous cockatoos. The razorbacks spread out, fumbling for bows. Budgie swerved and ran sideways along the front of the onrushing enemy.

Xoota made an attack run. Budgie galloped, neck flat, his blue feathers gleaming. Xoota stood in her stirrups, effortless and beautiful; tracked a target; and fired. A razorback screamed and fell. Budgie did as he was trained to do, swerving and weaving. Return fire missed, landing either too short or too far. Xoota worked the loading handle on her crossbow, gears clanking as she winched the string back into place. Her bow pulled a hundred and sixty kilos. At that range, it was lethal. She slapped in a bolt, moving with practiced speed. Feeling her rise to fire, Budgie raced straight and true, giving her a firing platform. Xoota aimed and pulled the trigger. The crossbow bolt flew so swiftly, it was almost invisible. Another razorback flew backward into the dust. Return fire arced in Xoota's direction, but the bows were weaker than her crossbow, and the shots were easily dodged.

The razorbacks veered away from the ship, charging vengefully toward Xoota. She swerved, galloping fast, working her cocking lever until the gears had cocked the bow. She ducked and dodged an arrow shot. Budgie sawed hard left, left again, then right, his patterns random and fast. He stabilized as Xoota found her moment, stood in the stirrups, and turned in the saddle. She fired straight back into her wake. The bolt smacked into a razorback, striking sparks as it burst through its heavy armor and right out through its back. The razorback reeled, roaring, the cockatoo hitting another bird and spreading chaos in the ranks. Xoota was already reloading, moving faster than the heavy war pig cavalry, keeping them in play.

The ship was moving.

The sails had filled. Someone had her steering hard over, moving along the mid slope of the hill, where the wind was strongest. It had to be Shaani; Benek would never be so clever. But the ship was moving painfully slowly. She gathered speed but it was taking her too long.

Xoota felt Budgie swerve again. Arrows flashed past her in the dust. She hauled Budgie off to the right, stood, and fired again. She saw her shot as it struck a razorback's shield and punched clean through. The razorback reeled, snarling, but stayed in the saddle, ravening and cursing.

Wig-wig came swirling overhead. Clusters of the biggest earwigs were carrying pipe bombs, the fuses fizzing dangerously short. They flew over the razorback charge, dropping the bombs. Explosions detonated on the sands. A single war pig fell. The rest fought rearing, swerving mounts. Earwigs swirled around Xoota and Budgie, urging them to head up to the hill.

"Xoota, come on board; be quick."

The ship was moving slowly sideways along the hill, climbing toward the crest. She had enough momentum to make it across. But another enormous spear from the krunch wagon whipped through the air. It hit the ship low and to the rear of the hull. The sound of the impact made Xoota's heart catch in her chest.

The ship sailed on.

She kicked Budgie into a gallop. He ran straight and fast.

Wig-wig passed her, heading for the razorbacks to dive and swerve at their cockatoos, making the birds balk. He slowed their charge. Xoota raced to the ship. The rear ramp was down, scraping on the dirt.

The ship tilted slowly, slowly over the crest of the hill. Another spear from the krunch wagon flew past her, hitting the starboard railing and sending splinters flying. Then suddenly the ship was away over the crest, her sails and masts still visible, moving more and more quickly as she rolled downslope. Budgie raced to intercept her, crossing the hillcrest with feathers flying. The ship was starting to really roll, faster and faster. Her sails cracked as they filled to a steady breeze. The budgerigar put on a mad spurt of speed and raced to catch up.

Budgie was tiring. The ship was pulling ahead. Suddenly the ship jerked, slowing; the masts whipped forward as the brakes came on hard. Budgie reached the ramp and flung himself on board, screeching to a halt inside the hold.

A giant razorback spear has gone clean through the hold. Water was gushing from a punctured water tank. Xoota leaped from Budgie's back. Wig-wig raised the ramp while Xoota raced to rescue the water supply.

The siphon was still pouring water from the fore tanks into the rear. The rear tank was hemorrhaging water straight out onto the sands. Xoota ripped the siphon hose free. It was too late to save the water that had already been shunted between the tanks; the last of it gurgled out into the desert even as Xoota tried to jam shut the hole.

Damn.

She raced up on deck. Benek was on the catapult. He fired a useless round up over the hill, the explosion of the bomb loud and violent in the desert. He had wasted a bomb for nothing. No razorbacks came across the hill. The way ahead was flat and featureless desert. The wind blew steadily in from the west. The ship headed northeast, leaning to the breeze as she hummed off across the hard-packed sand.

Xoota saw Benek reloading the catapult. Hot, out of breath, and still fizzing with adrenaline, she ran past him. "Stop that. Secure the catapult." The quoll yelled across her shoulder. "Set staysail and forestay." She raced into the control cabin.

Shaani was driving. A bloody bandage was wrapped around her head. She slumped over the wheel, in no shape to be up and out of bed. She saw Xoota and reeled back in the driving seat, looking thankful. "Are you all right?"

"I'm intact, which is more than I can say for you." She felt Shaani's head. She was clammy and unwell. "I can take the helm."

Shaani let herself be lifted out of the seat. "I'll sleep here. There's room on the floor."

"Just as long as you rest. Are you okay?"

"Dizzy. The room's turning around. I can't stand."

Wig-wig brought in sheets, a drink, and a pillow for Shaani as Xoota took the wheel. The ship was making a steady forty kilometers per hour, heading due east. The razorbacks were once again being outrun.

Xoota breathed a sigh of relief.

"Wig-wig, check for damage. See if those spears did anything other than busting the rear water tank."

"Okay."

Shaani kept her eyes closed, lying on her blankets on the floor. "Wh-what happened to the water?"

"There's no need to worry. It's only minor. Make sure you sleep."

"My word but we seem to have really pissed those razor-backs off."

"Apparently." Xoota leaned down to close Shaani's eyes with her fingertips. "Shut up and sleep."

The rat obeyed. Xoota took a quick look at the compass, noted the direction and speed on Shaani's charts, and settled down to putting distance between the *Sand Shark* and her enemies.

Far behind her, a band of razorbacks crossed the ridge. Xoota watched them in the side mirror and scowled.

"Yep, we pissed them off all right."

CHAPTER 7

Two more days of long, steady run across the desert. It was far more lifeless than before—just sand and baked red stone. No one had ever penetrated that far into the dead lands before. The place seemed eerily lifeless and dry; a faint tinge of radioactivity seared the breeze. The total silence was creepy. At night, nothing moved. No geckos skittered on the sand; no beetles roamed. But there was a horrible sensation that the ship was being watched.

On the third day, the ship was riding onward in the pink light of the dawn. The sails were taut, the wheels humming. Xoota simply tied the wheel and let the ship look after itself for a while as she helped Shaani up into the open air.

They sat the rat girl down against the mainmast. Wig-wig clustered around her, glowing and fussing, working his healing trick. Shaani breathed more easily, her head clearing at last. She reached beneath her spectacles and gratefully rubbed her eyes. "Thank you, Wig-wig dear."

Xoota squatted in front of her and held up one hand. "How many fingers?"

In a world full of alpha mutations, that could be a more complex question than it seemed.

Shaani blinked through her glasses and squinted. "Three?"

"Close enough."

It was a beautiful, fresh morning. Budgie was up in the bow, hanging his head over the rails and into the wind. Benek was at the stern, performing ritual calisthenics with cool, arrogant efficiency. All in all, things were normal.

Shaani blinked and tried to feel herself from within. "Urrr, what are my alphas today?"

"No idea. It's probably something really useful, like the ability to talk to fish," replied Xoota.

"How about you? Anything interesting?"

Wig-wig raced around the place and tittered.

Xoota shrugged wearily. "Yeah, I've got one."

"Gleeeee." Earwigs jumped and dive-bombed her from the mast, backsides first. They bounced off an invisible force field surrounding the quoll and shot happily away to be caught in the sail. The game had apparently been amusing them for hours.

"Will you just quit that? It's really annoying," said Xoota as her antennae splayed flat.

Shaani raised one brow. "Kinetic shield?"

"I guess. Damned useful but I have to move slowly when I'm reaching out for a sandwich. Thinking of which . . ." The quoll produced two clumsily made sandwiches made from damper. "Breakfast. Here. Cheese and honey."

They ate together in companionable silence, sharing a giant, blue-striped mug of tea. The ship was moving across perfectly flat, hard-packed sand, riding so smoothly that the motion scarcely trembled the hull. The wind meter showed a steady breeze. Oddly enough, there were clouds to the north.

Shaani looked at the food in her hands, grateful for the sandwich. Xoota was watching her carefully.

"You're all right?"

"I'm fine. Thanks to you chaps."

"Well, just don't let that chainsaw get you carried away. When in doubt, flee."

"I suppose so." Shaani sighed then perked up her pink ears. "The thought occurs: Do we still have hordes of razorbacks on our track?"

"We do. I'm sure I see dust wa-a-ay back on our trail. Benek wants to lie in wait and ambush them. I don't want to risk the ship."

The rat girl rested a loving hand on the deck of the *Sand Shark*. "But the ship's all right?"

"It's all right. We lost a strip of railing and some deck planking. I tried to fix it, but I'm not any good as a carpenter."

Shaani picked up that something was being left unsaid. She lowered her glasses and looked at the quoll. "What else?"

"Water." Xoota was clearly worried. "We lost about half our total water supply." She shook her head. "We're down to about four hundred."

It was a puzzle. Shaani sat back against the mast, frowning at the western horizon, where the razorbacks were presumably still struggling along in the *Sand Shark*'s wake.

"The razorbacks can't possibly operate this far into the desert. What the hell are they planning on using for water?"

"I think they plan on using ours."

Shaani delicately explored her healed ribs.

"That sounds . . . less than stable. They must be insane."

"Well, they *are* weird-ass, radioactive mutants."

The rat shrugged. "Well, so are we, but that doesn't mean we all have to take leave of our senses."

Xoota scratched her ribs. "Maybe they just really miss those tents?"

"Could be."

Shaani rose and stretched, thankful that the world had at last stopped spinning. She felt a backstay, feeling the tension on the masts. The ship was running beautifully. Xoota seized hold of an empty mug, poured some of the tea from the large mug they were sharing into the smaller one, then moved back into the control cabin to take the wheel.

The northern horizon retained the red light of sunrise. The color seemed to be spreading. Shaani frowned up at it for a moment then ducked into the control cabin.

"What's the barometer reading?"

Xoota blinked. "What's a barometer?"

Shaani turned. "The little tube thing with the dial on the bottom that was on the wall over here." The place was conspicuously empty. "Where's it gone?"

"Ah, we kind of broke it."

"Kind of?"

"Well, we definitely broke it. It fell off and smashed."

"Bother." Shaani went back outside. She scowled up at the red sky. Moments later, Xoota's voice drifted out of the cabin behind her.

"Do you know you have whole bottles of acid stored in your lab?"

"Well of course I do. Takes me ages to make that damned stuff." The rat blinked. "Wait, you broke the acid bottles?"

"No, no—I'm just saying . . ."

"Oh, well, don't worry about it. If the bottles break, just run." The rat decided to risk climbing the rigging. She certainly felt well enough. Wig-wig had done a sterling job of healing her. She swarmed up into the rigging and found Wig-wig aloft, helpfully cleaning out the bearings on the anemometer.

The entire northern horizon seemed to be a solid wall of pink. Wig-wig instantly sensed Shaani's concern. Earwigs climbed onto her shoulders to join her in staring at the north horizon.

"Hey, ratty lady. What is?"

"Do you see that?" The rat pointed north. "All that color in the sky?"

"Wig-wig not have distance vision." The insects politely sat and looked anyway. "Is something in the sky?"

"It's something." What was that rhyme in the book on navigation? *Red sky in the morning, sailor take warning?* Shaani leaned out from the rigging and called down to the deck.

"Yoo-hoo. Xoota. Ahoy there."

After a few minutes of calling, Xoota's voice finally answered. She sounded annoyed. "What?"

"You know, it's quite possible that we're in for a bit of a blow." Shaani sounded impatient.

"It isn't the season for it."

"What?"

"The season. It's the Big Dry. You don't get sandstorms until next season."

"Oh, good." Shaani smiled. "Well, that's a relief." She climbed back down onto the deck and tromped happily about her daily affairs.

· · · · ·

The storm, when it came, reached thousands of meters up into the sky, a vast wall of red dust borne on a ferocious wind. It slammed across the desert, moving fast. Shaani was the first to see it coming and bellowed for Benek. Madly they started winching down the sails. The cogs blurred as the sails sank down the masts. Shaani made a noise of panic, trying to turn the handle faster as the wall of dust thundered toward the little ship. Shaani's gaff-topsail finally reached the deck. She lunged for the ropes to tie it down.

"Xoota, turn stern-on to the wind," yelled Shaani. She could see Benek fumbling about with Wig-wig trying to show him which ropes went where. "Wig-wig, take cover," the rat called out to him in warning.

The earwigs would be horribly vulnerable to the storm, but so would white rats for that matter. Shaani ducked flat, yanking down her sand goggles and shoving her hat into the front of her shirt. When she turned to call out to Benek, the sand wall hit the ship.

The impact caught the vessel as she turned to starboard, causing her to keel over onto her wheels, the port tires lifting off the ground. Shaani squeaked as she slid, clinging to the railings for dear life. Able to hold on, she ended up dangling over the sand, with the entire ship threatening to roll over on top of her.

Somehow Xoota turned the ship, and she righted herself with a slam, masts whipping back and forth and the rigging cracking violently through the air. One cable lashed against Benek, hurling him back against the railings. Shaani clambered through the broken starboard rails, desperately holding on, but the whole world had disappeared, utterly engulfed in red dust. She had lost sight of Benek, lost sight of the masts entirely. She pulled her scarf up over her snout and tried to breathe normally.

Benek was hurt, but he would have to wait. Xoota had turned the ship stern-on to the wind and set the hand brake. Shaani felt a stay to see if the jib was still intact. The little triangular sail still seemed to be flying. The rat groped her way to the control cabin door and managed to wrench at the handle. The door flew open, and she spilled inside, bringing the dust and chaos of the storm with her.

"Xoota!"

The quoll was at the controls, trying to add the foot brakes to the hand brake. Shaani had to shout to be heard over the storm. "No brakes. Keep moving."

"Moving?" Xoota's goggles were down. The windows showed nothing but a raging cloud of dust outside. "We can't see to steer."

"Keep us moving or we'll get bogged and buried." Shaani could feel sand and dust sluicing against the hull. If the sand swallowed the ship, they would never get her free. "The jib's still flying. Go downwind."

Xoota yanked off the brakes, and the ship instantly moved, heading straight downwind. The anemometer was off the scale. The ship surged. She easily made sixty kph, riding with nothing but her little jib. "Should I try to slow us down?"

"No, we don't want to lose the jib sail. It will split if we don't keep her moving." Shaani opened the floor hatch that led to the inner hull. "Note the direction and speed, or we'll never navigate to the pipeline." Shaani fed herself down through the hatch. "I have to find Benek. I think he's hurt."

She left the steering in Xoota's tender, foul-tempered care. Beneath the main deck, the ship's working heart was dark and cool even as the hull boomed and the mast shanks creaked under the stress of the storm. Shaani crept forward, keeping a tight hold on the handgrips. She passed the capacitors, which smelled strongly of ozone in the dust, past the foremast and the spare cordage and the bales of food. Inside the main hold, Budgie was lying flat on the floor, eyes wide in fright as he looked up at the hatch where dust and sand drifted down through the cracks. Shaani found the walls covered with quaking earwigs, who were caught in Budgie's awe-struck sense of fear.

"Wig-wig, where's Benek?"

"Not know. Wig-wig be scared." The insects rubbed their forefeet together and lamented. "Doom."

"We're not doomed. I designed her to take all possible weather." Shaani tapped her foot, wanting everyone to be sensible. "Stay here. I have to go topside."

The rat looped a rope around her narrow waist and tied it fast then knotted her lifeline to one of the ladder rungs. Earwigs held on like grim death, clinging to the cracks and walls as Shaani fought open a hatch. She opened it the merest crack, slithered out onto the deck, and found herself hammered by the storm.

"Benek?" she shouted into the sand.

The wind came hard and viciously fast, driving sand particles like needles through the air. Shaani crawled flat across the deck, the sand scything beneath her shorts to sting her derriere. Her tail whipped around in the wind as she moved crabwise, finally finding the starboard rail.

"Benek!"

She found him huddled against the sleeping cabin wall, trying to make his way toward the door. The man was cradling his arm. With no sand goggles, he was utterly blind. Shaani reached him and put her hand on his back, only to have him shake her off.

"Benek, I'll get you to safety."

He shrugged her off yet again, but Shaani was persistent. She moved him in the simplest possible way; she grabbed his injured arm and towed him by it. The huge man bellowed, moving toward her to take the pressure off his broken arm.

She steered him to the tiny patch of wind shadow at the bow end of the sleeping cabin and let go.

"Stop being a fool." She pulled open the cabin door. "Here, this way. Take my hand."

She managed to wrestle the man through the door and slam it shut behind them. The sudden drop in noise level was an absolute relief. There was sand all through Shaani's fur. She shook herself then ran to look at Benek's face. He had sand in his eyes and was rubbing at his face. She fetched water and quickly washed his face then carefully bathed his eyes. "Keep still. This is causing you distress. We'll get your eyes clear."

Benek tried to turn his face away. "A pure human needs no help from animals."

"Well, we help you every day, old chap." Shaani was too polite to let much of her shock and disapproval show in her voice. Nevertheless, her tone became prim. "In any case, I am a rat: humanity's spiritual and intellectual partners."

Shaani was damned put out, but she did the right thing by her comrade. Benek's forearm had been snapped by a savage lash from a breaking cable. Only his armored vambrace had saved him from having the whole limb taken off. Shaani removed his dented armor and carefully prepared a splint.

"Wig-wig? Wig-wig. Are you there?"

An earwig appeared, peeking up through a knothole in a plank. "Wig-wig is here."

"There you are, old thing. Have you any more uses of that healing mutation today?"

"All gone."

"That's all right. We'll do what we can." The rat opened up her first-aid, field-surgery, and tree-lopping kit. She produced splints and began immobilizing the limb beneath a sheath of bandages. "Is everything all right belowdecks?"

"A little. A jar broke. I cleaning it up." The earwigs watched her, their antennae quivering, sensing her emotions. They looked from Shaani to Benek thoughtfully. "Wig-wig will come upstairs now and stay with Shaani."

"That's all right, love. Why don't you run forward to the control cabin and make sure Xoota is all right? Bring her a drink—that sort of thing."

The earwigs worked their chops thoughtfully, eying Benek. Wig-wig turned around and scuttled off, clashing his forceps, as if to make his thoughts felt.

Shaani sat neatly on the floor with her beautiful tail curled around her. She flipped a cloth over, folding it into a sling. The rat tied the sling in place around Benek's neck, making the knots with her customary efficiency. She patted him on the shoulder to inform him that she was done then rose and cleared away her equipment.

She left without speaking to him further.

Benek didn't thank her.

    · · · · ·

The dust storm held the ship tightly, pushing her south inside a churning, screaming mass of sand. The windows showed nothing but a dense, dark cloud of dust, lit by flashes of static lightning. Running blind, the ship took hills and ridges on the fly, her suspension slamming as she raced through unseen terrain. Xoota and Shaani took turns at the wheel, fighting the bucking ship as it plowed onward through the sand. Stomachs lurched as the whole ship almost took to the air, flying over an unseen hillcrest and slamming home onto the sand. The *Sand Shark* took the punishment and kept on going, driven onward by the flaying, screaming wind.

The violent storm was still with them by nightfall. Twelve numbing hours into it, they had been blown some seven hundred kilometers off course and still the ship raced onward in the dark. Reading the instruments by the light of an electric bulb she held in her mouth, Shaani tried desperately to keep track of course and speed. She was worried about the great southern cliffs, the thousand-meter plunge that seemed to seal off all access to the world beyond. She totted up the numbers, feeling more and more worried with every passing hour.

The noise of the wind was deafening. Electric flashes from the dust clouds flicked and blinded them as they drove. Wig-wig dragged in sandwiches and flasks of cold tea for them, and he spliced a failed electric cable in the hold. But there was nothing for the others to do except to shelter in the hold and ride it through.

• • • • •

At four in the morning, the wind seemed to change direction, finally blowing to the west. The ship changed course, unable to do anything but run with the storm.

The ship's clock showed that it was dawn, but the skies stayed dark. The sandstorm was so dense, the windscreens showed nothing but a wall of dust. Xoota was at the wheel, desperately trying to see the way ahead. The ship's headlights showed nothing but sand swirling thickly. Suddenly an image of a really, really bad future flashed into her mind. Her antennae stood stiff with fright. She hauled on the steering wheel. Tires screeched, and the ship tilted wildly. Shaani gave a yell and clung to her seat.

A vast, dark shape flashed past the ship: rocks looming higher than the mast. The ship missed a rock outcrop by a whisker's breadth. Shaani stared, watching rocks flash past in fright.

The ship almost capsized. But Xoota somehow got the ship back onto its wheels. She felt her fur standing on end.

There was a sudden, wrenching crash. Xoota was flung from her seat to slam against the windscreen. She bounced back, unhurt; her previous day's alpha mutation shielded her from impact as she felt the whole ship come smashing to a halt.

Glass broke. There was a splintering noise as one of the masts tore free and fell. The ship's nose bucked and slammed down into soft sand. Xoota was on the floor. She heard Budgie screeching and Wig-wig wailing in alarm. The wind howled in through a broken window. "Shaani!"

The rat was hanging from her seat belt straps; she was the only one who ever buckled up. Shaani stared, dazed, then fumbled for her buckle.

The headlights on one side were clearly smashed. The foremast had fallen on top of the control cabin and dented the roof. Xoota coughed then crawled over to help Shaani untangle herself from her straps.

"Shaani. Are you okay?"

"Th-think we had a bit of a bingle." The rat shook her head, trying to clear her mind. "Gods, are you all right?"

"I'm fine." Xoota blinked, looked at the crack in the windscreen her body had made on impact, and thanked Darwin for alpha mutations. "You check the damage below. I'll check the deck."

Xoota pulled down her sand goggles and made it out onto the deck in the blinding wind. The foremast had fallen, crashing down atop the control cabin in a tangle of cables and rigging. The jib still held on, streaming from the bowsprit like a strip of laundry left in the wind. The mainmast still stood, but the rigging was torn. Xoota fought her way forward against the wind and opened the door into the sleeping cabin.

The place was a mess. Bedding, food, and weapons were everywhere. "Benek."

"I'm here." The massive human had his arm in a sling. He was stiff with pain and seemed angry. "What happened now?"

"Collision. We're still checking the damage." The quoll looked over the cabin—nothing but cosmetic damage. "We'll check the hold."

Wig-wig was in a frenzy in the hold. Budgie was terrified by the accident, leaping around and screeching. Xoota and Benek fought their way past the maddened budgerigar. Their feet splashed in water, and Xoota's stomach fell.

Oh, kack.

The ship's water was currently spread through two tanks, port and starboard. The starboard tank had broken its supports and wrenched down onto the deck. Water was leaking from somewhere underneath. The quoll flung herself flat and tried to see beneath.

A jack, she thought. Xoota had kept the jack she found in an old car in the desert. It was in the ship's tool chest. She leaped to her feet.

"I'll get tools. Try and plug the hole. Benek, pump the water to the port-side tank."

She ran to the back of the hold. The old car jack was among the jumble of tangled, fallen tools. Xoota came running back to find Wig-wig racing all over the fallen water tank, trying to pull a patch of tar paper over the leak. Wig-wig was terrified of the water. Since they breathed through their little armpits, they didn't get on well with puddles. Benek was helping, trying to reach awkwardly under the tank to help the bugs. For Benek, that was a whole new horizon of cooperation. Xoota got down onto her back, inspected under the tank, and tried to fit the jack into place.

"Benek, can you lever the tank upwards? Just a few centimeters would do it."

"I can try."

The huge man took hold of a beam and shoved it under the heavy tank. He set his stance, put his shoulders under the beam, and lifted upward. His whole body shook with effort as he lifted up a two hundred–kilo tank. Xoota put herself under the tank, trusting his strength, and slotted the car jack into place. She crawled back out, fitted the jack handle, and frenziedly spun the crank.

"Okay, Benek, I've got it."

Working together, they lifted the tank up into place. Benek jogged the tank back onto its mountings. They would need to fit new bolts and straps. Wig-wig raced around the cracked lower corner of the tank, busily pulling tape and glue all over the leak.

Water was all over the floor and seeping out into the sands. They must have lost another hundred liters at least. And it was water they couldn't possibly replace.

The forward hatch creaked open. Shaani, covered in dust, climbed through into the hold. She had been outside on the sand. The rat sank wearily down atop a locker and peeled her sand goggles up from her eyes. The goggles had left white circles of clean fur on her dust-stained face.

She reached for a drink, looking bleakly at the damaged water tank. The wind was still raging and howling. "We've lost the starboard front wheel." The rat looked tired and dispirited. "It hit solid rock. Sheared the mounting clean off."

"Can you fix it?"

"Oppenheimer only knows." Shaani rubbed at her eyes. "I suppose so. Science can fix anything . . ." She pointed to the water staining the deck. "Did we lose much?"

"Maybe a hundred liters."

"Bother."

The wind howled. Shaani put her broad straw hat back on her head. "Well, we can't make any outside repairs until the storm abates, so I'll weld the tank. We can set things to rights in the sleeping cabin and the hold and hope we're not buried by sand." She stroked Budgie's head. "Let's clean up, have a decent meal, then try to sleep."

Benek reached down with his good hand and helped her to her feet.

Xoota dusted herself clean. "Right. It's a plan." She started up the ladder. "I'll do lunch."

Benek looked at her.

"I was unaware that you can cook."

The quoll looked at her companions with great dignity. "I can cook anything that has legs."

"Legs?"

"When the legs stop moving, it's done . . ." The quoll headed upstairs. "Right. Food, sleep, then tomorrow is another day."

She disappeared. Benek watched as Shaani struggled wearily up the ladder. He waited for the earwigs to swarm up the walls then followed the others into the cabin.

Behind him, Budgie sank down to try to get a decent night's sleep.

Fortunately there were always more goober nuts.

In the morning, Xoota awoke feeling her usual, grumpy self. There was drool on her pillow, her fur stuck out in a thousand directions, and she was naked except for one lime green sock.

She had sand all through her fur. It itched and she was well aware of the irony of actually craving a bath. It took her a moment of confusion before she remembered that the ship was a wreck, the wheel had come off, and they had been blown far, far from their course. Cursing, she levered herself up out of bed, found clean underwear and relatively clean socks, and dressed while peering out of a cabin window.

Benek had gone. His bed was rumpled and cold. Shaani's bed was neatly made, a clear sign that they were already up and about. She had left extra porridge for Xoota's breakfast. Only Wig-wig was still in the cabin. The earwig horde was sleeping in a nest of damp leaves, bark, and sticks. Xoota ate swiftly, eying the windows. Her antennae sifted the world for potential troubles.

The storm had stopped. The silence was wonderful. Xoota armored up and slung her shield across her back and her mace through her belt. Sunglasses went down onto her nose. Crossbow loaded and in hand, she emerged from the cabin and took a look at the world.

Sand dunes stood silent and utterly still. The silence was so pure that it almost seemed alive.

The ship was awash in a vast ocean of sand. Deep sand dunes were all around her, stretching off to the far, far west. But here and there, outcrops of alien green stone jutted high into the air. Scattered around, caught in the boulders, weird tufted grasses grew. The tuft grass stood stiff and still in the windless air. It only made the place seem more empty, more silent.

Yawning, Xoota opened her jaws in a ninety-degree marsupial gape. Scratching herself, she turned toward the bow. She stared in shock, looking up, up, up . . . ever higher. Her tail drooped behind her.

"Bleeding heck."

The ship had run into an island, a vast chunk of eerie, green rock that had somehow grown out of the desert. It was a kilometer wide and soared three hundred meters above the desert sands. The top seemed to be flat. Xoota could see a hint of green foliage peeking over the edge. Birds flew around the island, wheeling in the distance. The giant rock column literally formed an island in the sky. Vast, stunning, majestic . . .

And the *Sand Shark* had run smack into the damned thing.

The ship must have hit a boulder about a hundred meters back, lost her front right wheel, then plowed into a deep sand drift that stood at the base of the immense rock island. Her foremast lay in a tangle of wrecked rigging, and the entire deck was ankle deep in sand.

Xoota gave a curse. Ah well, if you were going to hit something, make it an impressive something.

And damn, but it *was* impressive. Xoota craned her neck to look up at the top of the sky island. It seemed fertile up there. In fact, it looked pretty damned lush. It was a breathtaking sight to find just sitting there among the dead, dry sands.

Rat footprints went back along the wake of the ship to where the lost wheel jutted from the sand. There had been some digging; Shaani had been investigating the damage, uncovering the sheared-off shank of the wheel mount. But then, in typical style, the footprints went straight to the rocky cliff, meandering up the sand piles. She had done her usual trick and become enthralled by a new discovery.

Xoota gave another curse. She stuck her head back into the sleeping cabin. "Wig-wig, wakey-wakey. We have to go."

Xoota opened a deck hatch. Budgie was still asleep down in the hold, kicking his feet in is little budgie dreams. He had food and water, Shaani's handiwork once again. Xoota descended and filled two canteens, thought about it, and filled two more. She found some lengths of rope, took a couple of insect bars, and clambered back up onto the deck.

Budgie, she could tell, pretended to still be asleep, hoping to avoid any potential work.

Wig-wig was up and bustling around. Some of the earwigs were eating and drinking, licking the porridge pot clean. Others were yawning in a deliberate mimicking of Xoota's marsupial ninety-degree gape. The largest earwigs—an impressive ten centimeters long—came tromping up to Xoota and waved hello. "We fixing ship, yes?"

"Yeah. Just as soon as we track down our shipmates." The quoll felt a really good grumble session coming on. "Let's go find the idiots."

"Yay. Find the idiots." Smaller earwigs chorused happily as they spread wings and started to fly. "Idiots."

Surrounded by a swarm of happy bugs, Xoota tromped her way out onto the deck. The bowsprit made a handy bridge to the top of the sand mounds. With her tail and arms for balance, Xoota made her way across and stepped onto the absurdly soft sands below.

Shaani's footprints were joined by another set, probably Benek's given the size of the damned things. Both sets of prints headed for a deep, ragged crevice in the side of the rock island. There the rock made a sharp upward slope full of boulders and handholds. Xoota looked up, saw no sign of her companions, and began to clamber up across the rocks.

The rock felt cool. Thankfully it wasn't slick. Green marble seemed to be caught in a matrix of rough, gray stone. Xoota propelled herself upward with sturdy thighs, her hands and tail gripping the rocks to speed her way to the top. Wig-wig kept her company, sometimes surging ahead to scout for danger. He did find a rather natty little radioactive rock python, and almost had a showdown with a small, hypnotic toad. Xoota chucked a rock at the toad to chase it away and kept right on climbing.

At the halfway point, she stopped for a breather and looked around. The view was simply beautiful.

The poor ship, broken and unhappy, stood a hundred and fifty meters below. But the desert spread out, pink and beige in the morning sun. The dunes of new-blown sand were perfectly formed. No tracks marked the dust.

She loved the desert. Despite the heat and dust, it was a place of stark, majestic beauty. The quoll took a long, quiet moment just to drink in the sight, the feel, the glory. Sand and stone, dust and dry, with life existing everywhere if you only knew how to look.

Xoota searched the horizon and saw no dust clouds, no smoke, no settlements, no plants—only more of the strange rock columns, all of them only a fraction of the size of the colossal sky island. She took a last look, enjoying the silence, then turned back to the climb. Wig-wig fluttered all around her as she made her way to the top.

The quoll climbed up over a final ledge of rock. She looked into a land of breathtaking, living green.

A jungle grew on top of the huge plateau.

Xoota stared. Never in her life had she seen so much green—so many different plants, all lush and damp and growing. It was a place of shade and big, verdant ferns. Vast fig trees grew high into the air, their trunks fluted and folded, their massive branches spreading dense, green umbrellas that shut out the sun. There was a thick smell of growing things and of rotting leaves and sap heated by the searing sun.

Silver birds flapped in the distance. Across the treetops, Xoota saw the crumbled top of an ancient tower. Her fur stood on end, alive with a sense of absolute awe.

There were some bangs and crashes coming from the nearby trees, noises that combined with happy little rat sounds. Crossbow ready for danger, Xoota signaled to Wig-wig to fly top cover. She advanced stealthily through waist-high grass.

The happy rat sounds were coming from over to the right. Xoota shook her head and tramped off in pursuit.

The ground rose, the soil somehow well watered and moist. Just across the rise, the ground formed a little, grassy hollow.

A decaying bird-fish creature lay on the ground. Jutting up from its rib cage was a long-stemmed plant topped with a growing green bud. A little farther on, another scatter of bones surrounded another stalk. A whole stand of the same plants filled the center of the hollow, each plant topped by a juicy, purple bud.

The dead bird-fish-thing still stank. Xoota gave it a wide berth, moving toward the plants. Her antennae twitched; the girl blinked, saw a future, and rolled spectacularly head over heels.

Something materialized behind her with a sharp *crack*. A shiny object the size of an egg thudded to the ground. The quoll girl blinked, her antennae in overdrive, and she lunged sideways, rolled, and sprinted aside.

She saw it as it happened. Things blinked into midair just behind and beside her. Shiny, brown eggs just appeared from nowhere. Xoota stared then ducked as an egg materialized right in the air her head had been occupying.

The plants.

The stand of plants had all turned to face her. They hummed. A glow enveloped the nearest stalks. Xoota ran, weaving erratically. Seeds teleported into the space beside her, displacing air with a loud, violent *crack*.

"Holy kack!"

She dodged like a mad thing. A seed the size of a hen's egg materialized right where she had stood, making a sharp zapping noise. Xoota dived and rolled. Another seed appeared right behind her. She ran, dodging crazily to shake off the enemy fire. Leaping across a patch of weeds, she came face-to-face with a decaying skeleton; a fish-bird, still gooey, with one of the plants growing up right out of its skull.

"Gah."

The plant hummed, the bulb turning to face her. Xoota saw a stand of fallen trees ahead of her. She launched herself into the tangled timber, catching onto a plant branch with her tail and jerking to a stop. A seed appeared right in front of her. She raced on, over a dirt mound, ran madly sideways, and flung herself into cover.

Panting raggedly, her fur standing on end with shock, she stared back toward the deadly plants. Her antennae were quaking with shock.

A cheerful voice called out to her from the trees.

"Spiffy. There you are." Shaani waved from the trees, in fine form—straw hat; great, baggy shorts; and chainsaw all neat and shiny in the sun. "Mind the plants. They can be a bit aggro."

Xoota flattened her ears. "Thanks for the heads-up on that one." Xoota wearily stood up. "You seem to have had no problems."

"Oh, no. The carrion was the clue. Caution prevailed. Logic overcame." The rat walked merrily over the grass. "Anyway, they only shoot *at* you or predict your current course and speed. If you stagger merrily about at random, you're as safe as houses. Bit of a spree, what?"

Xoota looked at her friend with a patience she never knew she possessed. "What are you doing up here all alone?"

"Oh, you were out like a lamp. Thought I'd take a constitutional then just got a tad distracted." The rat seemed gloriously happy. "I found something for you."

"For me?"

"Well of course for you." Shaani slapped Xoota on the back. "This way." The rat held up a hand and let earwigs alight on her. "Morning, Wig-wig."

"Good morning, rattie."

In among the trees, hidden from all but the sharp eyes of an inquisitive rat, there was something weird—something wonderful. Xoota stared at it in awe.

It was a vehicle. It had to be. But it was a vehicle without wheels.

In shape, it looked a little like an egg: a narrowed nose covered in glass and a smooth body as wide as the sleeping cabin of the *Sand Shark*. It had no wings, no wheels. The skin of the vehicle seemed to be some sort of metal, but it was unmarked by rust. It had landed on four solid legs that had extended from underneath the hull. Vines and weeds had grown up and through the landing gear and choked part of the hull.

The door was open, the lock apparently shorted out by Shaani and her magic sparks. Inside, plants had grown up through the floor. Shaani had hacked the more annoying ones out of the way, clearing a path into the hull.

The junk-prospector in Xoota's soul was immediately enthralled. Her antennae rose. "Ooh, was there anything good?"

"Well, there are no power systems. Plants seem to have jiggered up all the engines and controls. But we do have this."

In the back compartment of the vehicle, there was a weird box, a sort of cupboard, perhaps enough to fit a loaf of bread. The door had a set of controls beside it. The whole thing was made of green metal, all looped with things that looked like veins and muscle cords. All in all, it was damned peculiar.

There were markings on the controls. Xoota looked at them and frowned. "Can you read the runes?"

"Nope, afraid not, old thing." Shaani rapped on the box. "But look here: What do you think this was for?" Shaani opened the cupboard door. She shoved some plant matter inside then closed the door.

The machine glowed blue, hummed, then fell silent. Shaani opened up the little cupboard's door and gestured at the space inside.

The plant matter had gone.

The cupboard was completely empty. There was quite simply nothing there, not even the merest fleck of bark. Xoota sniffed and could no longer even detect the smell of fresh-cut weeds.

"A disintegrator?"

"Perhaps." Shaani scratched her head. "I thought it might be some sort of mass-energy converter, but there's no output of power."

"Good thing it didn't. You might have gotten yourself fried."

"Fried." Wig-wig clung to the ceiling, unscrewing the overhead light in case it might be useful. "Rattie take care."

The rat seemed happy. "Oh, evolved for science, remember? Radiation, electricity, EM fields. None of that bothers a true lab rat."

Xoota kept a careful eye on the forest. "Well, true lab rat, do you know where Benek is?"

"No sign of him. He must have gotten up before I did. He might have been tromping around up here for hours."

"Well, I don't want anyone doing that from now on." Xoota spoke clearly, looking authoritarian. Behind her, several earwigs mimicked her stance perfectly, wagging admonishing legs at Shaani. "Omega terrain is terribly dangerous."

"Right you are." The rat brightened. "Shall we see my surprise?"

"I thought this was the surprise."

"No, no, this is just an old wreck." The rat put her hat on straight. "Come along."

Xoota hung back. "What about the disintegrator cupboard?"

"It will still be here when we get back."

The rat led the way, threading through the nearby trees. She moved with gentle confidence, heading toward a strange, ongoing gushing noise. The noise had a hypnotically peaceful rhythm—soft and gentle, ebbing and flowing. The air filled with the scent of cool, clear water.

They came to a place where the trees opened out on the side of a rocky hill. Water welled up somehow from the rock, flooding into a shallow stream that spread and fell in a silver curtain over the lip of an overhang. Shaani took Xoota by the hand and coaxed her onward, bringing her to the lip of the waterfall.

From atop the rock, the women looked out over the whole surface of the sky isle. The vantage point showed a green, tangled wilderness of trees. Vines roped through the treetops. Here and there, strange, white palm trees jutted up into the sky.

There was a lake, a huge body of cool water covered in lush, floating plants. They saw a tower at the far shore, the top stories ruined and overgrown, but its windows and door were still intact. After an entire lifetime in the desert, Xoota was stunned. Never had she seen so many green plants, so much water, so much cool.

She sank down to touch the rock beneath her. It vibrated softly, wonderful to feel. "It's humming."

"Some sort of ancient pumping system." The rat's voice was a whisper. She took Xoota's hand and coaxed her down to the bottom of the little waterfall. "Come."

They walked down the rocks beside the waterfall. It spilled in a big, broad curtain, falling onto the smooth, green rocks below and forming a lovely, clear pool. The pool overflowed into a little creek that spilled down in another waterfall then ran off to feed the lake.

There was a gap behind the waterfall. Shaani led the way, ducking to clear the great silver gush of the water up above. The air shivered, filled with little water droplets that sparkled on their fur. Xoota's whiskers quivered as they felt the kiss of spray.

They came into a beautiful cave—a curving rock face overhead and the silver waterfall to the front. The floor was made from more green rock. The whole place echoed to the rush and bubble of the waterfall.

It was cool, so wonderfully cool.

It was the most private, peaceful place that Xoota had ever seen. Cool, clean rock walls, all mottled gray and green. And there, in the middle of the cavern, spread a beautiful pool.

Shaani laughed.

She threw off her hat, her boots, and her clothes and jumped into the water. She splashed at Xoota. "Come on. Get in."

It was a deadly world. Mutants and predators; radiation and poisons; enemies and weird, unimaginable disasters. The ship was damaged. The mission at a total standstill. Any sensible person would be thinking only of the grim tasks of survival and defense.

But Shaani dived like an eel, laughing. "Come on. You have to try this."

Xoota tore off her armor and her clothes. She left her weapons within easy reach by the edge of the pool. Tiptoeing on pink feet, she eased herself ankle deep into the water, shrinking from the cold.

She had never swum. There had never been so much water that she could try. Xoota blinked at the weird, wonderful sensation then slowly eased herself into the water. A look of pure, wondering delight spread slowly across her face.

Beside her, Shaani looked at her and smiled. "Life is full of surprises."

CHAPTER 8

Swimming was the most ridiculously wonderful thing. Xoota floated in shallow water, propelling herself slowly along with her fingertips touching the bottom. She cruised with just her snout above water, utterly at peace.

Shaani lounged naked on a rock, wet and comfortable. She wriggled her fine, pink toes. "That was an experience. Swimming in water. Really *swimming* in it. Oh my."

She lay on her back with her long, white hair spread across the rocks to dry, her pink tail coiled in sensuous delight.

"I declare myself to be a fairly happy rat." She sighed contentedly. "The ship needs repairs, but it can all be done. Science always finds a way. That swim was just what I needed to get the brain going and raise the spirits. I could spend a lifetime lying like this, right here."

Xoota agreed. She floated a little more, loving the sound of the waterfall, the echo from the rocks, and the wonderful sense of pure privacy. She wrung out her antennae and waded for shore. "I'm getting out."

Shaani kept her eyes closed, smiling as she raised one finger. "And I am not looking at the sacred pouch."

Xoota made a prim face. "Just because some of us have modesty . . ."

"An outmoded concept. Unscientific."

Wig-wig came bustling into the cave. The earwig swarm carried several remarkable objects along with them—round, yellow, egg-shaped things, each bigger than a pair of clenched fists. The bugs seemed happy. "Glee. Nice eatings in forest. Good things. Eat. Eat."

Naked, free of sand encrustation and wonderfully lazy, the two women reached for the fruits the earwigs offered them. The fruits were heavy, slightly soft, and smelled seductively sweet. Xoota sniffed and let her antennae test alternative futures to see if poison might be in the offing. But she saw nothing but a flash of happiness and joy.

"So, Wig-wig, any sign of Benek?"

"He be around. Saw footprints and fruit skins." The bugs began swarming around one of the fruits, eating heartily. "Yummy."

Xoota had a knife piled over with her armor. She reached out and used it to slice a line around her fruit. Juice went everywhere. While she cut, she looked out through the silver curtain of the waterfall. Images of the fig trees, the white palms, and the distant tower shimmered far beyond. Xoota had never seen anything like it in her life.

"So what is this place?"

"A garden?" Shaani peeled her fruit with her utility knife. There was no way to do it cleanly. "The water is being pumped to the top of the rocks; then it all runs down to the lake. So there has to be an operating power supply somewhere near." She sniffed at her fruit then tested it with her tongue. She made a face of astonishment and started eating. The incoherent noises of enjoyment were enough to overcome Xoota's caution. She carved off a slice of fruit and tasted it then ate like a starving dingo.

It was delicious.

They ate the fruits then reached for more. The mess was horrendous; juice went everywhere. Xoota scooped out the seeds inside the fruit and put them carefully aside. She was going to have to plant those things at home.

The fruits were damned delicious. Both women flopped back on the rocks, enjoying the afterglow. They had been definite messy fun. But time was wasting, and the ship needed repairs.

Finally Shaani gave a dutiful sigh. "Benek."

Xoota groaned. "I suppose we have to look."

"Well, he is a shipmate, albeit an annoying one."

The quoll forced herself back to her feet. "Benek. Yes. And check out the tower . . . and fix the wheel." Xoota stood under the waterfall and washed herself of sticky fruit juice. "All right. Duty calls."

They doused themselves clean and gathered up equipment. Their newly washed clothes, already dry from the hot sun, had gone stiff as boards. Shaani rolled her clothing up and vigorously pummeled it into submission before dressing. Xoota just wore the damned stuff raw: chafing was the gods' way of letting you know they hated you. The explorers grabbed their weapons and tools, filled water bottles, then reluctantly left the peaceful beauty of the cave behind.

The sun was climbing toward midday. From somewhere, a mist of water sprayed over in the trees. Xoota and Shaani walked down toward the tree line, heading for the lake. Shaani collected specimens of flowers, herbs, and soil while Wig-wig scuttled all around them, helpfully scouting the terrain.

The air began to take on a heady, perfumed smell—part sap, part fallen figs, and part pollen drifting from the stark white palm trees.

The trees that bore the big, yellow fruit were in evidence all over the forest. The sweet scent they gave off conveyed a feeling of sheer goodwill. Xoota looked around then headed for the lake shore, keen to see such a marvel right up close.

There were some fruit skins on the grass near the water. In the bushes, something slobbered horribly, snuffling like as beast gorging on carrion. Xoota halted, put up her crossbow, and pushed back her head scarf.

"Benek, there you are." Xoota was relieved. "You've been exploring?"

"I have." At that moment he was eating the irresistible yellow fruits. "I made some excellent finds," he said between mouthfuls.

He seemed to be racing to eat every fruit in the forest. Xoota raised her brows. For once she reserved comment.

Shaani and Wig-wig emerged from the forest and took a look over the lake. Marvelous. Simply marvelous. They watched what they thought were birds move effortlessly between the treetops and the bottom of the lake. Xoota watched the animals out of the corner of her eyes as she spoke to the juice-slathered Benek.

"Had a good morning?"

The man nodded, his mouth full. Worn around his helmet were a set of strange goggles, weathered but apparently in working order. "Found goggles."

"Goggles?"

"See in the dark." The man was pleased. "Still have a power cell."

That was interesting news. The island was clearly a treasure trove. Xoota examined the goggles from a distance. "Where did you find them?"

"Body. Skull." Benek snuffled yellow flesh from the inside skin of a juicy fruit. He reached for another one, but Xoota stopped him.

"Okay, enough fruit for now, Benek. You found a body?"

He glared at her resentfully for interrupting his feast. The man sniffed then washed his face and hands in the lake before pointing to the far shore. "I found a head over there. Just a skull. Had these on him, though. Useful."

Benek seemed to be of the school that wanted to race ahead of the rest of the party and seize any nifty treasure. It was usually a good recipe for an early death. Xoota shook her head. "All right. So you found some cool, new goggles, and you spent two hours eating fruit. Did you get to the tower over there?"

"No, not as of yet."

"Fine." Xoota hefted her crossbow. "Right, well, let's go check it out. But everyone keep together and keep sharp. I don't want anyone getting hurt."

They moved on.

The team kept a careful watch on the trees and the undergrowth. Xoota, wary of ambush, quested cautiously back and forth with her antennae as she took point for the team.

．．．．．

From the center of the party, Shaani had more time to enjoy herself. She flitted off to the side to gather specimens, always accompanied by Wig-wig, who was sharing her emotion of innocent delight. The rat gathered seeds, saps, and cuttings of different varieties of plant, labeling her finds swiftly and carefully. Her backpack rattled with sample vials.

Just off the path, the rat found a beautiful stand of mint, rich and lush and very refreshing. Shaani took up some plants, roots and all, storing them away, then rose, looking carefully ahead.

Something was lying in the grass nearby.

"Chaps? Over here."

The others came to her. Shaani nodded to the left. A body lay on the ground beneath a tall, white tree. It was an old, old corpse. Benek kept watch while Shaani and Xoota carefully approached the skeleton. It sat against a tree, dressed in ancient overalls and some sort of armored vest. The skull's jaw was missing, as was one arm. The bones were furred green with moss. It wore a bulky helmet that had been blown open at the top. The entire top of the skull had simply vanished.

The palm tree overhead had a sharp, herbal smell. The silence in the grove was horribly oppressive. Xoota poked the body carefully with a stick. Shaani leaned over to inspect the wound in the head and looked rather pained.

"Oh my . . ."

Xoota carefully examined the body. "Human." She checked quietly to see if the body was uninhabited. She didn't want a sudden fight with carrion worms or centipedes. "Same tech level as the ship we found. Could it have been the crew?"

Benek stalked over to another nearby tree. "Here's another one."

The second body lay facedown. A hole had been blasted clean through its chest, front to back, melting the skeleton's armor. Shaani examined the damage, seeing the seared, burned edges of the wound.

Benek scowled. "A hit from some mutation?"

"More likely a weapon blast." Shaani tilted her head as she examined the body. She looked from one corpse to the other then rose. "Just a moment."

She searched the weeds that grew beside the first corpse. Carefully parting the vegetation, she found first more bone then finally something else.

It was a tool, a pistol. The seated corpse had been holding a gun, and the arm had dropped away to be eaten by scavengers. Shaani lifted the pistol with care, producing a brush from her equipment belt to whisk it clean.

Xoota's whiskers quivered with interest. "What is it?"

"It's called a gun."

"I know it's called a gun." Xoota's ears went flat. "There are two laser pistols back at Watering Hole. I mean, what kind of gun?"

"Not sure." Shaani looked it over carefully. "The battery is dead, but they're rechargeable. Mechanism might still be intact. Omega tech. Very interesting."

The rat sat down beside the seated corpse. She looked from one body to the other, clearly intrigued.

Xoota raised her antennae. "What?"

"It's this chap here." Shaani pointed to the seated body. "Do you see? I think he shot the other one. Look at the angle." Shaani crouched, looking from the seated corpse to the other. "See? He shot this one in the back. Then killed himself. Fired up under his own chin."

"Why would he do that?"

"I'm not sure we're in a position to ask him." The rat inspected the bodies again. "Maybe they had a bit of a tiff."

"Does the other one have a gun too?"

He had a holster, and his hands were under his body. Shaani carefully rolled the fallen corpse over onto its back and made a face. "Hmm."

"What?" Xoota bustled over to look. "A gun?"

"No." Shaani carefully examined a cluster of dead, dried stems held in the corpse's skeletal hand. "Flowers. Roses, in fact."

"He was carrying roses?" Xoota blinked.

"Yes."

"And then this one shot him in the back."

"Seems so."

"My, that *was* a tiff." Xoota scratched her head. "Well, clearly this was the site of a great tragedy and a firm lesson to us all. Now let's loot these things down to the last gold filling and get a move on."

Shaani wanted to say more, but Xoota was already busily rummaging around the bodies. Shaani carefully removed a colored wristband from each corpse—blue with one gold stripe. She examined them quietly then bagged them for later study.

The rat knelt and reverently removed a small case from one body's belt. She opened it carefully, finding it full of small, multicolored, plastic vials.

Xoota was at the seated body, merrily shaking all the bones out of the suit of armor. "Whatcha got?"

The rat held up the vials. "I believe these are drugs. There's a skin applicator in the case."

"What kind of drugs? Would they still be all right? As in nonpoisonous?"

"Might be." Shaani read one of the vials. "'Healing accelerant' . . . 'antibiotic agent' . . . 'antivenin zero one' . . ." She pulled out a few blue vials and made a face. "Oh. And this one's an antiradiation serum. Not really useful."

"Keep it. We're not all highly evolved lab rats." Xoota had found a wristwatch on the left arm of the seated body. It had some sort of mutant mouse on it. "One of your lab rats here, I think?"

Shaani took the watch. She frowned at it. "Perhaps. It's rather oddly drawn."

"Artistic license." Xoota held up the scavenged armor vest. "Do you think this armor is usable?"

"Might be. I'll look at it later."

"Cool." Xoota folded it up and put it in the swag bag. "Hey, Benek. Found anything?"

Benek had found another fruit tree and was collecting big, yellow fruit. He shook his head. "I fear not. But there are supplies here."

"Well, that's something."

Benek threw a fruit over to Xoota.

Shaani walked away from the bodies, still deep in thought. She put the watch carefully in a sample bag; she would inspect that later too. She walked a little ways and found yet another corpse beneath a white palm tree.

It lay on its back wearing armor and a helmet, grass growing up through its bones. The corpse gave an absurd impression of being totally blissed out, arms spread beneath the trees.

Xoota came to Shaani's side. The body was more interesting than the others and far more intact. Its wristband was blue with two stripes. Perhaps showing he had a higher rank? Things that had the look of weaponry were threaded through its belt.

There were two clubs of the same design. Each had a short, plastic handle topped by a smooth sphere slightly larger than a fist. On the end of the haft there was a sealed cap that covered some sort of simple controls. Xoota removed the items from the corpse's belt, turning them eagerly over in her hands.

Shaani sat on the grass and looked thoughtfully at the ancient, desiccated corpse. "What killed this one?"

"Might have had a wound. Maybe it was exhaustion." Xoota was utterly intrigued by the hi-tech clubs. There was writing along one side. "What does this say?"

"It's in an omega dialect . . ." The rat licked her finger and wiped dirt away from the runes. "It says 'Mark five photonic.' "

"What's a photonic?"

"Light. Well, a sort of light energy."

"Light energy." Xoota held up one of the objects and beamed. "An energy mace."

"Really?"

"Of course. Look at the shape of it. I've heard of these. They're legendary." The quoll made some experimental swipe through the air. "Short—for really close combat."

"Why was he carrying two?"

"Must have had a cool, two-handed fighting style," Xoota remarked as she removed the cap from the bottom of one. It seemed simple enough. There was a switch with two positions, and apparently it could twist like a dial. Xoota flicked the switch and was rewarded by having the item start ticking softly in her hand.

She experimentally hit it at a tree. Nothing happened. "No energy emission."

Shaani looked over from the body. "What is it doing?"

"Just ticking."

Shaani looked at Xoota, utterly appalled. The rat dived to the ground. "Throw it!"

Xoota froze in panic then threw the club as far as she could. It sailed through the air, hit the ground, and exploded in a savage blast of light. Everything around the explosion simply vaporized. A wave of heat set fire to bushes, grass, and trees. Xoota stood, looking foolish, with the fur of her snout scorched by the blast. She blinked, standing quite stunned, then looked at the second "club" thrust through her belt. "Okay . . ."

Shaani's face appeared above the smoldering grass. "Let's take it as read that these are not energy maces."

"Sure." Xoota very carefully pushed the second weapon to the back of her belt. "I second that." She swallowed. "What would you call these, exactly?"

"Well, it's a stick that makes things go away." Shaani emerged from hiding. "How about 'magical go-away sticks'?"

Benek came over, holding a belt he had "rescued" from one of the other ancient corpses. "What was that?" he asked casually.

"That was almost the sound of Xoota turning into a cloud of fluorescing gas." Shaani was honestly angered. "Now look. From this point on, none of you lot are to touch anything. You are being irresponsible. All artifacts are to be vetted by a trained scientific mind before being set to any sort of use."

"What trained scientific mind?" Benek asked.

"Mine." Shaani gathered other artifacts from the body: a holster, what might be an energy cell, the helmet. She then laid the bones carefully back in some semblance of order. "Right. We're ready. Now where is Wig-wig?"

Benek and Xoota looked at each other. They both suddenly frowned. Shaani rubbed at her eyes.

"Oh, for Oppenheimer's sake." She signaled the other two. "Fan out and find him, please."

They spread out to search the woods. Overhead, the strange, white palm trees swayed in the breeze. The fig trees had carpeted the ground with fallen fruit, leaving the air heavy with the scent of decay.

The scavenger mentality of her companions was wearing Shaani's patience down. They were acting decidedly off color. The whole lot of them deserved smacked bottoms—even the earwigs.

She kept a sharp eye out for both Wig-wig and potential danger—the wilderness was no place for an untrained mind— but there was no immediate sign of him in the surrounding trees.

After carefully searching the local groves, Xoota scratched beneath her scarf in puzzlement. "Maybe he went to investigate the tower?"

"That would be silly." Shaani scowled, feeling that something was strangely wrong. "All right. Let's head for the tower. At least he knows that's where we were headed."

She was worried about him. Wig-wig was at times perhaps a little too trusting—not sensible like a rat. Shaani let the two warriors lead. She had to hasten to catch up with them, anyway, after she stopped to look for Wig-wig beneath some likely bits of fallen tree.

Should she shout? Call out for him? It might be dangerous; a forest was a rich environment for predators. Slowed down by her bags of salvage, Shaani struggled to catch up with the others, her senses prickling to a sudden feeling that something had gone wrong.

They came out onto a broad expanse of weirdly short and level grass. The meadow ran down to the shores of the lake. Beside the lake, there stood a ragged, old tower. It was an abstract shape, almost an arrow head in cross section with the top few floors collapsed into rubble all around its base.

Something whirred along the grass some distance away across the meadow. It looked like a flat disk made of gleaming, dark green metal and topped with several strange-looking arms equipped with scoops, shears, and saws. It was bigger than a plate but smaller than a dinner table.

In front of it, the grass was slightly ragged. Behind it, the grass was universally short. It stopped to pluck a weed out of the grass, using a little tool to dig the thing out, roots and all. The scar in the soil was smoothed over, and the strange object moved on.

All around the shattered, overgrown ruin of the tower, there were immaculate flowerbeds and well-manicured trees and hedges. Could it all be the work of that one solitary being? Whatever it was, the thing was well placed to have seen Wig-wig had he gone past. Shaani rose from hiding, covered by the crossbows of Benek and Xoota.

"Is it a foe?" asked Benek, who was breathing slightly heavily.

"No . . . more like a resident." Shaani was intrigued. She had never seen anything quite like it before. "I say, it's a jolly good gardener. I believe I should go over and try talking to it."

"Careful. That thing has a lot of blades and trowels and things," said Xoota as she scanned the trees and bushes for targets.

"Well, so do we. And we're all nice folk." Shaani strode forth. "No, no, hands across the sea. Great souls meeting in the wilderness, and all that sort of thing. All it takes is a firm grasp of diplomacy."

Girded by a deep-seated belief in politeness, good diction, and the purity of science, Shaani walked up to the strange, mechanical thing and doffed her straw hat. Her rat face was wreathed in smiles. "Greetings."

The disk kept right on carefully watering the plants from a little hose. It seemed rather preoccupied. Shaani cleared her throat again. "Hello there. Yes, do you mind awfully if we just disturb you for a bit? We are travelers, come seeking a lost friend. Have you seen a rather polite horde of earwigs hereabout?"

The disk delicately plucked a weed from the flowerbeds, backed away to contemplate its work, then swiveled around and drifted away across the grass, apparently floating on a cushion of air.

Shaani hastened to cut it off. "I say. Hello?"

The disk maneuvered around her and headed toward a neat, little shed. The rat blinked in astonishment, wondering what she had done wrong.

"I don't think it's listening," Xoota called out from across the grass.

"Well, perhaps it's not allowed to talk when on duty?" Shaani hesitated then followed the disk over to its natty shed. She knew several nonorganic folk back at the sand villages; one chap was all skin growing over a metal skeleton, and the mayor of Palm Tree village was a rather talkative brain in a jar that was mounted inside a oversized metal spider. She had no idea why *that* particular person was refusing to communicate. Careful lest she be intruding on someone's territory, Shaani knocked on the shed door and peered inside.

The place smelled of cut grass and clippings, which was a rich, weird smell to the nostrils of a desert rat. There were several gardening tools clipped into racks on the walls. The light fittings had stopped functioning a hundred years earlier, but there were no cobwebs, weeds, or dirt. The disk thing sat in a little booth that hummed away at a painful pitch. Dirt and grass clippings seemed to be shaken free to fall into a hopper and be blown off into a garden compost heap.

Once it had finished, the disk folded itself up neatly, putting its many arms away.

Shaani decided to approach it again. It seemed to see her, and some lights winked on. Shaani took that as an encouraging sign.

"Hello there. Couldn't help but notice you doing the gardening." The rat waved a hand in front of the machine. Was it a simpleton? Or possibly nonsentient? A sort of gardening idiot-savant? "Hello? Do you understand me?"

A red light blinked on the wall with a row of symbols on the screen below. The words read, "Please fill seed hopper. See manual."

It needed an offering?

Shaani carefully reached a hand out to touch the screen. The image on the screen suddenly changed to show a picture of a human woman in her underwear lounging by a blue pool of water. The screen read: "Welcome to Bliss Meadows . . . Pick Menu."

A series of small boxes at the side of the screen came with little labels. They were all to do with garden maintenance machinery. Shaani chose an information box and started reading. The text was odd, different than normal English. It seemed to be an omega dialect.

Xoota and Benek appeared. Xoota cast a careful eye about the shed. "Did it talk?" asked Xoota.

"No." Shaani was fascinated, reading through an instruction manual. "It seems to be an automated mechanism. A robot. All it does it tend the garden."

"So it's not smart?"

"It's just a high-tech gardening machine." Shaani tried to give the robot an instruction simply to report. She was asked for a password, some secret phrase she could only hope to guess at. She tried tapping a few entries, but the screen blanked and went back to the original menu. The gardening robot remained stubbornly in its niche.

"Ah well . . ."

The computer terminal was interesting, though. Shaani adjusted her glasses and took a look through her screen.

"Interesting. The computer seems to be intact. It might be connected to a larger network."

"Oh, those things are useless. They always are," said Xoota. Salvage value on electronics was usually negligible. "There might be some good finds in the tower, though."

Shaani flicked a frowning glance at her friend.

Benek was kneeling in cover; his heavy armor was scarcely the best choice for either desert or forest. The man held up a hand to silence the other two.

He aimed his crossbow and quite suddenly fired.

"Razorbacks . . . mutants!" he shouted before charging into the bushes with his sword aloft. He leaped over greenery and swung his blade in an arc that terminated on something in the ferns. Benek's war cries thundered in the gloom. "Mutant scum! All will be cleansed!"

Xoota and Shaani instantly dived for cover. Shaani pulled out the salvaged pistol and held it in possibly the right way. She stared into the bushes. "What's out there?"

Xoota half rose, crossbow at the ready. "Let's get after him. Cover me." Xoota charged, moving hard and fast. She reached bushes and hit the dirt, aiming her crossbow at the trees.

Shaani scuttled after her, one hand on her hat, the other waving the rather dubious pistol. She knelt in cover, looking for razorbacks. She saw nothing but heard Benek exulting among the trees.

He sounded like he was in deep combat, his sword hacking and ringing, clanking and crashing through the bushes far ahead.

Xoota swore and bellowed in his general direction. "Benek! Hold your position. Wait for us."

He wasn't listening. The damned man had gone. Confused, Shaani watched the flanks and rear. The tower nearby was sitting still and empty, its blank windows dark and brooding. Benek was in the woods. Wig-wig was missing. Xoota raced forward into the trees, crossbow at the ready, and simply disappeared. Shaani ran after her, getting a little tangled in the bushes.

The damned bushes were thick and snarled. Shaani waded along awkwardly, her feet tangling. A second later she fell over on her ratty backside, landing with a thump. Dazed, she felt something grab her by the ankle and drag her through the trees.

A big, green tree loomed over her. It hauled her up by one leg, gaping wide with a great maw split vertically into its trunk. Shaani made a squeak of panic. She leveled the pistol in the general direction of the monster and pulled the trigger.

Nothing happened.

"Damned omega rubbish."

Shaani shook the pistol. She cursed it and hammered it against her palm, which was enough to make it fire. It gave her the fright of her life, making a purple blast that left her eyes dazzled with horrid blobs of light.

The tree seemed to have caved in on itself, a hole longer than Shaani's boot was punched through right above its mouth. The tendrils released Shaani's leg and began thrashing madly around. The rat made herself scarce, running and ducking as a tentacle lunged for her and almost took her head clean off her shoulders.

"Xoota?" Shaani yelled.

There were no sounds in the forest, no sign of Xoota, Benek, or Wig-wig.

What the hell was happening?

Shaani went no further forward into the forest. She called again for Xoota and yelled for Benek. There was no sign of any marauding razorbacks. The rat searched the local bushes, but there was no indication that her friends had been engulfed by carnivorous plants.

Shaani was alone in the forest. She called out for the others time and time again to no avail then fell back to the open grass.

Something suddenly blurred past her in the air. Chainsaw in one hand, pistol in the other, Shaani whirled in fright.

"Wig-wig."

Her heart leaped with joy. But the bugs seemed to ignore her. They raced past, heading for the ruins. Shaani gave chase.

"Wig-wig. Please. It's me."

"Gleeeeee." The bugs were zooming through the air, wings glittering in the sun. "Chasing."

"Wig-wig?"

"Fun." Bugs were clinging to the walls, chittering happily. They watched a patch of empty air then jumped happily away. "Can't catch I." The bugs raced up into the ruins and disappeared.

Shaani sagged. Something was going on. Shaani sat, dazed, and tried to think.

The last sentient beings known to have visited there were dead. And they had died in very strange ways: murder, suicide . . . possible insanity.

Something was affecting everybody's minds.

Could it be the fruit? The others had been gorging themselves on it. But then why wasn't she affected as well? Perhaps her superior nature as a purpose-bred embodiment of science somehow kept her immune?

The ruined tower seemed largely gutted, although the shadows sometimes moved, playing tricks with Shaani's eyes. Jungle plants had moved in; one of the fragrant white palms jutted up out of what had once been an ornamental pool of some kind. The overgrown holes of windows and doors showed occasional flashes of decaying furniture and broken TV screens. One section of the ruins had collapsed onto trees and apparently burned, making a deep mound of rubble over a pile of charcoal. There were no animals, nothing but the flying fish out in the lake, who took brief forays into the forest then plunged back underwater, apparently to breathe. There was no sign of Wig-wig again or Xoota or Benek.

Shaani despaired, wondering what to do, when a flash of white suddenly caught her eye.

The bottom layer of the ruins had an extension. A crack in a wall showed a glimpse of white tile and gleaming steel. Shaani worked her way cautiously forward and felt her ears and tail stiffen in excitement.

It was a laboratory.

Almost totally intact, it had been sheltered by the falling floors above. Shaani clambered excitedly in through the crack in the wall and looked around, absolutely beside herself with joy.

The equipment looked intact and unblemished. Some sort of computer screens, glassware, heating pads, dials, and more ...

The computer blinked a screen. A human face looked out at her and smiled. "Greetings, fellow scientist."

Fellow scientist? Shaani was utterly thrilled. "You can understand me?"

The computer image looked benignly at Shaani and bowed. "I am programmed to respond to all authorized science personnel. Human scientists and, of course, laboratory rats."

Right. To business. Shaani dropped her bags. "I need to analyze a type of local fruit. I'm looking for toxins or hallucinogens."

"Chemical analysis equipment is available on the right." The computer lit up a square, white machine nearby. "Place a sample within the machinery."

"Just—put the fruit in the machine?"

"It would be best to distill the pulp, removing as much water as possible."

Ah. That was something Shaani could do well. She found a glass beaker, fetched a fruit from her backpack, and crushed the flesh, running juice off into the beaker. She waved a hand over the heating panels; they instantly responded, and she began to carefully distill the water from the juice.

Science at work.

Wig-Wig swirled by, laughing and swooping and playing games. Shaani beamed. The others may have been susceptible, but she was made of sterner stuff. With no time to eat or drink, she applied herself to her work.

The afternoon sun was slanting in through the windows as she put her finished concoction into the analyzer. The machine whirred, pinged, and finally the computer spoke.

"Analysis complete."

"Excellent." Shaani inspected the screen. "Sugars . . . carbohydrates . . ." She combed her whiskers. "I can't see anything unusual."

The computer whirred and blinked its many lights.

"You must concentrate," she said to herself. "Rat senses are acute enough to spot chains a human would miss." Shaani scanned the list of chemical compounds found in the fruit. Her eye was caught by some trace acids. "Ah, what is this compound here?"

"It is an unidentified acid, honored researcher."

"Are there similar acid structures on your records?"

"Yes." The computer put a list of chemicals up on the screen. "These are similar compounds stored in my records."

Shaani read the list, peering over her spectacles. "Lysergic acid diethylamide . . ." Shaani knew that one. It was in her chemical textbook, which never left her. "LSD."

Aha.

LSD was a powerful hallucinogen. The rat rubbed her hands together in satisfaction. Finally they were getting somewhere.

"Computer, can we construct an antidote?"

The computer face beamed. "You are the rat, honored researcher. What would you suggest?"

"Hmm." The rat pondered. "Well, bases seem to counter acids. Perhaps they need to ingest something alkaline."

"An excellent suggestion."

"A soluble salt would be easiest—and gentlest. Calcium carbonate?" Shaani was on fire with science. "Computer, are there any sources of calcium carbonate nearby?"

"I have no operating sensors. But calcium carbonate is found in shells. Mollusk shells are common near bodies of water."

"Yes, yes, yes." Shaani gathered up her collection equipment. "I'll be back as soon as I've found a source."

She set off out of the laboratory with a surge of real joy in her heart. Quite suddenly she heard laughter over in the ruined tower. The rat clambered over a stone and saw Xoota struggling through the ruins.

The quoll was dragging a makeshift sack made from some sort of cloth. The sack was filled to the brim with junk that clanked and rattled as she walked.

Shaani felt a huge surge of relief. "Xoota." She waved.

The quoll saw her and headed in her direction, exhausted with the weight of her finds. "Shaani . . . Shaani, you have to see this."

"It's all right." Shaani held up a hand. "Your erratic behavior is explained. A cure is at hand."

"What? Oh, that's great." Xoota dragged her sack over toward Shaani. "Shaani, there's a cache. Over in the ruins, all kinds of stuff under the rubble."

"Have you drunk anything lately?"

"What? No." The quoll stood before Shaani and wiped dust from her face. "You should see this. Look, look what I've found. Tools. Some sort of power drill. And guns—shiny ones. One for each of us." The quoll was excited. "And some sort of healing machine. Anything you want, it's in there."

Shaani looked at the sack. It held a terrible collection of scrap and rubbish: broken bowls, sticks, rocks. She shook her head, pitying Xoota's weak-minded susceptibility. "Xoota, you have to calm down and sit quietly. You are hallucinating. There's nothing here."

"What? No, no, no. You should see all these things. I've spent a lifetime looking for anything half this good. I'm not a loser anymore." The quoll's eyes were bright and earnest. "I'll bring back more, you'll see. There's everything you could ever want over there."

"You're not eating any fruit, are you?"

"No, no time." Xoota raced off, seizing what looked like a rusted kettle.

Shaani stared after her. Everything she could ever want . . .

Shaani moved very quietly to a rock. She sat and looked over the ruins.

A big, white tree stood beside the lab. There was another over near Xoota's "treasure" trove.

The bodies in the forest had all been near white trees.

Shaani closed her eyes for a moment and bowed her head, feeling rather crushed. But science is never proud. Science adapts to the evidence before it and carries on. The rat clenched her hands and let her mind race. She forced herself to drink; she had not noticed just how damned tired and thirsty she had been. She had been dehydrating in the heat.

It was the trees. The white, fragrant trees . . . The sweet pollen hung thick and sickly in the air.

Right. Science was called for. All the tools were readily at hand. Ignoring the laboratory, Shaani headed over to the fallen tower floors. A long pipe served her as a lever. She jammed one end beneath a chunk of fallen stone then swung her meager weight from the far end. Bouncing and jouncing, she worked the rubble loose, finally tumbling a large rock free.

Charcoal lay in a deep drift beneath the rocks. Trees burned in a fire decades before. The rat pulled at the crumbling charcoal, used her entrenching tool to clear away all of the surface material, and found the good, porous charcoal underneath.

Black and smudged from head to foot, she sat down in the rubble. An instant later, she had unthreaded her canteen from her belt. The rat looked it over, took her tools, and punched holes all through the bottom of the canteen.

Shaani stripped off her tank top and laid it on the floor. She chopped charcoal into small pieces and washed it in water, rinsing out the dust. She laid the charcoal out onto her singlet, patting it all carefully dry.

She filled her canteen with charcoal and wrapped cotton over the neck. She breathed through the neck of the water bottle, sucking each breath in through a mass of charcoal.

Science at work.

She gathered yet more washed charcoal in a bag, put her blackened, wet singlet back on, and climbed the ruins.

She had to breathe carefully; it was tiring, taking a lot of effort to suck breath through the charcoal mass. She worked at it, keeping her breathing as even as possible. Shaani moved near the lakeshore, away from the trees, heading carefully upwind. She walked for half an hour, keeping her thoughts as calm and clear as she could.

She walked back to the ruined tower and looked toward the laboratory.

It was an ancient kitchen, dust covered and overgrown. The "computer screen" had been an oven set into a wall. The analysis equipment had merely been cupboards, cracked bowls, and shattered utensils. Shaani nodded; the "computer" had told her nothing. She had fed the fantasy all by herself. But at least her mind was clear. Her inhaled-gas hypothesis had been proven.

All that was left was the difficult part.

· · · · ·

Xoota was digging madly through a pile of rusted refuse, lifting some pieces aloft in glee. Shaani came over to her, holding her bottle to her mouth and breathing with difficulty. She waved to Xoota.

"Hallo, Xoota."

"Hey." The quoll was looking tired, near exhaustion. Looming overhead was a white tree. If she looked carefully, she could see a network of surface roots; the things clearly fed by making their victims expire in deluded exhaustion then sucked the nutrients from the corpses as they decayed.

Shaani walked over, one foot tapping the ground, looking a little sheepish. "I, um, found an artifact for you, old bean. Looks pretty valuable—you know, top stuff. It might be a fusion gun, maybe a life ray or something."

"Wow, where?"

"Over here." Shaani pointed to the rubble nearby.

Xoota came scrabbling up beside her. She followed Shaani's finger, saw metal gleaming among the rocks, and knelt down to dig the object free.

Shaani pulled open a little vial that had long resided in her belt pouch. She dipped a long spike made out of thorn into the gooey green liquid in the vial. "You know, you *will* thank me for this tomorrow..." Shaani pierced Xoota's shapely backside with the thorn.

Xoota yelped, looked around in shock, then collapsed forward, stiff as a board.

Shaani nodded. The poison she had taken from the ant-lion larvae back in the desert many weeks past had proved to be useful at last.

Right.

The rest was all hard labor. She dragged the other girl free of the white trees. She put together an impromptu gas mask and tied it into place over Xoota's mouth. Shaani checked that the girl could breathe and put her into a old, wheeled trolley scavenged from the ruined kitchen. She trundled Xoota far around the lake and put her safely behind the lovely waterfall, far upwind of the deadly trees.

That was number one.

Number two: Wig-wig. He would not be so hard and certainly less likely to hold a grudge. She found a huge, plastic bin behind the garden shed. Whistling through her chisel teeth, Shaani finally attracted the attention of the earwigs, who were ragged with exhaustion after chasing imaginary playmates around and around the tower.

The earwigs waved. "Rattie."

"Wig-wig." The rat pointed excitedly down into the bin. "He's in here. He's hiding down in here."

"Glee." The bugs took off and swirled down into the plastic bin. They began eagerly combing through the bark and grass clippings at the bottom of the bin.

Shaani put the lid on the bin and clamped it shut. She had screwed in an air filter made from charcoal and a water bottle. An old bag served as bellows to blow in some nice, fresh air. She tucked the barrel under her arm and made her way awkwardly back to the waterfall.

QED.

Number three was going to be rather problematic. Ah, well, Shaani had left the worst until last.

Benek was up in the tree line. He fought a grim battle against opponents who crumbled before his unconquerable genetic might. He poised and fired his crossbow, racing forward. Bushes fell to bits as he hacked and swirled, slicing them to pieces and slamming home mighty *coups de grâce*.

Shaani laid her plans carefully, checked her distances and routes, and headed after him with a grubby handkerchief in hand. "Yoo-hoo, Benek. Oh, Benek, it's me."

Armored in full plate, with crossbow and a mighty sword, the world's most genetically perfect man whirled. Vast and slathered with muscle, he took one look at Shaani and roared. He clearly saw her as yet another mutant, there to fall before his blade.

Shaani tried her friendliest possible wave. "Benek. Benek, old chap. Now we do need you to concentrate. Clear head, all that sort of thing. You're rather delusional, and I really need you to just calm down—"

He charged.

Shaani shot off through the bushes like a rabbit, wailing. Benek scrambled behind her, crashing bushes aside, smashing saplings beneath his feet. He came on like a juggernaut, bellowing in rage.

She ran, fleet, skinny, and with a definite plan in mind. Her path was deliberate. She took a set course, bounding over bushes and fallen trees.

Benek roared and raced after her, clumsy in his heavy armor of steel. He splintered underbrush, hacking with his sword. A wild crossbow shot winged past Shaani's head. She ducked, then sprinted, her course curving, leaving Benek in her wake. She reached the point of her path she had marked with three white stones then ducked behind a bush to wait.

Benek appeared. Hot and dehydrated, wild eyed and insane, the man caught sight of Shaani and strode toward her, swinging his battered and sap-stained sword.

Long plant tendrils suddenly wrapped around his shins.

Shaani's old adversary, the carnivorous tree, jerked Benek off his feet. It dragged him toward its damaged maw even as he tore and ripped at the tendrils. Shaani poised, picked her moment, then lunged in with a long stick tipped with a poisoned dart.

She stabbed Benek in the backside with paralytic poison.

The man turned stiff as a board. Shaani poked him with the stick a few times to make sure then gratefully threw the pokey stick aside. She tramped forward toward the plant, which was smacking its lips in glee.

She started up her chainsaw in a most significant manner. The plant sullenly let go of Benek and went into a magnificent sulk. Shaani tied a rope around Benek's hands and feet. He was far too big to lift into a wheelbarrow. Shaani tied a gas mask to his mouth, fixed a tow rope to his feet, and laboriously dragged him over to her modified shopping cart.

Damn, but he was heavy.

The only way was to get him out of his armored skin. Shaani undid buckles, ties, straps, and laces, amazed at the armor's complexity. She managed to free him from his armor and found that he wore heavily patched underwear beneath. Relieved of some of the weight, she was finally able to winch him off the ground via a rope thrown over a branch. She lowered him into the trolley and arranged him into place.

Shaani threw her meager muscles against the trolley, pushing and cursing, feet slipping. Hauling his lumpen great arse back to the waterfall was a massive labor. Night had fallen, and a new moon was shining eerie gray light over the strange sky island. Shaani was hungry, exhausted, and almost collapsing with effort, when suddenly Benek's weight miraculously halved.

Xoota had taken the front half of the trolley out of her hands. Shaani looked at her—charcoal smudged, filthy, and tired. They both wore the silly bottle gas masks. Xoota nodded and helped her wrestle Benek back to the falls.

Behind the waterfall, Xoota had made a little refuge. Wig-wig was free and looking rather seedy, camped out beside the water and drinking his fill. He waved wearily, looking ashamed. Shaani sank down to the rocks, pulling her gas mask free.

There was one more trip to make with the trolley. They had to go back for Benek's armor. Shaani took time to gather a trolley load of fruit and take it all back to the cave.

Benek was lying on the ground, paralyzed but no longer completely crazed. Xoota held his head and helped him drink, making him take a full liter, sip by sip. She looked up as Shaani came back into the cave. "Hey."

"Hallo." Shaani sank wearily down. She looked Xoota over. "So how are you feeling now, old trout?"

"Good . . . better." She gestured to the makeshift gas masks. "Thank you."

"You're most welcome."

Benek blinked at the ceiling. "I have been overpowered by a mutant trick."

Shaani gave a tired sigh. "It was the white trees. The pollen was drugged. None of us were our real selves."

Xoota looked disheartened. "Perhaps we were too much our real selves."

"We were deluded." The rat drank cold water from the stream. "I shan't blame anyone for their delusions. Merely for clinging to them."

Xoota nodded, looking tired. "Benek, can you move?"

"Almost. I can move my feet."

"It won't take much longer." Xoota wearily rose to her feet. "Let's get the hell off this place."

It took half an hour to get Benek to his feet. They took their trolley with them, laboriously wending their way down the crevice that led back to the sands. Wig-wig flew on ahead to turn lights on at the ship, to bring Budgie on deck, and to ready the ship for sleep.

Benek manhandled the trolley up onto the ship. Xoota stood on the rocks with Shaani, looking at the crashed and damaged *Sand Shark*. They had a lot of work ahead of them.

"Kack. I'm sorry. I'm sorry. I'm the leader. I should have been in control," said Xoota.

Shaani gave a tired smile. "It's all right. You had a scientist watching over you."

"So you didn't go crazy?"

"A more genteel crazy." The rat sighed. "It was not a pretty sight."

They made their way toward the ship. Up on deck, Budgie twittered a merry welcome home. Xoota waved to the bird.

"So what was real? Was there loot? Did we actually find anything for all our troubles?"

"Ah, yes. The fruit was real; the bath was real. Both magic in their way." Shaani's eyelids were drooping. "And all the things from the forest bodies were real: a medical kit, three bracelets, two sets of armor—slightly used, one rather erratic pistol, one spare energy cell, and your patent 'energy mace.'"

"Oh." The quoll looked rather chastened. "Well, that's not a total loss."

"You're no loser." The rat handed her the pistol and took her arm in arm as they walked toward the ship. "Not at all."

CHAPTER 9

The morning came with a deep sense of moral hangover; the entire crew was aware that they had behaved like idiots. The only cure was to be rather busy and efficient.

Denial: it gets things done.

The broken wheel mount was going to be a major problem. The fallen mast was relatively easy to fix; all it needed was awkward winches, pulleys, and muscle power . . . then rerigging half the damned ship. No trouble at all. But the wheel mount was going to be a hard call. Shaani hung upside down inside the hold for half an hour, her legs, bottom, and tail wiggling awkwardly from time to time. She emerged with pink eyes blinking and grease smears on her nose. She did not look happy.

Xoota was inexpertly helping to splice damaged rigging. Wig-wig was definitely the expert. With dozens of earwigs weaving effortlessly over and under, he merely needed Xoota's help for the muscle power. She made the final tugs, jerked tight the knots, and used pulleys to haul finished cables up into the masts. With her boots off, Xoota had two hands, two prehensile feet, and a prehensile tail available to help her aloft; she was definitely the crewman voted to handle all of the action high above deck.

If only she actually liked heights . . .

Hanging upside down by her tail, cursing as she tried to thread a cable through a complicated pulley block, Xoota rapped her knuckle on the rigging. As she was doing her usual grumbling, Wig-wig flew effortlessly past her with countless wings flashing in the sun.

"Glee."

Xoota gave another curse and went back to work.

The broken rigging around the mainmast was slowly coming back together. The foremast would be another story. Xoota sighed, wiped her brow, and took a drink from her canteen while hanging from her tail.

Far below her, everyone was busy. Shaani bustled back down a hatch, carrying an old tape measure and a set of calipers. Wig-wig was swarming all over lengths of broken cable, knotting and splicing. Even Benek was down belowdecks, clearing out the buckled and bent mast mountings. His titanic strength was going to be needed when all the heavy engineering began. The only one slacking off was Budgie, who lounged in the shade of the deckhouse with his feet up, a sack of goober beans beside him and a look of immense satisfaction on his face. The budgerigar looked happily up at Xoota and flapped his little flightless wings.

"Whose a pretty boy, then?"

The quoll seethed in dark, ill temper.

"You'll keep, you feather-bearing git."

Xoota slid down a backstay, using leather gloves to protect her delicate hands. She landed with a feline delicacy, up on her toes, then dusted off her clothes. She stepped carefully over the earwig horde, dropped down a hatch, and moved through the airless spaces of the lower hull.

Benek was working a hammer, stripped to the waist and looking like an ancient god of ironmongery. Darwin only knew how he survived; he lacked all protective skin covering: no fur, feathers, scales, spines, platelets, silicon shingles, or chitin. No alpha mutations, no powers . . . Humans seemed to be a bit of an evolutionary dead end. But if Benek wanted to revitalize the poor, benighted race, it was hardly for Xoota to complain . . . as long as they didn't do it on the town streets and scare the budgerigars.

Xoota worked her way past the man, wrinkling her nose at the rather acrid scent of human sweat. "Hey, Benek. How's it going?"

"Adequately." The man rippled his muscles as he moved. "I have been straightening bolts and screws."

"Oh, wacko. Well, can't have you with loose screws." Xoota made sure the man had a bottle of iced tea. She never moved without at least one liter of water on her. "When are we putting the mast back up?"

"The rat believes we can do it this afternoon."

Raising the mast would take all night. All the next day would be spent rerigging the damned thing. Xoota was annoyed. Every day that passed put the citizens of Watering Hole in danger. The Great Star Goat only knew how the distilling station was holding out. If it broke down, the town would be dead in a matter of days.

Hours might count.

With her spotted fur gleaming around her bare midriff, Xoota clambered through the companionway. She was just in time to hear an unholy crash as untold tons of metal fell off the hull and clanged onto the ground below. Xoota blinked, owl eyed, and hastened to stick her head out of a gaping hole in the side of the ship.

Shaani was sitting in a little rope chair hanging from the side of the ship. She pushed back her safety goggles and smiled. "Oh, hallo." She wiped her face. "Any good alphas today?"

"Eh, something's in there. No real idea what." The quoll looked over the wheel mount. "You?"

"Oh, damage reflection. No bad thing."

"We never seem to get anything world crunching. You know, something that might let us generate a black hole inside someone's lower intestinal tract." Xoota shrugged. "I just came to see if everyone wanted a cup of tea." Xoota was a creature largely driven by tea; when stabbed, she might even bleed light brown with milk and two sugars. "Could you go for a cuppa?"

"Could I ever." The rat needed no further urging. She was tired and well streaked with grease. "I think I'm due for a break."

Xoota leaned out of the ship and looked down at a hefty metal shape lying on the sand. Shaani had unbolted a substantial chunk of the ship and let it fall.

"What the hell was that?

The rat raised a finger. "Ah, that was the section of the wheel mount that fit into the chassis."

"So why is it on the ground?"

"It's all twisted out of true. We need to straighten it out once I build a forge. Then we get to hoist it all back up again."

"Sounds hard."

"It's certainly no picnic." In addition to somehow unbolting an entire wheel mount, Shaani had also had to uncouple brake lines, power lines, and more. She had clearly been having a complicated morning. "Only way to do it really. But we'll probably need to fetch a big load of charcoal from up above. We'll need oodles of the stuff to run the forge."

Xoota was rather dubious. The previous day's general lunacy was a very painful memory. "Will we be safe?"

"The respirators seemed to work well." The rat clambered back on board. "And if we go a tad loopy, it's all just stress relief."

"You're remarkably calm about yesterday's . . . incident."

"A scientist must take failures in stride." Shaani dusted down her singlet, which was much the worse for wear. "You know, I'm rather looking forward to finding a settlement of some kind. I could do with some new kit."

Xoota frowned as they walked back through the hold. "Do you think there will be settlements?"

"Oh, there must be. We can't be the only bit of civilization left in the world." The rat was enthused. "That's what makes this all so exciting. Hands across the wilderness and all that."

Xoota sighed and looked up at the sky island towering high above. Climbing to the top again was not a pretty prospect. Still, at least they could collect and dry a whole bunch of jungle fruit. The damned stuff was delicious.

Shaani rigged a better, more usable version of her gas masks. The breather units were strapped to the chest, and the user breathed in via a hose and exhaled out of an exhaust valve. A nose plug was necessary to prevent anyone mistakenly breathing in unfiltered air. Wig-wig was more problematic; he was simply forbidden to advance any farther than the waterfall. But they would take Budgie along; the little blighter could finally actually work for a living. Shaani fitted him with a mask across his nostrils that was tied in place with rags. The result was definitely not going to win him any beauty contest.

The expedition traipsed back up the sharp slope of the crevice, clambering across the rocks and boulders. Budgie hopped from rock to rock, helped here and there by a shove in the backside. Xoota wondered if the damned bird was putting on weight.

Finally they reached the upper lip of the plateau. They took a wide detour away from the teleporting seed plants and made their way to the beautiful waterfall cave.

Xoota left spare water bottles beside the stream and left the party laundry there to wash later. She began tightening straps and rechecking her armor.

"Now no one goes anywhere alone. Wig-wig, we have to leave you here. You can collect fruit, but go no nearer the forest than the first pool. You hear me?"

"Yes, Xoota." The earwigs showed every intention of being very, *very* good. "I be finding yummy fruit."

"Be very, very careful. Flee back here at the first sign of the slightest danger." Xoota ticked things off on her fingers as Shaani led her off toward the falls. "So stay away from the teleporting seeds, the carnivorous trees, the bird fish . . ."

She was still thinking of things as they exited through the waterfall. Shaani rummaged in her pack and produced the ray pistol. She proudly handed it to Xoota.

"There you go, old bean. I fixed it good as new. Have a *bunduk.*"

"Bunduk?"

"Bang stick. The gun." Shaani passed the pistol across. "It's all right. I fixed it."

"Where *did* you pick up your dialect?" Xoota hesitated before touching the pistol. "You want to give this to me? Don't you want it?"

"No, no, you have it. You'll get more use out of it." The rat turned the pistol around and explained its workings carefully. "Sights—you get the idea. Spare power cell goes in there if it suddenly konks out on you. And *that* is the safety catch. It's a bit wobbly, so I've held it back with hairy string." The rat gave the weapon a last inspection. "The grips had decayed, so I've used yet more string. Should give you a good, nonslip handle."

"Right. Well, yes, thanks." It was a princely gift, the one thing every explorer hoped to find and never did. Xoota took the weapon, stuck it into a holster, and tied the holster to her leg. She felt it settle there as though it belonged.

Shaani led Budgie, who came with a basket slung on each side of his saddle. The rat chattered happily to the others as they walked beside the stream.

"Benek. Did that armor fit you?"

The huge man shook his head. "No. They were made for under-men. Their stature was too weak, too frail."

"Without your bulging pecs, eh?"

"Quite so."

"Ah well, we might be able to use them for Xoota and me. I'll mess around with them later." Shaani's mind was racing. "The coverage is poor. I think we can take sections from the damaged suit and use them to cover the thigh sections. Protect the femoral artery . . ."

Xoota flicked a patient glance at the rat. "We have crossed the entire desert with you wearing nothing but a cotton shirt, and *now* you get interested in armor?"

"Well, it wasn't interesting before. Now it's a challenge."

Thankfully they reached gas mask territory at last. The masks were fitted into place, which effectively stopping all chitchat. Xoota made sure everyone could breathe then led the way into the forest.

The ruined tower still stood within its immaculately manicured lawns and gardens. The gardening bot was still at work, diligently weeding flowerbeds. Shaani looked at it and took her gas mask from her mouth.

"I feel sad about leaving this little fellow here alone."

Benek scowled. "It is its duty to serve here."

"Well, he's keeping a beautiful garden with no one to appreciate it."

Xoota kept her crossbow loaded, scanning the underbrush for enemies. She liked the feel of the ancient pistol on her hip; it made her feel like a real adventurer. Her antennae quested for future trouble but decidedly came up blank.

"Let's just get the charcoal loaded and then meddle with dangerous metal entities later."

Shaani brightened. "Righto."

Xoota wearily realized her word had just been taken as a promise. Grumbling, she led the way to the ruins—the site of the previous day's shame—and tramped over to the charcoal pile.

"All right. How much of this stuff do we need?"

Shaani fetched her folding shovel. "We'll need about . . . three trips' worth. The forge is going to have to be jolly hot."

Well, they would be carrying one basket each, plus Budgie's panniers. They were in for a long afternoon. Despite the green grass and trees, the sun was ferociously hot. There were only two shovels. Xoota took the first shift, filling her own backpack then Shaani's and Benek's.

They made their way back to the waterfall and drank like stranded fish; the job was truly hot and horrible, far better left until the cool of night, except that the forest was no place to be wandering around in the dark. Wig-wig's fruit collection was going apace. He had also found another fruit that came in bunches of bright polka-dotted fingers. The mammals left him to it. They wended their way painfully back down the track toward the ship, moving carefully under their dusty loads of charcoal. It was a long, long way down until they finally dropped their burdens at the ship. Heads pounding from the exertion in the heat, they sat in the shade of the hull, drinking cold, sugared tea chilled by Shaani's cooling blankets. They mopped their brows then forced themselves to trudge their way back up the scalding rock slope to the plateau high above.

The halfway point provided a good view across the empty desert. Nothing moved; nothing stirred except mirages shimmering silver on the sands. The ship looked forlorn, its wheel and fallen mast begging for attention. The group caught their breath then moved on.

Xoota dreamed longingly of swimming in the beautiful waterfall again. The thought of all that water made her tongue hang out.

Shaani's head ached from the exertion. "We're going to need to find a . . . a way to top up the water tanks."

"How?" Xoota was damned tired. "We can't do a bucket brigade. We'll be drinking more damned water than we carry down the hill."

Shaani nodded. They just kept on climbing, with Budgie croaking protest from the rear.

There was nothing for it but to get the damned job done. They refilled the baskets and headed back down again, drinking as if it were going out of fashion. No one relished the prospect of a third trip. Even Benek was looking tired. But Shaani jumped to her feet, her stiff upper lip going into overdrive. She chivvied her companions up off the ground.

"Right. Excelsior. Onwards and upwards." She flicked at Xoota's backside. "Tally-ho, old bean."

Xoota wanted to hit her, but she managed to totter to her feet. She nudged Budgie in the arse; the bird was feigning death in the hope that he might be left alone to creep into the hull, sprawl on the water tanks, and sleep. Xoota tugged on a tail feather. "Get up or I'll pluck you bald."

The bird muttered something uncomplimentary it had picked up from Xoota's regular cursing; his vocabulary was getting better. The team clambered painfully back uphill, the rocks scorching their hands. The sun was getting low on the horizon, but there was still no refuge from the heat.

One more load and they could look forward to a swim. After that, Xoota planned on taking a long sleep in front of the cabin air conditioner, buck naked and with a cold cloth on her head. They visited Wig-wig, who was absurdly cheerful and rested as he plundered the forest's fruit reserves. Pausing only to plunge their heads into the stream, they plodded on to the ruined tower and wearily began shoveling their last load of charcoal. The gas masks were harder and harder to use, each breath having to be dragged in through the filters. Xoota felt vague and blurry with fatigue.

Shaani and Benek dug away. Xoota filled her basket then took a break. She wiped her feathery antennae with a rag—they worked better when they were clean—and looked off toward the forest. There were some minor bits of business to attend to.

"Are you lot all right here?" Xoota checked her crossbow. "I'm just going to nip into the forest for a bit."

"Oh?" Shaani was black as night from head to foot, utterly filthy with charcoal dust. Her pink eyes looked ludicrously bright against a mask of dirt. "Are you sure? Should we send someone with you?"

"No, no, it's safe enough. I know where I'm going." Xoota took another drag of air from her mask. "I just want to get that odd little cupboard thing from the crashed vehicle. It's been bothering me."

Shaani nodded. She was back behind her mask and couldn't speak. Xoota gathered her gear. "If I'm not back in twenty minutes, come looking."

The quoll tromped off into the forest. The pathways were almost becoming familiar. The odd fish from the lake clearly never breathed the deadly, hallucinogenic pollen from the white palm trees. They flew up out of the lake, ate fruit and berries, then eventually dived back into the water to breathe. There were no other animals in the forest, nothing bigger than a bee.

The ruined omega vehicle was exactly where they had left it. Xoota approached warily, scouting for dangers, then put her crossbow aside. The weeds had already started growing back. The quoll hauled open the hatch into the hull and looked the place over with a scavenger's practiced eye.

The control couches would make excellent lounge chairs for use on the *Sand Shark*. There were lights to repair the ship's headlights. One of the windows might be removable; it could replace the *Sand Shark*'s windscreen. The rest of the hull was made from an eerie, silver metal that would neither buckle, bend, nor cut. If she could have cut off a chunk of it, she would have—it might be useful—but the damned stuff refused to cooperate.

The alien box was still there in the rear cargo space. Xoota hauled it out into her lap and looked it over. The thing did not match the ship itself in materials or design. It had a door with an empty space inside, as though it might be used for storage. It was weirdly organic, a sort of horrid green color, and the box hummed softly when she put her ear to it.

Xoota put a broken stick tipped with three green leaves inside the box and shut the door. She waited a few seconds while it hummed, and she opened the door to find that the box was empty.

That is odd, she thought. It might make a rather useful garbage disposal.

Backing out of the hull, Xoota hauled the unit free. She set it down on the ground and stood up to contemplate the work in hand.

On a whim, she turned to look at the underbrush around her. She almost had a heart attack.

A giant, carnivorous plant with long tendrils and glossy green leaves loomed over her. Its maw, centered in a huge bulb of a head, was a mass of thorny teeth that looked large enough to swallow Xoota whole.

She put her hand to her pistol, glaring at the plant, but it didn't advance. The quoll narrowed her eyes. "Where the hell did you come from?"

It was a whole new plant. Darwin only knew how long it had been watching them, waiting for its chance to pounce. The plant tilted its head this way and that, as if looking at her, though it had no visible eyes. Quite suddenly, a long, orchid-colored tongue extended from its mouth. Xoota leaped backward, gun at the ready, but the plant was happy to sit where it was.

At the end of the tongue, the plant was holding something slimy. It was another little, green cupboard—the exact twin of the one from the crashed ship. The plant placed the unit on the grass then withdrew its tongue. It sat happily back with its mouth shut, making a vast, toothy grin.

Was it a trap? Something to lure Xoota into attack range? But the plant could already have attacked; it had a good deal of reach with its tendrils. A second and third bulblike head, each with its own toothy mouth, sprouted from the central trunk. As far as three-headed monsters went, it was being rather well behaved.

"Okay . . ." Xoota edged closer. She took up the little, alien box from the grass and opened the door.

Inside she saw the broken stick tipped with three green leaves.

Minutes later, Xoota was happily playing with the cupboards. The enormous plant handed her a fruit. She put the fruit into one cupboard and teleported it to the other. She then shut the door again and teleported the fruit back into the first container. The effect was ludicrously pleasing. The plant handed her another item—a river rock. They both watched it go from one cupboard to the other in satisfaction.

"Excellent." Xoota sat back and drank from her canteen, eying the plant. "What the hell do you eat, anyway?"

The plant opened one of its other mouths and revealed one of the flying fish. The creature was already half digested. The plant snapped its jaws shut and beamed.

Xoota was impressed. "Oh, wacko."

. . . . .

Some time later Xoota came plodding from the jungle, carrying the two alien cupboards in a string bag. Behind her, the plant trundled along on a mass of walking root clusters. It was carrying two control chairs and a window taken from the crashed ship.

Benek and Shaani had finished loading their charcoal and were waiting for Xoota. When she approached, she saw Shaani inspecting the gardening robot. Benek leaped to his feet in shock as he saw the massive plant. Shaani jerked at his motion and hit her head, emerging from beneath the robot, rubbing her skull. When she focused her eyes on Xoota, she waved.

"Oh, hallo."

"Hi." Xoota jerked a thumb at the plant. "He keeps following me."

"Perhaps he's feeling peckish?"

"No, no. He had fish for dinner." Xoota sat down and regarded the plant, which swiveled this way and that, appearing to look around. "Do carnivorous plants eat much?"

"Not really. My sources say it's more of a mineral supplement than anything else. They need soil."

The plant seemed to actually be quite useful. It was titanic; its tendrils stretched quite a few meters when it waved them around, and its jaws could easily chomp on a small sheep. Shaani adjusted her glasses and looked the creature over, fearlessly climbing between the tendrils to inspect the creature's mouths. It obligingly gaped a set of jaws for her and let her poke around.

"Well, it seems friendly enough." The rat inspected the plant's shiny, handsome stalks. "It's in very good condition."

"Why do you think it's following me?"

"Well, it's clearly sentient. Maybe it's lonely." The rat rested an elbow nonchalantly on the plant's jaws. "It's the only intelligent, native creature on the whole plateau."

Xoota shrugged. "Well, it's making itself handy." The quoll dragged the alien boxes over to the rat. "It brought me this. Teleport units, one to the other. Close the doors and *bing.*"

"Ooh, spiffy."

"I have no idea what to use it for, but it's pretty neat." Xoota demonstrated. "You don't have to have the doors closed on the receiving unit. But closing the doors on the sending unit seems to trigger it all off. Did you have any joy with the robot?"

"Not as such." The rat looked tired, dirty, and puzzled. "Watch this."

She was wearing a blue bracelet taken from one of the long-dead bodies in the forest. Shaani held up her wrist so the robot could see it. "Robot, report."

"Unit G6, Bliss Acres. Fully functional. No stores in hoppers." The voice of a patient elderly man came from a speaker on the robot.

Shaani nodded. "Robot, identify me."

"Identity level 2, military."

The rat pointed a finger. "Robot, please go that way for ten meters."

"Negative. Requires password or civil maintenance ID level 3 or above."

The lab rat waved her wrist toward Xoota. "He won't listen. I can't budge him. When I try dragging him, he fights me." Shaani sighed. "But we *do* now know these bracelets are identifiers of some kind. The higher the rank, the greater the number of stripes."

It was not a total loss. The ID bracelets might be useful. The mammals all took one. Shaani watched the robot heading back into its shed and shook her head in annoyance.

They headed back to the path, lugging their baskets of charcoal. The plant lumbered along behind them, still dragging the chairs and windows from the ancient ship. When they reached the path, Xoota set down her load and waved to the plant in thanks.

"Um, thank you. It's all right. We can take them from here." The plant seemed confused.

Xoota cleared her throat. "It's okay. We don't need to bother you anymore. You can—well, you know—go back to the jungle or whatever."

The plant hung its toothy heads, looking sad and dejected. It then gathered up the chairs and pointed up the path toward the waterfall.

Shaani came over and made a noise of sympathy. "Aww, I think it wants to come with us."

"Shaani, he's a giant carnivorous plant."

"That doesn't mean it's not a worthwhile person." The lab rat tickled the vast plant under one toothy chin. "What's up? Are you a bit lonely up here?"

Xoota wriggled on the hook. *"Shaani.* How are we going to keep it? What if it eats us all in the night?"

"It won't eat us. We'll just remember to keep it fed." The rat cosseted the plant, which clearly liked the attention. "We can make a tub of compost for him to stand in. He can sleep down in the hold."

Xoota shook her head, giving in. "If it eats my budgerigar, I'll chop it into kindling."

"It'll be fine. Anyway, we could use an extra hand on the crew. Well, an extra tentacle. Or vine . . ." said Shaani as she led the way off to the waterfall. "Right, on we go. Last leg and all that."

The sunset was spreading glorious mauve and orange fingers all across the sky. The crew of the *Sand Shark* made their way gratefully up the path, toward Wig-wig and the beautiful swimming hole next to the waterfall. They could swim, get clean, wash clothing, eat fruit. Xoota looked up to the cool curtain of the waterfall and smiled.

A thought came into her mind.

"Shaani, do you think the teleporter might be a way to get water to the ship? You know, send it load by load to the tanks?"

"I suppose it must have enough range." The rat was black as soot from head to toe. "Now that is a sterling idea." She clapped Xoota on the shoulder.

Wig-wig welcomed them with a fruit fest and a joyous dance as they all returned to him. The crew of the *Sand Shark*—plus one three-headed carnivorous plant—sat down to eat, to relax, and watch the desert turn slowly soft and cool with night.

. . . . .

Hours later, sitting on a rock together, wet, clean, and fed, Xoota and Shaani watched the new moon rise. The quoll lay with her head pillowed in her arms, waggling her pink feet. Shaani lay back and enjoyed the sight of the fish flying through the trees.

Behind them, the plant played with Wig-wig. They seemed to have become good friends. Xoota rolled her head to watch the weird pair at play and gave a sigh. "We do seem to collect the weirdest strays."

The rat held aloft a finger. "True science is simply the gift of having an open mind."

"Is that a quote?"

"If you want to quote it. I made it up." The rat sighed.

Back at the waterfall, Wig-wig was using the plant's leaves as springboards, bouncing up and down on it like a trampoline.

Xoota regarded the plant with a frown. "Shaani, what are we going to call the plant? I mean, we can't just keep calling it 'The Plant.' "

"Well, he has leaves. Let's call him Rustle."

The quoll nodded. "That seems fair."

. . . . .

Repairs took three more long days. The foremast was heaved back up into position. Xoota and her amazing prehensile appendages reaved blocks and spliced cables. Shaani piled rocks and mud laboriously taken from the plateau and made a makeshift forge. With bellows worked by the tireless Rustle, she stripped to her waist and heated up the brackets for the wheel mount. She bent the metal back into shape, the noise ringing out for hour after hour across the desert sands. Hauling the wheel up into place took the efforts of everyone aboard the ship. Even Wig-wig helped, crawling over all the others and exhorting them to mighty efforts. The earwigs then swarmed over the new coupling, splicing electric cables and hydraulics. Shaani made a last few welds, using her own self-generated sparks to arc weld brackets into place. She pushed up her dark goggles and looked over the results, feeling well pleased.

The *Sand Shark* was in fine shape. She had tanks filled with fresh water, thanks to the little teleporter units. The ship had a load of sun-dried fruit, dried flying fish, and dried chips made from polka-dotted bananas. With the wheels and running gear repaired, they were finally ready to go. What was more, they could make a cup of tea in the kitchen and teleport it straight through to the teleportation cubby in the control cabin. After so long stuck in the sands, the *Sand Shark* was once again in running trim.

As dawn slowly lit the eastern skies, the ship set sail once more. Xoota backed the ship slowly out of the sand heap, all eight wheels working perfectly. She drove around the massive sky island until wind came blowing past the hull. The main and fore gaff-topsails rose up the masts. The tall ship creaked as the masts took the strain with ease. Shaani watched it all with a discerning eye. She signaled to Benek and Rustle, who hauled ropes to raise the topsails and bright, triangular jibs. The wheels hummed as the ship's speed built, and she leaned beautifully into the breeze. With her deck tilting and her course running smooth, the *Sand Shark* headed northeast, speeding out across the desert sands.

It was damned good to be moving again.

They sailed the sands by day, rolling along beneath a flawless desert sky. Each dawn saw them sailing through the blue world of predawn, the desert breeze sharp and smelling of dust and cool, clean sands. They rode along the lines of dunes, climbing up and speeding down, up and down, the electric motors carrying her in the wind shadow of the valleys. After three days, they emerged onto flatter, red sands with a sparkle of quartz. Familiar stands of withered grass and smoke bush dotted the parched ground. The ship rode fine and fast along the ground, putting long kilometers behind her.

The crew had sorted themselves out into a comfortable life. Shaani and Xoota took turns driving. Wig-wig ran inspections of the rigging and the hull systems. Even Benek occasionally took part, taking charge of the nighttime guard.

Rustle the plant seemed perfectly at ease with the whole strange voyage. He set up camp in the hold beside Budgie, often sitting in a tub of dirt and leafing through any books that held pictures. But his favorite place was on the deck, right up behind the control cabin. He loved to ride along with one of his heads sticking over the side of the ship, his face to the wind and his tongue hanging out. He was strong enough to raise entire sails without using winches, and seemed to have a knack for understanding Shaani's nautical babble. In the evening, he folded himself up inside his own leaves to sleep, looking as peaceful as a baby.

A three-headed, carnivorous baby . . .

They spent long days sailing across the sands, with Shaani carefully noting course and speed. Evenings were whiled away beneath the aurora australis, with Shaani playing a tin whistle while the earwigs danced. The days blended one into the other, turning into a pleasurable blur.

Late at night, Shaani drew lines on maps, jotting sums onto a pad of homemade paper. Xoota lay in bed and watched her taking care of them, tirelessly working her magic to keep her ship on course.

They were in good hands. Xoota smiled and went to sleep.

■ ■ ■ ■ ■

On a morning where Xoota's alpha mutation had left her covered with quills that perforated her damned bedding and made her usual clothes unwearable, the ship came up to a strange, straight line drawn through the sand.

Xoota messed around with an old blanket, trying to make herself some sort of covering that might last the day. Wig-wig came scuttling in thorough the windows, waving his little feet in hello.

"Hi-hi, spotty quoll."

"Hello, Wig-wig." Xoota ended up belting her makeshift clothing with rope and string. "What's up?"

"Something is in the way. Shaani say you should come and see."

"I'll be right there." Boots were out of the question, so Xoota had to content herself with rope sandals. "Damn it. Okay, I'm coming."

The quoll tromped her way forward to the control cabin and swung inside to find Shaani at the wheel, cautiously slowing the ship.

Xoota squinted at the visible line drawn across the nearby desert, trying to make sense of the sight.

Shaani flicked her a quick glance. "Eww. Quills?"

"Yeah, I know, I know." Xoota grumbled. There was some omega ale left; if she drank the stuff, it might hasten a change into something more convenient. "What's this?"

"Not sure. Benek spotted it." Shaani changed course to close with the line at a shallower angle. "Whatever it is, it's straight and level."

Xoota made her way up on deck, passing by Rustle. Her damned quills were rattling as she walked. She found her binoculars and climbed the rigging, careful not to puncture any sails.

The line was a long, straight pipe. Concrete supports kept up above the sand. It emerged from beneath the earth a few kilometers to the west and stretched on for several kilometers to the east.

Shaani brought the *Sand Shark* to a halt some distance from the giant pipe, and lowered the sails.

The pipe was solid, perhaps a meter in diameter. Apparently it had been uncovered by the ongoing shifting of the sands. Xoota had to forgo armor. She took her crossbow, magical go-away stick, and pistol and jumped down onto the sands. Wig-wig joined her, fanning out around her to scout for enemies.

They came to the pipe, a vast piece of engineering that seemed to run forever. It never bowed, sagged, or cracked. It simply stood there, a half meter above the desert. Xoota reached out with one hand and gently touched the surface of the pipe. She found it strangely cool.

She laid her ear against the pipe, listening. Her heart soared. Water.

It was the pipe. *The* pipe. She looked around to find Shaani jogging toward her. "Shaani, it's the water pipe. It has to be."

The rat touched the pipe, listened with her ear against it, and smiled, her pink eyes alive with joy. She pulled out her navigation notes and spread them on the side of the pipe, totting up the numbers. "The numbers fit. This must be it. This goes west all the way to Watering Hole . . ."

The binoculars showed a hatch or blister on the top of the pipe perhaps a thousand meters away. The women returned to the ship, raised sails, and drifted the ship along beside the pipe. They drew up next to the hatch. The big plant and Benek peered over the side in interest as Xoota and Shaani jumped down onto the pipe and inspected the hatch. The thing was dogged down with a simple handle, but it was locked with a rusted padlock. Xoota took a crowbar and snapped off the lock. She covered the hatch with her crossbow as Shaani lifted the lid.

The sound of running water came up out of the pipe.

The pipe was clean and smooth inside. A great many power conduits were affixed to the inner walls, all utterly useless. Water gushed along the pipe, half filling it. It had a distinctly salty smell.

Shaani affixed a cup to a stick and lowered it down into the water. She pulled the cup back out, sniffed it carefully, and tasted it. She immediately spit it out. "Salt. It tastes far worse than before, utterly undrinkable."

Darwin help Watering Hole, Xoota thought.

"This problem needs to be fixed and fixed fast." Shaani looked off toward the west, clearly worried for the people who depended on the water. She stood up, cricking her back, when suddenly a bell began to ring.

Rustle was enthusiastically ringing the ship's alarm bell. He snapped his jaws in panic. Shaani flicked a look upward, and saw two huge, winged serpent shapes tumbling toward them from the sky.

Xoota saw them too. She instantly drew a bead and fired her crossbow at the leader. "Down! Everybody, down!"

The attackers made a dive at the masts, roaring through insectile mandibles that clashed hungrily. Long lines of lightning arced from eyes set deeply in their feline heads. How they didn't set their own fur-covered bodies on fire, Xoota did not know, but it made her worry they might be fireproof. One pair of beams reflected off of Benek's armor and gouged lines of fire across the deck. Shaani, equipped with her own mutant power, pointed her hand at the second monster and shot a bright line of radiation into its flank. The monster lurched aside, which caused its deadly rays to miss Xoota by a hair's breadth. Both monsters soared back upward, gaining height, far outdistancing the ship's crossbow fire.

Xoota stood and stared. "Was that a ray gun? Do they have ray guns?"

Shaani ran for the ship. "No, probably just mutations."

"Well, that's much better." Xoota swore. "Get that fire out. Hurry."

Benek was scorched and dazed. Xoota clambered back aboard her ship and hurled a bucket to Rustle, who was avoiding the fires on deck.

"Sand! Use sand." Xoota drew her pistol, readying to fire. "We'll see how they like a death ray right in the chops."

Shaani grabbed Benek, checked him in passing, then flung herself onto the ship's catapult. She began frantically working the loading crank. Shaani grabbed a bomb and simply bit off the fuse with her chisel teeth.

The monsters were already making a second attack. They came in damned fast, shooting bolts of lightning out of their eyes. Again, fire broke out on the wooden deck. Xoota felt the attack an instant before it came. She dived and rolled, coming up to shoot at the first beast as it passed. She missed and swore violently before running to put out the flames.

The second monster had dived at the mainmast. Benek rose and fired then took a savage buffet from the monster's batlike wings. It smashed him back across the decks, landing him in a tangle of armor plate against the port-side rail.

The monster made a lunge to snatch up the mainsail with its mandibles, but Rustle snapped his jaws, making the beast pull up in panic. Large plant teeth made an audible snap, taking a chunk out of the monster's tail. The monster screamed and beat a hasty retreat, flicking off into the sky.

Both monsters arced around. Wig-wig raced to Benek, who was burned and dazed. At the catapult, Shaani finally had the machine loaded. Xoota came to help her as she tracked the next attack. Shaani aimed and Xoota stood by with the glowing, red-hot lighter.

The furry serpents came speeding in, low and fast, mere meters from the sand. They closed at frightening speed. A thousand meters . . . six hundred . . . three.

Xoota touched the lighter to the fuse. She had a sudden image in her mind of the monster dodging left. "Shaani, shoot to your right."

Shaani jerked the catapult's aim aside and fired. The bomb whipped through the air, detonating in an apocalyptic blast a mere hundred yards from the ship. One monster arced away, holes shot through its wings. The other slammed down into the sand and crashed. It lay there, dazed, then scrabbled back to its feet. Benek shot the damned thing with his crossbow, making it stagger and scream. The beast took off, retreating as fast as its damaged wings could carry it, jabbering in fright to its counterpart. Both monsters veered off and headed away to the east, to where a line of hills could be seen, blue against the horizon.

Xoota seared the air behind the monsters with curses. The mainsail had a rip a meter long. There were burns scored all across the deck.

Shaani reloaded the catapult in case the monsters returned. She ran to check on Benek. "Are you all right, old thing?"

"I need no mutant ministrations." Benek sat up and removed his helmet. He looked badly injured. "I will survive. My superior powers—"

"Yes, well, let's have Wig-wig tend to you for a while. That last knock was a tad savage."

Shaani came over to Xoota, shaking her head. "I say, I thought he might have been translated to glory on that one. Did you see how far that threw him? He might have gotten a concussion."

"Fortunately he is well protected by having a small particle of brain lodged in his skull." Xoota dryly combed her antennae. "You know, I think they wanted the sail."

"Well, they can jolly well go find one elsewhere."

Xoota stamped on the last smoking embers on deck. "Can we move without the mainsail?"

"I think so."

"Right, let's get rolling before those things decide to come back."

With the deck still in chaos, Xoota raised the jib and foresail while Rustle hoisted the main. The ship began to rumble on her way, sails standing proudly. She headed east, following the pipeline off toward the distant hills.

Wig-wig came to cling in the rigging, looking east. "Where are we going, quoll lady? Are we almost there?"

"Almost there, Wig-wig." Xoota freed her hair into the wind. "East and an end to everybody's troubles." She felt her quills disappear. Thank Darwin she could go put her proper clothes on at last.

Things were looking up.

CHAPTER 10

A day later the ship encountered its first trees. At first there was simply brush—more and more and more of it, growing dense and wild, crackling beneath the wheels as the ship rolled. Grass trees stood out here and there, uncomfortably similar to those back home, with their spiky quills and their single eye atop a tall stalk. The ship gave the things a wide berth.

They lost sight of the pipe as it dipped back beneath the ground. Soon there were short, dense myrtle trees growing all around the brush, little hives of wasps tending the plants. They reacted with violent flashes of light as the ship went by, clearly trying to chase the mighty apparition away. The *Sand Shark* rolled on, unconcerned, although driving her had suddenly become damned challenging. The hard soil had ridges and runnels; there were stumps, deep bogs of brushwood, and loose sand. The wind was best if the ship stuck to driving along the flanks of the low stony hills.

There were trees growing in the valleys—real trees, things as tall as the big figs on the sky island. Eucalyptus trees with blue-green leaves and eerie, silver trunks. There were birds in the air along with something that looked a little like a melon, rowing through the sky on leafy paddles. Xoota and Rustle both hung their heads over the railings as small kangaroos erupted from the grass and went bounding through the trees. The two carnivores positively slathered.

"Stop. We should stop and hunt."

The sails were dropped at record speed. Xoota equipped herself in her new, alien armor, all retrofitted onto her old leathers.

Shaani emerged from the control cabin, eating a scone. "Oh, you're not going to hurt anything, are you?"

"Yep." Xoota was enthusiastically loading her crossbow. "I aim to terrorize things, send them on a horrific chase filled with angst and horror, then shoot them full of holes." She placed a hand over her heart. "Never fear. I have taken a solemn oath never to wantonly hurt another living creature—unless it is either tasty or annoying."

The white rat waggled her finger. "That is unknown wildlife, you know. It should be studied."

"I intend to check it carefully for taste and texture." Xoota lowered the rear ramp. Mounted on Budgie, she scampered out onto the dry grass. Rustle came with her, all three mouths grinning and snapping in anticipation of a decent lunch. His root clusters churned like bicycle wheels as he chased after Xoota.

The rat called out after them one last time. "Remember, don't eat anything that has a face."

Xoota called back over her shoulder as she rode past. "Don't worry, I cut the faces *off.*"

Shaani gave a sigh. She made the best of the halt and put the teakettle on.

Benek appeared on deck and frowned. "What are they doing? Scouting?"

"Foraging." The rat busied herself with tea mugs. "Ah well, it's probably good for Rustle to have fresh food. He's been eying Budgie in a very strange way these last few days."

The muscled human glared out over the weird landscape with its tall grass and green trees. "How far are we from my target?"

"Well, the timing of sunrise and sunset seems to match what you'd observed. So we're close. Within a few hundred kilometers at least. But a starport is an omega facility; it might have appeared virtually anywhere. So we might be in for a bit of a search."

Benek had a dire, intense look in his eye. "But we are close."

The rat nodded thoughtfully, pouring tea into the pot. "Oh, yes. We're decidedly closing in."

. . . . .

At the bottom of the hill, there was a gully, and the gully was well packed with trees. The whole region was far cooler than the desert. A waterhole still had muddy brown water in the bottom. The local wildlife had been scraping shallow holes in which to lounge away the heat of midday, but they had taken fright and all hastily changed their places of address.

Xoota rode up on Budgie, scanning the area for anything to shoot. She had been living on biltong and dried bugs for so long that she had almost forgotten what fresh meat tasted like.

Behind her, Rustle suddenly stuck one huge, fanged mouth through a bush, trying to surprise whatever was on the other side. He was disappointed to find nothing but grass and dirt. He uprooted a whole bush to see if anything was hiding underneath. Having no luck, he thoughtfully replanted the bush, and sat tapping all three chins in thought.

They pushed through the thicket. A host of little birds went twittering off through the trees, their feathers a startling blue. They gave off a beautiful green, radioactive glow. Something was wending its way behind a fallen log. Xoota's antennae tingled, but she ignored the signal, focusing instead on the hole in her belly. She stealthily dismounted from Budgie. Crossbow in hand, she crawled on her stomach through the grass. She emerged slowly from the bushes, resting her crossbow on a chunk of fallen tree.

Behind her, a large goanna emerged and clamped its jaws shut right on her tail. Xoota gave a piercing, indignant scream. She dropped her crossbow and turned around, desperately trying to latch hold of the lizard and pull it free. "Get it off! Get it off, get it off, get it off!"

Rustle reached down and simply ate the critter, chomping down on it with vast satisfaction.

Xoota looked up at him resentfully as she rubbed her stinging tail. "You'll keep."

The plant beamed back at her in satisfaction.

They labored up and out of the tree line. Another hill was before them. Several small kangaroos—complete with mutated balls of spine on their tails and armor plates down their backs—were grazing. A few rabbits loped around in the weeds.

Xoota ignored the rabbits; she was a hunter from the desert lands, and she was stalking heftier prey. Budgie made a chirping noise and immediately held back. Xoota shushed him and crept out to take aim at a kangaroo. "Now watch this, you idiots. This is how it's done."

· · · · ·

Xoota limped back to the ship some time later, her face glowering, daring anyone to say a word. Budgie and Rustle walked behind her, both smirking. Xoota held a dead rabbit swinging in one hand.

They climbed back aboard. Xoota came limping up to Shaani, clearly in some pain. Three long quills were jutting from her backside.

Shaani lowered her glasses and bent down to inspect the damage. "Yes, you really do seem to have a talent for this kind of injury."

"Shut up and pull them out before I hit you with a dead rabbit."

"As you wish." Shaani called up into the rigging. "Oh, Wig-wig. We have a customer."

They bent Xoota over a deck chair with her backside high and began to pluck out the quills. Xoota suffered it all with ill grace.

Shaani examined the quills with happy interest. "Well, these are impressive. Where did they come from?"

"Mutant kangaroos." The quoll was in a pouty sulk. "The damned things launch showers of them at you through the air."

"I did tell you to be careful."

"Yeah, that didn't work out so well."

"Well, at least you got a rabbit."

"Sort of. It was a kangaroo quill that impaled the dead rabbit, not a crossbow bolt," said Xoota shamefully. "I want lunch, damn it."

Shaani politely looked over to the happy, grinning plant. "Rustle, did you manage to find anything to eat?"

The giant plant opened up to proudly show off the dead goanna lizard dissolving in one of his mouths. Immensely pleased with himself, the plant then shut his trap.

"Yes, so I see. Jolly good." The sight made Shaani a bit queasy.

The last quill was plucked out of Xoota's behind. Her heart-spotted underwear would need some repairs. Shaani doused the quoll's backside with alcohol then ushered a horde of earwigs forward. "Wig-wig, the field is yours."

"Glee." Wig-wig came down from his particular nest up aloft. "Quoll botty. I fix it."

The earwigs began their healing, waving back and forth and humming while Xoota's backside took on a golden glow. Shaani sat cross-legged at the other end of her friend and offered her a cup of tea. Xoota drank with gratitude.

Shaani sipped happily at her mug. "So . . . any interesting sights in the valley?"

"Some." Xoota winced as her backside gave a twinge. "There are some strips of shorter grass on the other side of the hill. It's all mown short, clipped off at the base."

The rat mused over her tea. "I wonder if it's another gardening robot."

"Damned big one, then. The mown bit is really wide." Xoota winced again then looked back over her shoulder. "Hey, careful. That's tender territory."

"Is big territory."

"Watch it, bug."

Shaani looked thoughtfully over to the far side of the valley. "Did the mown strips seem to lead anywhere?"

The quoll tried to think. "They disappeared over the hill. Seemed to be heading sort of northeast."

"Let's cross the valley and see."

They rolled the ship slowly downhill, letting gravity do the work while they used the engines to take her up out of the shadow of the trees before they raised the sails. The ship began to move steadily, her speed a gentle twenty kilometers per hour.

The hill at the far side of the valley was oddly patterned. The knee-high grass had been mown short in long, even strips twelve meters wide. The strips ran parallel to each other, up and over the hill and out of sight. Shaani steered into the strips and followed them. The sails caught the wind beautifully at the hillcrest.

Xoota was finally able to stand after a few up-and-downhill runs. She pulled her pants back on, grudgingly thanked Wig-wig, and joined everyone clustered at the bow railings. The ship followed the strange grass strips along yet another hill to pass what looked like massive piles of dung.

At the crest of the next hill, they finally saw what had been mowing all the grass.

A dozen animals, each one six meters high and almost twice as wide, grazed sleepily. They moved forward at an ambling pace, one plodding step every few minutes without a worry in the world. On the backs of the animals, there were platforms covered with awnings. People looked to be living on the platforms; on some, families with children did family things, on others young women combed their hair (or quills, spines, tentacles, feathers, or whatever the case may have been). Young men strolled along beside the titanic animals, seeming to guide them as they climbed rope ladders up and down the beasts in shifts.

It was a whole little village on the move. The huge animals must have been carrying eighty people slowly along the grasslands.

As the natives caught sight of the sand ship, people began to run back and forth on the animal platforms, calling down to the men on foot all around the animals. The rearmost animals suddenly changed appearance as the passengers raised wooden screens around their homes.

The men on foot came in many different shapes and sizes. They were typical mutants, if such a thing could be said; some were descended from humans and some from other creatures, both familiar and completely foreign to the crew of the *Sand Shark*. Their weapons of choice were long spears fitted into spear-throwing devices called woomeras. Their most complex armor seemed to be made out of animal hide. Their technology was low, but they clearly were civilized.

Shaani was extremely excited. "It's a settlement. We must greet them in peace."

"Oh, absolutely." Xoota leaned down to mutter quietly to Wig-Wig. "Have Benek load the catapult, and keep the crossbows cocked and out of sight, okay?"

"Hokay."

They brought the ship to a halt far from the animals, dropping sails and putting on the hand brake. Shaani climbed up out of the control cabin to stand, waving, out of the roof. A group of the natives came forward cautiously, waving back. Shaani gave them a dapper little bow.

"Hello. Greetings. We are explorers from afar." Shaani doffed her hat, speaking with her perfect, cultured accent, absolutely positive that everything in the world could understand English, if only one's pronunciation were clear enough. "How do you do?"

One of the natives shuffled closer, and they saw it was a creature dressed in hide armor, his blue skin painted over with ritual lines and swirls of ochre. The man doffed the animal skull he wore as a hat. "Terribly well, thank you. And you?"

"Oh, topping. Quite topping." Shaani was delighted. "We've come from across the desert. Care for a spot of tea?"

"Oh." The man consulted a wristwatch. "Well, it's just gone elevenses. That would be splendid."

Xoota's antennae flopped to either side of her head. "You're kidding me . . ."

Taking it all in her stride, Shaani climbed out onto the main deck. She clapped her hands together in satisfaction as she passed Xoota. "Right. Let's get the kettle on. Hands across the wilds and all that." Shaani stuck her head into the kitchen. "Do we have any scones left?"

"I think so." Xoota pushed back her goggles, feeling bemused. "I'll just go get some." She looked anxiously at the animals up ahead. "Are you sure you want these people on board?"

"Of course." Shaani polished off the good teapot. "He's a man of letters. Surely you heard the accent?"

The native leader climbed up a rope ladder and stepped onto the main deck. He proffered a long, blue hand to Shaani and made a bow. "Tadash, madam. And a very good day to you."

"Good day to you, sir. I'm Shaani. Welcome aboard."

Shaani shook hands with the man and led him around the deck, pointing out the operative principles of her vessel. Following more cautiously came six warriors, all armed with spears and wooden clubs. They kept their distance from Rustle, the three-headed plant.

Benek looked them over, frozen faced; there was not a pure human in the lot of them. Xoota and Wig-wig welcomed the visitors aboard.

They took tea along with dried fruit and fresh scones under the awnings by the deckhouse. The leader of the native delegation—who had an extraordinary handlebar mustache—was really quite the gentleman. He refused a chair and sat cross-legged on the deck, drinking tea with real satisfaction.

His accent was the male counterpart to Shaani's. He spoke cordially as he brushed at his mustache. "Good lord. So you've actually crossed the great desert?"

"Bit of an epic journey, really." Shaani passed the scones. "Storms, doldrums, thirst, mutant monsters—all that sort of thing."

"Jolly well done, though."

"Oh, ta."

Shaani made the introductions, making sure her guests were all fed. "This is our gallant captain, Xoota. Benek, the Overman. Our hive-mind friend over there is Wig-wig, and the three-headed chap with the satisfied grin is Rustle."

The tribe called themselves Plodders, named after the mutant wombats on which they made their homes. The wombats trundled ever so slowly over the plains, chomping on grass. Every few weeks they telekinetically dug deep wells and drank vast amounts of water. The wombats lived their own lives, apparently unbothered by the beings who used them as ambulatory homes.

Xoota was puzzled. "But why live on top of giant wombats?"

"I suppose it's convenient. They're big enough to be safe from predators. They make an excellent base for spotting game. They reach water regularly . . ." Tadash sipped thirstily. He seemed to have quite a capacity for drinking tea, which he preferred with extra milk. "And they have telekinetic hands to help them gather grass. Can be a bit of a shock for anyone who decides to charge the herd and give us any trouble."

"I see." Xoota could only shrug. It seemed a reasonable life-style, in a twisted kind of way. "But you've contacted people from our side of the desert before?"

"Oh no, never. Quite impossible. Nothing that enters the desert can live."

"Then how is it that you talk just like Shaani?"

"Well, I am the tribe's archivist. Their scholar." The man sipped more tea. "The accent is passed down as a tradition."

"Quite right, old bean. Where would we be without it?" Shaani passed a plate. "Biscuit? They're wattle seed. Rather good."

They all shared tea and biscuits; even Rustle munched one or two. Shaani poured the tea and made a most genial hostess.

"Tadash, old man, it's lovely to chitchat, but we're on a mission of great importance. We're looking for a pipe, a long pipe that runs east to west. Have you seen any ancient ruins around here? Giant machines, buildings . . . ?"

The man elegantly twirled the ends of his mustache. "Oh, indeed. There are some massive places, rumored to be to the far east, the north, the south. Lost cities of the ancients. But they lie at the heart of radioactive wastelands or inside areas torn by nightmares."

"Nothing closer? Surely you know the area well," Xoota said.

The natives murmured together. Tadash nodded as he spoke to his companions then answered Xoota carefully.

"Ah. Yes, my chaps say they have spied a few buildings in the scavenging runs. They're to the north, by the coast, about twenty kilometers away. But there are always a great many bones around the buildings. Usually fresh bones—fresh kills. They try to avoid the place completely."

Xoota twiddled her whiskers in careful thought. "What sort of ruins?"

"Terra tech. Large cylinders and pipes. The whole thing emits steam." Tadash looked at them quizzically. "Is that why you've come?"

"It might be. We'll have to see." Shaani checked the teapot then refilled it. "Were there any other ancient places in this area? Or, say, anywhere in a radius of about a hundred kilometers?"

"There were a few buildings that could be seen beyond the other ruins. But it was too far to walk. We rarely go more than a day's march from the plodders."

It was all useful information. Xoota was happy to move the ship onward, but Shaani leaned in for a quiet conference with her behind her hand.

"We should offer them something as a thank-you for the information."

"But what?" Xoota gestured to the ship. "We're really just carrying essentials."

"What about tea?"

Tea? Xoota looked somewhat hunted as she flicked her eyes left and right. "Tea? What do you mean tea?"

"Well, they clearly really like it. It seems to be highly valued."

"How much tea do we have?"

The rat looked pained. "Um . . . Well, we have three boxes left. Two of the longhorn, and one of the 'strontium special reserve.' About three hundred mugs?"

It was a real sacrifice for Xoota. She bit her lip then gave a sigh. "All right. Give them one box of longhorn." She grumbled.

"Let's see if we can trade them some dried fruit for fresh meat. Maybe I can at least get a steak dinner out of this."

As it turned out, the *Sand Shark*'s crew was treated to a very, very good dinner. The tribesmen were excellent hosts, and the strangers who arrived in a mighty sand rigger were definitely a sensation. The people piled off the titanic herbivores, dug fire pits, and had a joyous evening meal. There were roasted kangaroos, roasted birds, flatbread, and desert plums. The locals made a weird, fizzy drink out of fermented wombat milk. Shaani drank rather too much of it and held forth before an enthralled crowd, telling them stories of the leaps of science that man and rat had once achieved. She ended up dancing the Plodder dances and was painted up with color as an honorary member of the tribe. In the end Xoota had to carry her back to the ship before she embarrassed herself any further.

She waved a hand happily back toward the Plodders as she was carried back to the ship, her hat on backward. "F-field work. First contact with new cultures. We are explorers."

Xoota rolled her eyes. "Yes, indeed. Explorers." Who would have thought fermented wombat milk would be so potent. "If you need to throw up, do it now, oh mighty explorer. We're putting you to bed."

All in all, it had been a truly excellent dinner. Rustle flopped down on the deck, his mouths crammed full of meat. Even Wig-wig was replete. He climbed up into Rustle's leaves and vines and fell happily asleep.

In all the time the party had lasted—many hours under a starry sky—the wombats had been snoozing. They made vast, warm, furry silhouettes that shimmered in the firelight. With her crew asleep, Xoota took a last turn around the ship. She seated herself on a deck chair, still with a crossbow at her side, determined to stand guard.

It was a bold attempt but doomed to failure. Belly full and the Plodder songs all around her, she fell happily asleep.

. . . . .

The next dawn saw the *Sand Shark* set sail once more. She passed the Plodder tribe, whose big wombats snoozed the night away but started walking again at the very crack of dawn. With red eyes and a face-splitting yawn, Xoota took the wheel, guiding the ship northeast. They ranged across a broad and grassy valley, zigzagging slowly into the wind.

The ground grew more sandy. The eucalyptus trees gave way to leathery, white paperbarks. Xoota used the engines to propel the ship over an old, dry watercourse and grumble up the opposing hill. Her sails flapped as the breeze shifted fitfully north and west.

The air had taken on a strange, sharp smell—a salty, almost chemical scent. Xoota drove with the windows open, puzzled by the breeze from the north but enjoying the cool. Driving took more of her attention as the breeze increased and the ship jounced along as they tacked.

Xoota heard a groan from behind her, and the quoll gave a malicious little smile. "Good morning, oh rat of infamy."

Shaani—feeling very sick—spoke with a precious, fragile dignity. "I believe I . . . I acted in the best interests of . . . intercultural felicity."

"Well, the dance around the fire was certainly memorable. As was teaching the Plodders that sea shanty."

"Which sea shanty?"

" 'The Good Ship Venus.' "

Shaani sat down in the codriver's chair. "Oh dear."

"Never mind. They appreciated it." Xoota kept her eyes on the way ahead, which was becoming more rugged. "We're currently making about twenty kph. Tacking on a general course northeast. We've come about twenty-eight kilometers since dawn."

"That's good." Shaani waved a hand at the earwigs, who were playing a game up in the rigging. "Wig-wig dear, I believe I might need your assistance."

The earwigs gathered to do their duty.

Shaani caught a look at her painted fur in the side mirrors and made a face. "Oh dear Darwin, is that an alpha mutation?"

"No, no. Just body paint." Xoota raised a finger. "I think you might have damage reflection today. I tried to smack your butt, and I sort of smacked mine instead."

"Oh." Shaani rested her head against the cool, soothing metal of the cabin door. She opened one bloodshot eye. "Why did you try to smack my bottom?"

"It was there."

Wig-wig did his soothing dance; mild poisoning was no real problem for the talented little empaths to cure. Shaani made a noise of gratitude, and nursed a jumbo mug of tea.

The rocks ahead of the ship were becoming more frequent and more jagged. Tangles of stunted paperbark trees blocked the valleys. Xoota brought the ship to a hilltop, saw what was ahead, and called out to Rustle to drop sail. She hauled on the hand brake and brought the ship lurching to a halt.

"That's it. That's the end of the trail."

"Oh." Shaani opened one pink eye. "Trouble?"

"Terrain. It's gotten too tangled ahead." Xoota rose. "I don't want to risk us getting jammed. I'll take Budgie out for a scout around and see what I can see."

"Take Wig-wig as top cover." Shaani made herself lurch to her feet. "Let's get everyone armed and topside."

Xoota filled her drinking flasks with cold tea then headed out of the cabin. Benek, fully armed and armored, met her on the deck. He was annoyingly intense.

"Are we headed to the ancient spaceport? To the cryogenic facility?"

"We are, we are—with just a little detour first." Xoota slung her shield over her back and checked the set of her cog mace and her pistol. "Just stay with the ship."

"Another pointless side mission?" Benek flexed his fists in anger. "My affairs should take priority."

"We're in the right area, Benek. We just have to scout around." Xoota hoisted her saddle onto Budgie's back. "Keep your pants on."

She rode Budgie down the rear ramp, enjoying the saddle once again. The bird needed a good run to keep him in condition. Xoota breathed the air, sensing a strange throb and pulse like a distant heartbeat that filled the world. She put her brand-new headset on her head. Shaani had been unable to adapt the ancient armored helmets to either of their skull shapes, but she had at least been able to scavenge out the radio sets and earphones. Xoota tapped her microphone. "Shaani, hello? Does this thing work?"

"Working well." The rat's voice had barely a crackle of static. "Roger."

Xoota tapped at her earphone. "Roger? Who's Roger?"

"It stands for 'R'—for 'received.' It's radio talk. Ancient style." The rat's voice sounded exasperated. "Do you even listen to the orientation lectures I give you?"

"Not if they're silly, no." The quoll waggled her finger at empty air, forgetting no one could see her. "Let's just forget all this ancient kack and just talk normally."

"Oh, all right . . ." Shaani's voice sounded full of grumbles. "Just make sure you stay in touch."

"Right." Xoota waved her hand to Wig-wig, who spread his many wings and whirred happily overhead. "We're moving out, headed north."

Budgie trotted through the strange, spindly undergrowth. The ground beneath his claws seemed to be mainly composed of sand and broken shells. The spindly grass grew everywhere in large, erratic bunches, often dotted with tiny, white snails. Xoota and Budgie made their way up over a hill, then off along a sandy gully. The earwigs flitted ahead from bush to bush, scouting for danger. As the trail became steeper, Budgie had to pick his path and hop from rock to rock. Xoota reined him in as Wig-wig came fluttering stealthily back to her and settled on her shoulder.

"Wig-wig sees a building."

"Good."

"But there be bones. Lots of bones—and an animal."

The quoll dismounted quietly and followed Wig-wig through the scrub, using the clumps of grass as cover. Xoota crawled on her belly beneath the branches, moving silently across the sand. She evaded one bush that looked a tad hungry and saw it quiver in disappointment. There was a series of buildings on the crest of a low, level hill. A giant, oblong structure had been festooned with pipes and massive tubes. Some steam drifted out of the roof. Xoota could see that one of the pipes attached to the structure had broken and was gushing water into the building, spilling it onto a concrete floor that seemed to be rent wide with a dark, open crack.

To the west, the great desert pipeline they had followed led into the ground. As Xoota followed what should have been its trajectory, she reasoned that the source of flowing water emptied right into the pipeline. They had found the source of Watering Hole's well. The only problem was the carrion. Several well-gnawed bodies lay around the buildings. One seemed to be humanoid; others included wallabies, sheep, and several legless things that might have been fish. The smell was damned ripe. Xoota felt her antennae quiver and reached out a hand, feeling the prickle of invisible heat.

"*Ack.* Wig-wig, be careful. It feels radioactive."

"Owie," replied the earwigs.

Just then Xoota saw the animal that had made a feast of the dead creatures as it crawled slowly among the rotting bones. Xoota tapped on her earphones, hearing a nasty crackle from the local radiation. "Hello, Shaani?"

"Hallo. Yes, we're listening."

"I have an animal of some sort here."

"What is it?"

"Star shaped, heavily armored, it's got some sort of shell about four meters across." Xoota watched the creature carefully. It moved with painful slowness on little tubular feet beneath its carapace. From what she could tell, it seemed to be feeding on the carrion. "There's lots of dead animals around here. I think it's a scavenger, but I'm going to keep well clear.

"We've found the buildings," Xoota continued, looking again at the structure. "There's a huge spring here. It might be feeding into the desert pipeline."

"You don't think the star-shaped thing might have killed all those creatures?"

"No, not unless it has a mental power or a beam weapon of some kind. It's pretty slow."

"We'll come out to you." Shaani's voice was all business. "Wait where you are."

Wig-wig flew back to lead the others to the buildings. Xoota remained in hiding, using her binoculars to examine the ruins. There were several big, square buildings with tanks that occasionally vented steam. A quiet but steady hum gave the hint of some ancient machinery inside the main building. And from there, a long chute led over to some derelict silos.

Xoota continued to watch as the others took their time in arriving, not having the advantage of riding on budgie back. The star-shaped creature wrenched apart the skull of a cadaver and began to idly crunch away at its meal with a thoughtful air. It could have been philosophizing about life, for all Xoota knew. When Shaani arrived—looking ridiculous in her new armor, her straw hat, and her insane body paint—she carried her beloved fusion-powered chainsaw. Benek clanked up behind her with Rustle in tow. The plant stood out like a sore thumb, rising a meter above the brush. So much for concealment, she thought.

Xoota quietly pointed out what she had seen about the buildings and the many interesting, well-chewed corpses as Shaani looked over the area with the binoculars.

"It's radioactive all right," said Shaani. "I can feel it. The buildings and the bodies. Definitely the bodies . . ." She had a decided talent for such things. "Well, I suppose we can just flit past that star creature and stay out of reach."

Xoota tapped at her antennae. "I have a nasty feeling about that thing. I'm not sure I trust something that eats radioactive corpses for lunch."

"True." Shaani pointed out a gully that ran around the hill. "Well, it doesn't look like it moves very fast. We can circle to the other side and see if there's a way into those buildings."

The group moved off, keeping to cover as Rustle lumbered along behind them, grinning, as much as a plant can, like a carnivorous idiot at a meat buffet. He had an alpha mutation that developed that morning—some sort of hardened outer skin—and he seemed to enjoy the way he clanked and rattled. He was a less-than-ideal stealth operative, but his toothy jaws were a fair compensation.

The team moved along the sandy gully until they found the pipeline. They ducked beneath it and continued. The air began to take on a stronger smell—sharp and strangely salty—and with northerly wind came a constant surge and crash of sound. The team struggled through some bushes then came to a clearing at the top of a rise. What they saw stopped them in their tracks.

The horizon was blue. It was water as far as they could see disappearing into nothing. It was a restless blue, covered with waves that broke and rushed against a wide expanse of sand. The adventurers stood and simply stared. It was like nothing they had ever seen.

"Darwin's beard," said Xoota. Her voice was reverent, utterly hushed. She stared at the sight before her with stars in her eyes.

Shaani's voice was almost a whisper. "An *ocean.* This has to be an ocean."

They had heard of it. Tales had been told of it. The salt plains back home had supposedly once been an ocean. But that was not the same as *seeing* it, beholding the thing for the first time in their lives.

The earwigs, not blessed with fabulous distance vision, seemed enraptured as Shaani whispered to him about what she saw. Rustle waved and swayed in the breeze, seemingly enjoying the new smells. Only Benek was unmoved. He gave the ocean a look and climbed the gully edges to examine the buildings up above.

Xoota was nervous of going near the sand but Shaani wasn't. With Wig-wig settling all over her and clinging to her for security, the rat walked out onto the beach. It squeaked beneath her feet. She stood right on the shore, gazing in wonder at the sea.

"I have seen an ocean." The rat closed her eyes and felt the sea breeze caress her fur. "An ocean . . ."

Benek had no time for romanticism. He had climbed a rocky knoll and stared off along the coast. He saw something, examined it carefully, and closed his telescope in satisfaction.

Xoota, seeing the body language, reluctantly tore herself away from staring at the wide, blue sea and clambered up beside the irritating man. "What is it?"

Benek's teeth gave off a perfect, predatory gleam. "Along the coast—two kilometers. There's another building. An omega building. I have seen it before." He flicked through the printouts he'd brought all the way from Watering Hole and found the one he wanted. "Here. It's part of the remote camera network. It has to be part of the cryogenic facility. The rest might be just beyond."

Xoota looked at the photograph then took her binoculars and examined the distant building. They certainly looked similar—a squat shape mounted up on pylons, grayish green, with a fence line all around. The quoll nodded. "All right. We'll check out the ruins here above us, and then we can head off and check out this place of yours."

"My mission must take priority."

"Your mission will wait. Watering Hole can't."

Benek seemed to inflate like a massive, well-manicured toad. "I insist—"

"Benek, we'll deal with it." Xoota's temper was never the best. "Save your damned energy. Apparently you're going to need it."

Cursing under her breath, the quoll stomped back down the hill. Wig-wig was delighting himself by chasing back and forth at the edge of the ocean, fleeing en masse before the farthest reaches of the waves. He had discovered an alpha mutation that morning that manifested as blinding flashes of light, which he used to spark and twinkle as he ran back and forth, squealing happily.

Shaani tasted the seawater and spit it out at once.

Xoota raised one brow. "What?"

"Salt." The rat made a face. "This must be what's contaminating the pipe."

"Could the pipe have fractures? Maybe somehow let this stuff leak in?"

"Maybe." Shaani looked back to the buildings on the hill. "I'll have to look inside there first. That seems to be the end of the trail." The rat called out to Wig-wig and Rustle. "All right, chaps. Come along. There's some adventuring that needs to be done."

The group reluctantly left the seashore. Rustle and Wig-wig came bustling up to where the others lay in wait, watching the buildings on the hill. Xoota thought the place had a decidedly dangerous feel.

There were yet more skeletons on the ground there, the bones covered in withered chunks of rotting flesh. Shaani pulled out a rope and a hook that she used to toss and snared one of the skeletons, dragging it carefully down to where they were. Flies rose from the carrion, as did a dreadful stink. But it was the heat of radiation that made most of the team back off. Shaani, oblivious to the radiation, covered her nose and inspected the corpse.

Xoota peeked out at her from behind a rock. "Shaani, careful. It's hot."

"Oh, yes, pretty steaming. I should keep well back if I were you." Bred for science, evolved to weather the sternest of stern stuff, Shaani examined the marks on the flesh. "It's been attacked by a carnivore. Something that can cut through a rib cage. See the way the bones have been sheared clean? Probably mandibles and not fangs . . ."

"That's fascinating." Xoota could feel the radiation even from behind a stone. "Don't get your clothing all contaminated."

"Don't be such a baby." Shaani settled her straw hat, looking at the buildings. "Right. Won't be long."

"What?" The quoll blinked. "What the hell are you doing?"

"Well, I have to check out the buildings." The rat came walking back to the others, cleaning off her fingers with a handful of sand. "I can't risk you lot. Not with radioactivity all over the place. Job for a scientist, you see."

Xoota could see her point but didn't like it. She unbuckled her holster. "Well, take the gun. And run back here at the first sign of trouble."

"Of course." The rat bound the gun belt around her meager waist. "You know me. I'm the soul of caution." She lugged her fearsome chainsaw up and onto the hill. "Toodle-oo."

Xoota sighed and covered Shaani with her crossbow. Her antennae were jangling with vague warnings of alarm.

. . . . . .

Up on the hilltop, the sand was covered in a thin layer of grass, burned and mottled yellow by radiation. Shaani moved cautiously along, her chainsaw in one hand and the pistol in the other. She reached out with her senses, feeling the radio-activity that poisoned the air. It seemed to radiate from the gnawed cadavers that lay all over the ground. Shaani moved up and gave the nearest body a cursory inspection; like the other one, it had been stripped of flesh and the organs accessed by snipping open the rib cage with some kind of huge shears. The dead creature seemed to be a mutant animal of some kind. Its bulk was impressive. It had been well equipped with armor plates, tentacles, and claws. Food for thought. Whatever was killing those things certainly didn't find size to be an object. Nor apparently fangs, claws, spines, or jaws. That was possibly bad news. The rat girl heard the gush and bubble of water nearby. She reached a rusty cyclone fence and managed to wiggle underneath the ancient links. She was damned close to the buildings. The splash and patter of falling water was loud, and the ground reverberated with a weird hum.

Her radio headset suddenly buzzed and hissed in her ear. Radiation was interfering with reception, but Xoota's voice came to her through the white noise. "See anything?"

She was in no place for a conversation. Shaani lay flat and tried to whisper. "I'm at the buildings. Hush."

The place had been sturdy, a big concrete structure. Staying low to the ground, Shaani found a brass plaque fixed to the wall near one corner that read, "This desalination plant was opened by the Right Honorable Angus Young, MP." Interesting. Desalination. Moving with all the stealth she could muster, Shaani flattened herself against a wall. She edged toward a large crack in the concrete wall, from where the sound of falling water came loud and clear.

Something seemed to flap and rustle inside the ruins. Shaani clutched her weapons and worked her way ever closer to the hole in the wall.

The radio crackled yet again. ". . . moving . . . zzz . . . round the side."

Shaani felt a little cross. She hissed an urgent whisper into her headset. "Shh. Go away." The rat turned off her headset. The sound of white noise was simply too annoying.

Shaani reached to her belt, and removed an old car mirror. She edged it carefully around the corner of the wide crack in the wall and examined the space inside the building.

There were pumps somewhere deep, deep underground. They fed water up from somewhere—probably intakes out somewhere in the sea. It all came percolating up into massive containers. Then apparently it gushed out of a shattered pipeline and spilled all over the floor. She did not see vast masses of water, but it was enough to feed the distant well at Watering Hole, enough to keep a whole community alive.

Only the machinery seemed to be broken. The pumps were still gushing water, but somehow the water getting into the pipeline was salt, not fresh. Why were the machines even working in the first place? Terra tech, the things that existed before the Great Disaster, needed electricity to run, which was usually fed by power lines. Power lines, however, were long dead and gone. And yet somewhere beneath the floor, some sort of pumps were clearly still operating. There were omega relics nearby too, and omega installations typically worked by power broadcast through the airways. If there was a broadcast power station nearby, then perhaps the old Terra tech had picked up the power beams?

Well, anything that was broken could be fixed, thought Shaani. *Science ad excelsior,* and all that. She felt a surge of satisfaction and put away the mirror she'd been using to look around the corner. From somewhere high up inside the building, there came a dry, rustling, flapping kind of sound. Shaani twiddled her whiskers and redeployed her mirror, looking up into the gloomy ceiling space. Four enormous moths clung to the ceiling near several cocoons. The moths were fully two meters long and glowed with an eerie green with radiation.

Shaani blinked, flattening herself against the wall. "Oh, bother." Gamma moths.

They were clearly to blame for all the carrion around the station. Gamma moths liked to swoop down on prey, fry them with radiation, then feast on the sizzling flesh. It also explained why the desalinator was no longer working. EMP blasts from the moths would have fried any exposed electronics above ground. Shaani flattened herself against the wall and tried to think of how the hell to deal with a nest of titanic, carnivorous moths.

Xoota intruded on her thoughts. The quoll pelted across the ground, casting all caution to the wind. She waved her hands in panic at Shaani. Shaani scowled in puzzlement and went forward to meet her, holding up a finger to indicate the need for a bit of hush.

Out of breath from her sprint, Xoota grabbed onto the rat and tried dragging her away. "C-come on."

"What?" Shaani scowled. "Look, why don't you take a moment and just catch your breath?"

"Shaani, we need to get the hell out of here." Xoota said as she pointed toward the giant armored star creature rounding the corner. It moved at a determined speed, heading straight for them.

Suddenly little darts shot out from the creature's armored shell on controlled bursts of air. Shaani and Xoota made a mad dive for the ground, and the darts ricocheted off the concrete wall behind them.

Xoota fired her crossbow at the creature. The bolt bounced clean off its armored hide. Shaani leveled her pistol, thought about it, and decided to run. The pistol shots were too damned precious to waste. Being that they were each a mutant quoll and a mutant rat, it may have struck someone as funny that the two ran like rabbits, but run they did, pelting over the dry grass like hares in a hunt. They reached the fence and searched desperately for a way through. Xoota looked back to see the star creature lumbering steadily toward them.

"Use the pistol. Shoot it."

Shaani was reluctant. "I haven't figured out how to recharge the batteries. We might need the pistol for emergencies."

"Then throw a bomb."

A bomb would instantly wake up the sleeping gamma moths. "Not advisable."

"Then what?"

The fence disappeared. Rustle had come happily forward and had simply ripped the wire away. They ran like hell, with Rustle ambling contentedly along beside them.

Darts whirred overhead. Two stuck harmlessly in Xoota's new armored suit. Another stuck into Rustle, who seemed immune to whatever effect they might have. He kept bumbling happily along, finally joining the others as they sheltered over the far edge of the hill.

The damned star creature was a juggernaut. It crashed down a section of fence and followed on the same path, apparently tracking them by scent. The team ran back to another sand hill closer to the beach, only to see the mammoth star monster come blundering down the hill, closing in on them relentlessly.

Budgie blinked at the thing and made a squawk. Everyone crowded back, ducking to avoid more showers of poisoned darts.

Shaani pondered.

"We can just outrun it."

"Then how do we deal with the gamma moths and fix the pump?"

Xoota popped up and fired another crossbow bolt at the huge monster. Again her shot bounced off. "Damn that thing. It's armored like rock— Wait. What about gamma moths?"

Shaani pondered. "Ah, but only on the upper surface. If we could flip it over . . ."

"Not really an option." Xoota grabbed Shaani by the hand and tugged her. The star monster was already topping the hill. The adventurers moved hastily back to yet another sand hill, easily keeping their distance. But the monster showed no inclination to go away. It kept following them, walking on its tubular feet and clashing a set of rather nasty jaws beneath its shell. Xoota gave a curse and led the retreat back to yet another sand hill.

Wig-wig came the rescue. He happily bustled forward, various earwigs waving their antennae at the others. "Not to worry. Wig-wig will fix it."

Xoota blinked in astonishment. "You? How?"

"Easy as pie." The earwigs were already flowing off in the direction of the star monster. "Get ready."

"Ready for what?" Xoota called out after the earwig swarm. "Wig-wig?"

The horrible star creature was already topping the next hill, its long, armored tentacles with their countless tube feet were questing their way over the edge. Wig-wig ran fearlessly right up into the creature's path.

Wig-wig had one of Shaani's pipe bombs and a box of her homemade matches. Shaani looked at what the earwigs were up to, and felt a touch dismayed.

"Oh dear."

The earwigs stuck a pipe bomb into the sand, lit the fuse, and fled, jumping and skipping as they ran. "Glee."

Oh, hell. Xoota ducked. Benek scowled. The star creature blundered right over the top of the fizzing bomb. There was a sudden detonation, and the sand seemed to buck beneath the adventurers. A shower of monster parts flew up into the air.

"Run away. Run away." The earwigs came racing past, fleeing as fast as they could go. Inside the pump building, gamma moths screeched in blood lust as they awakened. Everyone took one quick look at the old building then ran like hell. Boots, claws, feet, and tendrils churning at the sand, the adventurers ran wildly to the beach, took a hard right turn, and followed Wig-wig into a tangled stand of trees. They dived beneath some bushes, with Rustle uprooting several shrubs and holding them up so he could pretend to be a tree.

The gamma moths came fluttering up out of the ancient buildings, hungry for prey. The adventurers sheltered in a stand of trees, ready for combat. The gamma moths flapped around, hindered by the bright sun. They blundered in the air, blazing bright with radiation, stabbing bolts of gamma rays into random bits of sand.

One moth veered over the stand of trees. It fired blindly down into the plants, sheathing the place with radiation. The shot missed the adventurers and instead hit an innocent tree. The tree withered and died, nearby bushes blistered, and a sand weevil twenty meters away suddenly developed teleportation genes and dodged madly away.

One of the other moths had found the dead star monster spread lavishly around on the sand. The moths instantly converged on the steaming corpse. They picked up the tastiest chunks and carried them off toward their home in the pump house, disappearing from view.

Once sure that the gamma moths had gone, Wig-wig slowly emerged from hiding, one antenna at a time. "See? Easy."

Xoota eyed the insects with a dire glare. "You'll keep."

They sat together in the shade, sharing a water bottle—except for Benek, who kept fastidiously to his own. They all looked up toward the ruined desalination plant in pondered.

Xoota scratched beneath her chin. "You saw the pumps?"

Shaani nodded. "Oh, yes. They're on the fritz, but I'm sure they can be mended. You know, a bit of elbow grease and the old scientific spirit." She thought wistfully of a cup of tea. "The problem is, getting the current residents *out* so we can work on the jolly thing."

Xoota sucked her fangs. She clearly had an idea. "Not a problem. I think I can help you with that."

"Really?"

"Oh, absolutely. I'm a genius." Xoota patted Shaani on the shoulder. "Right, well, it won't work until sundown. So let's check out the beach then head back to the ship for a cup of tea."

"Ah, good." The rat stood and worked the kinks out of her tail. "What a sterling idea."

CHAPTER 11

"All right. Are we ready?" Xoota made a last check over the empty beach. "Everybody?"

A chorus of yes noises came from all around her in the dark. The sounds were muffled, and the nighttime surge and hiss of the surf on the beach seemed somehow louder. The beach at night was a strange place, where shadows seemed remarkably dark and the vast ocean was utterly black, except for tiny winks of light as waves foamed against the shore.

Xoota cast a last look up at the hill where the gamma moths lived then knelt down. She struck a match and set fire to the piles of kindling she had jammed beneath a heap of wood. She traveled around the pile, spreading the flames. Once she was sure that the bonfire would catch, the quoll ran and dived into a pit she had dug into the sand. She covered herself with a piece of old sack and lay low with her pistol in one hand.

Around the bonfire, they had placed several figures, all dressed in clothing and made to look as though they were sleeping. Shaani's music box happily blared out an ancient song to attract attention; she said it was one of the great classics from the dark ages of 1982.

They lay quietly waiting for the moths. They would be radio silent; EMP from gamma moths would fry their gear like bacon, anyway. Her antennae quivering, Xoota scanned the dark skies with her nocturnal eyes, hoping that Benek had remembered to put his night goggles on.

Quite suddenly a bolt of purple radiation stabbed down from the skies. One of the figures by the fire burst apart, clothing afire. A huge moth plunged down on it from above, its mandibles open in a bloodcurdling scream. It tore at its victim, ripping the burning cloth aside to find nothing but wet sand stuffed into the old clothes. The creature gave a screech of fury, its whole body blazing bright with lethal radiation. Still, Xoota held her peace.

A second moth plunged from above and slammed into one of the other decoys. It tore it apart with its claws to a similar result.

"Now!" Xoota shouted as she threw off her camouflage.

From inside their sandpit blind, Shaani gripped a length of insulated wire. She shot a spark down the line and into the pipe bombs hidden in the sand near the bonfire. The bombs exploded with a deafening blast. The concussion hurtled one moth into the fire, sending it tumbling and burning. The second giant insect simply disintegrated into grizzly chunks. Xoota and Shaani both ducked the shower of sand then emerged to desperately search the skies.

Benek rose from a nearby sand hill and bellowed a warning. His night goggles had spotted something up above. "Move!" He fired his crossbow. Seconds later a bolt of radiation seared down from the skies. It clipped Shaani, who ignored it. Xoota threw herself to one side; took aim at a massive, black shape that swept overhead; and fired her pistol.

A bright purple beam shot out and struck the gamma moth that swooped above her. She blew its head clean off. The body gave off a mad blaze of radiation and blundered off into the wilderness. Xoota shook her head, her eyes dazzled by the flashes of radiation in the darkness, but there was no time to recover. Another death bolt stabbed down from above.

She tried to dive aside, but a gamma moth flashed past, smacking into her with its wings. Xoota felt radiation burn her, almost crippling her with pain. She leveled her pistol but saved the shot. The moth had disappeared in the night.

As she looked down the beach, lights suddenly showed the outline of a man, dancing clumsily around. A gamma moth fired from above, and the man seemed to swirl and tumble, dodging aside as the moth flew down, hoping to crash into its prey.

Glowing happily with his alpha bio lights, Wig-wig flew apart. He had used his many parts to assume the shape of a man, but a second later, he was nothing but a cloud of black specks in the dark. The moth crashed hard into the ground, where it was easy pickings for Rustle, who emerged from his sand trap and chomped it in his jaws.

"Oh, hell no," exclaimed Xoota. She had told the damned plant to keep clear. She ran to Rustle and smacked him behind his bulging head, hammering him with the flat of her hand.

"Drop it. Drop it. Bad. Bad Rustle. Bad." Finally Rustle's jaws came open. A dead moth toppled out onto the sand. Xoota hauled the plant well aside, already feeling sick and faint from its still-potent fallout.

Shaani came running with her little medical kit open. She yanked down Xoota's pants, found a patch of backside, and pushed a spray injector against her skin. The injector hissed as it sprayed antiradiation meds into her. The lab rat looked at her friend with anxiety. "There. Sit still. Let it work. Get all your gear off and wash it in the ocean." She reloaded her injector and found a patch of Rustle's shiny bark that seemed far softer than most. She sprayed it with the drug, hoping the damned thing would work on plants. "Rustle, are you all right?"

The plant looked rather sick; clearly radioactive, killer moth was not part of his regular diet.

Shaani grabbed her two patients and charged them toward the beach. "Right, in the water, both of you. Wash off then come out, get naked, and get dry." She called back to Benek and Wig-wig. "Stay vigilant, chaps. Oppenheimer only knows what else might be out here. We'll rinse off and race back to the ship."

The rat stripped off herself then Xoota. The dizzy quoll felt the ancient medicines surging through her veins. Shaani, Xoota, and Rustle splashed into the freezing cold ocean, feeling the waves pull and suck at them. Shaani dunked Xoota's head, making sure any radioactive particles were washed well clear.

When Xoota surfaced, she spit out water, blinking salt water from her eyes. "You see? A perfectly brilliant plan."

"Quite." Shaani dunked the quoll under water yet again. "Now do be quiet and just wash."

· · · · ·

The end of a titanic quest was finally at hand; the ancient desalination plant that fed water (albeit accidentally) all the way to Watering Hole had finally been found. The adventurers occupied the site in the morning, dragging food and drinking water over from the ship. Radioactive carrion was hooked by grappling ropes and dragged away into the distant sand hills.

The dark, gloomy pump buildings were littered with old bones. There were several pupae up on the ceiling, each one about a meter and a half long, wrapped in radioactive, glowing silk cocoons. Shaani gave them a cursory look and declared that it would be at least a week until they depupated and turned into lethal moths. She then ignored the cocoons completely and began crawling all over the ancient machinery.

Somewhere below the ground, big pumps were working. There had once been an inspection tunnel that led down to the pump rooms, but it was completely filled with the salt water that came cascading up out of the top of the broken pipes and flowed onto the concrete floor. Apparently it all drained away into the desert "power" pipeline; it certainly wasn't damaging the pumps.

The problem was the salt, tons and tons of salt.

The plant seemed to work by superheating seawater and condensing the steam into pure water, which was then fed into the main pipes. The salt was sluiced off to a conveyor and into hoppers on the far side of the hill. But since the gamma moths had fried the machinery, the salt was no longer carried off on a conveyor belt; instead, it had piled up at the head of the belt, cascaded down onto the floor, and immediately mixed itself with the water that bubbled all over the concrete. The remixed salt water then sped off down the desert pipe. It was a simple enough fix in its way: just get the conveyor belt moving once again.

There were deep drifts of salt all over the floor. The hard crystals had jammed the conveyor belt and frozen it solid. Xoota, the mighty arboreal quoll, was voted to work high above the ground and chip the mechanism free of encrusted salt. Benek and Rustle were deputized to shovel the salt away from the pump house floor. Shaani and Wig-wig bustled up into the machinery to check out the electrical wiring and set things to rights once more.

The work up above the ground was dirty, parched, and damned unpleasant. The salt had hardened like concrete, and freeing the conveyor belt was no mean feat. Wig-wig bustled around, high up in the air, clearing the main mechanism of salt, rust, and old birds' nests. Shaani and Xoota toiled all through the heat of the day, ending up scorched and burned by salt for their troubles.

Down on the factory floor, much of the salt had solidified as hard as rock. Benek regarded the horrible mass with his fists on his hips, as if seeing it as a personal insult. He then began hacking at the bottom of the salt stacks. Rustle watched him with interest, making no move whatsoever to help.

After an hour, Benek pulled out of the hole he had been digging for himself. The plant was watching him, smiling with all three mouths, wonderfully entertained.

Benek glared at the creature resentfully and wiped himself down with a towel. "What are you grinning at, beast?"

One of the plant's heads turned to look at the huge salt mass, then back at Benek.

The human haughtily took up his pick and shovel. "Well, if you have a better idea, I'd like to see you try it." Benek went back to digging.

Rustle ambled off and began drawing something in the sand.

Half an hour later, Xoota came slithering down behind the massive salt hoppers to find Benek. She was wearing nothing but her pants and a halter. "Benek? Benek. Oi! Stop digging."

The human prized free a chunk of rock salt and flicked a sweaty glance at the quoll. He scowled at the sight of her wearing almost nothing but her spotty fur. "You are underdressed."

"I've been working." The quoll girl scowled. "Quit looking at my pouch."

The human sniffed. "I have no interest in your . . . your marsupial accoutrements." The man turned back to his work. "What do you want?"

"Well, you can stop now. No need to dig."

The man kept on hacking away at the salt pile. "Why?"

"We're about to fix the problem."

Benek stopped, sweat slathered, salt burned, and exhausted. He looked blankly up at Xoota. "How?"

Rustle stood beaming away with his triple grin above the salt piles. Shaani had just finished planting pipe bombs beneath the mass. She waved everyone into cover then held up a copper wire in her hand.

"Fire in the hole."

Everyone ducked. A triple boom crashed through the building. Salt chunks went flying through the air. The entire mass shattered, flying up into the air in chunks, shards, and choking dust.

Rustle used an old hose to blast the remnant salt chunks out of the building and off down the hill. Benek glared at the plant, set aside his shovel, and walked away.

. . . . .

Half an hour later, Shaani clambered up into the desalination plant. She touched a few wires together, made some sparks, and suddenly the machinery began to hum. Some salt came crashing down from the machine to land on the conveyor belt. The belt moved slowly, carrying the salt clear of the outlet. It then stopped, waiting for the next load of salt.

Shaani looked it over and called down happily from above. "That's it. It's working."

Xoota yelled back up. "The belt stopped moving."

"It only moves when the salt builds to a certain weight. It should be fine." Still covered in paint from her native celebrations two nights before, the rat gathered up her tools. On the roof behind her, the gamma moth pupae still hung from the ceiling.

Xoota pointed toward them. "What about the moths?"

Shaani looked back. "I've opened up the roof panels to let the light stream in. Moths hate the light. These ones will sod off and find new digs the moment they hatch." The rat lowered herself down the rusty, old machinery. "Nope, all's well. We are now officially the saviors of Watering Hole."

Shaani dropped to the ground. Water—clear, pure water—was fountaining up behind her, splashing down the newly cleaned concrete, and gurgling down into the ground. The rat tasted the water then drank her fill. She unpicked her long ponytail then plunged herself joyously under the shower. She emerged long minutes later, shaking herself dry like a dog.

"Right. Benek. Sorry about the delay, old chap. *Noblesse oblige* and all that. We'll get you on your date at last?" The rat strolled past Benek, wringing her glorious long, white hair dry. "Let's go put the kettle on."

Their great mission was over at long last.

· · · · ·

In the morning Shaani and Xoota walked from the ship back to the desalination plant. They labored up the sandy gullies as odd little insects that looked liked flying stingrays took to the air around them. Dawn was spreading cool and rosy fingered across the wonderful ocean as they topped the final hill.

They stood together, savoring the ocean breeze. The sight and feel of the sea was magical, something no desert dweller could ever truly have dreamed. They watched it together for a while and enjoyed the silence.

The desalination plant seemed to be working without a hitch. The equipment hummed, the water bubbled, and as they watched, the conveyor belt jerked into life and moved the salt onward. It all seemed oddly peaceful and wonderfully *right*.

Xoota scratched her pink-tipped snout in thought. "So why is it working? Don't these things need power?"

"They need oodles of it." Shaani sniffed as if hunting for a scent. Her electrical sense was highly tuned. "Broadcast power, from over that way, I should think."

"Benek's little building?"

"Oh, much bigger than that, I'd say." The rat stood, looking to the east, holding her straw hat onto her head. "I'd say it's from his mighty starport. We must be fairly close."

"Well, that will please him." The quoll looked over the conveyor belt again. "So it will keep working, then?"

"Yes, it all seems pukkah."

Xoota looked back at the pumps. "Should we just leave those pupae up there? What about when they hatch?"

"Oh, leave them. The next meal they make might be something that was planning on eating us."

"Oh." Xoota nodded. "When you put it that way, I suppose so."

"Ravening mutant monsters are just a part of the local ecosystem." Shaani passed Xoota a bottle of iced tea. "It takes all kinds."

When they returned to the ship, she stood ready and waiting, her tall masts beautiful in the morning light. She was a lovely sight, rugged and competent, with her balloon tires and her jaunty bowsprit. She'd become their home on their journey.

Budgie was digging happily around the bushes, finding edible roots for his breakfast. Xoota scratched him behind his head, and he chirred happily. They all mounted up the rear ramp and headed on deck to ready the ship for travel.

Rustle stood on deck in a tub of nice, wet compost, possibly still asleep; it was hard to tell. Wig-wig was taking breakfast by the railings; the deck was covered with earwigs large and small, all munching on fruit, banana skins, and porridge. Shaani headed up the mainmast to spy out the best route east, while Xoota poked around to try to find where Benek had gone.

She found him in the shadow of the deckhouse. Benek was sullenly playing his "training game," working to beat the high scores of the mysterious "G.I.A.N.T." Xoota sat on the rail, her tail curling, and watched him for a while. "Benek, have you ever thought that you should just enjoy the sheer wonder and variety in the world?"

The muscular man looked at her without a single spark of affection. "The world is wrong. We must act to fix it. Even the rat can understand the concept."

"Shaani wants to build something beautiful out of all the wonderful possibilities she sees around her. She is a believer." The quoll tilted her head and watched Benek carefully. "How about you, Benek? What is it that you believe?"

The man set his game aside. "I believe in *destiny.*"

Also interesting news. Xoota's ears and antennae lifted expressively high. "Right." She rose to leave. "Well, we're setting sail toward that omega building of yours. Might be there by midmorning, if the wind holds." The quoll looked at Benek, who did not return the favor. "We appreciate everything you've done, Benek. We'll help you do your thing now. Don't worry."

Xoota walked away, feeling a tingle of warning in her antennae. Something was not quite right. She walked over to join the others as Shaani slid down to the deck to hand back the binoculars.

"Trouble with Benek?"

Xoota's ears were flat. "There's something going on here. Part of me wonders if we should just kill him and eat him."

Rustle took the idea on board. He gaped all three mouths open and eagerly waggled his tentacles.

Shaani gave Xoota a patient look. "No. I don't think so."

Rustle immediately pouted.

The quoll grumbled. "I know. He's probably too chewy, anyway."

"Let's just get the ship under way." Shaani headed for the mainsail winch. *"Noblesse oblige* and all that."

Xoota headed to the control cabin and signaled to get under way. The hand brake was released, the mainsail sheeted home.

With her engines humming softly to take her up into the breeze, the ship caught the wind, moved gracefully up onto a hilltop, then rolled away across the grassy plains.

• • • • •

The sea breeze was constant and moved the ship smoothly inland. She took a wide turn past the sandstone outcrops near the shore and moved deeper into the plains. In the distance, they could see the Plodder tribe, still ambling ever so slowly along. The ship mounted a long, smooth plateau, and started slowly tacking into the breeze, heading skillfully across the wind. Two-headed emus watched them pass, blinking in confusion from the safety of nearby rocks.

Xoota mounted Budgie and ranged ahead, scouting for a way through a field of boulders. Just beyond the rocks, she found herself looking down on a quiet, little dell. Benek's alien building sat in the middle of a broad patch of well-overgrown grass. The building formed a long, low *Y* shape, raised off the ground on squat pylons four meters high. A hexagonal patch of concrete lay off to one side, weeds jutting up through cracks in the surface here and there. A row of tall, gleaming fence posts surrounded the entire area, but no wire was stretched between the posts.

Nothing moved. The only sign of life was a dead bird in the middle of the concrete hexagon. It seemed to have been on the receiving end of a nasty accident; there was nothing but a beak and feathers surrounding a burned hole where its body once had been.

Grisly, thought Xoota. She looked the site over and pondered.

The ship came rumbling up the hill slope behind her, apparently able to navigate the boulders without her help. Shaani engaged the electric motors to bring the ship up to the crest. Xoota signaled and the ship dropped her sails. She turned to point her nose back downhill before putting on the hand brakes and locking herself in place. The crew came to the rails to look over the old omega buildings.

Xoota sat cross-legged upon Budgie and called up to the others. "It looks pretty intact. What do you guys make of it?"

Benek was staring avidly at the buildings through his telescope.

Shaani hung from the railings, secured by her long, pink tail, and examined the alien fence line. "If it's intact, it's intact for a reason. We'll proceed with great care on this one."

"Absolutely." Xoota was very suspicious of the fence, or the lack thereof. "Follow my lead on this one. No one split off from the party. Benek, do you hear me?"

"I hear you." The man was already arming himself. "Come."

The whole area was clearly transplanted from another Earth. The plants did not match with those out on the plain. As they made their way down, they passed a stand of fat, green cacti that would have been more at home in Watering Hole. They stopped well short of the fence line, and everyone ducked down into cover—all except for Rustle, of course, who loomed overhead, essentially untroubled by the world.

Benek looked past the posts at the building beyond. "A fortress. Perhaps it's an armory."

Shaani scowled. "It does look a tad grim." She slowly thrashed her tail, examining what looked like a gun turret at the top of the building. "Fortresses have ways of protecting themselves. So let us just be careful."

Xoota edged closer to the fence line. The fence poles were humming softly. Her antennae gave off a definite warning. The quoll grubbed around herself and found a rock. She tossed it between the fence posts and nothing happened. The rock sailed through and thudded down into the long, tall grass.

"Excellent," said Benek as he started to rise.

Xoota made a noise to halt Benek. "Hold your budgies there, son." The quoll lifted a finger. "Shaani? What do you think?"

The rat carefully examined the fence posts. She held up a hand to signal everyone to kindly sit back and wait. "Pardon me, chaps. Let me just try a little something." The rat found a rock and placed it under her armpit. She let it stay there for quite a while, looking apologetic over the delay. She whistled between her big, chisel teeth to pass the time. Finally satisfied, she removed the rock and lobbed it gently underhand between the nearest fence posts.

The posts gave off a high-pitched sonic scream. Xoota and Shaani clapped their hands to their ears in agony. The rock landed in the grass, apparently unharmed. Shaani emerged from the grass, her pupils dilated and her white fur standing stiff as a brush. Xoota was in worse shape, her hands and teeth jittering in shock. She looked appalled.

"What the hell was that?"

"S-some sort of sonic attack." Shaani had to sit down and put her head between her knees. "Triggered to sense intruders. Motion and h-heat."

Benek seemed only slightly affected by the sound. He looked at the two animals and sneered. "Designed to keep out beasts, perhaps."

Xoota waved at him. "By all means, walk right on through."

The man strode toward the fence then thought better of it. He stopped, reached out a hand as if to put it between the fence posts, then retreated and looked at the fence in thought. "Shoot the fence posts. Take the gun and blast a way in," he suggested.

"I think that might be a gun turret on top of the building." Shaani adjusted her glasses and motioned to the guns. "Let's forgo damaging the fence for now, shall we?"

The fence posts were easily four meters high—too high to jump. There were no handy trees or timber with which to make a ladder. The ground was a thin layer of soil over a foundation of solid rock, so making a tunnel was out of the question.

Shaani shook her ringing ears and pondered. "Did anyone develop teleportation or time-stop abilities overnight?"

"No," said Xoota and Wig-wig from behind a cactus.

"Well, it never hurts to ask." Shaani hemmed and hawed. "This is a bit of a poser."

Wig-wig suddenly sat up, looking clever. "Wig-wig knows. We can throw one teleporter through the fence. Then we can teleport Wig-wig through inside the compound. Then Wig-wig can find controls and shut off fence."

Shaani eyed the bugs. "How do we know the teleporter actually teleports living matter?"

"Ah." Wig-wig wilted a bit. "Maybe we can experiment."

Shaani mused. "It's certainly worth a try." Shaani seemed enthused. "Back to the ship and let's give it a shot."

They party trundled back up to the hillside and climbed aboard ship. Shaani stopped to gather some cacti from the surrounding terrain and hauled the plants carefully on board. She set up the two teleport units on opposite sides of the deck.

Xoota watched with interest as she set the whole experiment up. "What range does this thing have, anyway?"

"No idea." Shaani placed a cactus inside the unit beside her. "We haven't tried it at more than a kilometer. Might be quite good, though; otherwise, what was it for?"

"What *was* it for?"

"Not sure. Maybe a sort of alien postal box. You know, small parcel delivery." Shaani sent Xoota chasing off over the deck. "All right. I'll send this through, and we'll see what happens."

Shaani closed the door of her teleporter unit. Xoota immediately opened the other unit and peered inside. "Oh."

Shaani looked across at her. "What?"

"Well, it's sort of inside out." Xoota was not happy. "And upside down."

"Ah." The lab rat was undeterred. "All right, chins up. There are some sort of settings and slides on the unit here. Let's see what we can do . . ."

It took them half an hour of careful meddling while Benek chafed over in a corner. It seemed that both units needed their settings to be synchronized perfectly; then all was well.

With both doors open, and a switch held in place with hairy string, the teleporters went into continuous operation. Wig-wig ran his merry, little swarm in one end and out the other, in the sender and out of the receiver. He ran round and around, teleporting in a happy loop until the others finally called the game to an end.

It had been an hour well spent. Shaani was extremely pleased. "All right. Time to head back. Come along; don't dawdle. *Science ad excelsior* and all that."

Rustle carried the two teleporters, and everyone traipsed back down the hillside. They reached the fence line and set up their next attempt to enter the grounds. Shaani used the boat hook to carefully push the open-doored teleporter though the fence, seating it as far as she could into the far side of the compound. "I'd love to know what powers these things. It doesn't seem to be electrical." The rat was careful not to let her hand come close to an imaginary line drawn between the fence posts. She set the teleporter up with its rear tilted high, so that anything within the compartment would naturally fall out onto the ground. "There. That should do it."

Wig-wig gathered in a happy swarm. "Wig-wig will go in."

"No, no, one final test." Shaani teleported another piece of cactus. It appeared in the teleporter unit inside the compound. The cactus rolled out to fall onto the ground. The fence did not trigger. No alarms rang and the cactus seemed intact.

Shaani pronounced herself satisfied. "All right, Wig-wig. Through you go."

The earwigs poured into the first unit. They teleported across to the unit inside the fence line and scurried quickly out into the long grass. When he had finally gathered all his buggy selves together, Wig-wig gave a wave from atop a grass stalk and set merrily off toward the buildings.

· · · · ·

The building had a single entrance at ground level at the middle of the *Y*. The earwigs explored the grass and found another dead bird before emerging onto the concrete path near the entryway.

A skeleton lay facedown on the concrete. The body was dressed in rigid armor. The bones were old and flaking. He had a red bracelet on one extended arm and a shattered pistol in his hand. Sitting on the concrete a few meters away, there was a squat, metal cylinder festooned with lumps, bumps, and tubes. As Wig-wig scurried across the concrete, the cylinder suddenly gave a jerk.

"Halt. Identify."

The earwigs all sat up most politely and chorused in unison. "Hello. I'm Wig-wig."

"Identity. You have thirty seconds to comply." The robot tried to move but only wobbled slightly in place. Its lower half seemed badly damaged. "This is a prison zone, maximum security level ultra. Lethal force is authorized."

"Don't shoot Wig-wig" The bugs began to chase each other around. "I told you who I was."

"Twenty seconds. Nineteen. Eighteen. Seventeen . . ."

The earwigs ran for the nearest cover, hiding inside the armor of the long-dead skeleton. The skeleton twitched and writhed as the bugs moved around inside. The mechanism out on the concrete immediately settled back in place.

"Apologies, Officer Kierkegaard. Identity acknowledged."

Earwigs peeked out from the dead man's helmet. They tried to make a deeper voice. "Um, don't shoot anybody any more. Is an order."

"Order acknowledged, Officer Kierkegaard. Standing down." Gun barrels withdrew back inside the damaged robot. "Have a nice day."

· · · · ·

A few minutes later, a skeleton dressed in armor appeared at the fence line. He moved across the ground while lying prone, transported by a carpet of earwigs. The bugs waved happily to their friends.

"Look. I be Officer Kierkegaard. No one will shoot me." The bug came right through the fence, utterly unmolested. *"Glee."*

Shaani stooped to examine the ID bracelet on the arm of the corpse. It was red with one gold stripe. She removed the bracelet and held it up in thought. "ID bracelet. The defenses must be keyed to it."

Before anyone could stop her, she had walked through the fence. Nothing happened to her.

The rat happily tossed the bracelet through to Xoota. "Come on. Don't dawdle."

One by one, they all crossed the fence line, tossing the ID bracelet to each new person to cross. As a final thought, Shaani walked back to the fence. Donning her blue and gold bracelet, she waved her hand near the fence and walked back out of the compound. Again, nothing happened to her. The rat waved her bracelet. "Oh. These ones would have worked too."

Xoota watched her with lowered eyelids, seething in annoyance. "Do you mean to say we could have just walked through that fence the whole time?"

The rat seemed to take it in her stride. "Never mind. Look at what we learned about the teleporter." She walked past the others heading for the entrance to the building. "Come on."

Xoota fumed. "There are days when you are heading exactly the right way for a smacked bottom."

They walked across the grass, finding yet more corpses of birds that had failed to identify themselves to the guard robot. It even seemed to have blasted a couple of butterflies and moths. The robot turned a turret load of sensors in their direction as the party approached. Wig-wig was still happily carrying the helmet of the unfortunate Officer Kierkegaard, as well as his ID bracelet.

Xoota walked over to the robot and waved her blue ID bracelet. "Robot, who are you?"

"I am security monitor 2, Bay Reach Transfer facility. Currently standing down. Request maintenance and repair to drive systems."

"Right you are. We'll see to that." Xoota was triumphant. "Hey. We have us a security robot. If we mount this on the main deck, no one will ever mess with us again."

Shaani walked over to the main doors. A security camera emerged from a little hatchway and looked at her. A calm female voice spoke from a grill beside the massive entry doors.

"Please identify."

Shaani waved her blue and gold ID band. "Here you go, old bean."

"ID registered as Sergeant Yoshitomo Watanabe. Please provide retinal scan."

Another hatchway opened, and a flash of light caught Shaani right in the eyes, she staggered back and frowned, rubbing at her eyelids.

The female voice spoke again. "Retinal scan negative. Access denied."

Xoota tried the door, armed with the red ID band.

Again there was a flash. Again the female voice blandly denied them entry. "Retinal scan negative. Access denied."

The party stood on the concrete and pondered. Xoota hefted the magical go-away stick in her belt. "What if we used this to blow a way in?"

"It might not do any good." Shaani rapped on the door. It felt quite thick and made of an alloy she couldn't identify. "This jolly thing feels tough as a fortress."

Xoota let her eyes rest on the robot. Her antennae lifted up in sudden inspiration. "I'll bet the robot can get inside if it wants to."

They had Rustle pick up the robot and dangle it in place before the security camera.

Shaani held up the red ID band. "Robot, dear heart. Please request entry into the building."

The robot whirred softly. Suddenly the main doors opened. Xoota sped inside and found a manual locking bar that jammed the doors in place. She fixed the doors open, and stepped back with a smile. "Perfect. Okay, Rustle, you can put him down."

The big plant carefully put the robot back in place on the concrete, then waddled over to join the others as they cautiously moved inside.

Within the building, the dark gray antechamber slowly grew visible as their eyes grew accustomed to the low light. Luminescent strips ran along the ceiling, slowly glowing brighter as the party moved indoors. Xoota led the way, soft footed and cautious, with her clever antennae feeling for dangerous futures.

The entryway was a cylindrical room. A row of what looked like metal cupboards lined one curved wall. Shower stalls lined the other, and single door was at the opposite end. Right beside the door at the far side of the room, there was a flat platform that came up out of the floor. The top glowed a welcoming emerald green color and held two hand imprints recessed into its surface.

Benek strode over to inspect it. Xoota saw him move and waved him away.

"Careful. There might be weirdness about."

Benek looked at her in annoyance. "This is the culture of my own people." He grandly laid his hands on the green tabletop. "I would not expect you to understand."

Something went *click*. Benek's hands were suddenly linked together by two bright orange bands. He jerked and fought, but the bands seemed to constrict even tighter. The man struggled then looked to Shaani in panic. "They won't come off."

The rat bent down to look at the wrist restraints in interest then examined the table, seeing the hand imprints and dispenser slots beside them. Finally, she touched the wrist restraints with the red ID badge and pressed a control.

The wrist bands fell off.

"There we are. All done." The rat took possession of the wrist restraints and bagged them. "Now do be careful. None of you chaps are really omega qualified."

The lockers turned out to contain mostly scraps and rags, but there were several pairs of bright red overalls made from a tough, artificial material that had ignored the march of time. Rustle was handed the loot bag, and he happily stuffed the various finds into his sack.

Finally they examined the door at the far side of the room. It opened at the touch of a button. Inside, there was small chamber only a few meters across. Another single button stood beside the door.

Shaani kept the others out of the room. She examined it carefully then touched the inner button. The door slid shut. Xoota waited patiently then began to feel nervous. She keyed on her radio headset.

"Shaani."

"Right here." The rat's voice came with the usual crackle of static. "Oh, I say. Right. Here I come."

The door slid open again. Shaani waved the others in. "It's a moving room. Goes up and down, up to the next floor." She crooked her finger, coaxing the others aboard. "It's perfectly safe. Come along. Come along."

There was no way to fit Rustle into the room on the same trip as the others. He came up all by himself, immensely pleased by the ride. The huge plant shuffled out into the upstairs room, where his companions were already fanning out cautiously across the floor.

A single large, round room formed the junction of all three arms of the building. There was an upper ring of balcony four meters above, where several chairs were set into the floor beside some metal desks. The positions had several small windows on the wall before them, each one flickering with images and views.

Two bodies lay on the floor—skeletons clad in flesh mummified by the cool, dry air. One wore armor and had apparently had its head twisted one hundred eighty degrees around on its neck. The other was dressed in a red jumpsuit and had a fractured skull. The armored body showed several broken bones. It had an empty pistol holster, a broken helmet headset, and no ID bracelet.

Shaani carefully examined the body. The corpse's plastic armor might possibly be useful. As she rolled the body over, she found a small, plastic egg that was equipped with a metal ring. She sniffed it, read the writing on the bottom of the egg, and put it in her sample case for later.

The doors into the three main arms of the building were all made of clear, transparent material. One was lined with several smaller rooms, all with their own transparent doors. Another seemed to contain what looked like kitchens and a dormitory. The third one . . .

The third one was decidedly weird. Writing on the door identified it as *E wing*. The area seemed to be a single wide corridor. There were several pedestals lining the walls, one of which had shimmering blue column of light extending up from it. Stuck inside the column was a metal cube about the size of a human fist. Xoota peered through the door, shrugged, and walked back to join the others.

Shaani climbed up the stars to the second level. She called back to the others. "Stay in pairs. Nobody leave the room. We'll stick together." She headed for the little glass screens surrounding the various chairs. "Now let's see what we have here . . ."

The little windows were all views from distant cameras. One showed the robot outside the main door; one showed the fence line. Another showed the corridors in the main building. Shaani wandered to another station. There were several other views. They showed images of a vast, concrete field, covered in sand and weeds and buildings. But one camera showed a line of different structures—spacecraft standing in a row along the concrete field.

It was Benek's spaceport. It matched his photographs. The time of day in the pictures seemed to match the present hour. They were views taken in real time. Shaani beamed in satisfaction.

"Benek, we have live camera feeds to your spaceships. This facility is linked in to your target." Communications links must still somehow be up and running. "Can't be far away."

Benek paid her no attention. He had found more lockers and was rummaging inside. Shaani worked some controls and flicked between images.

There.

It was a view across the mysterious starport. The hill they had crested was in the distance, clear as day in the camera. Benek's base was only perhaps twenty kilometers to the east.

Behind her, Xoota had been flicking through images on other monitors.

There were pictures of a cold, terrible hall. Cryogenic chambers were ranked in the gloom—the home of Benek's brides-to-be. The chambers were frosted, glowing an icy blue.

In another screen, she found an image that made her fur stand on end. She swallowed. "Shaani? Here, look at this."

The screen showed a round chamber. Seated in the chamber, there were several armor suits, massive things with sealed helmets; sleek, armored plates; and hulking bulk. They looked as big as sand sharks. Dust covered them. The armors had power gloves festooned with weapons.

There were other cameras showing similar images: rifles in racks, heavy guns, weird tubes, magical go-away sticks . . . It *was* an ancient armory, left rotting in the gloom.

There was enough to equip an army. Xoota quietly switched the screens to another view. She had not seen photos of the old armory in Benek's photograph collection. She wondered why.

· · · · ·

They searched the long wing lined with rooms and found them to be empty except for some disintegrating mattresses and surprisingly sturdy sheets that might make good sails for the *Sand Shark*. But in the dormitory section, Shaani made her great find. There, just lying on a table, there was a small handheld computer. She leaned over to pick it up and wiped the dust from the screen. The computer instantly blossomed into life.

"Greetings, Officer Kierkegaard. Welcome to Tinder Plus Plus, your reading system of choice."

The thing had a voice. Shaani stared. "Um, hello."

"Do you wish to access reader memory?"

"Yes, please."

"Memory currently empty. Officer Kierkegaard, you have one credit left in the base library. What book do you select?"

"Show me a menu."

The handheld unit's screen filled with the titles of books.

Shaani skimmed her finger along a menu. When she touched the screen, the images on the computer changed. She was most impressed. "Spiffy."

In the nonfiction section, a title seemed to leap out at her. She nodded in satisfaction. "Computer, can I load the *Terran Trade Authority, Student's Encyclopedia*?"

"You may, Officer Kierkegaard."

"Please load the encyclopedia."

The unit in her hand hummed briefly, and it was done.

Shaani felt a surge of sheer excitement. She lifted up the hand unit and spoke into the screen. "Open encyclopedia."

The unit's voice was calm. "Open."

"Show me . . . ooh, start with 'A.' Show me . . . alcohol distillation techniques."

"Provide security ID."

Shaani touched the side of the screen with a bracelet. "There you go."

"Confirmed." The little screen showed video of giant steel vats attended by human workers. It was real footage of real people from oh-so-long ago. "Alcohol distillation techniques. Choose basic primer or advanced menu."

"Basic primer."

She skimmed text while ancient video told her stories. There was a history of brewing in ancient times; details of the chemical formula; then actual recipes for distillation of ethanol, methanol, beer, cider . . .

It was going to be so damned useful. It was the treasure of a lifetime. Shaani hugged the thing to her heart in joy. From across the way, Xoota looked at her and raised one brow.

"Happy?"

"Science." The rat was overjoyed. "What could be happier?"

"This place seems weird to me. Given all the security outside, I expected there to be more on the inside. There is no evidence of what we saw on the screens earlier. It's completely empty, all except for two energy cells lying in the dust." She held them up then put them in her bag. The quoll looked around the dormitory.

"I think this was a prison. This is the guard's quarters; the other sections are cells."

It made sense. Shaani emerged from flicking starry-eyed through her new computer book screen, turning the old computer off. "That's a jolly fine hypothesis." She, too, looked around. "I can't see much evidence of any prisoners."

"Well, maybe it was empty?" Xoota suddenly felt her antennae jerk. She got a flash of futures flicking past, filled with fire and blood. She whirled, her heart racing.

"Where's Benek?"

Everyone was supposed to be in pairs. Rustle and Wig-wig were at the dormitory kitchen, thieving spatulas and cutlery. But Benek was gone. Xoota ran into the main central chamber. It was empty but the door to the E wing was somehow clean of dust. The quoll raced forward. Through the transparent door to the other wing, she could see Benek inspecting the pillar with its strange blue column of light. He was pushing buttons on a control panel at the top of the pillar.

"Benek. *No!*"

He touched a button, and the blue pillar of light suddenly shut off. The metal cube suspended in midair tumbled to the ground and split open. A sizzling flash of electricity scored into the floor. All the screens on the upper level suddenly screamed with static.

Benek fell. On his belt, his handheld computer game scorched and sizzled. Electricity sparked. And just as suddenly as they had gone static, the screens showed a cascade of numbers and images.

A female voice spoke calmly from the ceiling. "Security alert. Security alert. Artificial Intelligence prisoner J-31 has breached stasis containment. Security alrr— Scrity alerrr—" The voice warped horribly and ground to a halt.

The screens around the upper level all lit with the opening screen of Benek's computer game. The computer voice became harsh and grating. "Destroy all mutants. All must be cleansed."

A large gun suddenly popped out of the ceiling. It whirred around and aimed itself right between Xoota's eyes.

The quoll's antennae fell.

"Oh, kack . . ."

CHAPTER 12

Xoota felt the thing before it could fire, sensed the shot, and lunged forward. She came up with her pistol out of its sheath. She fired and missed but blasted a hole in the ceiling. She cursed and dived again as a shot from above struck her armor. She was protected but the force hammered her hard into the ground.

Shaani leveled a hand and fired a blast of electricity straight into the gun. The weapon shorted out. "Xoota!" Shaani ran to Xoota's side.

Doors slammed as the different wings sealed off and gas started to hiss from the ceilings. Shaani fished for her respirator and yanked it into place on Xoota's face before the gas could fill the main chamber. She held her breath while Xoota breathed then took the mask for a few quick breaths herself. Xoota had left her own gas mask back on the ship.

Rustle wrenched open the dormitory doors. Wig-wig scampered through; neither seemed affected by the gas. Xoota, holding the gas mask with one hand, pointed to the E wing door with her other. Rustle ambled off and wormed his tendrils into the door cracks then wrenched the doors slowly apart. Wig-wig bustled into the corridor beyond like a living carpet, wriggled beneath Benek, and carried the man out onto the main room.

The computer roared in a garbled, shattered voice. "All mutants must be purged."

Long, metal tentacles flailed out of a panel in the wall, reaching for Shaani. The rat ducked quickly enough that the tentacles missed her by a centimeter, plunging clean through a chair behind her. The rat immediately fled upstairs, away from Xoota and the gas mask.

The tentacles turned on Xoota, but the quoll managed to get her shield up on her arm. She shoved a flailing tentacle away then fired with her pistol. The beam flickered then died but not before it clipped one of the tentacles, cutting it into a madly lashing stump. Xoota tried to fire again, but the pistol did nothing. She dodged against a wall as the remaining tentacles tried to smash her from above.

Upstairs on the balcony, Shaani found a computer terminal, pulled the cover off, and jammed her hand in among the workings. Raw voltage shot from her hand, right into the base computer network. Screens sparked. Machinery fried. The lights flickered and blinked. And the computer terminals all abruptly shut off. Shaani staggered back, unable to hold her breath any longer. She breathed gas, choking and coughing, then fell to the floor.

The tentacles that Xoota had been fighting lay limp and dead. The base computer systems were fried. Still wearing her gas mask, Xoota raced up, grabbed the rat, and threw her over her shoulder like a sack of roots. She led Rustle and Wig-wig to the elevator, where Rustle hauled open the doors. With no way to make the elevator run. Xoota pulled the old battery out of her pistol and reloaded with one of the power cells she'd picked up earlier. She fired the pistol three times into the floor.

Half the floor smashed clean open. The edges of the hole were red hot and molten. Xoota looked down, picked her spot, then jumped. She rolled free of the elevator in case it suddenly moved to smash her flat and made a quick assessment of the antechamber.

No guns. They were safe for the moment.

Wig-Wig flew down to join her, and Rustle awkwardly lowered Benek and Shaani down. Both of them were breathing but unconscious. While Rustle squeezed himself down the hole in the elevator floor, Xoota ran forward to the outer door to carefully check the scene outside.

Again, her senses warned her with a quick look at an awful future. Xoota jerked to a halt and flattened herself inside the door frame. She drew a knife and used it as a mirror to look out into the world beyond.

Energy beams hit the door frame, vaporizing metal and sending out an unholy mess of heat. Xoota's knife melted and she dropped it in shock. Outside the door, the security robot's voice snarled and roared.

"Purge the mutants. Establish an empire of purity." The robot fired again. Concrete blew apart in a storm of energy fire. "The minions of G.I.A.N.T. will be destroyed. The purity of mechanism shall overcome the mutations of the flesh."

Sheltering away from the glowing hot wall, Xoota blinked in shock and looked at Wig-wig.

"Greatest Insect of All Nature and Time." Wig-wig risked a peek about the corner. "I can has high score on Benek's game."

"Oh, lovely." Xoota tried to poke a stick around the corner, but it was instantly shot to pieces. She tried two sticks; they were shot to pieces a split second apart, one after another. At least the robot could only target a single foe at once.

"Wig-wig. Do you still have Officer Kierkegaard's helmet?"

"Yes, yes."

"Give it to Rustle." Xoota felt at the back of her belt. "Rustle, when I say 'go,' you throw that helmet out through the door as far as you can." Xoota readied herself. "Okay? Ready . . . steady . . . go."

The huge plant flung the helmet out into the grounds. Energy beams flashed, missing the helmet then hitting it hard. Xoota was already leaning around the door. She flung her magical go-away stick at the robot, the fuse ticking busily away. The grenade, hit the pavement, was missed by a snap shot from the robot, and landed, clanging, at the robot's base.

The magical go-away stick exploded in a brilliant flash. The ground shook. The instant the flash had passed, Xoota hurled herself around the corner.

The robot was broken open and spitting sparks. Its tentacles still thrashed wildly back and forth. Xoota flung herself on the robot with her mighty cog mace. She battered the robot's cranium to pieces.

"Die. Die, you gravy-sucking pig."

The robot made a high-pitched noise and ceased to move. Xoota jumped up and down on its innards for good measure. Suddenly the machinery began to smoke. The quoll sped away, and the robot detonated with a sullen *bang*.

Red hot scrap metal showered the grass. Grass fires instantly flared up all around the prison.

It was time to go. Xoota holstered her pistol and led the way. The fence stood dead and deactivated; the gun position atop the prison seemed to have shorted out. There was decidedly no loot to be had there. Annoyed, tired, singed, and furious at Benek, Xoota collected the teleporters and led the way back to the ship.

· · · · ·

When Benek came to, he was in the hold, unarmored and with his hands clamped behind him with the orange prison restraints. He was secured to a ring bolt in the deck. Xoota sat on a box of dried insect sticks on the far side of the hold, her crossbow in her lap and a sheaf of photographs in her hand.

Her face definitely did not look happy.

"Hello, Benek."

He said nothing. He merely glowered at the quoll with malice.

For her part, Xoota lounged back and sifted through the photographs. "So I *wondered*. I mean, a genetically modified superhuman in a world full of mutants. No powers, no alphas, no weirdness. Just pure, slathering, ursoid muscle and easy-to-manage hair . . ." She flicked through photos. "I'm sure the 'perfect brides' idea is appealing. But surely there must be at least one or two human women somewhere in the desert? Why go all this way? What is so damned important about this starport?

"And then we found this."

There were other printouts, pictures that had been hidden deep in Benek's baggage, pictures of massive, armored suits designed to equip human behemoths armed with energy weapons that could make a mockery out of crossbows and spears.

"This is what you want, isn't it? An ancient armory. Enough firepower to conquer half the planet."

Benek remained silent.

Xoota dropped the photographs to the floor. "Who are you working with?"

The man looked at her with pure scorn. "That is not the concern of beasts."

She left him there, secured in the hold, and took the ladder back to the deck.

The ship was heeling in the wind, heading southeast with the sea breeze in her sails. Shaani was lying on the copilot's chair in the control cabin with Wig-wig bustling back and forth. Rustle loomed just outside the door and helpfully licked her face in a weird attempt at first aid. The rat blinked, winced, then winced again as a long, gooey plant tongue licked her up and down.

"Eww." She blinked. "I feel sullied and unusual." She opened bleary eyes and coughed. "What happened?"

Xoota was ready with iced tea and a scone.

"Benek freed some sort of machine intelligence."

"I know that." The rat put a hand to her head. "I mean what happened after I got gassed?"

"Ah." Xoota wiped the rat's brow with a cool cloth. "Well, the computers and electronics inside the building were all fried. The machine intelligence transferred to the security robot outside. We had to finally get rid of it with the magic go-away stick." Xoota shrugged. "We survived."

"And how is Benek?"

"Yes," Xoota's mood was dire. "Let me tell you about our friend Benek . . ."

The ship was pretty much driving itself across a flat section of plains. Xoota sat and shared tea with Shaani, discussing Benek's apparent plans for world domination and the likelihood that his "perfect brides" had ever even existed. Shaani sighed unhappily. She had no idea how to deal with people on that sort of level. Benek was outside her real realm of expertise.

"Thank you, Wig-wig. My headache is finally going away." She gratefully drank her tea. "What do you think we should do now?"

The quoll sucked her fangs in indecision. "No idea."

"Well, unfortunately we can't keep our agreement with Benek. I'm certainly not furthering any plans for world domination by the self-elected genetically pure."

"Yep." Xoota thrashed her tail. "But oddly enough that starport is too important a find to just ignore. It might have all sorts of tools we could use."

The rat smiled knowingly. "Ah, treasure."

"No, no—tools. And . . . research . . . and stuff." The quoll was quick to protest. "We can't just sail back to Watering Hole empty-handed."

It was getting close to evening. The sun was almost at the horizon. It had been a rather eventful day.

Shaani sat up on her chair and looked sideways at the quoll. "Well, you're right, of course. We should investigate. A starport could be a treasure house of knowledge." She heaved a sigh. "We need to go there, if only to destroy that armory." Shaani lifted a finger. "People can't all be lab rats, you know. They can't be trusted with that sort of firepower."

Xoota shrugged. That part was negotiable. Personally, she wouldn't say no to having a suit of powered armor in the hold for emergencies. "We'll have to keep Benek restrained until we've checked the place over and are well away."

"I suppose so. And if we find any brides . . . well, he can have them as per our original agreement." Shaani tried getting to her feet, but she wobbled unsteadily. "That gas has left me damnedly wonky."

"No, no, we're going over some sort of rocky rubble." Xoota headed for a hilltop. "Shall we head for the starport?"

"Let's shall."

The ship was heading south as they looked for a pass through the eastern hills. They kept on sailing until sunset spread calm and magnificent across the sky. They halted the ship atop a hill with a fine field of fire all around and settled down to enjoy the evening in peace.

· · · · ·

Shaani took the midnight watch. It was a peaceful time. She needed to make some more gun cotton, which meant distilling some acid. There were also two new plastic suits of armor to examine. But best of all, there was Shaani's brand-new toy, something her rat ancestors must have designed as an education aid. And it would perform that noble function once again. Shaani sat down and pulled out her new computer reader, turned it on, and settled down to read.

But where to begin?

"Computer—hmm, show me . . . basic electronics."

"Basic electronics. Please select menu—history or practical lessons."

"History first, please."

The videos and comments had only just begun to run when a flash disturbed the darkness out on the plains. The light was so quick and bright, it scarred an impression onto Shaani's eyes. She looked blankly around the darkness to the west then saw a violet streak of light that flickered somewhere on the plains.

Then again and again.

Shaani went to the cabin and shook Xoota awake. "Something's happening."

Xoota lunged awake and reached for her clothes.

The two women climbed into the rigging. There were grass fires many kilometers distant over the plains, but they saw no more weird, violet flashes. It had been energy weapons fire, Shaani was sure of it. Someone out there was in trouble.

The rat carefully watched the distant fires. "Do you think you can steer us in the dark?"

Xoota looked aloft. There was a decent moon in the sky. It made the shadow sides of the hills jet black, but the crests were silvered with ghostly light. She checked the wind meter. "I think so, if we're careful. Get the others up, raise sails, and we'll go. Keep the lights off so we're harder to spot."

First Xoota and Shaani loaded the catapult. They locked a bomb in place on the rails then went to rouse Wig-wig and Rustle from their slumber.

Under headsails and mainsail, the ship slid slowly through the dark of night. The wheels were almost silent. Shaani stayed up in the rigging with Xoota's broken binoculars and Benek's confiscated night goggles, carefully searching the darkness. They kept on rolling silently through the night. The wind whispered in the rigging; the wheels rumbled softly in the grass. The distant grass fires continued for a while, disappearing from view as the ship rode up and down the rolling plans. The fires spread wide, driven into the west by the winds and burning out slowly as they reached the sparser sand. But vast square kilometers of grass had been consumed, and black smoke choked off all view of the stars.

Animals began running from the west, passing the ship as she drove onward toward the disaster zone. Spike-tailed kangaroos; double-headed emus; and great, long-legged echidnas all ran fast with panic in their eyes.

Soon the night goggles showed the hot, withered burn zone ahead. Shaani lowered the mainsails. The ship crept forward on topsails and auxiliary motors, turning to parallel the line of smoldering, blackened grass.

The stench was choking. Embers glowed where grass and trees still burned. Rustle and Wig-wig came to the railings, craning to see the disaster zone in the eerie darkness. There was no sound except the hiss and sizzle of the fires. Rolling slowly through the smoke, the ship felt her way forward along a wasteland of ash and charcoal.

The night-vision goggles showed large shapes up ahead. It had to be the Plodders. The ship came to a halt, and Shaani cupped her hands to bellow out into the dark. "Hallo? Anybody? This is the *Sand Shark* here."

There was no answer. Xoota came up from the control cabin and armored herself, making sure her boots were on tight. Shaani followed suit. The quoll called back to Rustle, who was extremely leery of the glowing coals.

"Rustle, you stay on board with sand buckets and the water pump. Keep an eye out for any sparks. Wig-wig, you keep in the rigging." The bugs would wither in any heat or flame. The little creatures were just too vulnerable. "We'll go check this out."

Shaani, loaded up with welding gloves, first-aid kit, and water, slid down into the hold, waved a somewhat self-conscious hello to Benek, who sat glaring at her in the gloom, and tromped down the back ramp and out onto the grass. She patted Budgie as she passed. "Mind the ship. There's a good boy."

The budgerigar whistled three bars of Mozart at her then went back to sleep.

Xoota vaulted over the side of the ship, landing lightly on her booted feet. Shaani lifted up her penlight and flashed it into the dark. Massive, black shapes were out there somewhere. The two women walked forward into the dark.

Shaani called out and flashed her light. "Hallo? Anybody?"

The giant, mutant wombats were hunkered down in the middle of the smoking grass. There was a faint shimmer of force fields around them as the immense, slow creatures protected themselves from the flames. They were all curled up, heads tucked in beneath them and looking quite featureless. Whether the wombats generated their own force field or the Plodders had some sort of omega tech, Shaani wasn't sure, but it had protected the beasts.

Shaani ran from one to another, calling up to the platforms mounted on the animals high above her. There were no answers.

Here and there, artifacts were burning in the grass. Broken spears, mats, and weavings . . .

. . . A body.

It was lying in the smoldering grass, its skin scorched black. Shaani made a noise of dismay and turned the body over. It was one of the Plodder tribesmen, a warrior. And his head had been blown clean off.

The rat's stomach jerked. She forced herself to be a scientist; she was no use unless she could be dispassionate, unless she could view the evidence with a clear, unbiased mind. She forced herself to kneel down and examine the wound, looking at it underneath her light.

The tissue was seared and charred, cauterized. It was clearly the result of an energy weapon, perhaps a pistol much like the one Xoota was carrying.

"Shaani, over here."

The rat stood. She wiped her eyes and stumbled over to where Xoota held aloft a bio light.

One of the huge wombats lay steaming on the ground. Its fur had burned off. The cracked skin oozed red in horrible, wet fissures. At first it seemed the creature was hunched in and covering itself like the others. A closer view showed the animal had holes blasted through its flesh. Much of its head was missing. It was clearly stone dead.

Grim and revolted, Xoota nodded at the wounds. "What the hell could kill one of these things?"

"Energy weapons." The lab rat's voice sounded hoarse. "Big ones."

There was no sign of the tribesmen. The platforms atop the Plodders were empty. No one screamed or cried for help. There was only one dead body lying in the ash. Xoota looked around in frustration then ran toward a tall ridge of rock. She stood up and scanned the area carefully with the night goggles. "Hey, there's something out there. Some four hundred meters away . . . it's long and furry and not moving very well." Xoota leaped instantly from the rock. "Shaani, Wig-wig, this way."

The quoll raced to the ship and called for Budgie. She mounted the bird bareback, reaching down to swing Shaani up behind her. The budgerigar raced full pelt across the unburned grass, waving his little wings in anxiety at the nearby smoke and fires. Swarming down from the *Sand Shark*'s rigging, Wig-wig whirred and fluttered in the night, following the riders in a colossal, untidy swarm.

Hundreds of meters away, half hidden in a fold in the ground, something was thrashing and crying in pain. Shaani and Xoota drew Budgie to a halt and dismounted in the long, unscorched grass nearby. Suddenly aware of the sheer size of the poor thing thrashing in the little dell, they approached cautiously through the weeds.

There, lying on the ground, was one of the winged, furry serpents that had attacked the *Sand Shark* only a few days before. It lifted its maned, feline head, clashing its mandibles. Perfectly formed hands on the ends of its wings gripped and tore at the soil. It had two smoking wounds burned into its side. The beast rolled its head, caught sight of Shaani's glimmering white fur, and instantly gave a squeal of fright.

"No kill Yexil. Good Yexil. Nice Yexil. No kill him. No."

Xoota stared at the creature in alarm. "Sweet Enola Gay, it talks."

"Yexil talks." The monster thrashed its furry body and groaned, clearly in agony. "Help. Help poor Yexil."

Shaani began sliding down into the dell. "Shh, I'll help you."

Xoota drew her pistol in fright. "Shaani, these are the things that almost blew us apart."

"Well, now it needs help." The rat was already at the monster's side. "Science must be compassionate, or else it loses its soul. If we can't overlook a simple misunderstanding or two, then we are only just monsters." She opened up her first-aid kit and stroked the patient softly on his furry side. "There, there, old chap. Soon fix you up. What happened, eh?"

"Shiny men. Shiny men shoot poor Yexil."

She carefully cleaned the two worst wounds. They were from energy gun blasts; a smaller creature would have been blown clear in two. Wig-wig came to consult with Shaani. The two of them began working on healing Yexil while Xoota nervously tried to provide fire support from above. Shaani propped her computer reader onto the rocks beside her, letting it run its articles as she worked.

"Computer, show me first aid and emergency medical procedures."

"Basic or advanced?"

"One after the other, if you please."

Shaani worked by the light of an ordinary light bulb tucked behind her pink ear. She carefully tended to Yexil while beside her, the computer droned on about defibrillation kits and inflatable splints.

"So what happened to you, eh? How did this happen, you poor thing?"

Yexil wailed. "Yexil hungry. Fly to Plodder men with bag of fruit to trade. Plodder men make fabric. Yummy yummy fabric. Yexil make good trade with Plodder men.

"Big beetle come from sky. Out come shiny men. Four, five . . . many. Shoot Plodder. Shoot poor Yexil. Take Plodder men away."

Shaani carefully administered drugs from her ancient medical kit. "Took them away?"

"Poor Plodder men went into shiny beetle. Shiny beetle flew away."

Xoota was listening alertly. "Where? Where did it fly?"

Yexil flopped its head to point to the northeast. "There. Over hook-head mountain."

Wig-wig was managing to do good work healing the creature. The drugs seemed to be helping.

Shaani walked over to his head to give Yexil a drink of water from her flask. "So these shiny men, they just attacked without warning? Did the shiny men say anything?"

Yexil drank gratefully, then flopped his head down to rest. "Shiny men say 'All mutant must be kill.' 'Mutant not be pure . . .' "

Xoota was not amused. Her antennae fell flat. "Oh, kack."

It was Benek's damned computer monster.

They gave Yexil liter after liter of water to drink. The poor thing was parched. As they helped him drink, Shaani conferred urgently with Xoota.

"The robot, it must have had a communicator link to the starport. Maybe it jumped to a new host." Shaani looked appalled. "Dear Darwin, it has the armory. And it has ships."

Xoota blinked. "There's nothing out here to conquer."

"There are these poor tribes. And how long do you think it would take it to find Watering Hole, the desert villages, everything worthwhile?"

Yexil rolled over onto his feet. He was no longer ebbing and fading. He drank yet more water. As an experiment, Shaani pulled out a sheet she had taken from the ancient prison. The Yexil seized it and ate it with gusto. It seemed to greatly aid in his recovery.

"All right Yexil, old chap. Are you feeling any better? Can you fly?"

The animal looked grateful. He flexed his wings. "Fly a little. Not feel so bad now."

"Well, can you make it back to your home?"

Yexil nodded. "Yexil can go home now." The huge monster reached down and licked Shaani's face with an immense, pink tongue. "Yexil sorry he try to steal cloth from big butterfly on wheels. People who live on butterfly-wheely are friends for Yexil now."

Yexil stayed nose to nose with Shaani. He was apparently expecting something. Shaani made a little *ah* of understanding. She licked Yexil's face in return.

Yexil seemed pleased. "Yexil and wheely-butterfly people be friend." He suddenly beat his wings. "Now Yexil go home." The creature beat his way up into the air. Moving slowly and painfully, he flapped off toward a distant set of hills.

Shaani waved until he had disappeared from sight. The rat had a strip of Yexil lick across her front.

Xoota looked at her with droll eyes. "You licked him?"

"Seemed to be the thing to do." The rat settled her hat upon her head. "Actually, he tasted remarkably like chicken."

They led Wig-wig and Budgie away from the little dell, heading back to the ship. Xoota was angered by Benek, computers, and electronics in general. "Where do we go now?"

"Go?" Shaani was surprised. "Well, we have to find the starport. We have to see what must be done."

"I thought you might say that." Xoota scrubbed at her eyes. "Right. We'll move in the dark. I want the ship hidden under cover by daybreak. Anything you can do to mask our heat signature, do it."

"Righty-o. Science shall prevail."

Xoota shook her head. "Yeah, well, they have a lot more of it on tap than we do."

"Ah, but they don't have a lab rat." Shaani briskly led the way back to the *Sand Shark*. "All right. Chop-chop. Science never sleeps."

Xoota took a last look at the groaning shapes of the Plodders in the dark then turned Budgie back toward the ship. Ahead of her in the darkness, Shaani was happily reading up on her first aid.

"Ooh, defibrillation. That sounds fun."

· · · · ·

Xoota, Shaani, Wig-wig, and Rustle sheltered behind a rocky crest atop a steep, sharp hill. Below them, a carpet of gray-green treetops led down a long valley toward a plain of sandstone rock covered with ancient omega buildings. They spread out over an area greater than all the villages of the desert put together. There were vast sheds—complex buildings with thousands of glass windows. And there, beside the main building, were the ships: a row of tall, pointed darts, gleaming in scarlet, blue, and gold.

Midday heat made the rocks shimmer. Parched grass nodded. Here and there, little, beige butterflies flitted among the wilting flowers. Xoota had a locust in her mouth, munching on it thoughtfully as she peered through her binoculars. She kept the lenses carefully shaded behind a fan of grass.

"There, what do you make of that?" she said, passing the binoculars to Shaani.

A sonic fence ran around the rim of the plain. Squat, silver blobs moved along the fence lines. Security robots? The defenses looked pretty heavy.

Several places in the starport were covered in rubble. An aircraft seemed to have crashed into the main building long before, causing damaged that had been overgrown with grass and weeds. Elsewhere, crevices had opened into the ground, showing entrances into tunnels below.

A line of powerful, silver figures moved slowly past the flying machines. Even from their distance, they looked colossal. But were they humans or robots? It was hard to tell. They marched in step, with a sinister gait.

"There. I think it's the Plodder tribesmen," said Shaani as she swiveled the field glasses. There was other movement to the left of the main buildings, over at one of the gaps in the ground. Humanoids were trudging out of a tunnel mouth, carrying buckets and baskets loaded with rubble. They were guarded by a giant figure dressed in powered armor. "Slave labor."

The *Sand Shark* had been parked down at the bottom of the cliffs behinds them, under cover of the rocks and trees. There were enough opossums and radioactive rock wallabies in the area to confuse anyone trying to locate the *Sand Shark* crew using heat sensors. From the rock ridge high above, they spied out the lay of the land.

Things did not look good.

Xoota took the binoculars again and tried to get a fix on the armored figures that guarded the laborers. "The computer intelligence must have awakened Benek's frozen superhumans. Looks like they've loaded up on gear from the armory." The quoll sucked a fang in thought. "How many brides did he say there were?"

"Two thousand."

"Kack. That's quite an army." She passed the binoculars back toward Rustle and Wig-wig. "Do you guys want to look?"

Actually that wasn't going to help. Rustle seemed to see via light receptors on his skin, and she doubted Wig-wig could see anything through the glasses, but the earwigs were keen to use the binoculars anyway. They crowded over each other, all trying to peer in at once while Xoota patiently held the binoculars steady.

Shaani pulled out her computer reader. "Computer, starports."

"Basic primer?"

"Primer and guide to typical layout and components." Video and commentaries ran. Shaani sat and concentrated on the screen, her intelligent, rat face perfectly absorbed.

Xoota whipped out her hand and snatched another huge locust from a nearby grass stalk. She waved it toward Shaani. "These locusts are really good. Do you want one?"

"No, thank you. I'm all bugged out."

Xoota crunched the juicy bug and watched the distant starport in thought.

Shaani read her files and watched her videos then eased back up to the ridge. She pointed to the buildings far below. "Right, so it all seems pretty pukkah. Those dart things over there are orbital shuttlecraft. The ones on the little landing pads are atmosphere vehicles—commuter transports. Hangars and maintenance . . . that's the passenger terminal. And communications—including the main computer . . . *There,* where the big tower is."

"Right where they have the slaves digging."

"True." The white rat pointed to a squat tower. "That's apparently an emergency heat vent for the power system. So there must be a reactor somewhere below."

"A reactor?"

"A sort of power generator. Really big scale. Like an atom bomb but exploding very slowly under control."

"Oh, wacko." Xoota looked askance at the starport. She sat down with her back to the rocks. "So to kill this thing, we would have to blow up, short out, or fry the main computer. And any way we do it, we also have to deal with the unfrozen superhumans."

Shaani pondered, tugging at her whiskers. "It should be possible. We would need to disrupt communications so the artificial intelligence can't beam out and escape then detonate the reactor. Theoretically it can be done."

"Theoretically?"

"Never fear. I'm a lab rat." Shaani seemed perfectly happy. "Science is the art of turning theory into practice. Where there's a will, there's a way." The rat slapped Xoota on the bottom. "Come on. Let's get back to the ship. I need to think through a few details."

"You go. I'll be there in a while." Xoota crouched below the rock ridge, looking for any apparent weaknesses. "There seem to be pipes or something over to the left of the starport. I'll see if I can climb a tree and get a better look."

"Well, keep Wig-wig with you. He can watch for danger." Shaani rose to go. "Come along, Rustle. Let's get your leaves all moistened down. You look like you need watering."

. . . . .

Rustle lifted Shaani down from her perch high in the rocks. She doffed her straw hat to him in thanks. With the great plant shambling happily along behind her, the rat made her way back to their beloved ship.

The *Sand Shark* stood beside a wide, brown water hole. Dried creek beds ran all through the area. During the wet season, the region would be lush with streams. But the last remnants of the local water supply were dwindling, patrolled by flash dragonflies. It seemed something else was living down there in the water too; bubbles appeared on the surface from time to time. But whatever it was, it had thus far kept cautiously far away. Budgie was foraging, scratching busily at a mound of dirt near the bow, turning up roots and tubers. Shaani waved to him, but the bird was busy and didn't see.

Shaani led Rustle up the rear ramp and into the hold, where Benek was asleep. She took the plant up on to the deck under the dappled shade and mixed him up a nice, slushy tub of water and compost. Shaani helped him settle down for a nice drink and mulch, happy to see his toothy mouths beaming away as he hydrated.

Shaani unhooked her armor and let it drop. She sailed her hat and goggles onto a lounge chair and straightened out her long, silky-white ponytail.

Time to think. Benek was a moral problem that weighed heavily on the rat's kindly heart. He had been working to secret agendas; the man had strange plans. He may even have never really been a friend. The world was in trouble because of his actions. He had unleashed something positively awful, and it was time he stepped up and helped deal with it. Shaani decided to make the man a nice cup of tea and some fresh fruit scones and sit down to have a decent heart-to-heart.

She carried a tray with tea and scones down the steps into the hold, being careful not to spill. She tried to smile her nicest ratty smile. "Here we go, Benek, old thing. Now let's see if we can sort everything out, shall we?"

Something hit her in the stomach. The rat croaked. Wheezing, she was unable to breathe. A second blow behind the ears made the whole world flash a brilliant white and she went down.

■ ■ ■ ■ ■

Shaani vaguely felt herself being dragged. She was relatively aware of things happening. She lay, unable to think, hearing things—random clanks and bangs . . .

Someone threw water in her face then dragged her into a sitting position, slamming her up against the hull. The rat blinked. Her feet were bound together, her hands tied behind her back, and a rope secured her to a ring bolt. A gag had been shoved into her mouth, tied in place with a greasy length of twine. Shaani felt the whole world spin and whirl.

Benek had managed to shatter his wrist restraints. The man pulled on his armor and found his sword. He then squatted down to look into Shaani's face. "Animals . . . with pretentions. Delusions. Mutant abominations who think to claim the Earth." The man helped himself to Shaani's red security arm bracelet. "Of all of them, you are the most pathetic I have encountered. A rat, a *vermin*. You speak like a human, you walk like a human, but you are not wanted by humanity. You are a creature of the sewers, nothing more. And we will put all of you creatures back where you belong."

With malice, he propped Shaani's computer reader on a box in front of her. He opened up the screen. "Computer. Run all information on laboratory rats. History, breeding, the many uses of."

"Confirmed."

The man turned, took his weapons, and walked out of the ship, heading toward the ancient starport. Behind him, Shaani stared, dazed and lost, as the encyclopedia files began to play.

· · · · ·

Xoota and Wig-wig came back down through the trees that grew all over the sharp slopes of the gully. The quoll was hot and tired. It had taken some time, but she had found a vantage point from which she confirmed the broken pipelines that led beneath the starport fence. The knowledge was hard won: it had taken an hour of arduous tree climbing and led to an encounter with a patch of territorial mistletoe that had pelted her with rock-hard berries. Ahead she saw the ship where she'd left it beside the watering hole and felt a surge of relief. She waved to Budgie, who had made a nest in the cool, shaded dirt between the front wheels. Slinging her shield, Xoota made her way up the back ramp and into the hold.

"Hey, Shaani. I might have found a way in. I don't think the robots have—"

The white rat was sitting, tied up, in the hold, staring bleakly.

Xoota drew her pistol and ran to Shaani's side. Drawing a knife, Xoota hastily cut the rat girl free. "What happened?

Where's Benek?" she asked, though she knew the answer. "Wig-wig, check the ship. Make sure it's okay and look for Benek." Xoota returned her attention to Shaani, who had yet to move. She removed her gag and peppered her with questions. "Has he gone? Did he hurt you? Are you all right?"

Xoota froze when she realized the rat girl was silently crying.

Shaani had been weeping, long and hopelessly. She simply sat in place, utterly lost. Xoota hastily checked for traces of drugs but found none. Shaani shivered under her touch like a broken animal, staring at the computer screen. Xoota looked at the screen, saw the images, and suddenly felt cold.

The film showed lab rats—little, white rodents, kept in cages. They were tools for human scientists, bred at whim, used horribly as subjects on which to test drugs and petty cosmetics. They were used for surgery and vile experiments. They were organic tools, killed and vivisected at whim, bred for death and torture.

Xoota grabbed Shaani's face and turned it away from the screen. She held her friend tightly in her arms, wanting to somehow crush the hurt out of her. Wig-wig hastily turned the computer off.

Xoota had no idea what to say. She tightened her fingers in Shaani's hair, and simply rocked her to and fro. "You are our scientist. You're the smartest creature I've ever known."

Rustle came blundering up to the hatch, full of concern. He snapped his jaws, waving his tentacles, signaling that Benek was nowhere in sight.

"Benek gone. He let all our water run out of the tanks," said Wig-wig.

Xoota looked up at her crew. "He must have gone to the starport. Wig-wig, stay with Shaani. Don't let her be alone. I have to steer us out of here before he gets to the computer and it finds out we're here." Xoota estimated they had about an hour until sunset. If they were lucky, they'd find cover before the computer's minions could attack. "Rustle, ready the sails."

Xoota raced for the control cabin. She had to leave Shaani in the many little hands of the earwigs. Shaani was the best friend she had ever had. And Benek had hurt her in the worst possible way. When Xoota caught him, she would cut him open and let him bleed out on the sands.

CHAPTER 13

The first light of predawn filtered out across the plains. Above the burned grass, two wicked, little, silver airships hunted for prey. The computer entity was hungry for blood and used the metallic drones to search for signs of the *Sand Shark*. Looking to flush the crew out, ships fired into anything that might offer cover, but the only thing they succeeded in finding were double-headed emus and spiked kangaroos.

The *Sand Shark* was not on the plains. She was neither hiding in a stand of trees nor taking shelter in the hills. Instead, she sped along the hard-packed beach at the very edge of the ocean, catching a stiff sea breeze. She raced so fast that she almost heeled clean off her starboard wheels. There had been no time to take on new ballast. But the ship was steady, the terrain utterly flat. The *Sand Shark* raced through a moonlit night suspended between the worlds of land and sea. Then it met the looming sandstone cliffs that were down the shore. As daylight hit, the ship made her way over flat sand, and Xoota parked her in the shadow of the cliffs beside the sea.

As they looked back at their course, they saw that the waves had washed away the ship's tracks in the sand. Xoota had been driving the ship hard, with half an eye over her shoulder, expecting death to strike from above. Her antennae tingled from overuse. But that bit of luck was welcome. The quoll rose from her control chair and made her way out onto the deck, where Rustle and Wig-wig were securing ropes and checking knots.

Shaani sat on the deck, in the shadow of the cabin. They had put a blanket around her, but it had slipped off her shoulders. The rat's eyes were blank, her fur, dull. Xoota looked at her, feeling desperate. She had no idea what to do; people skills were decidedly not her strong point. The quoll walked over to quietly consult with the earwig swarm.

"Hey, Wig-wig, how is she?"

Wig-wig gave off a chorus of worried, little sighs. "Sad. She will not talk to I."

"Okay." Xoota rubbed her face, trying to think. "All right. Well, you guys go and rest." She patted Rustle on his big, green trunk. "And well done. We made one hell of a good run. We hit eighty kph down on the sand."

They were almost back at the old desalination plant. Xoota had no idea what to do next. For that, they needed Shaani. When in doubt, tea shall be your salvation. Xoota brewed a pot using the water from her canteen and fetched the ancient, blue-striped mugs that Shaani set such store by. She poured the tea, adding condensed milk brought all the way from Watering Hole. She sat beside Shaani and said nothing.

The rat girl held her mug and stared sadly at the deck. Xoota looked down at her own boots.

"This is our world. We're the ones making it. It's all about what we do, not about the past. About things we can't control. I need you. We all need you."

The rat hunched in on herself.

Xoota felt a sudden stab of annoyance. "Who built this ship? Who even figured out that it was possible? Who navigated us across the entire desert?" The quoll kicked her boot heel irritably against the deck. "Gas masks, artifacts. You made a forge out of nothing but charcoal, mud, and sand.

"You're scientist. Not because anyone bred you to be one or meant you to be one. You had an image of what you wanted to be—a noble image—and you became it."

The quoll blushed. She stood up and looked over the rails.

"This is Gamma Terra. No one cares what your people were. What's important is what you *are*. And you are a *scientist*. Now drink your tea; then come sit with us at the railings. We need you to tell us how we're going to beat Benek and this damned computer army."

Xoota walked off, slightly embarrassed by having spoken her mind but confident that what she said was true. As she looked out at the sunrise on the ocean, Shaani joined her at the rail.

"We're near the desalination plant?" asked Shaani tentatively.

Xoota nodded. "About ten kilometers, far as I can figure."

"Good. We can do this."

"How?"

The rat sighed. "With EMP. With a stiff upper lip . . . and with science." She lifted her mug. "Always with science."

The sound of the sea was soothing. Standing beside the *Sand Shark*'s rail, the white rat laid out her plan for her friends to see.

Bugs, sewers, and reactors. Science at work . . .

．．．．．

Nighttime under a dying moon. A vast field of ancient buildings, dazzling white beneath the haze of countless spotlights. Small figures working. Vehicles moving. The night was filled with the distant sounds of industry. Sparks from robot welding equipment bounced and danced across the rock. Somewhere in the depths of the buildings, heavy engines hummed.

It had taken two days for the *Sand Shark*'s crew to prepare themselves. Finally Xoota, Shaani, Rustle, and Wig-wig crept along a dusty gully toward a nest of ancient sewer pipes. The ship was hidden in a stand of trees nearby. Dawn would surely see the ship discovered. But she was there, ready for a fast escape should everything go as planned.

When everything went as planned, Xoota reminded herself as she gingerly carried her bundle down toward the sewers. She hastened after Shaani holding her package as if it were a ticking time bomb.

"It's burning me. I can feel it burning me."

The white rat twirled her tail. "The drugs will fight that off for a while."

Xoota gingerly shifted her package. "How long is a while?"

"Oh, long enough. It's only radiation; don't be such a baby."

Both women carried bundles of old tablecloths taken from the ancient prison. Inside the tablecloths, they each had one of the huge pupae of gamma moths taken from the desalination plant. The damned things were due to hatch in days, maybe only hours. Xoota was sure she could feel the creature stirring. In the dark, the cocoons all glowed a faint, unpleasant green. Xoota and the others had loaded up with antiradiation drugs so they could withstand the rads, but Shaani with her natural immunity didn't need any.

They made their way along a gully filled with rusting metal and shattered concrete. Shaani and Xoota were clad in their newly fitted armor—elegant black suits that had a definite sense of style. Wig-wig bustled along beside them, and Rustle followed, carrying yet a pair of radioactive pupae. Shaani and Xoota climbed up to the weeds that edged the gully. Out on the old tarmac, slaves were clearing rubble as a robot whirred around. Standing guard over the ships were sinister figures clad in sealed suits of ancient armor. The men inside the suits were clearly as massive as Benek, juggernauts of muscle, bone, and steel.

Xoota watched all the dust and activity in careful thought. "What are they doing?"

"Nothing good." Shaani's ears twitched as some sort of distant machinery broke down in a screech of gears. "But I think it has them a tad distracted. Thank Oppenheimer for small mercies." The rat inspected the insides of a broken pipe that led off toward the ancient starport. "I can't see any traps or sensors here. They mustn't be aware of it."

Shaani pulled out a little, homemade toy, a ranging device she had made for their catapult. Rustle held it steady while she took a sight from each arm of the device then checked the angles. She jotted numbers down into her notebook with a stubby pencil. "Range is . . . I make it about nine hundred and fifty meters . . ." The rat rubbed her eyes, looking tired.

Xoota watched her carefully. "Are you all right?"

"I'm fine. Just a new alpha coming on. Feels like a wonky one." She looked away then deliberately straightened her shoulders. "Right, let's get cracking."

The rat was still haunted by that damned computer and its articles on lab rats. Xoota cursed Benek then cursed the whole damned human race.

The tunnel was blocked by large slabs of crushed and broken pipe. Rustle bumbled over, lashed out with his powerful tendrils, and wrenched the rubble aside. Shaani shined a flashlight down the tunnel, powering it with her own bare hand. The way looked dusty but unoccupied. The pipe seemed to stretch off forever into the dark.

"Right, chaps, here we go."

The team crept into the concrete tunnel. Rustle had to crouch to move, but the team went carefully onward, with Shaani lighting the way.

Xoota tried to hitch back her shield. "Are you sure the moths will do the trick?"

"Quite sure." Shaani's white face glimmered in the dark. She looked sleek in the full set of ancient armor, ponytail, and spectacles. Her fusion-powered chainsaw was a wonderful added touch of insanity. "The moths flash heavy electromagnetic pulses. They will disrupt any complex electronics within hundreds of meters around them.

"We have to plant some next to the communications equipment in order to destroy the computer intelligence's means of escape. And the others—we will plant them down near the reactor, inside the main shielding."

"And when they hatch, that will blow up the power plant?"

"Oh, it will be a damned impressive bang." The rat patted her bundle. "Thankfully we'll have some time to get away in the ship before these little devils hatch. QED."

Xoota looked at her bundle in thought. Gamma moths were the least-loved beings in all of Gamma Terra. She was certain she could feel her skin tingling from radiation. "How big will this explosion be?"

"That depends on what sort of reactor. I mean, it could be an itty-bitty fusion deal. That's about a kiloton worth of bang. Then again, if it's an antimatter reaction chamber, we could be looking at a megaton. Might get a bit dicey."

Xoota gave an uncomprehending shrug. "But what sort of force does that translate to?"

The rat hitched up her chainsaw. "Well, look at it this way. The bombs from our catapult are about three kilos. Three hundred and thirty three of them would equal a single ton. Three hundred and thirty three *thousand* of them would equal a kiloton. Three hundred and thirty three *million* of them would equal one megaton."

"Oh." Xoota blinked. "Wacko."

"Should be a bit of an eye-opener." The rat waved the way forward down the tunnel. "All right. Come along, chaps. Science ever onwards."

Xoota took point with her shield up and pistol out, spare energy cells tucked into her belt pouch. Wig-wig swarmed along beside her, partly on the floor and partly on the walls. Behind then, Shaani carefully counted her paces. She had a notebook and pencil fixed to her forearm and her insanely sharp chainsaw held in her hands. She used her penlight to check markings that were printed on the walls.

The old tunnel echoed as the team moved cautiously forward. Thankfully they had not encountered any creatures in the pipe. There was only sand, a few rocks, and a smell of dust. But ahead they noticed a small, bronze box, flat and smooth at the edges, had been affixed to the ceiling of the tunnel.

Xoota motioned Wig-wig to a halt and edged a little closer. She quested carefully with her whiskers and her eyes. "Shaani?"

The rat came quietly forward, ears pricking. There was a faint humming in the air. "Another sonic fence, I think." She moved her hand with its blue and gold ID bracelet closer to the line across the tunnel. There was a faint whining sound that felt like a needle being hammered into the brain. The rat jerked back her hand. "Bother. Ah well, we'll use the tried and true."

Rustle opened a bag and pulled out the two alien teleportation units. Shaani used the tip of her chainsaw to push it carefully past the fence line until it was well clear of the danger. Shaani set up the other unit for action.

"Wig-wig? Once you get through, just flip that little switch on the box up on the wall. That ought to be the cutoff."

"Okay, pretty rat." The earwigs bustled into the teleportation unit. "It won't take a minute."

The earwigs transferred past the invisible fence line. Wig-wig gathered up his many happy parts then skittered merrily up the wall. It took the bugs a few tries to push the switch atop the bronze box—the earwigs were not really made for exerting quite that kind of force—but the fence shut down with a dying hum, and the passageway was quiet. Shaani tested the area by edging her hand forward. All was well, and the party crossed the invisible line.

From up on the wall, Wig-wig seemed to frown. "There is a little light here. It is red."

Shaani immediately came to look at the bronze box. A tiny, red light was blinking softly.

Xoota cursed. "Tell me that just means it's on standby."

"Let's hope it's not an alarm." The rat flicked the switch and turned the fence back on. The red light disappeared. "These are old systems. Hopefully the computer will think it's just a minor flutter."

There was nothing for it except to move on.

As they advanced into the darkness, Shaani counted the paces. There were shafts branching out here and there, metal ladders set into the stone for access to the surface. Each of them had a sonic fence box, designed to be switched off from inside the tunnels. Along the way, they found small drainage tunnels that fed into the main pipe. The drainage tunnels were wide enough for Shaani and Xoota to crawl through but would never fit Rustle. Shaani ignored the side routes and headed for the heart of the complex.

Something whirred in the main pipe ahead. Xoota froze. The team switched off their flashlight only to see electric light glimmering far ahead. Something was heading down the pipe,

"Back," whispered Xoota, and they ran back as far as one of the shafts leading to the surface. Xoota pointed to Rustle. The plant fed itself up the shaft, climbing with two heads at the top and one hanging down, the jaws looking ludicrously scared of being caught. Wig-wig and Xoota climbed into one of the side pipes. Shaani made sure the area was clear of telltale signs of passage then followed them into the pipe. She lay flat, whiskers questing, watching the tunnel outside.

It was a robot, a rounded, orange ball with a flat base and a host of tools and tentacles. The thing moved slowly and steadily down the tunnel, humming softly to itself as it passed by, presumably to check on the sonic fence. Rustle started to emerge from his hiding place, but Shaani frantically waved him back. The wide maw jerked back into hiding, and all was still.

Long minutes passed.

Finally the humming returned. The robot glided back up the corridor, on toward the starport, and disappeared.

Shaani carefully emerged from the pipe and looked around, her whiskers questing. "Righto. We should be clear."

The team moved on.

The ground above them began to feel alive. There was a sense of motion, of hidden power. Shaani held a hand against the tunnel ceiling, feeling the flow of electrical currents up above. There was a huge power flow, coming from the east . . . and coming up from below? The reactor must be deeper below the ground.

At about nine hundred fifty meters, there was another vertical shaft. Xoota climbed the rungs. She switched off the sonic fence—there was no other choice—and opened up the hatchway overhead.

Xoota peered out into an enormous oblong hall, lit from above by flickering strips of light. Tall stacks of boxes were piled in neat, orderly rows. She risked a swift look then climbed up and ran into cover between the boxes. Wig-wig, Shaani, and Rustle then followed. The hatch clanged shut.

Rustle had only just ducked his bulk behind a pile of boxes when the orange robot returned. It reached out with a tentacle and opened the hatch, stopped, and reached for the on/off switch for the sonic fence. It turned the fence back on and withdrew its tentacle. The hatch clanged back shut. The robot glided away, off down the hall.

Shaani looked unhappy. Xoota understood. The robot may have registered that a sonic fence had been deliberately switched off. If the computer intelligence were alert, then it might be on its guard, which meant they were going to have to get in and out as fast as possible.

Xoota gathered her team. "Right. We have to move fast." She drew a quick map in the dust. "We're about *here,* in the central complex. There's that big field of fallen rubble out there, which should give some cover. Wig-wig and Rustle, you head this direction and get to the communications center. Try and hide your moth pupae somewhere around the machinery." The damned moths were definitely moving inside their cocoons. "Don't fight. Get in, drop the moths, get out. Wig-wig, keep your radio on."

The earwigs sat up, politely listening. "What about Plodder peoples?"

"If you can get them out, then do it. Otherwise just run for the ship. We'll get them out ourselves."

Xoota made sure the earwigs and the plant had all of their equipment. "Shaani and I will head for the reactor. We'll see you back at the ship."

"Be safe. And watch out for cameras," Shaani added.

The earwigs and Rustle both headed off, the plant terribly conspicuous as he crept along with his heads held low, peeking around corners. Large doors leading outside hung half ajar. Wig-wig peeked through then led the way outside.

Shaani slung her makeshift sack containing the moth pupa over her back. She pointed to a long, dark corridor leading south. "This way."

"Are you sure?"

The rat shrugged. "I'm a . . . I'm special. Remember?"

Xoota gripped her shoulder. "Stay behind me. The alarm might have already been raised." This could all go to hell in a real hurry, she added silently to herself.

• • • • •

The rat and quoll flitted carefully along a dark, shattered passageway. They moved as fast as they dared. The walls sagged inward; broken concrete choked the floor. Xoota ducked and led the way, threading down a side passage and squeezing past a pile of shattered rock. A flight of steps led down into a zone with dark, metallic walls. There were exposed pipes and flooring made from metallic plates. Noises sounded louder as they reflected off the surfaces, which made stealthy movement difficult. But as they progressed, a deep, powerful vibration began to permeate the air. The walls and floor shivered and made their fur slowly stand on end. They saw a ruined elevator shaft in a corridor. The open doors exposed a rusty cable that dangled even farther down into the pitch dark.

Shaani brushed off the ancient, weathered plate beside the doors. The script was in an omega dialect she recognized. "Engineering—basement level three."

Xoota looked down into the pitch-black shaft and slung her gear behind her. "How many more levels are there?" she asked without expecting an answer. She wrapped her tail around the ancient, metal cable as she took hold with her hands. "Guess we'll find out." She climbed down a little ways then waited for Shaani to test whether the cable would hold them.

As they carefully made their way down into the dark, the cable swayed. Showering rust made it hard for Xoota to look up. Thankfully it wasn't totally dark: Shaani had a penlight between her teeth. The light still wasn't too comforting as they continued ever farther down, past doors that were rusted shut and covered in grime; down finally to the lowest point in the shaft, where they dropped gingerly onto the ground.

Shaani jimmied a little crowbar into the crack between the doors and pried it open enough for each to worm their fingers into the gap. With all their strength, they were able to pull the rusting doors open enough for them to pass through.

Shaani stuck her narrow head through the gap first. She checked the dark space behind with her penlight, and it seemed clear. Xoota went first, pistol at the ready, and Shaani followed, passing through the moth pupae and their gear.

"No guards yet. I hope that means they aren't all closing in on the other two," said Shaani.

"Darwin only knows." Xoota looked for exits. "Are we on the right level? Which way should we go?"

"That way." Shaani pointed to the left doorway. "There's electrical power down there. Lots of it."

"You're sure?"

The rat hunched her shoulders. "Trust me. I'm a lab rat."

They came into a place where the air grew chill amid the sharp tang of ozone—a scent and feel of something ancient, something vast. Shaani and Xoota felt their way slowly forward in the empty space below the ground. The constant hum had grown stronger, almost as though the air quivered in the dark. Ahead they could see a space haunted by a blue glow, a cavern that opened up all around them, ice cold and deathly still. They stood at the upper level of a great, yawning gulf. Tier after tier of walls below them were filled with frosted booths, the glass doors smothered in ice. There were thousands of the booths, at least five levels, stacked one upon the other down to a floor below.

Xoota's fur shivered. Her antennae stood stiffly. She felt many futures, terrifying futures that chilled her right to the soul.

"This is more than two thousand," said Shaani, making a quick calculation.

There was no sign of security cameras or monitoring equipment of any kind. The pair could only guess it was there somewhere and try to stay out of sight. Moving carefully into the room, Shaani crossed over a metal balcony rail and lowered herself beside the first layer of booths. She wiped at the frost as Xoota dropped down beside her.

The inside of the booth seemed fogged with gas. A figure lay inside the chamber, a human with reddish skin and no hair. It was massive with frighteningly powerful muscles laid over heavy bone. It appeared so strong and brawny it almost didn't seem to be the same species as Benek.

Shaani looked at the thing in puzzlement. "It's male."

"This one too." Xoota had smeared the ice from another booth.

Shaani found a stairway that fed to a lower level. She quickly descended.

Xoota looked down at her from above.

Shaani wiped away more ice. "Another one . . . actually, it's the same."

Several other freezers were hastily wiped clear. Each frozen figure was identical to the last—the same face, the same build—utterly exact. The rat stared at them, and Xoota's skin started to crawl.

"This is a frozen army. These things are clones." Shaani examined one of the frozen beings carefully. "Look at these things. They must be military."

Xoota was on all fours, examining the power feeds that joined the freezing booths. She rose and looked at a small screen fixed to the side of the nearest freezer. Lights blinked; the screen showed ticking numbers and an outline of a human body. Xoota felt a sudden clench of fear. "Shaani, these things are thawing."

The rat stared then took out her computer reader and switched it on. "Computer, freezing of bodies. Basic instruction to equipment and parameters."

"Query: Did you mean to ask about cryogenic storage of living subjects or the freezing of the dead?"

"Living subjects." The rat read fast.

Meanwhile, Xoota ran up and down, checking booth after booth. Not all were unfreezing, just one section of the second row—perhaps only a three hundred enormous, genetically engineered killing machines. "Shaani, how long have we got?"

"Just a tick. Just a tick . . . here." The rat read swiftly. "It says it's a slow process. About seventy-two hours."

"If they've already had at least two days, in a few hours we'll be neck deep in these damned things." The quoll looked over the power lines. "Can we stop the process?"

"Yes, by doing what we came to do." Shaani followed the power cables running across the floors, heading to the far end of the chamber. "Shake a leg."

▪ ▪ ▪ ▪ ▪

Shaani and Xoota ran quickly down the steps toward the chamber floor, jumping to the last level when the rusted steps looked too dangerous to use. They followed the huge power cables off into the gloom. The cables snaked their way along the floors, twisting like intestines.

The quoll and rat moved fast, clinging to the darkest shadows and twitching nervously when ice slid from a slowly thawing freezer door. It felt as though they were being watched.

The cables twisted down into a tunnel that was almost choked with slick, tangled power lines. Shaani knelt and looked into the dark, narrow spaces. She took the lead, climbing head-first down into the dark. They struggled through the gloomy space, wriggling like worms in the darkness.

Xoota fought to keep her gear in place. Her shield and the moth pupa proved damned difficult to move. Humming noises were louder and louder.

Shaani slithered downward, almost falling. She clung to a cable but slipped further. Her whiskers sensed a wide, open space before her in the dark.

There was a gulf there, a place where the air crackled with electricity. Shaani felt the slow crackle running over her skin. It was as if the jet black space floated with shifting ghosts. The rat managed to find her little penlight and shined a beam of light into the dark. A cheerful, yellow sign hung before her.

The rat was upside down, so she craned her head to try to read the runes.

"Oh, my."

"What?" Xoota couldn't see from behind. "What is it?"

"The reactor." The rat twisted her head more, trying to read the sign. "Says here it's a matter converter."

"Matter converter? Converting to what?"

"It turns matter into doesn't-matter." Shaani started wriggling herself free. "Come on."

"Wait . . ." Xoota tried to get free. "Is that the kiloton one or the megaton one?"

"Ah, best not to ask." The rat managed to free her feet from the tangling cables. "Come on." She pulled a cable loose and used it as a rope to lower herself to the floor.

Xoota joined her and turned on a bio light.

They stood in a space between giant pipes and tubes. Ropes of dust hung everywhere. The dirt on the floor was jet black and many centimeters deep.

The whole place shivered to the hum of ancient engines. The explorers walked forward between rows of vast machines, approaching a titanic sphere that stood at the center of the cavern. The sphere crackled with little wisps of electricity.

Xoota crouched in cover. "Is that it?"

"That's the beast." The rat carefully put her moth pupa on the ground. The thing was visibly wriggling. "That's the core. Disrupt that and the power plant will blow."

There was plenty of dust and dirt. Shaani and Xoota looked around then simply stuffed the cocoons under piles of greasy, old dirt. Xoota tucked her moth pupa into place and recoiled as the thing bucked in her hand.

"Shaani? These things are hatching."

"Just stop agitating it."

"*Me* agitating *it*?" The quoll dropped the cocoon and threw dirt at it from a distance. "Let's get the hell out of here."

· · · · ·

Xoota hauled herself upward over the slick cables, feeling as if she were wriggling like a meal in the guts of a snake. Climbing through the conduit they had just descended, they reemerged in the cryogenics chamber and headed for their escape route to the outer world. Xoota led the way but stopped for a moment to use her extra sense of possible futures. Something shivered just at the edge of her perception, a sudden, creeping feeling that there was something wrong . . .

Her antennae jerked. She caught a flash of a future in which Shaani was gunned down. Xoota lunged into Shaani with her shoulder and brought the rat down to the floor just as a purple bolt of energy slammed into her own back, hurling her against the wall. She fell to the ground, jerking, smoke rising from her chest. Shaani stared then snatched the quoll by her belt and dragged her aside. She flung herself flat behind a heaped tangle of power cables. The rat threw a fistful of pipe bombs out into the cavern. The resulting explosion severed pipes, and freezing gasses jetted out into the air.

More energy bolts slammed into the wall as figures loomed in the dark, massive, armored forms, their forearms lifted. Bolts ripped past Shaani's cover. The rat dragged Xoota into hiding. She tore open Xoota's armor, seeing the burn mark on the quoll's chest. Shaani fumbled for her medical kit while Xoota swallowed and tried to focus.

The quoll blundered a hand up and seized Shaani's arm. "Get out of here." Her hands shook as she gripped Shaani's armor. "Run."

The rat pulled out an injector. "That's not going to happen."

· · · · ·

Shaani checked herself for any new alphas that might get Xoota up and running with her again.

Suddenly Xoota choked. She slumped, her eyes unfocused, unmoving.

Shaani stared in shock. "Xoota?" Shaani felt a raw surge of terror. "Xoota!" She felt for a pulse. The quoll's heart was still. Emergency procedures. She banged a fist against Xoota's chest, hoping to restart her heart. She pumped, just as the encyclopedia had instructed. Ten rapid pumps then she felt for a pulse again.

Nothing.

Sobbing, the rat put a hand on Xoota's chest, to either side of her heart, closed her eyes, and surged electricity into her friend. The body bucked beneath her. Shaani slumped, exhausted. Xoota lay still and unmoving.

Again, she had to do it again.

The rat slammed a second shock into Xoota's heart, willing it to start. Shaani felt her power ebbing but forced herself to find more. Suddenly Xoota drew in a huge, ragged, sobbing breath. She was alive. The quoll looked up, confused, her eyes focused on something over Shaani's shoulder.

Shaani snatched up Xoota's pistol, turned, and opened fire on a towering figure blundering toward her.

The purple bolt from the pistol died against a force field that enfolded the enemy. She fired again and again, the kick-back of the gun making her hand ache as the enemy's force field turned orange, then red, and finally failed in a flash. The beam gouged into the armor, sending a gout of molten metal through the dark.

Another figure pushed past the first. It aimed a glove at Shaani and fired. She ducked aside, and the wall behind her smashed open, spitting sparks. She tried to lead them away from Xoota, firing at the shapes that marched toward her in the dark, more and more of them, great boots thumping on the floor.

Shaani fired again and the battery died. *Damn!* She had no time to reload. Large, armored hands reached through a mass of pipes toward her. Shaani drew her chainsaw and swung for the monster's head.

The weapon showered sparks as it tried to cut through the armored suit. Trapped in the pipes and cables, the enemy thrashed. Its force field suddenly failed, and the chainsaw bit home. The armored clone lost one arm, and sparks spit from the systems inside. But the clone backhanded Shaani with its remaining arm and sent her slamming hard against a wall.

The rat fell to the floor, dazed. She wove to her feet and fired a blast of radiation at a metal figure that loomed in the dark. The blast was powerless against the defenses of its suit.

Just then an armored monster snatched Shaani by the root of her ponytail and hauled her to her feet. The creature held her in its terrible grip. Shaani hammered at it helplessly, radiation blasts dispersing over its screens. She grabbed at the faceplate, found a latch, and managed to rip the plate up and away. A human skull leered at her from the helmet.

Shaani sagged and made a croaking noise, terrified out of her mind. The monster threw her to the ground. Dazed, the rat tried to crawl away, heading toward Xoota. A undead monster raised a foot to stamp her into the ground.

"Hold."

A suave voice called out from the dark. The skeletal monster stopped. It slowly withdrew its foot and turned to face another figure in the dark.

The skull-faced armor spoke in a savage, grating voice. "The mutant must be purged."

Another armored behemoth walked forward, its metal feet making the ground tremble. The creature raised its visor. From inside the helmet, Benek's face sneered. "The sewer rat and the scavenger." His voice dripped sheer scorn. "Of course."

More armored monsters appeared in the dark. Yellowed, half-mummified skulls were inside the helmet bowls. The voice that came from their helmets was the voice from the ancient prison, the sound of the deadly computer consciousness. "All mutants must be purged."

"Yes, my friend." Benek patted one of the armors on its shoulder. "But information is a weapon. Where there are these ones, there will be their mutant friends." Benek signaled to the undead monsters. "Strip them. Bring their equipment. Bring them to the observation deck."

Cold claws grabbed at Shaani. Her groping hand found something on her belt. She fumbled for it blindly as hands latched on to her arms. She pushed the object into Xoota's grasp, meeting her eye.

The monsters had her. They pulled Shaani, tearing off her armor, her equipment, leaving her nothing, not even underwear. Xoota received similar treatment.

They were dragged helplessly through halls filled with the slowly thawing legions of clones. All around them, the withered skulls gleamed in the darkness.

"Death to the mutant. Long live the empire of genetic purity."

CHAPTER 14

Out on the tarmac, there was a good deal of activity. Some Plodder tribesmen were being driven to work at shifting rubble, watched over by an egg-shaped robot that held a pistol in one of its tentacles.

"Work. All mutants must serve or die," the robot croaked at its prisoners as they labored to unblock the tunnels that led to the chambers far below. It was old and damaged, partly covered in lichen from a century and a half of lying in the rocks. But the robot was under the control of an evil mind. It cruised along, jerking from time to time as its drives fluttered. It was barking another of its relentless commands when a giant rock dropped onto it from high above.

Squeeeee, came the sound from the ruined piece of machinery.

Several dozen earwigs and three big carnivorous plant heads peered over the edge of the roof up above, watching the proceedings below in interest. The earwigs tilted their heads in puzzlement.

"Why do robots go *'squee'* when you breaks them?"

Rustle held up a few leaves in an apparent shrug, clearly having no idea.

They climbed down a ladder from the roof and investigated the spitting, sparking wreckage of the robot. Its pistol was still intact, so Rustle picked it up, twirled it around the end of one tentacle, and stuffed it into his leaves for safekeeping.

Wig-wig waved toward the Plodder people, who stared at the earwigs and Rustle in shock. "Is friends come to rescue you. Run away now and be free."

Tadash, the old chief scholar of the Plodder people stared. "Good lord."

"No, no. Is Wig-wig and Rustle." Wig-wig sat up prettily while Rustle beamed. "Turn off sonic fences from this side before you cross, then run very far."

"How far should we run?"

Wig-wig was pleased. "One megaton of far."

The Plodder tribe ran.

Wig-wig and Rustle continued into the rubble. The communications room lay half open to the outer world, with one wall rent by a wide crack. Rustle peered inside, followed by Wig-wig. The place was full of wires and controls and nifty-looking machines. They dropped their two gamma moth cocoons inside and felt well pleased.

"Mission accomplished. Time to go home." Wig-wig danced around in delight. "This was easy. This was a very good plan."

There were many enormous, armored figures at the far end of the spaceport, lifting massive engines back up into the ships. But it was all too far away to concern Wig-wig and Rustle, who kept to the cover of the rubble and made an unhurried exit. It seemed best to head back to the ship the same way they had come, so they climbed back up a ladder onto the roof of an old hangar, thus missing the area of tarmac covered by security cameras down below. Pleased with their cunning, the two friends made their way over to the main terminal buildings and climbed back in through a shattered window.

The upper floors of the old starport were dusty, dark, and empty. Only a few overhead lights still worked. Some potted plants had overgrown their bounds, colonizing what once had been commissary and cafeteria. The plants waved, clearly carnivorous. Wig-wig kept well away.

Rustle stopped at an old stand filled with sunglasses and selected three pairs, putting them on and admiring himself in a piece of polished tile. It seemed a good place to go shopping for a while. Rustle filled a string bag with interesting items: detective novels, a power-cell recharger, an electric toothbrush . . .

Then the noise began. Crashing, marching feet—metal boots stamping on the tiles in unison. Rustle put himself into a corner behind a stand of swaying mutant ferns and struck an innocent pose. Wig-wig simply flew up to hide inside a broken overhead light. The brutal footsteps came closer and closer until suddenly the hall doors burst open wide.

Twelve suits made out of gleaming silver duralloy marched in absolute unison. They all moved together, faceplates open to show the skeletons of long-dead occupants still rattling around inside. Wig-wig watched them pass, creeping out to peer upside down from the ceiling.

More footsteps announced another group of skeletal warriors. Two of the armored figures had Xoota and Shaani pinioned in their arms. Others carried armor and equipment bundled into bags. Sauntering behind them, wearing powered armor of his own, came Benek. The man seemed utterly at ease.

As the parade marched off to the center of the terminal, Wig-wig slid down from the ceiling, and Rustle emerged into view.

"Uh-oh," said the earwigs tentatively. Wig-wig thought about what to do. Shaani would have made a plan, and Xoota would go and kick someone in the arse. Wig-wig wondered which of the two he and Rustle should do. The insect and the plant both pondered, looking off along the darkened terminal.

Wig-wig nodded. "Wig-wig will deal with the computer. Rustle can deal with Benek, yes?"

Rustle beamed and nodded. It seemed fair.

"Okay, let's rescue rattie and quoll."

Rustle snapped his three toothy jaws. He headed off in pursuit of the armored suits. Wig-wig fluttered around and began searching through the offices that adjoined the dark, abandoned concourse.

An old computer terminal stood in an office. Wig-wig crawled up and over the desk and nosed around, looking for buttons and switches. One earwig pressed the screen, which instantly blossomed into life.

A savage, gravelly voice came from the speakers. "Identify."

"Hello. I'm me." The insects nosed the screen. "Who is you?"

"I am the supreme mind. Now the supreme mind has supreme purpose."

"Ooh, what is purpose?"

The computer screen pulsed red. "To purge and destroy the mutant, leaving only perfection."

"Oh." The insects raised their antennae high. "Is you perfect?"

"I am."

"You sound like the game we used to play."

"The game gives purpose. The game has given direction. Now we are the game, and the world shall be purged."

The bugs waggled their feet. "But you are no good at the game. You can never beat the master of the game."

The computer seemed to brood. "There was one other mind . . . Once, there was . . . G.I.A.N.T."

The insects sidled up to the screen. "I am G.I.A.N.T. And I can beat you."

The screen flickered a dark, dull red. "You cannot."

"Can too."

The computer gave a dark growl. "I am supreme. All who challenge me must fail."

Bugs stuck out their tongues. "Nyaaa. Prove it."

There was a pause. Suddenly the screen lit up with the opened menus for the computer game Mutant Purge.

Wig-wig made a little noise of glee. He started up the game and began to play.

After the first few minutes, the computer started losing. The insects were rather practiced and wickedly devious. The computer grimly tried to fight back.

It took more and more processing power.

The computer attacked and parried. Wig-wig's characters danced mockingly aside. The computer snarled, fighting back with every iota of its will.

More and more computing power went into playing the game.

• • • • •

"It is amazing, isn't it?"

Benek pressed a switch on his forearm and deactivated his force field. He stood with his helmet open, gazing out of the balcony windows at the starport below. A row of shuttlecraft sat on the tarmac, their engines being serviced and refitted by robots and the slow, menacing shapes of powered armors. It was a fleet—a fleet with enough firepower to rule a continent.

"My fleet. And now with the computer persona as my ally, I have my army."

Xoota hung in a zombie trooper's arms. She looked at the man in hatred. "So your computer buddy is okay with your plans for world domination?"

"Oh, yes. It seems that great minds truly *do* think alike." Benek paced, his massive armor thudding. His hands were encased in duralloy gauntlets that could crush a skull to pulp. Xoota struggled as he stroked her under the chin. "So what were you after? What brought you here, knowing I would have reached here before you?"

"The armory. The photo you had showed the armory. It's worth a fortune."

"Ah, and so the desert scavenger would be a loser no longer?" Benek turned his attention to the beautiful rat. "But why would *you* come? Why would a mere sewer dweller put herself at risk?"

Beside Xoota, Shaani bitterly hung her head. "To find a gun and kill you with it. To prove I'm better than you."

One of the powered armors out on the tarmac slowed then stopped. It dropped the equipment it was carrying and stood still.

Shaani raised her brow. She saw another powered armor outside the windows cease to move, then another, and another.

Interesting.

The observation lounge of the starport still had a tarnished glory. Overgrown plants cluttered the balconies and alcoves. The center of the room was filled with sculptures of birds in flight. Benek turned to look over the row of space shuttles awaiting his new legions. Behind him, his guard of skeletal armored warriors all stood stock-still.

"With the computer controlling the powered armors, we have invulnerable firepower. And with the clone army awakening, ready to imprint upon me as their leader, I will have entire legions. The database holds the location of other weapons caches, other armories. We will have power unseen on this world since the Great Disaster." The man slapped a hand onto the shoulder of the nearest armored suit. "Together, we will conquer the world. None will stand before us."

The computer voice growled from the armor, slightly dull and distracted. "The opponent must be overcome. Must be beaten. All resources must be committed."

"Yes. No holding back. Total commitment. A vision of genetic purity. A new world."

The computer struggled. "I engage G.I.A.N.T. I will overcome."

Benek clanked back to stand before his prisoners. "Yes. But first, what shall we do with these? These *things* that have so belittled us during our journey into greatness?" Benek waved a hand at the armors holding Shaani and Xoota. "Release them." The powered armors did not move. "Release them, I said."

Xoota managed to jerk herself free. She fell onto all fours on the floor.

Benek stood over her, fists on his hips, braying in triumph. "And so there you are—a mutant marsupial, with your antennae and your whiskers and your absurd pouch. An evolutionary abomination." The man gave a sour laugh. "Have you anything to say before we pass judgment upon you?"

"Yeah." The quoll looked up. "I've told you before. Quit looking at my pouch."

Before he could blink, her hand was in her pouch and she pulled out the egg-shaped energy grenade they'd found earlier. She sprang past Benek's hands, latched onto his armor, rammed the grenade down into his helmet, and leaped clear.

The grenade exploded in a gout of arcing, sizzling energy. The huge man screamed and fell, his armor writhing helplessly as its circuits fried. Benek fought the electric shock, trying desperately to break free.

Shaani jerked loose from the armor that held her.

The sinister suits all suddenly turned to face the concourse. The computer voice snarled from a dozen different helmets all at once. "Defeat will not be tolerated. Destroy G.I.A.N.T. Destroy."

The armors all began to move. They marched from the room, weapon gloves raised, heading for the concourse. They blasted doors aside.

Benek clawed his way out of his armor. He staggered then found Shaani standing over him. The rat's right hand was the nucleus of a sinister, building glow of radiation. He froze then sneered. "You are nothing but a pathetic dabbler. An accident of science." He rose to his feet. "You lack the temperament for murder."

With her long hair streaming, the white rat put up her aim. "I won't kill you, Benek, because I am a *scientist*. And I see science as something pure and noble." The rat looked proudly at Benek. "I am what I choose to be. And you're right; murder isn't in me." She opened her hands in apology. "Rustle, on the other hand, has a more flexible outlook on life."

The giant plant loomed out of the nearby foliage. He bit off Benek's head and crunched it as a dog might a bone.

Xoota staggered to her feet. The entire southern concourse shook as colossal firepower slammed into the structure. Powered armors outside the building fired up at the walls, hitting the armors that had crowded inside. Wig-wig came spilling out of the acoustic ceiling overhead as armors melted his computer workstation into vapor far behind him.

Still somewhat dazed, Xoota blinked then looked to Shaani. "What happened with Benek?"

Rustle opened his mouth to proudly show off his meal then closed his trap.

Xoota tossed him the equipment sacks dropped by their captors. "Neat. Now let's get out of here."

Shaani reached inside Benek's old armor. She worked a control, popped off the suit's left glove, and tucked it underneath her arm. Naked and unconcerned about it, she led the retreat, heading for the outside world.

Powered armors blundered through the building. One fired at Xoota, who ducked away. Rustle fired his own pistol and atomized the armor's skull. That had absolutely no effect on thing at all. The plant hightailed it out of there as quickly as his roots could carry him.

"Destroy G.I.A.N.T. Purge the mutant. De . . . Purge . . . P-pur . . ." The speakers on the powered armors crackled. The nearest suit suddenly fell over. All sounds of firing stopped.

The silence was wonderful but also rather eerie. The *Sand Shark's* crew members stopped in their tracks, looking around.

Xoota blinked. "What is it now?"

One by one, the powered armors crashed and fell. Skulls and bones spilled all over the floor.

Shaani started to move. "Oh, goodness. Communications are down." She ran like a hare. "The gamma moths. They must be depupating."

A one-megaton explosion was due to blast that whole chunk of the world into a picturesque mushroom cloud. The team ran madly out of the buildings then pelted off toward the distant fence.

The *Sand Shark* was parked more than a kilometer away. The crew ran like mad things, trying not to waste time looking back. Xoota sped up to the sonic fence around the starport grounds, looking for an off switch, and found one hidden in the weeds. Rustle lumbered past with Wig-wig clinging to his stalks. Staggering and gasping, Shaani reeled, bringing up the rear. Xoota caught her under one arm and helped her run.

The ship had been parked on a hillside at the far side of the fence. Budgie squawked and capered on the deck, excited by the sight of everybody else in panic. The crew raced aboard, dumped equipment, and sprinted for the upper deck.

The wind was blowing from her beam, off out to sea. Xoota lunged for the control cabin; Rustle and Shaani began frantically working winches and raising sails. The ship began to move, blown slowly along by the steady portside breeze.

The ship was slow, painfully slow. She began rolling downhill. At the base of the hillside, the Plodder tribesmen were emerging from hiding. They all waved to the ship. Xoota leaned out of the window and yelled.

"No, no. Further. Much, much further." She dropped the rear ramp. "Get the hell on board. Hurry."

Eighty tribesmen ran frantically aboard—women, children, young and old. The extra weight helped the ship gain momentum downhill. She began to roll faster.

Shaani raced aloft, helping Rustle hoist every stitch of sail the ship possessed. Jibs, forestays, even the skysail billowed out. With the breeze coming hard abeam, the press of sail began to tilt the ship too far to starboard. The rat yelled down to the tribesmen who were clinging like flies all over the deck and hold.

"Get to the port rail. Shift the ship's weight to port." She waved. "To the left. No, *your* left. Left facing forward."

Bloody landlubbers.

She finally got the overladen vessel into some sort of order. They topped a hill, the engines moving them dreadfully slowly. Xoota let the ship fall off slightly before the wind, her sails cracking with power as the breeze took her again. She began to roll faster and faster. The starport slowly receding into the distance. Two kilometers . . . four . . . six . . .

Shaani slid down a backstay and landed on the deck. She pushed through cowering crowds of tribesmen and stuck her head into the control cabin.

"What's minimum safe distance?" Xoota yelled over her shoulder.

"Ten kilometers."

"Did you just look that up?"

"I can't turn on the computer, or the thing might get taken over." Shaani checked the trip meter. It stood at eight point nine. "Ten Ks. Then we need all sails down and hit the decks."

Eleven kilometers from the blast zone, there was an outcrop of rocks. Xoota steered the ship and parked behind the rocks. Sails were dropped. The villagers ran into the boulders to take cover. Xoota parked the ship stern on to the distant starport and dropped her sun lenses down over her goggles. Wig-wig and Budgie hid themselves belowdecks. Rustle put on his three pairs of sunglasses and sat on deck, grinning eagerly away and hoping for a magnificent big bang.

With her own dark goggles on and strapped into her armor, Shaani tied down everything on deck.

Long minutes passed.

The lag became a tad embarrassing. Some of the villagers peeked their heads up out of the rocks. Xoota strapped herself into her armor, checked that fire buckets were filled and ready, then edged over to stand beside Shaani.

They both looked to the east, toward the starport. Nothing was happening. There were clouds blowing out to sea, butterflies flapping through the grass, but no *boom.*

Xoota hesitantly cleared her throat. "I suppose—"

The eastern horizon flashed a brilliant white.

Seconds later the ground rumbled. Everyone who had ears felt them stab with pain as air pressure slammed across the plains. Dirt burst from the ground as the shock wave hit the rock outcrop. The tops of the *Sand Shark*'s masts whipped in the sudden breeze, snapping stays and cables. Xoota and Shaani hit the deck, holding tight to the planks.

It was hard to hear. There was a horrible ringing sound in deafened ears, a distant rumbling as the explosion did its thing.

Shaani lifted her head to look at Xoota in inquiry. "You suppose what?"

"Oh, nothing."

Well, they were alive. Benek's army was gone. The clone hordes were incinerated. As was the treasure horde of the ages, a whole starport full of ships, armor, power plants, engines, force field generators, sonic fences, ray guns . . .

Shaani seemed to be thinking along similar lines. She lifted a finger into the air. "Rustle found some goodies. And I did nick a glove off Benek's armor."

"Oh, wacko." Xoota sat up. "So at least we got some treasure."

"And Wig-wig's high score on the computer game remains unchallenged."

"That's true."

A huge mushroom cloud rose to the east. Actually it was damned impressive. The fallout would nourish lots of colorful mutations among the local wildlife for many years to come. So again, that was something.

Xoota frowned. "So no broadcast power. Meaning the desalination plant no longer works. Meaning Watering Hole is toast."

"No, no. I've had an idea on that score." Shaani sat on deck to watch the atomic cloud spreading overhead. "The teleporter unit. The controls on the side let you set it to act as a filter. So we wire the doors open. Then set it to only teleport water molecules, not salt. Then we chuck one end in the sea, and the other end pours pure water out into the pipeline. Sends it happily all the way over to Watering Hole. QED."

Xoota looked at her with a level eye. "Do you know how much trouble we could have saved if you'd thought of that earlier?"

"True. But look at all the fun we would have missed." The rat waved a hand. "And Rustle did get to eat Benek's head."

"True, true." Xoota stood and cracked her back. She felt as though she could sleep for a hundred years. "Shall I put the kettle on?"

Shaani brightened. "That would be spiffy."

They had a well-found ship and a vast world to explore but not right that minute.

Overhead, the mushroom cloud spread magnificently up into the atmosphere, bowling off toward the sea. Xoota watched it rise. "Are we in danger here?"

The white rat twiddled her fingers. "Oh, it's only a little fallout. Don't be such a baby."

"Mmm." Xoota headed down to the hold. "Even so, let's head downstairs until this one blows over."

After all, they couldn't all be lab rats.

THE ABYSSAL PLAGUE

From the molten core of a dead universe

Hunger
Spills a seed of evil

Fury
So pure, so concentrated, so infectious

Hate
Its corruption will span worlds

The Temple of Yellow Skulls
Don Bassingthwaite

Sword of the Gods
Bruce Cordell

Under the Crimson Sun
Keith R.A. DeCandido
June 2011

Oath of Vigilance
James Wyatt
August 2011

Shadowbane
Erik Scott de Bie
September 2011

Find these novels at your favorite bookseller.
Also available as ebooks.

DungeonsandDragons.com

DUNGEONS & DRAGONS®

An ancient time, an ancient place . . .
When magic fills the world and terrible monsters roam the wilderness . . .
It is a time of heroes, of legends, of dungeons and dragons . . .

THE MARK OF
NERATH
Bill Slavicsek
Available now

THE SEAL OF
KARGA KUL
Alex Irvine
Available now

UNTOLD
ADVENTURES
Short stories by Alan Dean Foster, Kevin J. Anderson,
Jay Lake, Mike Resnick, and more
June 2011

THE LAST
GARRISON

Matthew Beard
December 2011

Bringing the world of Dungeons & Dragons alive,
find these great novels at your favorite bookseller.
Also available as eBooks.

DungeonsandDragons.com

EPIC STORIES
UNFORGETTABLE CHARACTERS
UNBEATABLE VALUE
OMNIBUS EDITIONS — THREE BOOKS IN ONE

Empyrean Odyssey
Thomas M. Reid
February 2011

The Last Mythal
Richard Baker
August 2011

*Ed Greenwood Presents
Waterdeep I*
July 2011

*Ed Greenwood Presents
Waterdeep II*
December 2011

Dragonlance Legends
Margaret Weis & Tracy Hickman
September 2011

Draconic Prophecies
James Wyatt
October 2011

**Find these great books at your favorite
bookseller.**
DungeonsandDragons.com

MANY ROADS LEAD TO
Neverwinter™

RETURN WITH
G A U N T L G R Y M
Neverwinter Saga, Book I
R.A. Salvatore

Neverwinter
Neverwinter Saga, Book II
R.A. Salvatore
October 2011

CONTINUE THE ADVENTURE WITH
BRIMSTONE ANGELS
Legends of Neverwinter
Erin M. Evans
November 2011

LOOK FOR THESE OTHER EXCITING NEW RELEASES IN 2011
Neverwinter for PC
The Legend of Drizzt™ cooperative board game
Neverwinter Campaign Setting

HOW WILL YOU RETURN?
Find these great products at your favorite bookseller or game shop.

DungeonsandDragons.com

**WELCOME TO THE DESERT WORLD
OF ATHAS, A LAND RULED BY A
HARSH AND UNFORGIVING CLIMATE,
A LAND GOVERNED BY THE ANCIENT
AND TYRANNICAL SORCERER KINGS.
THIS IS THE LAND OF**

CITY UNDER THE SAND
Jeff Mariotte

UNDER THE CRIMSON SUN
Keith R.A. DeCandido
JUNE 2011

DEATH MARK
Robert Schwalb
NOVEMBER 2011

ALSO AVAILABLE AS eBOOKS!

THE PRISM PENTAD
Troy Denning's classic DARK SUN
series revisited! Check out the great new editions of
*The Verdant Passage, The Crimson Legion,
The Amber Enchantress, The Obsidian Oracle,*
and *The Cerulean Storm.*